G. P. Taylor is the author of several bestselling novels, including *Shadowmancer*, *Shadowmancer: The Curse of Salamander Street*, *Wormwood* and *Tersias*, as well as the *Mariah Mundi* trilogy. A former vicar of Cloughton in Yorkshire, he has enjoyed a varied career, moving from rock music to social work to ten years in the police force before his ordination. He now lives with his family in Scarborough.

Praise for *Mariah Mundi*:

'When Harry Potter hangs up his wizard's cloak, booksellers will be looking to G. P. Taylor's *Mariah Mundi*emily, to keep the cashtills ringing.' *BBC News*

'It really is wonderful, wonderful stuff . . . *Mariah Mundi* surpasses Potter on just about every level there is. Highly recommended.' *The Bookbag*

'The book that combines the big story of C. S. Lewis and the plot of an Indiana Jones movie. We could genuinely be looking at the book series that will replace Harry Potter at the top of every child's wish list.' *BuddyHollywood Review*

Praise for *Shadowmancer*:

'The biggest event in children's fiction since Harry Potter.' *The Times*

'The adventure unfolds at a vivid and breathless pace.' *Observer*

'Shadowmancer is flying off the bookshelves as if a wizard had incanted a charm on it.'*Herald*

'A magical tale of vicars and witches.' *Daily Telegraph*

'A compelling and dark-edged fantasy . . . highly recommended.' *Independent*

2244 ← IPod Pin

G. P. Taylor

MARIAH MUNDI
and
The Ship of Fools

faber and faber

First published in 2009
by Faber and Faber Ltd
Bloomsbury House
74–77 Great Russell Street
London WC1B 3DA
This paperback edition first published in 2010

Typeset by Faber and Faber Ltd
Printed in England by CPI Bookmarque, Croydon

A CIP record for this book
is available from the British Library

ISBN 9780-571-25188-9

2 4 6 8 10 9 7 5 3 1

MARIAH MUNDI
AND THE SHIP OF FOOLS

[1]

The *Triton*

THE long black line of railway carriages stopped suddenly. Steam hissed viciously from the engine and mingled with the stench of smouldering coal that now filled the dark tunnel. The train shook and tremored as if it had been struck by an earthquake. The metal wheels screeched against the iron tracks. Shards of bright blue sparks flashed against the dripping brick walls. Mariah Mundi was unexpectedly thrown forward from his sleep. He crashed against the empty seat opposite before sliding to the floor. In his sudden waking he heard the faraway screams of frightened children. The train juddered. Carriage battered against carriage as the echoing madness rolled on and on like a coming thunderstorm.

Twenty-eight miles from Liverpool Mariah had sunk into slumber. For the six-hour journey from the town-at-the-end-of-the-line, only he and Captain Jack Charity of the Bureau of Antiquities had inhabited the compartment. Charity was a tall man with a muscular frame and a thick scar across his right cheek. He had filled the seat opposite Mariah and sprawled across the compartment as he read his penny dreadful. The blinds had been pulled down, the door had been locked and a sign stating *Out of Order* had been placed in the window.

'Don't want to be disturbed by people . . .' Charity had whittered as he slipped the ticket collector a neatly folded and ironed five-pound note.

That seemed like another day. Now, Charity had gone and the train shook again as it briefly juddered along the track. The hissing of the engine subsided. All was then silent. Mariah looked up, waiting for Captain Charity to reappear. The gas lamp that illuminated the First Class carriage flickered. It dwindled in luminosity and then, like a September firefly, abruptly died.

Mariah could see nothing. The gloom of the tunnel was like a double blanket to the darkness of the night outside. It was completely black, eerily silent with the stench of sulphur. Getting to his feet Mariah reached out like a blind man to find the door handle and took hold of the brass lever.

Footsteps clattered outside the compartment. Steel-capped heels cut against the wooden boards of the narrow corridor that ran the length of the carriage. Mariah listened as they stopped outside the door. It was as if whoever was outside was snooping intently before moving on.

Mariah stood still. He tried to hold his breath.

'This one?' asked a gruff voice outside the door.

'Can't tell,' replied another voice as a dim light flashed against the faded, rolled-down blinds.

'The Captain is locked in the khazi – won't be going anywhere. Got our chance now to find the lad . . .' the first voice said, grumbling each word.

The handle of the door rattled. The lever dropped as someone pushed against the door.

'Locked,' the voice sniffed. 'Out of use,' he went on as he shone his lamp towards the hastily made sign on the greasy pane of glass.

4

'Must be the next door,' whispered the other man as if he choked on his words. 'Thought he said it as the first compartment? You know what to do . . .'

The footsteps paced quietly away and then hesitated, the two men walking as one. Mariah pressed his ear to the window of his compartment, shielded from view by the drab blinds. He could hear the door next to him open slowly. Something inside him made him want to shout a warning, as if he knew what was going to happen. The door trembled on its metal runner and then clicked open.

'HE'S THERE!' screamed one of the men, and two loud shots from a military pistol broke the silence. The hand lamp swayed violently back and forth as screams rang out. Passengers leapt to their feet and filled the dark corridor.

'He's been shot!' screamed a man as Mariah pulled the handle of the door to be free from the compartment.

'Guard! Help! MURDER!' Mariah heard another man shout as the news of the attack filled the train.

Mariah pulled on the handle once more. It held fast. He reached up to the baggage rack. His hands scrambled to grab hold of the first travelling case that came to his grasp. Taking the handle of a small Gladstone bag, which Captain Charity had so neatly packed that morning at the Prince Regent Hotel, Mariah smashed the window. Within a few seconds he had knocked out every shard of glass and, jumping from the seat, had leapt into the corridor.

'Who has been shot?' he asked the shadowy man blocking the passageway.

'In our carriage. I saw the flash of the gunshots . . . he's slumped to the floor.'

'Get a light,' Mariah insisted as he pushed by the travellers and stepped inside the compartment.

A man in a plaid suit, with tiny feet and uncomfortable

shoes, struck a match and held it high above him. In the faint light Mariah saw the face of a young man. His lips were tinged blue and already the colour had drained from his face. He was the same age as Mariah, no older than sixteen, and wearing a dark suit. Next to him, holding his hand was an older woman.

'Is he dead?' she asked Mariah, her eyes firmly shut as if unable to look at him.

'I don't think so,' Mariah replied softly. 'He's unconscious. The bullet has grazed his head.'

'He's my son. We are going to America with my husband. We were to meet him at Liverpool docks,' she said as tears rolled down her face.

'Shot him, shot him in the head,' said the man, holding the burning match in the tips of his fingers. 'Never looked, just opened the door – flash of light and then shot him.'

'He's alive – but badly wounded. Did you see them?' Mariah asked.

'Just the hand and the pistol . . . a revolver,' said the man nervously.

'Quickly,' Mariah said as he got to his feet. 'Find the guard!'

The train lurched forward. There was a shrill hiss as the winding pump pushed gas through the pipes again. Without speaking, the man with the matches lit the wick of the lamp and rubbed the soot from his singed fingers. The gas lamp lit the drab walls and blinded windows of the carriage. It began to billow gusts of hot air that rolled across the painted ceiling of the coach and out of the open door.

'Best leave them be,' Mariah said as he stepped towards the door. 'We need to get him to a doctor.'

'Stay,' said the woman. 'I don't think I can be alone.'

'Mariah! Mariah!' shouted Charity as he stormed through the passageway.

'The boy's been shot,' bawled the man by the door as Charity

6

forced his way through a gaggle of people all trying to stare inside the compartment.

'SHOT?' Charity shouted as he pushed harder against the mob blocking the corridor. 'Let me through!'

Soon Charity had forced his way through the crowd. He stood in the doorway of the compartment, his immense frame casting a deep, dark shadow.

'They said you had been shot,' Charity said.

'Not me,' Mariah replied as he saw Charity's eyes cast upon the lad behind him.

'Let me see to him,' Charity said. He stooped down and lifted the lad and lay him across the long bench seat opposite. 'Just a graze . . . Boy, can you hear me?'

'He's called Lorenzo . . . after his father,' the woman said as Charity attempted to wake her son. 'Lorenzo Zane . . .'

Charity raised his head for a moment as if in recognition of the name as he felt for a pulse in the boy's neck.

'He seems well to me, a strong lad – he will come to no harm. Tell me, Madame Zane, do you know of any reason why someone should want to shoot your son?'

'I know of nothing. My husband lives a quiet life. He is an engineer, an inventor,' she replied as she sobbed.

'The creator of the Zane Generator,' Charity said as her son regained his mind. 'Like father like son – he is with us again.'

'Mother,' said the lad feebly.

'Did you see who shot at you?' Charity urged as he propped the boy against the seat.

'Just for a moment. I think I have seen the man before. I can't recall where. There was the darkness of the tunnel and then a blinding light.'

'They ran by me,' said the man in the uncomfortable shoes. 'Two of them, ruffians and squalors . . . jumped from the train as they pushed me out of the way.'

'Won't they still be in the tunnel?' Mariah asked.

'They will be long gone and far away,' Charity replied as he nodded for Mariah to leave the compartment. 'We will soon be at the harbour and there is sure to be a doctor to take care of young Lorenzo. Keep your son calm,' he said to the woman. 'It should only be a matter of minutes before we arrive.'

Charity took hold of the man in the plaid suit and sat him next to Madame Zane as if he were a lap dog.

'I would be grateful if you would care for them whilst we are gone,' Charity said. He patted the man on the shoulder, then turned and pushed Mariah from the compartment. 'Things are not what they seem to be,' he whispered as they entered their own compartment.

'I know,' Mariah replied. 'I heard the men in the corridor – they were looking for the first compartment.'

'And I was locked in the lavatory. Not the most convenient convenience, but locked in I most certainly was.' Charity shrugged in his usual way and raised an eyebrow.

'That is what I heard the man say – the Captain was locked in the khazi . . .'

'Then it must be that they wanted me out of the way,' Charity replied as the train juddered yet again. 'They had pulled the emergency cord in the next carriage. When the train stopped it was plunged into darkness. They took no chances and must have known they had just three minutes before the train would start again.' Charity stopped and looked at Mariah anxiously. 'I have a great worry that they shot the wrong person.'

'Who?' Mariah asked.

'I think that *you* were their intended victim,' Charity replied solemnly.

'But why?'

Captain Charity paused. He turned, brushed away broken

glass and then sat down on the bristled fabric that tightly covered the seat.

'I have not been fully honest with you. This isn't just a trip to Liverpool, Mariah. I have taken the liberty to pack your trunk. We are going to America.'

'America? But that is another world away – an ocean and everything.' Mariah gulped excitedly.

'America – a place that if it didn't exist we would have to invent it. A colony stolen from its rightful owners.' Charity tried to smile. 'I had a letter from Isambard Black. This is Bureau business. We are booked on the *Triton* – the biggest and fastest ship ever to be built – unsinkable. It is to race the *Ketos*, a vessel that it is said can never be beaten. Whoever crosses the Atlantic first will win one million dollars.'

'So why is that the business of the Bureau of Antiquities?' Mariah asked.

'For such a prize, men will do many things and we are to ensure fair play. No one knows we are about to make the journey, but from what has just happened I think our presence is no longer a secret. An interesting coincidence is that Lorenzo Zane invented the means by which the *Triton* will be propelled. The Zane Generator – it is a steam engine so powerful that at full speed it will take the vessel five miles to stop.'

'And the Bureau of Antiquities is to guard the ship?' Mariah asked.

'Indeed. The prize money will be placed upon the *Triton*. Five hundred gold bars are to be stowed in its hold. They are guarded for the time being by officers of the Royal Navy. We put to sea at midnight.'

Charity shrugged his shoulders and rustled the collar of his coat to keep out the draught that billowed through the broken window of the compartment. Reaching into the pocket of the coat he pulled out a leather pouch. 'Your ticket for the ship.'

'What about the Prince Regent?' Mariah asked as he thought about the hotel they had left behind. 'Who will manage it whilst we are gone?'

'Taken care of. All will be well . . . if perhaps a little different.' Charity replied as if he were the keeper of an amusing secret. 'We mustn't think of it at all. But should anyone ask, you are a magician's apprentice and I the owner of Europe's grandest hotel.'

With that, Captain Charity closed his eyes and allowed himself to sleep as the carriage rocked back and forth.

The train ambled on between long grubby terraces of drab houses. It twisted and snaked past dimly lit streets as it approached the harbour. Mariah looked out of the window as he thought about the young Lorenzo Zane. He had an anxious and nagging doubt. He rolled the words of the assassin over and over – *the first compartment . . . the first compartment*. He realised that what Charity had said was true: Lorenzo Zane was a mistaken victim.

There was another shudder as the train crossed the double rails of a junction, then a blast on its whistle signalled the approach to Liverpool docks.

Mariah looked at the neat leather pouch that Charity had given him. It was embossed with a three-pronged spear held in the hands of a bearded giant with the tail of a fish. Mariah opened the flap and peered inside. The ticket for the *Triton* looked as if it was made of a wafer of solid gold. It was cold to the touch and sharp as steel. Beaten into the metal and painted in black was the number 395. Engraved below the number was just one word: *Triton*.

There was a gentle tapping on the door. Mariah hid the ticket pouch in his pocket as Captain Charity opened one eye, not wanting to be disturbed.

'Come in,' he drawled in a bored voice, his hand deep in the pocket where Mariah knew the Captain always kept a small dandy-gun.

The door opened and in stepped Madame Zane. Mariah noticed for the first time how incredibly tall and how incredibly beautiful she was. She looked at them both and smiled as, without being asked, she sat down next to Mariah.

'I have been less than honest with you,' she said. 'My son, Lorenzo . . . I was frightened he would not understand.' Madame Zane looked at Charity and then to Mariah as if asking permission to continue. Charity did not speak but merely smiled and nodded. 'My husband has made some enemies. It is purely by accident – an argument over the generator. He has been threatened, but he will not tell me who by. That is why we are travelling separately. He thought we would be safe.'

'Why do you tell me this?' Charity asked. 'We are just fellow travellers.'

'You know about the Zane Generator,' she stuttered in reply.

'So does everyone who travels on the ship. It promises to take us from Liverpool to New York in six days,' Charity snapped. 'Has your son recovered enough for you to sit and chat with us?'

Mariah was puzzled by the tone of his voice.

Madame Zane suddenly stood up. Her face changed. The smile vanished to a scowl.

'I presumed you to be different,' she answered quickly.

'Then your presumption was misplaced,' Charity replied as he looked again at the penny dreadful and unfolded the pages. 'Your son is safe and we have a boat to catch. Goodnight, Madame.'

Before he could finish speaking, Madame Zane had turned and gone. The door to the compartment was slammed shut. Charity smiled smugly to himself.

Mariah knew Charity well enough to know that it would be

no good to question him on the way he had spoke. He turned to the window and looked at the backs of the drab houses with their curtainless windows and unpainted sills.

In the dark night sky he could see the growing light of the docks. There, towering above the houses was the silhouette of a ship. It touched the very peak of the sky and blotted out the full moon. It was as high as a mountain, a monstrous ship that grew bigger as the train broke free of the terraced houses and approached the dock.

'Incredible . . .' Mariah said unexpectedly, as if he never meant to speak.

Charity passed a cursory peek over the top of the penny dreadful.

'That is the *Ketos*. Wait until you see the *Triton*.'

Mariah didn't reply. His eyes went higher and higher as he followed the decks and ladders up and up. Finally, when he could see no further, there was a long red flag dangling from the middle of the three black funnels.

'The Guptara Flag . . . given for the fastest Atlantic crossing,' Mariah said to himself in awe. He had seen the flag before. There had been a sketch in *The Times* of its presentation.

'And if it is to be believed, it will be the last time you will see it on *that* ship. In six days time it will be the property of the Marquis DeFeaux – the owner of the *Triton*,' Charity replied as he put down the paper to stare through the windowpane.

'But look!' Mariah said, astounded at the sight he gazed upon.

'Ah, the *Triton*. I thought you would be amazed,' Charity said.

The *Triton* was nine hundred feet long and two hundred wide. It towered above the dock cranes as high as St Paul's Cathedral. In the swirling spotlights it shimmered as if it were alive. Along the entire length of the walking deck was a brass handrail that even from that distance could be picked out like a gold thread against the black of the ship.

'We shall sail on that?' Mariah asked, unsure if anything so vast would ever be able to float.

'And sail we shall. Nothing is grander – bigger, smoother, faster – than the *Triton*. We have a cabin as vast as my room in the Prince Regent and, Mariah, they have a Montgolfier balloon for pleasure rides.'

Mariah laughed. He had seen a Montgolfier once before. It was a large hot-air balloon that had carried a cart across the London sky. He remembered seeing it one bright winter morning when he had watched from the gardens of the Colonial School long before he had met Captain Charity or travelled north to the Prince Regent Hotel. The Montgolfier had flown from east to west, nearly touching the clouds. In the cart a man had waved at him and thrown packets of sweets to the mass of people gathered below.

'A ride in a balloon from the back of the ship?' Mariah asked.

'Not for the faint-hearted – but imagine the view of the Atlantic.'

Mariah wasn't listening. All he could see was the *Triton*. The four gold funnels of the ship shimmered in the rays of a vast sodium light that burnt brightly on the quayside. It was festooned in ribbons and garlanded in flags. It was the biggest ship Mariah had ever seen.

'How can something that big, float?' Mariah asked.

'Science, my dear Mariah, and at midnight we shall see for ourselves.'

As the train drew to a halt on the long pier, it was as if the whole world had gathered to see the ships set sail. A hundred men waited on the platform with iron trolleys to carry the baggage of the passengers leaving the train. Mariah watched one man tap impatiently on his barrow handle.

The steam train stopped quietly, its noise drowned by the shouting of the crowd. As the doors to the train opened, the people waiting began to applaud their arrival.

'We shall wait until the last passenger has left the train and slip aboard quietly,' Charity said. 'We don't want to be seen if we can help it. Perhaps, whoever wanted you dead is still waiting . . .'

[2]

The Great Race

F OR the next hour Mariah and Captain Jack Charity sat in
the cold compartment of the steam train. Mariah stared
out of the carriage window. Madame Zane and her son were
quickly carried off in a makeshift ambulance, a donkey cart
covered in a green tarpaulin with their luggage stacked on the
back. Strangely, Mariah thought, they were taken to the ship
and not to the hospital. He could only believe that the lad
would be better cared for on board. What perplexed Mariah
was the way in which Sir Lorenzo Zane greeted his son. He
had been the first to approach the train and when he saw his
son being lifted from the carriage had tutted as if what had
happened to him was quite trivial. Then, when Madame Zane
had almost fallen to the platform, her husband had chided her
loudly.

Still, people were leaving the train. Some fought over their
luggage as porters grabbed whatever they could and stacked it
upon their barrows in search of a meagre shilling to push it
across the wharf to the awaiting crane nets.

Mariah stared at the quayside packed with people. They
shouted and moaned, waiting for the great race to begin.

Impromptu betting stalls littered the jetty as tattered bookies shouted the odds as to which vessel would win the race.

'Will we have to wait much longer?' Mariah asked, eager to be on board the ship as the shouting crowd pressed against the side of the train.

Charity reached into his pocket for his fob watch.

'I am waiting for a suitable diversion,' he said, as if he knew what was to come.

A gigantic crane lifted roped parcels of luggage high into the air, swung them out across the harbour and then into the rear hold of the ship. It laboured back and forth, its steam pistons churning and whirring in time with a brass band of uniformed men who played pompous military music. The vast lamps that lit the ship beamed back and forth. They cast deep black shadows high into the air and sparkled upon the newly painted gantries. From where Mariah watched he could even see the captain high upon the bridge of the ship. The man was looking down and pointing in a manner that suggested he was not pleased with the celebrations far below.

'I can see the captain,' Mariah said as Charity looked at his watch yet again.

'Tharakan, the old sea dog,' Charity replied without looking up from his watch. He was counting the seconds towards the eleventh hour. 'I met him a long time ago. It was in the Sudan – he knew your father. Tharakan was the captain of the vessel that your parents sailed out on.'

Mariah didn't reply. Charity's words brought back a cold memory. He remembered the day well when he had said goodbye to his mother and father and was then taken to the Colonial School, a neatly ironed five pound note in his pocket. He could still see them waving to him as the ship set sail from Southampton docks. Little did he know he would never see them again, and that soon Professor Jecomiah Bilton, headmaster of the Colonial School, would break the news to him that they were both dead.

'Did he know them well?' Mariah asked, gulping the words.

'They told me that they had dined with him. Tharakan is a compulsive man. I don't think that would have suited your father,' Charity replied.

'But Tharakan would have spoken to them, known them a little,' Mariah said, in his heart hoping that he could speak to the captain about them.

'Good people live on in the memories of those they have met,' Charity said.

'Do you think they could be –' Mariah stopped before he finished the sentence.

'Alive?' Charity asked. 'We would have heard by now, we would have had news of them. I believe they are lost to the desert and that we have to carry on.'

'I can't see my mother's face. When I think of her I can see everything but her face,' Mariah said. 'With every year it gets worse and I fear she will vanish completely from my memory.' He traced the outline of the ship in the misting windowpane.

There was a sudden roar of the crowd. Everyone rushed from the train and pressed towards the *Triton*.

'On time, just as I thought,' Charity said as he got to his feet. 'The gold has arrived.'

Mariah looked out as hordes of people pushed to get closer to the gates of the dock. Charity took his Gladstone bag and a small case from the rack and slid open the door.

'Time for us to leave. I have made arrangements for our trunk to be taken to the ship.'

'Is that really the gold?' Mariah asked, as the screams of excitement grew louder.

'It is whatever they want it to be,' Charity replied as together they stepped into the corridor and disembarked from the train.

'I did make a suggestion that the gold be put on board this afternoon and that what is seen to go on tonight is in fact just lead bricks, stamped and proved . . . covered in gold leaf, of course.'

'A deception?' asked Mariah as they walked quickly over the quayside and onto the long wooden bridge that led to a narrow steel door in the side of the ship.

Charity stopped on the gantry and pointed to the procession entering the docks. A long funeral carriage was flanked by a regiment of Marines. The crowd parted as it drew near and their shouting ceased as they gazed in awe at the bars of bullion. They were stacked neatly, to form a peculiar sarcophagus. The inside of the hearse was dimly illuminated by two red carriage lamps that swung back and forth as the wheels of the carriage rattled over the cobbled road. The dock fell completely silent. Men took their caps from their heads as the procession passed by. It was as if they were spectators at the funeral of a great statesman drawn by the black landau towards his grave.

'Quite spectacular,' Charity said as if pleased with himself. 'I thought of that myself. It was hard to convince the Bureau of Antiquities that it should be done this way.'

'So it's real gold?' Mariah whispered.

'To those who look on with greedy hearts, it is worth more than gold. See how they clamber to be in its presence, as if they stand before a god. In their silence they give reverence.' Charity looked at his fob watch. 'Now . . .'

At that precise moment the carriage stopped. The Marines took their rifles from their shoulders and stood to attention, forming a phalanx from the carriage to the gangway of the *Triton*.

There was a sudden loud blast on the ship's horn. It rattled the windows of the houses for miles and miles and sent a gigantic squall of squawking sea birds high into the night sky. They swirled above the ships like a host of angels that flew in and out of the searchlights. The crowd applauded as the doors to the hearse were opened and the gold bars were passed in a human chain from man to man.

'They look so real,' Mariah said as Charity smiled to himself. 'Do you think anyone will try to steal the gold?'

'Not tonight, not here. It would take an army to do such a thing,' Charity replied as they watched the gold disappear into the ship one brick ingot at a time.

'And it is really gold?' Mariah asked, hoping Charity would be truthful.

'I have arranged for it to be displayed in the grand entrance – suitably guarded, of course.' He laughed. 'Good Bureau business.'

Mariah had known Charity long enough to understand what he meant. The Bureau of Antiquities always went to elaborate lengths to hoodwink and misinform the world.

Aldo Rafden, he was told, had formed the Bureau of Antiquities a hundred and fifty-three years before. He was an explorer, collector and government spy. To those who knew him, he was a scandalous thief who loved nothing more than finding something precious and taking it for himself. He had plundered the tombs of the East and put the loot on display in Bloomsbury. Rafden had a particular interest in the mummified remains of animals and had so filled his displays with dead cats so that the whole museum looked like a charnel house.

The sole purpose of the Bureau, as it was known, was to find those mysterious objects of power and legend that were only spoken about in whisper. Often the objects the Bureau found were so secret that people would never dare mention even their names in public or admit to know of their whereabouts. The Bureau could not be bought for any price and those called to its service would rather die than give away its secrets.

'So why is this Bureau business?' Mariah asked.

'All will become clear when we are at sea,' Charity said quite sternly. 'I think this will be our most dangerous task yet. We do not know our enemy or why we are really here. All I have been told is that three weeks ago a strange light was seen in the far north of Greenland. It burnt as bright as the sun and it shuddered the ice. The Bureau received a telegram from one of our agents. It said that there was *death on the ice*. Five days ago the agent was found dead. He had been badly burnt. It looked as though he had spontaneously combusted.'

'Hexagenamite?' Mariah asked. 'Just like at the Prince Regent?'

'As if it were the same,' Charity replied. 'There have been reports in the press that the ice cap is moving. A catastrophe has occurred and a vast land of ice is in motion.'

'And what has that to do with the *Triton* and the *Ketos*?' Mariah asked.

'The Bureau of Antiquities looks at all these things with interest. It is our experience that whenever something of this magnitude happens, then a human element follows close by.'

'Then who could it be?' Mariah asked.

'Stew . . . I can smell beef stew,' Charity replied as he sniffed the air, picked up his bags and walked into the ship. 'I think they are serving beef stew for supper.'

Mariah took a final glimpse at the procession as the gold bars were loaded from the funeral cart to the ship. The crowd was still silent as they counted the ingots. Turning quickly, Mariah followed Charity through the small doorway and into the *Triton*. He nodded to the guard and showed him the ticket in the leather wallet. The guard grunted for him to follow on, muttering that it was highly irregular that guests should enter the ship by the crew hatch. Already, Charity was far ahead. He strode up the steel stairway two treads at a time with a bag in each hand.

'Quickly, Mariah,' he bellowed loudly. 'We shouldn't be here – crew only, didn't you read the sign?'

By the second landing, Mariah had caught up with Charity. It was as if he knew the ship as he walked on, coat flapping and cases clattering against the freshly painted white walls. They went up several decks and on and on through steel hatches with brass wheels to make them watertight. Then up a final flight of stairs.

'I wish we could have gone through the guests' entrance,' Charity said quite breathlessly as he stopped outside a closed hatch. 'All I will say, is that what is on the other side of this doorway is quite breathtaking.' Charity spun the wheel on the door and pulled slowly. The aroma of beef stew, red wine and cigars floated through the opening and into the stairwell. 'Delicious,' he said as the noise of excited conversation flooded in. 'I think you should go first.'

Mariah stared and stared. He could not believe what he saw. Opening before him was a sumptuous sight, a grand hallway with two golden stairways circling down from high above. Hanging from the ornate ceiling was a vast chandelier bedecked with tiny and yet dazzling white lights. Beneath his feet was a soft carpet embedded with golden unicorns woven into the fabric. In the centre of the room, below the circular balcony, was a grand piano, and next to that was a large catafalque. Two Royal Marines in uniforms of blue and gold neatly stacked the bars of Charity's bullion on a sheet of black velvet. The crowd of passengers now seemed to give it little attention. Its value paled against the vast majesty of the ship and the wonder and awe of all that was around them. It was as if the *Triton* were a city of the seas. There were avenues of small shops selling goods from around the world. Cafés and restaurants lined the upper deck, and thousands of people from every nation milled about in their finery.

'Did you know it would be like this?' Mariah asked.

'Never,' Charity replied, as if lost for words. 'Magnificent . . .'

A man tapped Charity on the shoulder. 'Captain Jack Charity and your young guest,' he said.

'Tharakan. It is years since we last met,' Charity said warmly. 'This is my godson, Mariah Mundi.'

'I heard much of you from your parents – I took them to Africa. Tell me, how are they keeping?' Tharakan asked.

'They are dead. Lost in the Sudan,' Mariah replied.

'And you, Captain Jack – how are you?' Tharakan asked as if he had not heard or wanted to hear what Mariah had said.

'Well, very well,' Charity replied as his hand squeezed Mariah's shoulder.

'I hear that you have already met Madame Zane. She told me that you had helped them on the train whilst young Lorenzo had his accident.' Tharakan's dark eyes flashed about the room as if he searched for someone.

'Did she mention me by name?' Charity asked.

'As if she has known you for a lifetime. But then again, once you have met Captain Jack Charity then he is never forgotten – eh, Mariah, do you agree with that?'

Mariah smiled as he examined the buttons on Tharakan's deep blue uniform with interest. Each one looked as if it had been carved from the pearled shell of a deep-sea creature. Engraved within each pearl was the three-bladed spear.

Tharakan was even taller than Charity. Mariah thought his eyes, suspended in deep brown circles of wrinkled skin, seemed lifeless. His long dark beard, flecked with blades of grey, hung down to his chest. It made him look like an ancient god of the sea.

'When do we go to our rooms?' Mariah asked.

'Rooms?' snorted Captain Tharakan. 'There is not a single room on the ship – every guest has a suite and nothing finer will you ever find in the whole world. Not even in Claridges Hotel. Ah,' Tharakan snorted as he finally saw who he had been looking for. 'Lorenzo Zane . . . I must speak with him. Come to the bridge at midnight – you will be surprised by what you see. And bring Mariah.'

Captain Tharakan walked off without saying goodbye. Mariah watched as he took Zane by the arm and led him away deep in conversation.

'He mentioned Claridges Hotel. Does he know about Room 13?' he asked anxiously.

'Even if he does then it will be of no consequence. Room 13 at Claridges Hotel doesn't exist. It is a code for the headquarters of the Bureau of Antiquities, not the place itself.' Charity didn't continue because there, coming towards them, picking her way through the hundreds of people in the room, was Madame Zane. As she walked through the crowd of eager sojourners every head turned to look at her.

'She's coming to talk to you,' Mariah muttered under his breath, as a small waiter with a scar across his cheek attempted to force him to eat what looked like the squashed remains of a dead crab.

'And we cannot escape.' Charity grimaced through gritted teeth.

'Captain Charity, I feel I must again try to give you my thanks,' she said politely as she held out her hand.

'No need – it was Mariah who was of greatest help,' he replied.

'And so like young Lorenzo – they could be mistaken for brothers,' she said. She turned to watch as the last bars of gold were placed on the catafalque and covered in a gigantic glass case. 'We will have to stare at all that gold for the next five days.'

'A fortune for all to see,' Mariah said.

'Yet so ugly,' she replied. 'I feel I have met you before, Captain Charity – do you remember where?'

Mariah noticed that Charity appeared to be embarrassed. He coughed and covered his face with his hand as if to wipe his brow.

'I can't say I do. But then I meet so many people. Perhaps you have been a guest at my hotel, the Prince Regent? Do you know of it?' he asked.

'A friend of my husband stayed there recently, an American . . . Dedalus Zogel – do you know him?' she asked.

'We met,' he said politely.

'I quite forgot,' she said, interrupting Charity. 'I have taken the liberty of bringing you a gift. I know it is something quite small but in terms of my thanks for helping me on the train it is just a token. I hope you both like it.'

Madame Zane reached into her purse and brought out a small wooden box. It was covered in thick black lacquer that made it shine like a mirror. Madame Zane held it in the palm of her hand like a dark offering.

'We couldn't possibly,' Charity tried to say.

'I insist – it is just a token,' she said with a giggle as she twitched her long nose and sniggered at the same time.

Charity instinctively held out his hand and Madame Zane slid the box on to his palm.

'See,' she said as she blew upon the box. 'It is full of surprises.'

With that the lid of the box began to move slowly until it suddenly sprung open to the sound of a chiming bell. From inside appeared a small ebony figure, half man and half beast, that flicked upwards and began to dance in time to the chimes.

'Amazing,'Mariah said. He watched the jewelled eyes of the bull-headed creature sparkle as it danced.

'It is an invention of my husband. It can dance with your mood – however you feel, the Minotaur will dance in that way.

If you are sad it will skip a lament and if you are happy it will dance a jig.'

'But how do you get it to stop?' Charity asked.

'Quite simple, just blow upon it and it will be gone.'

Charity blew upon the creature and just as she said, the beast stopped dancing and curled itself within the box as the lid slid tightly shut.

'An amazing invention. We can't possibly have such a gift,' Charity said as he handed it back to her.

'Once given, it cannot be taken back. I will be deeply offended.' As before, Madame Zane's manner changed suddenly. It was as if the wind had blown upon her and all her goodness had vanished in one breath. 'I will not have my charity rebuked by your Charity, Mariah,' she scoffed.

The *Triton* shook as a grave sounding of the horn rattled the glass case covering the gold.

'I think we are ready to set sail,' Mariah said as he took the box from the palm of Charity's hand and placed it in his pocket.

'Then we can go to our rooms,' said Madame Zane, again restored to politeness.

[3]

The *Bicameralist*

O N the bridge of the *Triton* Captain Tharakan stared out to sea. The ship towered above even the largest buildings of the city and dwarfed the quayside cranes.

'Soon be ready for the race,' he said excitedly as a tall, silent man in a neatly pressed uniform ushered Mariah and Charity onto the bridge. 'Thank you, Mr Ellerby,' he said to the chisel-faced officer before turning to Charity. 'I hear you have not met Lorenzo and I so much wanted you to experience the full force of the Zane Generator.'

Lorenzo Zane nodded from the far side of the bridge. He was in his shirtsleeves with the cuffs rolled back and the collar removed from the neck. Mariah thought he looked more like a servant than a famous inventor. He was tall and thin with a nar-row face that looked like a horse and did not fit on board a ship. All around him, officers of the watch checked the steel dials and gauges and shouted instructions into the mouthpiece of a brass speaking-tube that vanished through the floor. A guard with a pistol in his hand stood by the crisply painted doorway next to Mr Ellerby, the officer who had shown them on to the bridge.

'Thanks for what you did for my son,' Lorenzo said as he noted down the numbers on the dial in front of him. 'The generator has to be watched at all times – if the pressure becomes too great then the ship will explode.'

'Dangerous machinery for a passenger ship?' Charity asked.

'Not at all, Captain Charity. As long as this dial is maintained at a constant pressure then all will be well. You seem to be familiar with my work . . . Did you enjoy the gift from my wife?' he asked.

'Totally entertaining,' Mariah said as he took the box from his pocket and held it out for all to see.

'I have one myself, given to me by Lorenzo,' said Captain Tharakan appreciatively. 'It is in my stateroom and I shall keep it with me always.'

'I invented it for my son – to help him sleep. He says the music and the dancing soothes the mind.' Lorenzo handed his clipboard to the officer of the watch and muttered something under his breath. 'In two minutes we shall depart on the greatest adventure the world has ever seen.'

'I thought we were just going to the colonies?' Charity asked sarcastically.

'But at what speed and in what style!' Lorenzo replied. 'We are to race the *Ketos* – the fastest ship afloat, and we shall beat her.'

'Is your generator tried and tested, Lorenzo?' Charity asked.

'In the heaviest seas of the North Atlantic as far as Engronelant,' he replied.

'A truly amazing experience – we cut through icebergs as if they were cheese,' added Tharakan like an excited child.

'Then we shall be amazed also,' Charity replied, as there was a sudden shudder from far below. Slowly the ship began to move. At first it was hardly noticeable. Then as each second passed by, the lights of the city began to move away. 'I wonder if we could watch from outside?' he asked as Lorenzo Zane returned to peer at the pressure dial.

Captain Tharakan ordered the guard to open the doorway and Mariah and Charity were escorted to the long metal balcony that ran across the width of the bridge. From there they could see the two ships moving slowly from the quayside like waking sea monsters. On the pier below it looked as if the entire city had gathered to see them set sail. Thousands of people screamed as the *Triton* shuddered with the sound of its own horn. Without warning the sound came again and Mariah was blown backwards with the force.

Then, from high above them, a searchlight beamed from the clouds and illuminated the decks of both ships. The crowd on the quayside fell silent and stared towards the heavens as lightning sparked from cloud to cloud. From far away came the rumbling of what Mariah thought was thunder.

'It can't be,' shouted Charity as he ran across the bridge gantry.

'What is it?' asked Mariah, fearful that a creature was coming from the skies.

'Look!' Charity said as he pointed to the source of the light.

From the distant east, as if it had slipped through the peaks of the far mountains, came a bright light. As it drew closer the beam dimmed to a soft glow like a full moon. The crowd below cowered back, not knowing what was about to befall them. The *Triton* and the *Ketos* sailed slowly on into the deep Mersey.

It appeared that the ships were being followed by a gigantic, menacing shadow that cut across the night sky. Then, as the moments passed, Mariah could make out a long cylindrical shape as big as the *Triton*. It edged closer, as if it were about to strike. Around it sparked shards of jagged lightning as its murmurings turned to thunderous groans.

'What . . . what is it?' Mariah asked as he stared upwards.

'It is something that I never thought possible,' Charity said, straining to see the approaching manifestation.

The ship's horn shuddered once more, sending the crowd fleeing from the harbourside and screaming in fright. From out of the air the sound was answered as if a shot of thunder was blasted towards them.

Tharakan stepped onto the bridge gantry with Lorenzo Zane.

'I wanted this to be a surprise for you, Captain Charity,' he shouted above the noise of the fleeing crowd. 'It is another of Lorenzo's inventions. It has been waiting until we set sail.'

'A skyship?' Charity asked Lorenzo. 'How have you kept such a device a secret from the world?'

'I built it where no one would ever guess,' he said coldly. 'Inventing a sailing ship is one thing – inventing a skyship is another.'

'It is to follow the race across the Atlantic as far as New York,' Tharakan said proudly. 'Imagine it, Charity. With a skyship any land or sea can be crossed without peril – no more seasickness . . .' He laughed.

'My skyship can travel to any city in the world – nowhere is out of its reach,' Lorenzo said proudly as the skyship drew closer through the thunderous clouds. 'We shall tell it that the race is about to start.'

'How do you communicate with a ship that sails the sky?' Mariah asked as the wind blew around him.

'By light,' Lorenzo said eagerly as Mr Ellerby took hold of a large brass-rimmed signalling lamp that was on the corner of the gantry. 'We flash a code in light – it is translated and they will reply.'

'Like a telegraph?' Mariah asked.

'Exactly,' said Captain Tharakan. 'Mr Ellerby – tell the *Bicameralist* that we will be at the race line in five minutes.'

Ellerby nodded without speaking and appeared to look to Lorenzo Zane for confirmation of the order. Mariah saw Zane smile at Ellerby. The man then took hold of a wooden handle on the side of the lamp and clicked the shutter back and forth as if he was tapping out the notes of a song.

In the dark night Mariah saw the canvas of the skyship light up with each letter of the code. All then was dark again. The searchlight on the *Bicameralist* dimmed even more until it faded to naught. Moments passed. The *Triton* sailed on as the *Ketos* drew alongside. In the distance the people on the quayside became like tiny creatures wailing against the sea.

'They seem to be taking their time,' Charity said as he leant against the gantry.

'Presently, Captain,' Tharakan said quickly. 'They will respond . . .' His words were interrupted by five flashes of white light that lit up the sea, the land and the distant hills. 'They are ready!' he shouted. 'The race is about to start.'

Soon, both vessels were level with the Bidston Lighthouse on the dark Wirral shoreline. Mariah looked towards the *Ketos* as it drew close on the starboard side. He could see hundreds of passengers on deck and the bow wake spurning up from the cold black water below. It was like the back of a gigantic whale being chased by the ship, as it was about to dive to the depths. Both liners sounded their horns as if to bellow a warning to the sea. Then from the land came the flash of a cannon, then another and another. Twelve guns blasted, spitting fire and ash upon the water and lighting the dark lowlands with their flaming tiger-eyes.

From Bidston Hill, rockets shot high into the air. They burst with flashes of sapphire and crimson sparks. As the land was lit and then shadowed with each heaven-bound detonation, it looked to Mariah as if the sky would burst into flames.

The sound of the cannon rumbled across the channel as the

ships broke out of the Mersey and into open sea. The *Ketos* gave a long, loud blast upon her horn as she turned towards deep water. Everyone upon her deck was waving towards the *Triton*. Mariah could hear the faint sounds of a dance band playing upon her deck and see the misted shapes of people dancing and throwing streamers to the wind.

'She is somewhat faster, Captain Tharakan,' Charity said, stepping back inside the bridge as the salt spray billowed like snow from the sea.

'Only for tonight,' Lorenzo Zane replied as they all followed on. 'It takes time for the generator to reach full power. The *Bicameralist* shall keep us informed as to how many leagues the *Ketos* is ahead.'

Mariah listened intently as the man explained the finest workings of the Zane Generator. It appeared that the ship was powered by a steam boiler. It was made even more formidable by the seawater that it sucked in from jets in the keel, pressurised by steam pumps and then forced out from the stern.

'You are a man of another age,' Charity said to Zane when he had finished his long explanation.

'In making my inventions I am limited by the devices I have. It is a deceitful trick to have been born in such a primitive time as this,' Zane answered with a sigh.

'But not for long,' Tharakan said as he barked orders to the crew. 'Lorenzo Zane will be a name the world will never forget and the *Triton* shall go down in history as the greatest ship ever built.'

'How will the *Bicameralist* follow us so far from land?' Mariah asked as Ellerby opened the door for them to leave the bridge.

'That, dear Mariah, is a secret that I am not allowed to share with anyone.' Zane was obviously uncomfortable that he had been asked such a question.

'It is too late for talk of such a thing, Mariah,' Charity said to break the silence that followed. 'We have travelled the breadth of the country upon a most uncomfortable train and I feel in need of sleep. I am sure Zane will be willing to talk more of his inventions during the voyage.'

'I will make sure Ellerby takes your cases to your room,' Tharakan said as the bridge door was shut firmly behind them and they descended the stairway.

'Did you know the *Bicameralist* had been invented?' Mariah asked as they walked along the deck.

'There was rumour of such a craft, an amazing invention and far bigger than I ever thought possible to fly,' Charity replied as he counted the suite numbers outside each room. 'I think we are here. From the instructions I do believe you slide your ticket into the door and it will open.'

'Like magic?' Mariah asked.

'Like science,' Charity replied as Mariah slipped the metal ticket into a narrow slot next to the door. There was a sudden click and then the whirring of a small motor as the door opened without being touched.

'How does such a thing work?' Mariah asked.

Charity looked back. Mr Ellerby was at the far end of the passageway, watching them. He made no secret of what he was doing. He stood by the open door, smiling arrogantly.

'Ignore him,' Charity said as Mariah looked nervously towards the man. 'He wants us to know we are being watched. I don't think our presence is as welcome as I thought.'

'Do they know we are from the Bureau of Antiquities?' Mariah asked.

'We would not have been given this welcome if they didn't,' Charity said as he stared at the door. Mariah looked again and Ellerby was gone.

'There,' Charity said as he took a small magnifying glass

from his pocket. 'A fingerprint on the brass. And look there,' he said, pointing to a splinter of wood in the opening of the door. 'Someone has slid a knife into the lock.' Then he motioned for Mariah to be silent. He took a pistol from his pocket and clicked back the hammer. 'They could still be here.'

Charity pushed open the door with the tip of his boot as Mariah kept watch for Ellerby's return. The door opened slowly. Mariah looked in on a pitch-dark room. The whirr of the Lorenzo Generator dimmed as the ship moved gently back and forth in the growing sea. Charity reached in and flicked the brass switch on the wall by the door. A chandelier flickered into light.

'I think that we have had unwelcome visitors,' Charity said as he stepped inside.

Mariah followed and looked about the suite. The room had been ransacked. The large brass porthole swung open on its hinges. The doors to the two sleeping cabins on either side were unlocked and the contents of the sea-trunk had been tipped across the floor.

'What were they looking for?' Mariah asked as he sat on the lid of the trunk and sighed.

'That we will never know, but they have unpacked for us – even if we have to pick every garment from the floor,' Charity replied. He made safe the revolver and slid it back in his pocket. 'Whoever was here has left in a hurry,' he said, pointing to the porthole.

'But that goes to the outside of the ship – how would they have escaped without falling into the sea?' Mariah asked as he picked Charity's telescope from the floor.

Charity thought for a moment and looked about the room. He seemed to be searching for something quite invisible. He raised one eyebrow and scowled. Mariah had seen this many times before. It always came before Charity would announce some great idea or grand scheme.

'I am beginning to think that we should see Captain Tharakan. We should ask him to search the ship,' Charity said in a loud voice as he gestured for Mariah to get up from the trunk and walk towards the door. 'I will ask the steward to come and make the room ready whilst we are gone.'

Charity opened the door. He motioned for Mariah to stand on the far side. He then flicked off the light and slammed the door shut. For a moment they stood in the pitch black. The *Triton* moved gently in the swell. In the cabin, all was quiet and nothing stirred. They waited in the dark. Mariah realised that Charity thought someone was hiding in the room. He felt scared, his mouth was parched. He tried to breathe as quietly as he could as he listened for the slightest sound.

Then it came – a sound like the creaking of a tree branch. In the half-light, Mariah could see the lid of the trunk lift slightly. First a finger, then a thumb and another finger appeared from under the lid. Mariah watched Charity out of the corner of his eye. He stood back against the wood-panelled wall of the cabin-suite. There was a slight smile on his face, as if he were about to enjoy what was going to happen. A hand appeared as the lid of the trunk lifted even more. Then, bit by bit, a man cautiously stood up in the trunk and looked about the room.

'We have a guest,' Charity said as he flicked on the light switch and stepped towards him. 'Explain yourself!'

The man didn't reply. His hand darted to the pocket of his suit and then flashed a knife before them.

'I won't take you, Charity. I'll get the boy first. Take another step and you'll see,' the man said as his eyes desperately searched for a way of escape.

'You have me at a disadvantage,' Charity said. 'You know my name but I don't know yours.' He took a step in front of Mariah.

'You can hide the boy all you like – but you can't be with him forever. He should have just died on the train and saved us all the bother,' the man replied as he pushed back the sleeve of his jacket.

'Then put down the knife or fear the consequences,' said Charity.

The man laughed as he again reached into his pocket.

'I never thought I would have to use this so soon,' he said as he held out a small glass orb filled with a brown powder. 'I will have to take my chances.'

Charity stood his ground as he shielded Mariah from the assassin. 'If I am not mistaken then that is sodium hydride and if the flask is broken there will be a large explosion.'

'It goes bang, if that's what you mean,' the man replied. 'Out of my way, Charity. Just open the door and I'll be gone.'

'But you're on a ship with one thousand people – how will you ever escape?' Mariah asked.

'Now I know why they want you dead – and are willing to pay a price.'

'I'll open the door if you tell me who sent you here,' Charity said.

'You'll open the door or else will explode – there shall be no more questions,' the man replied as he sucked the air nervously through his teeth.

Charity pulled the handle and opened the door. The man stepped from the trunk and looked at Mariah.

'I'll be back for you . . . Some time, some place . . . Your death waits,' he said as he edged past Charity and into the corridor.

Then the door slammed into his back, knocking him to the floor.

'Get down, Mariah!' Charity shouted as he leapt towards the man.

In an instant the assassin spun out of the way and jumped to his feet like a cat. Charity crashed to the floor of the empty corridor.

'I didn't think you'd just let me go,' the man said breathlessly. 'They told me that Charity would want to fight.'

Charity kicked out with his feet, knocking the man to the ground. But again, as Charity dived for him, the man leapt to his feet as if he were an acrobat.

'You must be getting old,' the man scoffed. 'Let me go unhindered and give up your foolish games.'

Charity drew his pistol as he got to his feet, aiming it at the man's head.

'I never thought I should have to use this, but needs must . . .'

Before Charity had finished speaking, the assassin threw the circular flask of sodium hydride towards him. It spun like a forbidden planet through space. Mariah leapt from the doorway and seized the orb before it could hit the floor. The man jumped forwards, twisted and somersaulted, and snatched the pistol from Charity's hand.

'You are getting old,' he said as he stepped away. 'Perhaps it would be a good thing just to kill you both – here and now.'

The man clicked the hammer of the pistol and took aim. Mariah catapulted the orb as hard as he could. Just as the assassin fired the pistol the orb smashed on his forehead.

'Run!' shouted Charity as the assassin dropped the gun and staggered back, trying to scrape the gelatinous substance from his burning face.

The corridor shook as an incredible fireball exploded above them. It rolled like a thick black cloud along the ceiling of the passageway. Mariah turned to see the assassin shudder and then disappear in the smoke. He hid his eyes for a moment and then looked back again. The assassin was gone.

Charity got to his feet and wiped the dust from his coat. Mariah saw the bullet hole in his chest pocket.

'You've been shot,' he said, wondering why Charity wasn't injured.

'Spiderweb,' Charity said as he looked down at a pile of dust, all that remained of the assassin. 'Completely bulletproof and hand made in Huntress Row. A strange new material.'

[4]

The Lost Quatrain

MARIAH woke in the early hours of the morning, just as daylight was breaking over the horizon. It streamed into his cabin through the small circular porthole above his bed. The ship moved gently back and forth as it cut through the cold water. The bed appeared to stay immobile as the springs connecting it to the floor absorbed the ship's motion.

He thought of the night before. The terrified look on the assassin's face was still etched in his mind. Again and again he saw the final moments of the man's life and watched him explode and vanish to dust. Mariah had fallen asleep thinking of the man and wondering if he had been the one who had shot the boy on the train. He also wondered who had sent the assassin and why they wanted to kill him.

The night before, Charity had treated the incident in his usual matter-of-fact way. He had called the steward and informed the captain. Dutifully the pile of dust that was the assassin's mortal remains had been swept from the carpet. The corridor had been re-painted and before they had retired to their suite it looked as if nothing had ever occurred.

Captain Charity had taken out a bottle of liquor from his

travelling bag and poured himself a small glass. He had then opened a long black tin and buttered some biscuits. He had sent Mariah to bed with the words, 'Life is an adventure, Mariah, and sometimes we may not wake up from our sleep.'

Mariah had slept fitfully. The sound of the engine had droned for the first hour and invaded what dreams he had. He was aware that at one point in the night the ship had sailed through a storm. The glasses had clinked and chinked in the cupboard next to his bed and he had heard something rolling back and forth across the cabin floor as the ship rocked.

'I have taken the liberty of ordering our first breakfast in our suite,' Charity said as he opened the door to the sleeping cabin and looked in on Mariah. 'I thought we could plan what is to be done.'

'I can't stop thinking of the assassin,' Mariah said anxiously.

'If he had succeeded in his task, would he be thinking of you?' Charity asked. 'No, Mariah, he would not. The man would be at breakfast, eating his sausages – and so shall we . . .'

For a few moments Charity vanished into the bathroom. Mariah washed and dressed, then peered from the porthole at the vast desert of ocean that surrounded the ship.

Breakfast came on a silver tray. The steward slipped quietly into the room and placed the tray on the table, bowed to Mariah and then left the room. Within the hour, eleven sausages, six slices of bread, a jar of pickled onions and four eggs had all gone.

'I think it must be the sea air,' Charity said as he sank back in the divan chair and closed his eyes.

Mariah's mind was elsewhere. He looked at the jacket that Charity had worn the night before. The bullet hole was no longer visible.

'What is Spiderweb?' he asked.

'I don't rightly know.' Charity yawned his words. 'It was

developed for the Bureau some years ago. It is knifeproof, protects from bullets and will not catch fire.'

'Are all your clothes made from it?'

'Every one,' Charity replied. 'Even my undergarments.'

'Fireproof undergarments?' Mariah asked disbelievingly.

'You never know when they will be needed,' Charity replied with a snore.

'The bullet hole in your coat has gone – it's as if it never happened,' Mariah said.

'That is why it's called Spiderweb. Break the web of a spider and the next day it is as perfect as it was before.' Charity paused as he sighed with tiredness. 'Everything in your trunk is just the same. A precaution I thought I would take, just in case.'

'Did you know my life was in danger?' Mariah asked.

'A suspicion, nothing more,' Charity replied reluctantly.

'Do you think the assassin was alone?' Mariah asked as he ate the last pickled onion from the bowl next to the large but empty silver teapot.

'Possibly not, that is why you should carry this at all times.' Charity pulled a long leather case from under his chair. He placed it upon his lap, flicked the silver hinges and opened the lid. From where he was standing, Mariah could see that the box contained a pair of small pistols.

'So you think I will need a gun?' Mariah enquired nervously.

'Not one gun, but two. Strap one to your ankle and keep the other in your pocket at all times. Only use the ankle gun when you have to. And Mariah – your life could depend on it.'

'Why should they want to kill me? Who's behind all this?' he asked.

'The Bureau of Antiquities has many enemies. At the Prince Regent Hotel you met only two of them. Dedalus Zogel is a man beyond the law. He alone has good enough reason to see us both killed.'

Mariah took the pistols from the box and strapped one to his ankle. It felt uncomfortable and rubbed against the top of his boot. The other he slipped into the pocket of his coat. He had the urge to fire the gun to see if the Spiderweb would stop the bullet. His finger grasped the trigger.

'I should warn you about one thing,' Charity said. 'They are not *ordinary* pistols. Pull the safety catch back and it will fire – push it forward and it will spurt fire from the barrel.' His words were cut short by a knock at the door. 'Are we expecting anyone?' he asked quietly as he got to his feet.

Mariah stepped away from the door as he turned the handle to see who was outside. The passageway was empty. Mariah looked back and forth but could see no one. By his feet was a silver tray. On the tray was a small, neat envelope addressed to Captain Charity.

'Looks like an invitation,' Mariah said as he handed it to Charity. 'But whoever left it has gone.'

'Then we shall see,' replied Charity as he held the envelope up to the light to see what was inside. 'It looks safe enough,' he said, and he opened the envelope with his fingers.

Inside was a small green card with silver writing etched across the surface. It looked like a small emerald mirror. Charity studied it closely and then carefully handed it to Mariah.

'We are invited for dinner by the Marquis DeFeaux,' Mariah said as he read the words on the card. 'In his suite on Deck 13. Place the invitation into the steam elevator and access shall be gained . . .'

'And his messenger vanished before we could reply,' Charity said as he took the card from Mariah and looked at it again.

'I take it we cannot refuse?' Mariah asked.

'The Marquis DeFeaux is not a man to be ignored. He is the owner of the *Triton* and the one who requested the presence of the Bureau of Antiquities.'

'Perhaps he has heard about the assassin,' Mariah said.

'Perhaps he sent him . . .' Charity replied.

Mariah never mentioned the assassin again that day. The morning was spent walking the deck of the *Triton*, until they had walked for five miles. The promenade was packed with people of all sorts. Suited gentlemen followed skirted ladies like pet dogs. Mariah tried to listen to their conversations as he walked by, keeping pace with Charity's military stride. All the time he looked out for the assassin's accomplice, and every man who looked at him for more than a second was treated with suspicion. By lunchtime, the walk was complete. They ate together on the reserved foredeck, all the time watching out for some sign of the *Ketos*. The other passengers looked on, wondering why the man and boy had a place of such privilege. Far below, the Atlantic was calm as an old millpond. On the furthest horizon was a faint billowing of smoke – a sign, Charity said, of the funnels of the *Ketos*. Mariah peered through Captain Charity's spyglass, but could see nothing.

Above them, the *Bicameralist* sailed on majestically. At one o'clock in the afternoon it blotted out the sun and covered the ship in a deep shadow. With not one cloud in the sky, the skyship looked as though it were a broken piece of the moon floating upon the deep azure.

By late afternoon the skyship had sailed on faster than the *Triton* until it could no longer be seen. It was then that Mariah saw the ship on the port side. At first it seemed to be going the same way, heading out to the deep Atlantic and away from the Irish coast. Sometime later it turned and began to steam towards the *Triton* at full speed. Taking the spyglass he looked towards the ship and saw a man on the bridge of the ship flash a coded message towards the *Triton*. As if in recognition of what had been said, the *Triton* gave seven loud blasts upon its horn and then began to slow down.

Mariah looked again, and again a message in light was flashed from the ship and the *Triton* blasted its horn.

'I think we have an important guest,' Mariah said to Captain Charity as, wrapped in two large blankets, he dozed in a deck chair.

'Does the vessel have two funnels?' Charity asked Mariah.

Mariah looked at the ship through the telescope. 'Two funnels and a small mast,' he replied.

'And are they painted gold and red?' he asked without opening his eyes.

Mariah looked again. 'Gold and red with a band of black,' he said.

'Then our guest is the Marquis Lyon DeFeaux and that is his ship, the *Diablo*.'

It was not long before Mariah could read the nameplate on the front of the vessel that steamed full ahead towards them. On deck he could see several men with long rifles and an older man in a fur hat and matching coat that looked as though it had been forcibly taken from the back of a polar bear.

The *Diablo* turned slowly as it drew to a halt in the shadow of the great ship. Without any fuss, a wooden launch was lowered into the sea. The man in the fur hat stepped on board, followed by two other figures dressed exactly the same. They hunched together in the back of the boat as if to keep warm as a giant of a man took the helm and sailed the craft towards the *Triton*.

'They're about to come on board,' Mariah said, hoping to interest Charity in doing something other than sleeping on the deck.

'Really?' Charity replied without concern. 'Is there a Leviathan of a man steering the launch?' He had some mysterious way of seeing that which he could not see.

'Yes,' said Mariah, impatiently, 'and two others dressed exactly the same as the Marquis.'

43

'Then we shall be truly blessed at dinner,' Charity snorted with a laugh. 'The mountainous man is Casper Vikash – his bodyguard. The others will be his wife and daughter.'

'Do you know him well?' Mariah asked as the small launch came alongside and Mariah could see it no more.

'The Marquis Lyon DeFeaux has few friends and even fewer enemies,' Charity said mordantly.

'Fewer enemies?' asked Mariah.

'He has fewer enemies because he has them all murdered,' Charity whispered his reply, quite satisfied.

Within a few minutes the Lorenzo Generator was powering the ship towards the horizon. Mariah took a final glimpse of the *Diablo* through the spyglass. Far to the east, the sea swallowed the sun as, high above, a spectral carpet of stars began to appear.

Later, in Suite 395 Charity and Mariah dressed for dinner.

'Does this jacket have Spiderweb?' Mariah asked.

'Of course,' Charity replied. 'At dinner you can be attacked by the most perilous of creatures.'

Mariah thought about replying but didn't speak. In his mind he had strange pictures of being assaulted by a malicious kipper or disgruntled sirloin. He kept the thought to himself and was soon dressed in the image of Captain Charity. He wore a long tailcoat, a white starched shirt that rubbed his neck and a delicate cummerbund of black silk.

'You look like your father,' Charity said, smiling. 'He would be proud of you.'

'Did he carry a gun and wear Spiderweb?' Mariah asked as he thought of his father, unsure if he could ever imagine him ready to kill.

'I never asked and the circumstances never came about,' Charity said as he looked at Mariah, wondering what thought or memory had provoked such a question.

44

'He told me that life was sacred,' Mariah replied in a near whisper. 'I know that not to be true. It is to be taken, snatched and snuffed out. As worthless as a candle stub with no one to care for its passing.'

'Desperate words for one so young,' Charity replied.

'I can't get the eyes of the assassin from my mind – yet I know if I hadn't thrown the orb we both could be dead. He glared at me as if he willed me to kill him.' Mariah shuddered slightly, still unsure if he had done the right thing.

'Then you have found the answer to your question. You put your life – and my life – above his. We didn't go looking for the fight and we gave him opportunity to surrender. The assassin sealed his own fate.'

'If things could be so simple, then my heart would not be so heavy,' Mariah replied as he fastened his tie and looked at his reflection in the mirror. Yet something in what Charity said made him feel pleasantly reassured.

'We see life as a dim reflection in a clouded mirror – but one day we shall see it without our misted minds.' As he spoke Charity walked to the door and turned out the light before they left the cabin.

They walked silently along the passageway. Charity nodded to the crowds of other passengers who were leaving their cabins and going to dinner. He looked at his fob watch. Mariah saw that it said six-fifty. At the end of the passageway they took the crowded steam elevator together to Deck 13. It reminded Mariah of the elevator at the Prince Regent. A peculiar woman in a fur overcoat pressed close to him. She smelt of cucumber and beer. Her lipstick was smudged across her mouth so that she looked like a drunken clown. The man she was with was older. He was particularly thin, with a neat bow tie and silver hair that shone like steel. His moustache arched over his lips like a frozen waterfall of icicles below his

45

craggy, lined face. It was obvious to Mariah that they had been arguing. Their eyes never met and the woman looked as though she had been crying.

'An interesting journey,' Mariah said to her with a smile in the hope that she would turn from her remorse.

'Is it?' she said in a chirp. 'This is my honeymoon – but you wouldn't think so.' She spoke quietly, just loud enough for the man to hear her.

The steam elevator stopped on Deck 11 and the couple got out with the rest of the passengers to go to the large dining room at the stern of the ship. Mariah slipped the invitation into the slot beneath the buttons. Charity and Mariah waited as the doors closed automatically and the elevator rattled up two further decks.

'Deck 13?' Mariah asked before the elevator doors opened. 'Does the Marquis DeFeaux have his own dining room?'

'I think you will find he has his own deck at the very top of the ship,' Charity replied as the elevator stopped and the door slid open.

Mariah gulped twice. Stretching out before him was a marble floor that eventually met with walls covered in thick fur. A gold chandelier bedecked with electric lamps hung from the ceiling, whilst ancient gods fought with strange sea creatures within gold picture frames.

'Captain Charity?' asked a gargantuan man with a shaved head, three gold teeth and a face scarred by a thousand cuts.

'And Mariah Mundi,' Charity replied, as if it was an everyday occasion to be greeted by a human monster.

'The Marquis has asked me to meet you. If you would both like to take a seat,' the man said in a voice so deep that it was like the rumbling of a whale.

'He's a giant,' Mariah said as the man walked away into another room and closed two panelled doors behind him.

'Casper Vikash,' Charity replied.

'Did you see his face – all those scars?' Mariah asked.

'He saved DeFeaux in the Amazon. Rumour has it that he jumped in a river and rescued his master from a shoal of piranha.'

'And they did that to him?' Mariah asked.

'The Bureau of Antiquities was informed that Vikash was close to death for many weeks. DeFeaux had his surgeons rebuild the man's face the best they could, but they left the scars. You will never see DeFeaux without him. Vikash was a Legionnaire – that is all that is known of him. Be careful, Mariah,' he added as they waited patiently. 'We are dealing with dangerous men.'

'Does the Bureau make a business of knowing everything about everyone?' Mariah asked.

'There are certain people who we are *interested* in. DeFeaux is one of them,' Charity replied quietly.

The doors opened and Vikash stooped through and smiled warmly. 'The Marquis is ready to see you. I hope you both enjoy dinner.'

As the entrance hall was grand, the dining room was quite sumptuous. It was clad with oak panels as in a fine castle. A large window looked out across the stern of the ship. There were doors to a balcony deck. Everywhere Mariah looked was brightly polished wood and brass. Before them was a long table on which were five square plates of plain porcelain. Each had a set of silver cutlery. In the middle of the table was a simple candlestick with three candles. Each plate had a name etched on triangular card. Mariah could see his own name in black ink.

'Please be seated,' Vikash whispered eerily. 'They will be with you soon.'

Charity and Mariah sat and waited. The room was silent.

Mariah could hear neither the sea nor the generator. It was as if he was again on dry land, on a high mountain or at the top of the Prince Regent Hotel – yet far from feeling safe, the eerie silence gave him deep foreboding.

[5]

Biba DeFeaux

WHEN the Marquis DeFeaux walked quickly through the open doors and into the vast dining room, Mariah gave him little attention. Charity stood to his feet and held out his hand in welcome, but Mariah just stared. It was not the Marquis who stole his interest, but the girl who walked in his shadow.

Mariah had never seen anyone quite like this before. She was tall, thin, with skin that shimmered. Her face was white and her neck was wrapped in a long purple scarf of fine silk that fell to the floor. She wore a green velvet dress and riding boots, and a green suede jacket that was held back on the arms by heavily bangled wrists. Mariah could not help staring at the whirl of deep red ringlets that tumbled to her shoulders. He was aware too of the woman who walked behind her, smiling and nodding as if she welcomed an old friend.

'And this is Mariah Mundi,' Mariah heard Charity say as if he were being woken from a dream.

Mariah stood up and gulped, 'Hello.'

'I have heard so much of you from the Bureau,' the Marquis replied as he gestured for all to be seated. 'Captain, I believe you know my wife, Mergyn?' he asked.

Mariah saw Charity smile at the woman across the table.

'And this is my daughter, Biba DeFeaux,' the Marquis said proudly as he leant across and stroked her face. 'She is somewhat shy . . .'

'It is good to be with you,' Charity replied. He looked about the table as an army of waiters invaded the room with silver dishes and decanters of wine.

'I took the liberty of ordering for you,' the Marquis said as they all sat down. 'When you own the ship it is possible to have just what you want. I have even prepared a fish supper, just like they give you at the Golden Kipper.'

Mariah wondered how the Marquis knew about Charity's small café by the harbour of the-town-at-the-end-of-the-line. It made him think of all that he had left behind. He realised that he had given no consideration to travelling so far from the place he now called home, and a terrible thought assaulted his mind. It lasted only a second, but it was powerful enough to make him feel quite sick.

'You have been doing your homework, Lyon,' Charity joked. 'I am sure your chef will surpass anything we could prepare at the Golden Kipper.'

'On the contrary, Captain. I hear you serve some of the finest food in England,' said Mergyn DeFeaux as she sucked the juice from an empty oyster shell.

'Do you still keep a crocodile in the cellar?' asked the Marquis, as Biba giggled.

It had been the first sound she had made. She had not greeted anyone in the room nor said anything as they began eating. Biba DeFeaux had stared at the table as if she were the only person in the room. Mariah thought her to be a doll, a marionette with a clockwork smile. He could not fight the desire to speak to her.

'Do you always travel with your father, Biba?' he asked.

The table fell silent as if he had broken a great taboo. Mergyn looked at her husband as Biba pulled her napkin to her mouth and stared at Mariah through astonished blue eyes.

'My daughter had an accident, Mariah,' the Marquis said. 'She doesn't enter much in the way of conversation.' As he spoke his wife picked at her food like a sparrow with her long fingers.

Mariah was about to apologise when Charity spoke. 'I have both the best chef and the biggest crocodile in England. In fact, Lyon, it is a crocogon. An amalgamation of crocodile and a Java dragon. I found it on the beach not a few hundred yards from where I live.'

Biba giggled again as she took out a lacquered box from her pocket, opened the lid and watched the figure dance. It was as if balance had been restored. The rest of the meal was served and they all ate well. Mariah listened to long conversations about the *Triton* and how DeFeaux knew the ship would win the great race. A clock chimed the hours as plates were served, emptied and taken away. Throughout, Mariah tried to look interested and steal an occasional glance at Biba DeFeaux. He wondered what *accident* had taken away her speech and why she wouldn't look at him. There was something about her that was different beyond her silence. He could tell that she listened to all that was said. Not just to the words, but to the feelings of the heart.

'I fear I must speak to you alone,' the Marquis said to Charity sometime after the last crumbs of chocolate cake had been eaten. 'I would like to show you the balcony. The *Bicameralist* has returned and as yet I have not seen it at night. Mergyn will keep the lad company,' he went on as he pulled the lapels of his coat closer together and shrugged his narrow shoulders.

Charity and DeFeaux left the room. Casper Vikash followed them. He carried a bearskin coat over his arm. Mariah saw him lock the balcony door from the outside as Charity and DeFeaux leant against the iron railings and looked out to sea.

'Have you known Captain Charity for long?' Mariah asked Madame DeFeaux as the servants cleared the table.

'Before I knew my husband,' she replied. 'I met him in London – he would have been just a little older than you. He had just left the Colonial School – we were great friends. And you, Mariah, what is your acquaintance with him?' she asked.

'I work for him at the Prince Regent Hotel. He is the owner and I a magician's apprentice,' he replied.

'And what of the ship – is it to your liking?' she asked.

'I haven't seen much. Captain Charity insisted on walking the deck for most of the morning and sleeping for most of the afternoon.'

'Then Biba will take you for a guided tour. I will arrange everything. Be outside the lift on Deck 13 at ten in the morning,' she said.

'But . . . she doesn't . . .?' Mariah tried to ask in a whisper.

'Speak?' said Madame DeFeaux before going on. 'Biba was attacked by a polar bear – it was three years ago in Greenland. Vikash shot it just before it was about to seize upon her. My husband had it made into a coat for Biba to wear. Once she is sure of you, she will speak. Isn't that right, Biba?'

Biba didn't reply. She stared at the lacquered box and watched the dancer twirl and twirl.

'Is that from Sir Lorenzo Zane?' Mariah asked.

'Indeed, it was given to Biba by his son. They are very special friends. Biba takes it everywhere. She thinks it reminds her of him.' Madame DeFeaux watched her daughter as she spoke.

Mariah thought that Madame DeFeaux was the image of her daughter, even down to the clothes that they wore. For a moment, he wished the assassin's bullet had not missed Lorenzo Zane.

'He is on the ship – we met on the train,' Mariah said as suddenly Biba looked up.

'We did not know – we thought he was still in Greenland,' Madame DeFeaux replied.

'I met him on the train, he was travelling with his mother.' Mariah thought it not wise to mention the assassin.

'Then perhaps you could explore the ship together. Captain Tharakan has promised fine weather – not that it matters on a ship of this size, where there is so much to do,' Madame DeFeaux said.

'If Lorenzo joins us then that will be a fine thing,' Biba said unexpectedly in a fine English accent. 'Tomorrow at ten by the entrance to the lift.'

'I will see that Casper allows you an entrance. Deck 13 can only be reached in the steam elevator by invitation,' said Madame DeFeaux as the door to the balcony opened and Charity stepped inside.

'Then that shall be that and the gold shall be safe,' the Marquis said as he closed the door behind them.

'You speak as if you have won it already,' said Charity eagerly.

'I don't think the *Ketos* will be able to keep the pace she does. By tomorrow we shall be ahead of her. I want to sail as close as we can so as we pass by I can look the captain in the eyes and wish him well.' He laughed. 'A million dollars just for winning a race – what kind of world do we live in, Captain Jack?'

In the steam elevator on their way to their suite, Charity did not speak. He appeared troubled. Mariah knew that Charity was thinking about what had been said on the balcony. When the time was right Mariah would be told all he needed to know. He often felt that Bureau business was like a gigantic jigsaw. Each piece was scattered here and there and yet when it came together all would be revealed. Charity had told him that it is often dangerous to know everything – in case you should fall into the hands of the enemy. 'Know little, but know what you need,' is what he would say on the days when Charity would talk about the Bureau. Mariah would listen intently, something within telling him his life would depend upon it.

As they pressed the ticket into the whirring lock by the side of their door, Charity stopped. He looked pensive, as if he had forgotten something important.

'There is something I must do,' he said musingly. 'I will be back as soon as I can. Keep the door locked and answer it to no one.'

'Where are you going?' Mariah asked.

'I have someone to see. All will be well,' Charity replied as the door to the room opened. 'Just keep the door locked.'

'But I can come with you?' Mariah protested.

'I have to go alone. The one I go to see won't speak to me if you are there. No witnesses,' Charity replied.

Mariah felt concerned. He didn't want Charity to go, but could not speak his fears. He found himself saying, 'Don't worry for me – I have the pistols.'

He went into the suite. It was cold and lifeless. Somehow it was different from when they had left it hours before. Mariah looked about the room. All appeared to be the same and yet there was a strangeness to the air. The travelling trunk was still in the middle of the room behind the long leather sofa. Next to it was the lamp and the table on which was the black telephone. He could see that nothing had been moved, but Mariah knew that the atmosphere had changed. He racked his mind – he had felt this way before. Then he remembered. It was the night at the Prince Regent when the killer had stalked him. It was the feeling of being watched, just like before.

On that occasion Mariah had been by the fire in the hallway of the hotel. He had got up from his chair and stood by the fire-place. He looked at his face in the mirror and for the briefest moment he had been frozen to the spot. He couldn't move, his arms and legs were petrified. There, in the reflection of the mirror, as if the figure stood behind him, was the face of a masked man. For a fleeting second Mariah saw the bloodshot eyes and drivelling mouth half-hidden behind the golden mask of tragedy.

When he looked again, the face was gone. All he could see was the chair and a large aspidistra billowing from a brass pot. Mariah had turned; his eyes had searched the shadows for the faintest trace of the man. There was no one.

Now the feeling was the same. It was as if something within warned him of a real and present danger. His body tingled and his spine shuddered; the hairs stood on the back of his neck and a voice inside his head told him to run. Mariah locked the door and made sure the bolt was slid across. He went to each wardrobe in turn and, slowly opening each door, checked inside. The room was empty. Everything was just as it should be. Still the deep unease was there like before. He knew that someone was watching him, that eyes stared from hidden places . . .

Fearfully, Mariah opened the door of the sleeping cabin and looked under the bed. He then crossed the room and did the same in Charity's room. All was as it should be. The suite was empty. The wind whistled outside and whispered coldly.

For several minutes, Mariah sat in the leather armchair that was bolted to the floor. He stared about the room, looking for a miniscule aperture from where he could be watched. He took the pistol from his pocket, checked the chamber and pulled the trigger until it stuck against the safety catch.

'It's in your mind,' he said out loud to break the silence of the room. 'I'm alone, I know it . . .'

The words felt empty. No matter how much he tried to convince himself, he still had the nagging doubt that someone, somewhere, could see everything he did. It was an unfounded fear, but a voice within, an ancient perception of when danger was near, told him to make ready to fight.

There was the shrill ring of the telephone. Mariah picked up the receiver. Even before he could give a greeting he could hear the faraway sound of someone breathing.

'Who is it?' he asked. 'Suite 395, hello.' He hoped someone would answer.

There was silence. No one spoke. All he could hear was the sighing breath. It rasped and coughed as if it were about to die.

'Who are you?' Mariah asked, his hand shaking. 'Why are you doing this?'

There was gentle laughter, as if whoever it was had remembered a fond and happy memory.

'It's me . . . I've come back,' it whispered just as the line went dead.

Mariah put the telephone back on the table and checked the lock on the door and again looked in the wardrobes and the beds. He was alone.

Just as he returned to the leather chair, he noticed something quite strange. The mirror by his bedroom door appeared to be glowing. It was as if the glass were about to become aflame. It shimmered momentarily. He looked again, and the mirror was just mercurial glass in which he could see his reflection.

From the door came a tap-tap-tapping as if a tiger-claw struck the wood time after time. Then, as Mariah turned, there was a scratching as if a dog was in the passageway. Mariah listened as the scraping came again and again. He went to the door and put his hand upon the wood. He could feel it move with the tremor of the generator. The scratching came again, this time louder. Mariah could feel it against the door – something was on the other side. He listened as the creature sniffed the sill. Then, as swiftly as it had come, the sound had gone.

Mariah sat with his back to the door. He wanted to leave, to be at home. He didn't want to be on his own. Whatever haunted him seemed to know his mind and what he feared.

'Mariah . . .' He heard the whisper. 'Mariah . . .' said the voice of a child, calling him from the passageway outside. 'Come with me . . .'

He didn't know what to do. The room grew colder, darker . . . The lights began to fade in their brightness. Mariah could hear his heart beating as the blood rushed through his head.

'Who is this?' he asked, hoping the voice would be gone and he would be tormented no more.

'Topher . . .' replied the voice from outside, this time so clear that Mariah recognised its tone.

'But it can't be,' Mariah replied in total disbelief.

'You remember me. The Colonial School . . . I fell from the boat, in the Thames . . .'

Mariah could not forget that summer day five years before when his most perfect friend had fallen from a rowing boat by Chiswick Bridge. They had searched the water but he was never found.

'Why are you here?' Mariah asked, as if death could not stand in the way of their friendship.

'Come with me, Mariah. Jump the ship . . . We can play again, it's so easy to do,' the voice pleaded with him.

Mariah got to his feet, slid the brass guard from the circular spy hole and peered into the passageway. It was dark, as if the lights there had faded also.

'It can't be you, Topher. Not after all this time.' The memories of his friend blew about his mind like a breeze through an open window.

'You can't see me, Mariah . . . Not there . . .' The voice of the child now spoke from inside the room.

Mariah gripped the door, his face pressed against the wood,

too fearful to turn. He knew that Topher was there, right behind him, standing in a pool of golden light cast by the mirror.

'Do you wish me harm?' Mariah asked as he could see the room behind him begin to glow.

'I've come for you, Mariah . . . We all have,' the voice replied with chilled breath, as if spoken by an orchestra of spectres.

'But you're dead?' Mariah asked.

'What is death but a doorway, Mariah? I was given to the waters and from there I have to return. Join me, Mariah – jump from the ship . . .'

Mariah turned slowly. Streaming from the mirror was a golden light. It fanned out from its source to form a tight cone the size of a small child. There, before him, standing like a mirage in the darkness . . . was Topher. He was perfect in every way and looked just like the picture that hung on the wall of the Colonial School. Around his feet was a pool of water that dripped from the hem of his coat – the coat he wore on the day he disappeared.

'I'll wait for you,' Topher said, his lips unmoving and smile rigid as if he were but a hologram.

Mariah couldn't speak. The terror of the vision chained him to the ground. The image flickered with the golden light and seemed to come closer. A blue mist with the scent of almonds and seaweed filled the room. The vision of Topher began to fade. Mariah could hear him speaking but couldn't understand the words. He felt weary, exhausted. His eyes were heavy. His head drooped. Finally his knees buckled and he fell to the floor, overcome by a deathly sleep.

[6]

Naturum Muriaticum

THE Saloon Theatre was misty-thick with the smoke from a thousand cigars. Charity stood, crowded to the end of the long wooden bar. Three large windows gave him a view over the dark sea. High above, the *Bicameralist* kept pace with the ship, hovering like a dark cloud. A searchlight at the front of the skyship bathed the *Triton* in a pool of carbide light.

Charity looked down. The ship appeared to be surrounded by a ghostly phosphorescence that bubbled from the sea. Promenaders walked the deck arm in arm. Some stopped by the railings and looked out at the flat, calm Atlantic that enclosed them like thick green ink. In the packed saloon, old men drank absinthe and Angostura poured from tall jugs. The conversation was loud and raucous as they watched the dancing on the small stage by the curtained doorway.

Sipping from his glass, Charity waited. He had no interest in the burlesque or the milky-green cocktail, yet he held his glass so as not to appear out of place. With each faux sip, he looked about the room. It had been something that Casper Vikash had said to the Marquis on the balcony of their suite that had brought him to that place. Charity had been sure that he was not meant to hear that single word, but hear he had. As the night had gone on so the intrigue had grown and grown. By the time he and Mariah had got to the door of the cabin, Charity could bear it no longer.

As he had taken the steam elevator to the upper deck, Charity knew he was being followed. There had been two men at the end of the passageway near to his cabin. They had watched him intently whilst they conversed amiably with one another. Then as he left the elevator on the saloon deck, another man had followed him along the corridor and through the red velvet curtains. Charity didn't know who these men were, but his suspicion was that they worked for the Marquis DeFeaux. Each one was typically Continental, smaller than average, swarthy in complexion and with a thick Latino brow. Their clothes were to big for them, as if they had been hurriedly found for the purpose of fitting in with the aristocratic guests of the saloon bar.

Even as he sipped his drink in his gloved hand, one of the men watched him from the door and then, within minutes of his arrival, was joined by the two others. Charity knew that whilst he was in the company of so many people nothing would happen. As he waited, the dancing stopped. The stage was cleared of several disregarded Akomeogi hand-fans thrown down by the dancers. Into the bright limelight stepped a hunched man in a tailcoat and white spats. He carried on his arm a large leather-faced doll dressed as a Chinese Mandarin.

For a moment, he held the doll for all to see. It was lifelike in every way, although its skin looked as if it were tanned rawhide and the eyes were that of a large fish. A long, thin moustache flowed down from its lips. The man took a stool and sat with the mannequin on his knee.

'My name is Charlemagne. I am the keeper of secrets,' he said as he bolstered the doll against him. 'Shanjing is more than a mannequin – he is a thousand years old and has seen empires fall. This night, he will tell you the darkest secrets of your hearts.'

As the ventriloquist spoke in his Italian accent, the audience muttered in bored disapproval.

'We want dancers, not mind-reading bits of wood,' shouted a thin man with an obvious glass eye on the very front row.

'You want to know who is stealing from your business and how much you spend on horses?' Shanjing appeared to ask, as his wooden arms flailed in his embroidered silk jacket.

The man on the front row fell silent and tried to sink as low as he could, for fear that his secrets would be made clear to the world.

'Then tell me what I had for breakfast,' shouted another man as he struggled to keep his absinthe in his glass.

'You want to know what you had for breakfast – but I will tell the world the name of the one you had breakfast with,' Shanjing replied quickly.

Those around the man laughed as he fell back, stunned that a doll should know of his deceit.

It was then that the audience fell strangely quiet. Shanjing rolled his eyes and looked around the saloon. He seemed menacing, otherworldly and malevolent. It was as if he were no longer a doll dressed in gold silk but a tiny man, perfect in every way and seeing into the dark hearts of those around him.

'Who would ask Shanjing a question about their life?' Charlemagne asked. No one dared speak. Each man had too many secrets to behold. One man with a fresh scar on his cheek got to his feet to walk out of the room. Shanjing opened his eyes and stared at him.

'You!' he said. 'Leaving because you are frightened what Shanjing may know about you? Don't worry. Police in New York will not be waiting for you.'

The audience laughed nervously. The man stopped and put a trembling hand to his face as tears trickled over his cheek.

'How did you know?' he asked in horror. 'Is it so clear?'

'It is as plain as the scar on your face,' Shanjing scoffed. 'No matter what you do – the secret will follow you like a prowling tiger.'

The man looked to the floor as all around him faces stared, wondering what secret Shanjing had discovered.

'Who told you?' the man demanded. 'I have told no one.'

'You have told yourself every night as you have looked in the mirror. *Pity him – at least I have a face* . . . Isn't that what you say?' Shanjing asked, his Mandarin voice shaking as he spoke.

'Then you know too much,' the man said as he pushed his way through the silent crowd and left the saloon.

'I have a question,' Charity asked from the back of the room to break the silence. 'Who will win the race, the *Triton* or the *Ketos*?'

'Rather you should ask, Captain, will the race be completed?' said Shanjing melancholically. 'There are many miles of sea and the ice flows from the north like a dagger. The winds will rage and waters ravage. So do not be complacent. I look for the day when my feet touch dry land again.'

'Your feet don't even touch the floor,' shouted an absinthe-tongued young man who was standing by the red velvet curtains.

'And your heart will not beat after you celebrate your birth again . . . Go now before it is too late, before you all die . . . Go quickly. Death comes to kill you all.' Shanjing began to rant as he spoke curses in Mandarin.

Charlemagne held the mannequin as if it were a sentient creature. Then with one hand he smothered its mouth whilst with the other he held the struggling doll close to him as he ran from the stage.

The gathering looked ominously at each other. It was as if they did not want to believe what had been said. Quickly, the rotund impresario pushed the dancers back on the stage. The small orchestra played even faster than before. Waiters in white jackets hurried around the tables, filling each jug with fresh absinthe.

Charlemagne vanished through the curtains that hid the doorway at the side of the stage. Charity followed him closely. The man ran ahead, pushing aside a waiting magician and sending a sleeve of pigeons into the air. In an instant he was out of sight. To one side of the passageway was a narrow doorway. Charity stopped. He could hear voices arguing beyond the door.

'You said too much,' muttered Charlemagne.

'I can only speak of the visions I have,' Shanjing replied, his voice smothered.

'Then tell them things that will make them laugh,' Charlemagne insisted.

'But that will not help them – we must get from this boat before disaster comes.' Then Shanjing fell silent.

Charity banged on the door.

'I must see you,' he said.

'I cannot see anyone,' Charlemagne replied.

'Then I will stay here until you come out,' Charity vowed.

'Very well,' said a feeble English voice.

Eventually the door to the small dressing room opened and Charity stepped in. Charlemagne was sitting on a red sofa by the wall. On the floor at his feet was a coffin-shaped box. The room smelt sweetly, almost sickly, like boiled almonds and seaweed.

'You have quite a skill, Mr Charlemagne,' Charity said.

'It's not Charlemagne – that's just a name for the stage. I'm Eric Bloodstone, from Wigan,' he muttered.

63

'A convincing Italian accent – very Florentine. I was completely fooled,' Charity replied.

'I have had practice. I worked in Florence as a waiter for many years,' Charlemagne said as beads of sweat trickled across his forehead.

'Do you really see those things about people or are you just guessing?' Charity asked.

'Why should you want to know? If you want to see more come back tomorrow night,' he snapped.

'I am the owner of the Prince Regent Hotel, and I am always on the lookout for entertainments that will astound,' Charity replied.

'The Prince Regent – I have heard much of that place,' Charlemagne said, his eyes lighting up with the prospect of future employment.

'Then we should speak further.' Charity turned to go but paused. 'One thing – how did you find such an amazing creation as Shanjing?'

'He found me. Sometimes I wonder who is in control of the act,' he replied.

'May I see him?'

'No,' snapped Charlemagne. 'That would be impossible. No one has ever seen Shanjing in his box. I treat him as if he were a living person. That is the only way.'

'Perhaps another time?' Charity asked as he left the room and closed the door firmly behind him.

'You treat me like a dog,' Charity heard Shanjing's muffled voice plead. 'If I could escape from you I would be gone. He knows too much – he will bring misery to you.'

'You would never go – you need me as much as I need you. Just be careful next time – lie if you have to and don't frighten people.'

Charity listened as the man spoke to himself.

'Obviously quite mad,' he whispered as he entered the saloon through the stage door.

There was no music, no dancing – every face was pressed against the windows that overlooked the deck below.

'He's going to jump!' shouted the impresario as he looked on. 'He's just a lad, why should he want to throw himself from the ship?'

'That steward wants to catch hold of him,' said a man.

'He'll drag him over with him if he does,' said another.

Charity pushed through the crowd until he could see from the window. There, three decks below on a gangplank over the sea, was Mariah. His long curls blew in the breeze as he held out his hands – it was as if he were following someone he trusted.

'No!' Charity shouted as he pushed against the pack and ran from the saloon.

The entire ship seemed to be making for the place where Mariah stood. Crowds of people bustled through the corridors and blocked the exits. Charity ran on until he found a door to the outside deck. He climbed as fast as he could over a railing and caught a wire that ran from a funnel to the prow of the ship. Without hesitation, Charity leapt from the ship and slid down the wire.

'Mariah!' he shouted as he got to his feet and began to approach the boy.

Mariah didn't reply. He walked along the gangplank towards the sea below as if he couldn't hear him.

'Stay back!' shouted the steward as he edged behind Mariah.

'Topher?' asked Mariah as he looked to his invisible friend. 'Where shall we go?'

'Who do you talk to?' Charity shouted as he pushed the Steward out of the way.

Mariah stopped momentarily and looked back. Charity saw his glazed eyes that looked like burnished steel.

'It's all right, Topher, I'm coming to you . . . I must say good-bye to Captain Charity . . .' Mariah spoke as if he could see both worlds.

'He's not real, Mariah. It's an hallucination,' Charity shouted. He was scared to get too close for fear that Mariah would leap into the sea.

'Topher came for me – in the cabin,' Mariah said. 'He's not dead – he didn't drown.'

'Look at me . . . look at me,' Charity said desperately. 'I have something for you to take with you, something for Topher.' He held out his fob watch towards Mariah. 'Take it . . . you'll need this.'

Mariah stopped and looked. He could only see Charity as an apparition. It was as if his soul had crossed the Styx and now dwelt beyond death, looking back at life. The dangling watch spun on its chain, shimmering in the light from the skyship that hovered above them. Mariah looked back on a ghostly world. He could see the outlines of the people as they gathered near him on the deck. Below, the bubbling jade water looked warm and inviting. He could see Topher at the end of the gantry – so real, so alive, an old friend waiting for him. Charity began to fade until he was just a dim outline of the man.

'You have to take it,' Charity insisted as Mariah teetered inches from death. 'Topher wants you to have it.'

'I can't see you, Jack – where are you?' Mariah asked.

'I'm here, Mariah, just a few feet away. I will give you the watch,' Charity said as he edged closer.

For a moment Charity looked up. There on the balcony of Deck 13 was the Marquis DeFeaux and his daughter Biba. He could see them clearly in the light of the *Bicameralist*. The Marquis looked as if he were Caesar staring down at a gladiator about to die.

66

'Just one step and you will have the watch. Reach out, Mariah, it is just here,' Charity said as he reached out his hand.

Mariah stumbled a pace towards him and then stopped as if a voice were calling him back.

'Listen to me, Mariah,' Charity shouted. 'Just a few more inches . . .'

Mariah wasn't listening. Whatever had taken his soul called him on. Without a word, he stumbled forwards, clutched the wire rail of the gangway – and then fell back. Charity dived towards him and gripped him by the sleeve of his jacket. Mariah fell from the gantry. Charity held fast as the lad dangled above the sea.

'Take my hand, Mariah. Don't let go!' Charity shouted as he felt the gangplank slip from its mooring and dangle from the small crane over the water. The passengers began to scream in fear as both Mariah and Charity were suspended over the sea. The gantry swayed back and forth as Charity pulled Mariah to him.

'Let me go!' Mariah shouted angrily. 'I want to follow Topher.'

'It's an illusion, a phantasm – he isn't real,' Charity urged as he managed to grip Mariah by the hand.

Within a minute Charity had pulled Mariah back on to the gangway. A sailor on the ship had powered the steam crane and let down the gantry to the lower deck away from the onlookers. Captain Tharakan and Ellerby were waiting.

'Is he dead?' asked Tharakan as Mariah was dragged from the gangway to the safety of the deck.

'Very much alive,' Charity replied as he saw specks of purple powder in the lines on Mariah's hand. 'But from the look of him, I would say that someone has drugged him with *Lyzerjid*.'

'Who should do such a thing?' Tharakan asked. 'An assassin in your room and now this . . .'

'Someone wants him dead, and I do not know the reason why,' Charity replied. A steward helped him get Mariah to his feet. 'We shall take him to his room. Captain Tharakan, can you provide a guard for the night?'

Tharakan nodded to Ellerby, who disappeared into the shadow of a doorway only to appear moments later with three of his men armed with revolvers.

'We will follow you,' Ellerby said harshly. 'If we find anyone trying this again, they will be dealt with sternly.'

Charity didn't believe him. There was something about the man that he felt he couldn't trust. But this was not the place to question Ellerby as to his loyalty. As they led Mariah away, Charity thought that whoever wanted Mariah dead would need an accomplice. If Tharakan wasn't the one, then Ellerby could be.

'Mr Ellerby, do you have another cabin that we could take him to?' Charity asked as they got near to the open door of Suite 395.

'The ship is full, Captain. Not a single bed is left,' Ellerby replied without a glint of concern.

Then Biba DeFeaux stepped from the door of the room, followed by Casper Vikash. 'My father has sent me to see you,' she said. 'We have taken the liberty of packing all your things. The Marquis thought it would be wise if you both stayed on Deck 13. There is a private suite and Casper will keep us all safe.'

Biba DeFeaux smiled at Charity as she twisted the ringlets of her red curls. Here was the girl who but two hours before had refused to speak. He thought for a moment. It all appeared to be too convenient, too manipulated by the power of a wealthy man. He looked around the room and saw that everything had been packed into the trunks. Several of DeFeaux's servants stood, arms folded in their neat black uniforms, awaiting instructions. Biba looked at Charity and then touched Mariah's face.

'I think it would be best if we went to Deck 13,' she said with a click of her fingers. 'Casper will see to everything.'

[7]

Tiger, Tiger

MARIAH woke up and stared at the ceiling. He could see his dim reflection in the polished gilt that covered the ornate surface above him. This was not his cabin, he thought to himself as he tried to lift his head from the soft silk-lined pillow. Everything was bright and bold and glistened slightly. In the room were a narrow bed, a chair, a bookcase brimming with leather-bound volumes and a brass spyglass on a large stand. On every wall was an electric light set in an ornate tortoiseshell cover. There was a large window to his left. The glass was set in a brass frame that could not be opened and on either side were thick drapes of embroidered green silk.

For a moment he thought he was dead and that this place was heaven or even possibly hell. Mariah hadn't made his mind up as to which would be preferable. It was something he didn't feel he should consider until he was much older. Yet there was a nagging doubt in his mind that he could be nearer to having to decide than he wanted.

He was aware of every breath that he took. His lungs burnt and his eyes felt sore. Whatever had happened the night before had exhausted him. Pulling the covers to his face, he turned over. The room was so designed that from the bed you could look through the window. Mariah could see that he was high up on the ship. It was daylight and he could smell tea. By the window was his trunk and on that a silver tray, one porcelain cup and a large teapot. To one side was a covered salver and, next to that, two eggs wrapped in small knitted caps. Beside the eggs were plates of toast and neatly cut beef sandwiches.

There was a gentle tap at the door. The handle turned and Biba DeFeaux looked inside.

'I had them bring you breakfast,' she said, remarkably confident for someone who had once been terrified to silence by a large bear. 'Captain Charity told me what you liked.'

'Is he here?' asked Mariah.

'No, he and my father have gone to look at the gold bullion. Casper is here to look after us. They say that you were going to throw yourself from the ship,' she said as she walked to the trunk. She poured Mariah a cup of tea and handed it to him.

'I can't remember what happened. I just remember dreaming,' he replied.

'I was made to see a psychiatrist. They thought the bear had made me quite mad,' she said as she twisted the silver chain around her neck.

'Why didn't you speak when we met last night?' Mariah asked.

'I don't. Well, not when I first meet someone. I didn't like the look of you – you seemed ordinary. Lorenzo isn't ordinary, he has his own skyship and a boat that goes under water and a father who is a genius . . . What does your father do?' she asked, her words gushing like water from a tap.

'He does nothing,' he replied. 'He's –'

'That's why you are ordinary,' she went on clumsily. 'I even bet that you went to school. I had tutors and my father employed children to play with me.'

'I'm not surprised,' Mariah muttered, hoping Biba would be struck dumb with the fear of bears yet again.

'I think I should take you around the ship. My father owns it and soon the *Triton* will be seen as the fastest ship in the world.'

'I don't feel too well,' Mariah tried to say as Biba pressed a plate of toast and butter into his hands.

'Just a matter of food,' she said sharply. 'They say that if you eat, it makes you well. I try to avoid eating at all costs. I have a theory that we can get all the goodness we need from the sun – just like plants.'

'What if you live in Greenland? The sun doesn't shine for weeks,' he asked as he attempted to eat the toast that tasted somewhat unusual.

'It's not the eating, but the digestion that I don't like,' she went on as if she wasn't really interested in anything he said. 'Anyway, I will never go to Greenland again.'

'Were you there for long?' he asked casually.

'Just a few weeks. My father owns the harbour where Lorenzo Zane designed the *Triton*. That's where they built the skyship.'

'Did you see it?' asked Mariah.

'I flew in it,' she replied, and she spread out her arms like wings. 'It took us all the way to Nova Scotia and then we sailed back to England on the *Ketos*.'

'And what about the polar bear?' he asked dangerously.

The question silenced Biba. She took a boiled egg from the tray and held it in the palm of her hand. Biba looked at it for a moment and then crushed it in her fingers.

'Casper shot it. He said he'd shoot anything or anyone that tries to hurt me,' she snapped. 'Why were you on the gang-plank walking into the sea? I thought you would have drowned quite easily if Charity hadn't saved you.'

'I can't remember. It all seems so unreal. I can recall going into my room and then nothing else. I dreamt I was over the sea, following someone, an old friend – but that couldn't be, he's dead.'

'A ghost – is that what made you do it? A ghost . . . Who was it?' she gabbled. 'My father once paid a man to talk to the dead. We went to his house and furniture started to move and dance about. There were voices coming from the walls. He said he could converse with the departed, but Casper found his assistant hiding in a cupboard. So he locked them both in and left them there.' Biba paused for breath.

'Why should your father pay to hear people talk to the dead?' Mariah asked as a thread like a memory of the night before wound its way into his mind.

'Because he never does anything without knowing what they say,' she quipped as she skipped from the room. 'I think you should dress and then I'll take you on a journey . . .'

Mariah got up from the bed and dressed. Every fibre of his body tingled. He looked in the mirror and saw the face of someone older, a stranger. He remembered a moment of what had happened. It was a glimpse of Topher standing in the room, the pool of water about his feet. This time he could see the eyes of the boy. They were dark and empty. The life had been taken from them.

It took him longer to dress than he thought possible. His body ached and every nerve seemed to be on fire. It was as if he had shrunk in the night, for everything he put on felt as if it had been made for another. Remembering what Charity had told him, he strapped one pistol to his ankle and the other he placed in his jacket pocket.

Mariah realised that for some reason he was now a guest of the Marquis DeFeaux. Perhaps, he thought, it had been Charity's idea to keep him safe; or perhaps it had just been a coincidence. Whatever was the case, Mariah dressed and was eventually ready to leave the room. He took the meat from three beef sandwiches, folded it neatly in his hankersniff, rolled it up and put it in his pocket.

'Do you always take this long?' Biba asked as he stepped through the door into an even larger and more ornate room. She had changed her clothes and was now dressed as a Sultan. On her head was a silk turban with a jewelled brooch and in the belt around her waist was a curved dagger.

'I had trouble finding my things,' he said, not knowing what else to say and feeling underdressed.

'Then we shall all go on our journey,' Biba replied as she began to pull on a long gold chain that led from the room and into the corridor outside.

There was a low moaning sound that quickly turned into a growl. The chain tightened – whatever was on the other end did not want to be drawn near. Biba wrapped the chain around her hand and pulled harder.

'Is there something –' Mariah tried to ask.

'Rollo never does what I want,' she tutted as the growls grew louder. 'He's the kind of tiger that makes you very irritated.'

'Tiger?' Mariah asked, taking a step back to his room.

'A pure white tiger – he would make a lovely coat, but mother thinks that would be cruel. Just a kitten really,' she replied in her madly matter-of-fact way.

'Isn't it dangerous to have a tiger?' he asked.

'We have seven tigers – all snow white – and an ostrich. In fact on Deck 5 some of the animals perform in the circus.' Biba gloated as she spoke, as if this were something to be marvelled at. Mariah was not too sure. He had once seen a monkey locked in a cage in a department store. It was quite mad and spent its time spitting water at passers-by.

'So it lives in a cage – on a ship?' he asked.

'It knows nothing else. I did want to take it to Greenland but thought it might get lost or be too cold,' Biba replied.

Just then a large white face appeared around the door and looked in.

Mariah stared at the creature that stood before him. It had long white fur that looked to be tipped with silver flakes. The tiger stared at him through its yellow eyes as if it wanted to eat him. Then Rollo sat in the doorway. The gold chain was fixed to a studded collar around its neck.

'It's bigger than I thought,' Mariah said as the tiger twitched its nose.

'Just a kitten, really, not even a year old,' Biba replied as she went up to the beast and stroked its head. 'A big softie and not to be scared of. Although,' she said thoughtfully, 'it doesn't like small dogs.'

Mariah felt thankful he was not a small dog. He asked, 'Why doesn't it like dogs?'

'When I took it to Paris, we were walking by the Hotel Deville. A Frenchman came towards us with a small terrier. Rollo snapped it from the pavement in one bite. My father paid the man not to take us to court.'

'Ate it in one bite?' Mariah asked, astounded that a tiger could do such a thing.

'The man didn't seem to mind. He said the dog belonged to his wife and perhaps now he would be better treated,' Biba replied. 'I thought Rollo could come with us – I have to take him back to his cage. You will join us, won't you?'

Mariah did not like the idea of walking around the ship in the company of a girl whom he thought to be mad, and who was dressed as a Sultan, and a large tiger.

'Of course,' he heard himself saying with a smile.

'Good,' said Biba firmly.

They left the room and walked the long corridor towards the

steam elevator. Mariah realised that he and Captain Charity had their own apartment at the far end of Deck 13. They went through a regal lounge with gold sofas and chandeliers, passed the room where they had had dinner and eventually they arrived at the steam elevator.

'Isn't Casper Vikash coming to protect you?' Mariah asked.

'I don't need Casper when I have Rollo with me, not on the *Triton*. Everyone on board is a specially invited guest – my father knows them all.'

'Doesn't he have enemies?' Mariah asked, remembering what Charity had said.

'If he did –' Biba stopped speaking just as the elevator arrived. 'I think we should start at the circus,' she said as the three got into the compartment and Biba pressed the button for Deck 5.

It soon became apparent to Mariah that Rollo didn't like the steam elevator. The tiger pressed itself against him and growled loudly as they hurtled down the decks. Every thick white hair stood up on the creature's back as if it were just a frightened tabby-cat. It shook fearfully as the elevator stopped and the doors opened. Then, as soon as it saw the people waiting out-side, the tiger revived itself like an actor about to start a great performance.

The few passengers who had found their way to the lower decks parted as Biba walked towards them followed by the tiger and a reluctant Mariah.

'It's just here,' Biba said, dragging the now regal tiger along on its gold chain. 'I have the key to his cage and can come and get him whenever I want.'

'And how often is that?' Mariah asked as he followed her along the windowless corridor that led to a door marked *Circus*.

'Every day. Well, that is what I would like, but my father insists I study with my tutor and practise my shooting with

Casper.' Biba left her words in the air as she opened the door to the circus.

Inside the door was a man in a grey uniform. He had a large moustache that drooped down like the teeth of a walrus. He looked at Biba and tried to smile as if it were expected of him.

'Not open yet, Miss,' he said, but Biba ignored him.

'On the contrary, Mr Blake, it is always open to me. We are taking Rollo back to his cage.'

The man nodded. It was pointless to argue with Biba DeFeaux.

What he saw next amazed Mariah. It was as if the whole of the rear of Deck 5 had been magically turned into a colossal circus tent. The high ceiling was clad with candy-striped cloth. Ropes hung down for a trapeze and sawdust covered the floor. In the middle was a circus ring of wooden boxes surrounded by stacked seats. Mariah gawped. It was the biggest theatre he had ever seen.

'This is a real circus?' Mariah asked. 'With clowns and acrobats?

'And animals,' Biba said with a smile. 'The cages are there.'

Biba pointed into the distance, towards the far side of the auditorium. Mariah could see a row of neatly painted cages. Each one had a striped roof, walls of black iron bars and five wooden steps leading to a grille doorway. A tarpaulin hung like a thick, heavy curtain around the base of each cage, covering its wheels from view.

'They live in there?' Mariah said as he caught sight of several more white tigers, each in its own cage.

'They can hardly live with the passengers,' Biba replied as she slipped the chain from Rollo and he bounded across the circus ring.

They followed on and Biba took a key from her pocket and unlocked the door to one of the cages. She said, 'He doesn't like going in, but when he performed on the *Ketos* he was found in the kitchen eating all the meat.'

'The *Ketos*?' Mariah asked as he wondered why Rollo should have been on that ship.

'My father owned the *Ketos* as well as the *Triton*. He sold the *Ketos* to Lord Bonham. The *Triton* really will be the fastest ship in the world if father says so . . .'

Mariah didn't have to ask her what she meant. It was obvious to him that if the Marquis demanded, the *Triton* would win the Great Race.

'But the *Triton* still has to beat the record set by the *Ketos* to win the prize,' he said as Biba locked the door of the cage and left Rollo whimpering in a corner like a scalded cat.

Biba giggled and walked off. Mariah looked at the other tigers locked in their cages. They were all bigger than Rollo. A solitary old cat, pure white and tinged with grey, gazed at him. It seemed to plead with its eyes and looked forlorn and broken. The beast lay in its cramped cage in obvious and desperate misery. As Mariah walked by it twitched a lazy eyelid and showed its yellowed teeth.

'That's Eduardo – he's a killer,' Biba said proudly, admiring the once magnificent beast. 'My father found him in a circus in Milan. He had eaten his wrangler – but the man had been cruel to the tiger and tigers never forget. They had wanted to kill him.'

'So you have a man-eater in your circus?' Mariah asked.

'People love him. We never let him out – far too dangerous,' Biba replied as she walked on.

Mariah looked deep into the tiger's fireless eyes. He knew that they had never stared upon any forest of the night. He reached into his pocket and brought out the hankersniff. Mariah picked out the slices of beef in his fingers and put them in the cage.

'*Did He who made the lamb make thee*, Eduardo?' Mariah asked in a whisper as the tiger ate the meat and purred like a farm cat with a mouse.

'It's no use talking to him, Mariah. Eduardo is completely deaf,' Biba said as she took him by the arm and pulled him away. 'All he understands is a stick across the head.'

Mariah looked back to the tiger. Their eyes met again.

'And you have an ostrich?' Mariah asked.

'And three snakes and until last year a kangaroo – but he jumped overboard and was eaten by sharks,' she scoffed.

Mariah was amazed as the thought of an escaping kangaroo fleeted through his mind. 'Really? By sharks?'

'No, I was joking. He died of old age. He was a fighting kangaroo and one day didn't want to fight any more, so we bought another –' She stopped and looked seriously at Mariah. 'Shall we come to the circus tonight? It's an amazing show. I love it when the sea is rough and the acrobats fall from the trapeze. The circus is built into the stern of the ship. The wall is the hull; in some places, if you look closely you can see the rivets. You can hear the waves clattering against the sides. We'll have to see it. There are clowns and all sorts of things. Casper will look after us.'

Mariah was dragged on by the ever more impatient Biba DeFeaux. They nodded at Mr Blake as they left the circus. He twitched his long white moustache and eyed them nervously at the same time, muttering under his breath.

Instead of taking the steam elevator, Biba and Mariah walked up the stairs at the end of the corridor. A golden carved handrail spiralled up to the next deck. Biba talked as she went ahead. It was mostly about herself and Mariah quickly realised that she was manifestly lonely.

'I wish I had been visited in the night by a ghost,' she said as they got to the door to Deck 6.

'It was not as agreeable as you may think,' he said as he was suddenly confronted with hordes of smartly dressed passengers waiting in the lobby of the Oceanic Theatre. Mariah stared at the babble of elegantly attired women with their cosmopolitan companions. One thing he found strange was that there were no children.

'I guess there must be a luncheon matinee,' Biba said, unaware of the man in a drab suit who had followed them up the stairs and through the door and now waited in the shadows of the overhead stairway.

[8]

Dead Gold

'IT is strange that the Bureau of Antiquities should pay such attention to a few bars of gold, Captain Charity,' the Marquis said as they stood in the empty foyer of the grand entrance hall and looked at the glass-encased tomb of gold.

'We are here by your kind invitation, Lyon, and a million pounds is not just a few bars,' Charity replied. He looked up to the roof of the crystal atrium seven decks above them. The dim Atlantic sun streamed down and glistened on every landing. The atrium was the heart of the ship and took light to the darkest depths of the vessel. From where he stood, Charity thought it was like an ancient basilica, a holy place of glass and steel. Each floor was linked by a balcony and a sweeping staircase, which was joined on every deck by the long corridors that ran the length of the ship. At every door stood one of the Marquis's officers, stopping anyone from entering. 'This is a marvel of engineering, it is a cathedral of the age.'

The Marquis put his hand on Charity's shoulder as if to steady himself as he also looked up. 'I wanted it to be an experience and not just a journey. The air is cleaned and warmed, the water purified, and there is every technique to refresh the body. That was my desire – a pleasure-dome of the ocean, greater than that of Kublai Khan. Imagine it, to cross the Atlantic in three days, to join continents – what price will people pay for such a luxurious venture?'

'In that you have succeeded,' Charity replied as he checked the case that covered the gold.

The Marquis looked about him to see if they could be overheard and changed the conversation. 'Do you think the information about a robbery is true?' he asked quietly.

'If there are thieves, where would they take it? We are at sea. Who would be able to do such a thing and not be noticed?' Charity asked.

'I fear the plot may be greater than you think,' the Marquis said cautiously. 'I didn't say last night for fear of being overheard, but I have had grave . . . correspondence.' The Marquis stuttered his words and took out his handkerchief and wiped his brow. 'I am being held to ransom. A letter was in my room. Pinned to the wall. I am to deliver a million pounds in bullion or the *Triton* will be sunk.'

'And you have this letter?' Charity asked.

'It is here in my pocket. It is clear in its demands. I have to place the gold in a lifeboat at midnight tomorrow, fifteen hundred miles off the coast of Nova Scotia. The *Triton* is to sail on. If I do so, then my ship will be safe. If not, a bomb on board will take us all to the bottom of the ocean.'

'Do you have any idea who could have sent it to you?' Charity replied as he stepped closer to the Marquis.

DeFeaux rummaged in his pocket and handed Charity the neatly folded letter. 'There is nothing of consequence about the letter, but I know it is not a hoax. It also says that to prove their intent they will have your assistant, Mariah Mundi, killed.'

Charity took the letter. It was handwritten on a piece of

vellum paper. He held it to the light. It carried the familiar watermark of Claridges Hotel in London.

Charity read the words written in fine black ink:

Dearest DeFeaux, if you do not place all the gold in a lifeboat and set it adrift at midnight on the third night of your voyage then my agent will blow up the Triton *without warning. As proof of our intent we have selected a passenger from the roster and he will be killed. His name is Mariah Mundi.*

'I think they leave us without any doubt, Charity,' DeFeaux said, his concern etched in the lines on his brow.

'I would have said it was a hoax, had there not been three attempts on Mariah's life,' Charity replied.

'Three?' asked the Marquis.

'Someone shot Lorenzo's son by mistake, an assassin tried to kill us both, and when I went to Suite 395 I found this.' He held up a vial with grains of purple crystals stuck to the side. 'I found the dust on the inside door handle and on the telephone. It is *Lyzerjid ergotium*, a powerful hallucinogen.'

'Poisoned?' asked the Marquis.

'Mariah was taken to the side of the ship. I have a witness who says that a woman was with him just before he was on the gangplank. He was meant to jump – but he was too strong willed to give in without a fight.'

'Then you believe that this ransom note is true and a saboteur will try to sink the *Triton*?' the Marquis asked.

'You have a thousand passengers and not enough lifeboats. I counted them yesterday,' Charity said.

The Marquis looked to the carpet. 'Lorenzo Zane said they would blight the look of the ship – and that the *Triton* would never sink. We have enough for six, perhaps seven hundred people.'

'And the rest will be left to the sea?' Charity asked.

'We will have to do what the ransomer wants. I cannot see the ship destroyed,' he replied.

'Or people die?' asked Charity.

'There will always be people, Captain Charity – but the *Triton* is unique.' He muttered slowly as he thought of the consequences.

'Then we shall have to stop this before anyone is lost,' Charity replied as Captain Tharakan stormed down the cascading staircase from the deck above.

'It cannot be true,' he said loudly as Ellerby followed at a polite distance behind. 'The ship cannot be held to ransom like this.'

'I took the liberty of informing the Captain by letter and inviting him here,' the Marquis said to Charity as Tharakan stood by them.

'We must search the ship and the passengers,' Tharakan gabbled loudly. 'You must have some idea who is responsible.'

'We must tell no one. There would be panic,' Charity replied. 'If we are to search the ship then it must be done secretly. As for the passengers, they are to be watched.'

'But what about the gold?' Tharakan asked as he looked at the bullion behind the glass dome.

'It is to be put on a lifeboat and cast adrift just as they want. It cannot be left to chance,' Charity said.

Tharakan gasped with disbelief. 'You cannot just give away all this gold. It cannot happen. They are pirates,' he protested.

'And what if the bomb explodes? You only have enough lifeboats for seven hundred people. Will you allow the rest to die and the crew as well?' Charity asked Tharakan, staring him in the eye.

'But they will be able to hold every ship in the world to ransom. It will not be safe to put to sea. Do you not understand that money and gold is transported from country to country by ship? It is the way in which the world works. Giving in to these people will mean they could do this again and again.'

'The *Triton* is unique. I cannot see my ship go to the bottom of the ocean,' the Marquis intervened.

'I will not allow this. I am the captain!' Tharakan screamed as if he chastised two children. 'The gold will stay on the ship and we will find the saboteur.'

'As soon as the saboteur knows you are on to them, what is to stop them from exploding the bomb and blowing up the ship? Whatever is to be done has to be in secret. It is the only way,' Charity said, trying to reason with Tharakan. 'Nothing must seem to be different. We have until midnight tonight. Then we have to take the gold from the ship.'

Tharakan thought for a moment. 'Marquis,' he said urgently, 'you must reconsider. If we give in to these people it could have consequences for the whole world.'

'And if I don't it will have consequences for my ship, Captain Tharakan.' The Marquis spoke as if these were the last words he would ever say.

'I cannot agree. I will instruct my men to search the ship. The bomb has to be somewhere,' Tharakan said.

'If you mention that there is a bomb then the news will be out,' Charity said. 'I suggest you tell them it is contraband. Something hidden of great value. I'm sure that the Marquis will reward whoever finds it. Make sure, Captain, that when it is found, no one touches the device.'

'But what will such a thing look like?' the Marquis asked.

'It will most likely be a travelling case placed somewhere below the water line,' Charity said. 'There cannot be many places that are suitable and yet secret enough for the bomb not to be found. I too will search and will report to the bridge before dinner tonight.'

'You go alone?' asked the Marquis.

'I think it would be best if you all carried on as normal. If I cannot find the device by tonight then Captain Tharakan can have his men search the ship,' Charity replied as Ellerby listened eagerly.

'We cannot have a civilian wandering all over the ship, Captain,' Ellerby said to Tharakan. 'I will send one of my men with him.'

'It would only be right, Charity. The crew would wonder why a guest was below deck. This way it could be said that you are being given a guided tour.'

Charity thought for a moment as he considered what Ellerby had said.

'My assistant, Mr Sachnasun, will be able to help you, Captain Charity. He knows every part of the ship,' Ellerby said.

'Very well,' Charity replied. 'Have him meet me in one hour by the saloon. In the meantime, Tharakan, I suggest you get your men to start loading the gold into a lifeboat.'

He could see Tharakan bristle with rage as the gold braid shuddered on his black tunic.

'I don't like giving gold to criminals and murderers, Captain Charity,' Tharakan said as he picked at the thread on the sleeve of his jacket.

'You have no choice, Captain,' Ellerby said, quite out of place. 'But if Sachnasun helps him search the ship then we may not have to give the gold away.'

Tharakan did not seem to be appeased by what his assistant had said. He looked at the man with a sneer. It was as if Tharakan had to obey Ellerby without question. Charity noticed the look of insistence on Ellerby's face, and he thought it not right.

'So all will be done as you like, my dear Lyon,' Charity said to the Marquis as he turned to walk away. 'But I insist that no one should know of what we do – too many lives depend on it.'

'You trust a civilian?' Tharakan raged when Charity had gone.

'He is more than that,' the Marquis replied.

'The Bureau of Antiquities? The answer to every problem in life?' Tharakan scorned.

'Trouble,' muttered Ellerby under his breath.

'It's not for you to say, Mr Ellerby. I invited Captain Charity and The Bureau of Antiquities to protect the gold. After all – it is my ship and you both work for me.'

Charity listened from behind the closed door and smiled. 'Divide and conquer,' he whispered to himself as he walked the long passageway.

An hour later he was waiting by the door to the saloon. Mr Sachnasun was late. Charity looked at the dial of his fob watch. Inside the saloon he could hear the dancers rehearsing for the night-time performance, clumping on the stage in their iron tipped shoes as they stomped out another song. Passengers came and went, using the saloon as a short cut from the walking deck to the panoramic dining room.

'Captain Charity?' a man asked as he tapped him on the shoulder.

Charity turned. There was a man in full naval uniform. He was tall, wide and had a face that looked as though it had been chiselled from ice.

'Mr Sachnasun?' Charity asked, taken aback by the aspect of the man.

'Indeed. Mr Ellerby has told me what I am to do.'

There was something about the man's accent that seemed strange and yet familiar. His deep blue eyes peered from a hooded brow like those of an eagle. Flecks of pure white hair stuck out from under a black cap that was pulled tightly to one side.

'Then you will lead and I will follow,' Charity said as he gestured for the man to walk on.

87

'It is an unusual task, no?' Sachnasun asked. As they got into the steam elevator he pulled out his crew ticket and slipped it into the slot below the floor levels. He saw Charity look at what he had done. 'It is for the crew only. So that the passengers cannot get below the decks.'

'Does everyone have such a device?' Charity asked.

'Only if they are an officer. The only people you will see above deck are stewards and officers. The rest of the crew live and sleep below, in the gloom.' Sachnasun laughed as he spoke.

'Like prisoners?' Charity asked.

'Only of their poverty and lack of learning, Captain Charity. They all seem to be happy with their situation in life. Beware – it is a hot place. The Zane Generator burns with such heat that if we stay too long in one place it will boil the sea around the ship.'

'If I am not mistaken you are from Greenland?' Charity asked.

'You are the first man to notice. I often get mistaken for a Dane or an American.' He laughed again.

'More than that, I would say that you came first from Iceland – in fact from the town of Arborg?' Charity asked as Sachnasun nodded in agreement. 'Then I would say that at the age of fourteen you went to live in Greenland – Jacobshavn?'

'Indeed you are a clever man, Captain Charity. It is if I am an open book and you are reading my pages. You will be telling me what I had for breakfast, indeed.' Sachnasun patted Charity on the back with his gigantic hands.

'It is easy when you know the differences in people's voices. I own a large hotel and we get people from all over the world. Perhaps you have heard of it – the Prince Regent?'

Sachnasun laughed as the elevator slipped quickly below the decks and into a world of darkness. 'I have never heard of such a place. I worked on building this ship and now I travel upon it.

Mister Zane trained me in navigation and many other things. Otherwise I would still be at Jacobshavn.'

'I am sure that someone of your wit would have not been contained by the ice for too long,' Charity replied as the steam elevator stopped at the bottom of the shaft.

'Indeed, perhaps that would be true. But I have a lot to thank Lorenzo Zane for. He commands my loyalty.' Sachnasun reached into the inside pocket of his jacket and pulled out a long carbide lamp. 'This is for you,' he said as he handed it to Charity and twisted the ring on his middle finger.

The ring burst into a thick beam of light that shone from a narrow crystal tip. It brightly illuminated the dim, dungeon-like corridor that led from the elevator away into the darkness.

'You do not seem surprised,' Sachnasun said to Charity.

'Another of Zane's marvellous inventions?' Charity asked.

'Every officer of the crew has one. It is remotely powered by the Zane Generator. The lamp works within a hundred yards of the ship and the light is focused through the crystal.'

'Does the heat not burn?' Charity asked as Sachnasun walked ahead.

'Indeed not. It is like ice – a closely guarded secret,' he replied.

'And this is like a journey to the centre of the earth, Mr Sachnasun.' Charity shivered as he spoke.

The ship grew dark and deeply grim. A labyrinth of tunnels went this way and that. Each was lined in steel and every hundred feet was a watertight door and a dim, electric light. One long corridor led to another and everywhere the unfettered churning of the Zane Generator resounded. It whirred and moaned as if in constant anguish as Sachnasun and Charity searched the myriad of stores and rooms that led from each black, dripping avenue. Each room was lit by a dingy electric light that gave off a meagre glow. The air was thick with sulphur and vaporous oil. Every surface was glazed with a fine mist of viscous fluid. They saw no one and heard nothing but the generator and the thrusting of the steam jets that propelled the *Triton* through the sea.

'Indeed, Mr Ellerby said we are looking for something of importance?' asked Sachnasun as they searched another empty room.

'Property of the Marquis DeFeaux,' Charity replied.

'I can't imagine someone so rich being so forgetful with their property,' Sachnasun said as he turned down the power of the ring so that it was no more than a bright glow.

'Where do these go to?' Charity asked as they came to a criss–cross of tunnels.

'The right is to the far side of the ship and the engine room, the left to the outer bulkhead. The ship is designed not to sink,' Sachnasun said. He pointed to a small glass sphere punctured with three holes and containing what Charity thought to be a lump of cheese. 'If the detonator is submerged in water then all the doors will automatically lock. Water will get no further and the ship will stay afloat. This is my job, to maintain the defences.'

'Another of Lorenzo's inventions?' Charity asked as Sachnasun reached up and checked the alarm.

'My invention, Captain Charity, and one I discovered by accident.' Then Sachnasun stopped speaking and pointed back down the tunnel to a shaft of light and a thin black shadow. It appeared to move in and out of the light, but no one could be seen.

'Have we been followed?' asked Charity as he turned off the carbide lamp.

'It is best that I go to check. Stay here and I will come back for you, it is the only way we will find who plays games with us,' said Sachnasun, and he followed the tunnel towards the light.

Charity waited until Sachnasun was out of sight. He could hear the churning of the engine and the pounding of the water against the riveted steel plates. The cold sea dripped from above his head.

It was then that he heard a voice from far behind him. In the half-light he could see a figure the size of a small child standing to one side of the watertight door. It was too far away to make out any features.

'Help me – she is trapped inside!' The voice echoed eerily. Then the boy stepped through the door and ran away.

Charity followed at a pace. Soon he could see the boy ahead of him running in the shadows. He stopped momentarily to turn on the carbide lamp. When he looked up, the child had gone.

'I'm here. Help me!' came the voice of a woman from a near-by vault.

The voice came again, this time from behind the locked door of a room to his left. Charity spun the wheel handle and unlocked the door. He pulled open the seal and looked inside, shining the lamp. There in the corner was the slumped figure of a woman. Her head was pushed to the floor and her dress torn.

Charity stepped inside the room. He didn't hear the door begin to close quietly behind him.

He knelt beside the woman and took hold of her lifeless hand.

'A doll – a mannequin,' he said to himself as the door thudded shut. Charity realised he was now trapped. A spigot turned above his head as he heard the dull twisting of a valve outside. Very slowly, drips of hot bilge water began to flood into the vault. Within a minute the floor was covered in a large pool of oil-smeared water.

[9]

Bitter & Twisted

'AND now – directly from the Orient – a man who will amaze and astound – the Great Shanjing and his assistant, Charlemagne!' The ringmaster cracked his long whip and the lights of the Oceanic Theatre dimmed.

Mariah snuggled back into his seat. It itched through his coat, as if an army of biting fleas crawled at his back.

'What do you think it is?' Biba asked as a roll of the drums shuddered from the orchestra pit.

He shrugged his shoulders. A tall man walked on stage carrying a large and very lifelike doll.

'Ventriloquist,' Mariah muttered under his breath as a man came and stood in the aisle next to his seat.

'I welcome you into a world of magic,' said the man on stage. 'The world of the Mighty Shanjing where not even the thoughts of your mind are safe. I think I will have a volunteer from the audience – you, sir . . .' He pointed to a rotund Frenchman in the front row. 'If you would be so kind . . .'

The Frenchman reluctantly stepped on to the stage with the encouragement of the audience. Charlemagne asked the man his name and then looked to the puppet Shanjing, who appeared to be asleep. With a mechanical tremor, the mannequin came to life. It reached inside the front of its silk coat and pulled out a long mahogany pipe and began to smoke. The puppet studied the Frenchman and then gave a leathery smile.

'I take it that you will do everything I ask?' it said. Its head juddered as if it were on a spring.

The man nodded and laughed. He kept turning to his wife and smiling, as if pleased that his life should be lived in the limelight.

'Not everything, Shanjing?' Charlemagne asked as if in a Florentine conversation with the doll.

'I insist – everything,' Shanjing replied as he gave a puff on his pipe and blew deep blue smoke across the stage. The smoke enveloped the man as if he were in a cloud.

The man dropped his head, mesmerised. His jowls wobbled and moustache sagged. Charlemagne gave a surprised gasp and then went to a small table set at the side of the stage. With his free left hand he picked up a long-barrelled pistol.

All the while, Shanjing ranted. 'This man will smoke the pipe of Shanjing. On my command he will raise his head and my assistant will fire the pistol and blow the pipe from his mouth. He will be blindfolded – though even with the use of his eyes he could cause fatal injury . . .'

The man never moved as Charlemagne took the pipe from Shanjing's mouth. Placing it in the man's teeth, Charlemagne took ten deliberate steps backwards, stopped, put the gun in his pocket and then put a blindfold over his eyes.

'Raise your head,' the puppet said to the man. 'I will tell Charlemagne when to fire,' Shanjing shouted as Charlemagne took the gun from his pocket, raised the pistol towards the man's head and took aim. 'One . . two . . . three . . . Fire!'

The gun exploded and the pipe shattered in a cloud of thick blue smoke. The Frenchman vanished before their eyes. The crowd was silent and then everyone stood to their feet and applauded.

A woman in the front row began to scream.

'My huzbend, where is my huzbend?' she pleaded as laughter began to explode in the theatre.

'We have done the world a service,' giggled Shanjing, 'and rid the world of a troublesome Frenchman. Surely, Madame, the thought *had* crossed your mind? What you would have done with poison . . . I have done with magic. Consider it a crime of passion.'

The woman screamed even louder as the crowd cheered. She attempted to bite Charlemagne on the leg and drag him from the stage with her teeth.

'Geeve me bark my huzbend,' she snarled like a demented poodle.

'Very well, Madame,' Shanjing replied as another small explosion blew the woman back to her seat and into the lap of her naked husband, who had appeared in a cloud of smoke as quickly as he had disappeared.

'Arrgh, whet hev they durn to yew?' she demanded to know from her subdued spouse.

'You didn't say you wanted him to be awake as well,' sniggered Shanjing as the crowd roared with laughter. 'Very well, Charlemagne – snap your fingers and revive the man.'

Charlemagne did as he was told. The man opened his eyes and looked at his wife. He could see the tear-wet streams of make-up smeared across her face and for a moment wondered at her distress. And then he realised he was naked but for a large hat decorated with tropical fruit. The man jumped to his feet and ran towards the exit, followed by his frantic wife, who was trying to give him decency with a large top hat that she had stolen from a man in the next row.

'And there you have it,' Charlemagne bellowed as the crowd

stomped their feet in time with the crescendo of music. 'The world of the Mighty Shanjing . . . I can promise more tomorrow and every night of our voyage,' he said as Shanjing flopped like a lifeless doll in his arms and hung motionless.

Mariah and Biba applauded with delight as the curtain slipped across the stage and the lights grew brighter. All around them people laughed – all except the man who stood nearby.

'My father found Charlemagne working on Wigan pier,' said Biba. 'He is the finest ventriloquist in the world.'

'The doll seems so lifelike, almost real,' Mariah replied.

'Don't ever call Shanjing a doll,' she said with surprise. 'Charlemagne insists he is a god.'

'Made of leather and wood with strings that pull his words,' Mariah replied.

'Well, Mariah Mundi – if you are so clever then we shall go and see him for ourselves.'

'Mariah Mundi?' asked the man stood by them. 'Are you Mariah Mundi?'

Mariah turned to see who spoke to him. There in the aisle was a man in a plain suit. He looked distinctly out of place and too ordinary to be a guest on such a ship as the *Triton*. The man smiled at Mariah and held out a piece of folded paper. His fingers were grubby, as if they were coated in oil.

'I'm Mariah Mundi,' he replied as the man offered the note again with a smile.

'Max Arras,' the man said as he handed Mariah the note. 'I work with Jack Charity.'

'The Bureau?' Mariah asked, leaning forward and hoping that Biba wouldn't hear him mention the name. 'And you know Captain Charity?'

'He asked me to give you the note – said something has come up and I had to find you.' Arras took Mariah by the arm and led him away from Biba so she could not hear. The man then went on. 'I'm undercover – looking after the gold. Jack has told me to find you and make sure you do what it says.'

Mariah broke the wax seal and opened the note. It was written by Charity. He could tell that the ink was the same purple and red concoction of crushed beetles and borage stems that Charity always used. It smelt sweetly, even when dried on to the paper. Each letter was clear and distinct as if laboured over by a tired hand.

Mariah stepped back so Arras could not see what had been written.

Dear Mariah,
    How things have changed. I need to see you alone at 2 p.m. Come to Lifeboat Station 13 on the rear boat deck 11 –
    Jack Charity

He read the note several times before screwing up the paper in his hands.

'Are you going?' Arras asked him, still smiling. 'I have to give him your reply – Bureau business.'

'I will be there,' Mariah replied, his mind racing. He had never heard of Max Arras and was sure that Charity would have told him. 'You work for the Bureau?'

'Last five years,' Arras replied, shrugging the shoulders of his jacket and looking around the emptying theatre.

'From Claridges Hotel, Room 31?' Mariah asked.

'Just the place,' he replied. 'Better be going. Keep safe, Mariah, keep safe . . .'

Max Arras turned and mingled with the crowds as they left the theatre. He stopped momentarily at the door and turned back and smiled.

'He looked shifty,' Biba said as she edged closer. 'What did he want?'

'I have to meet Captain Jack in two hours,' he said as the thought resounded in his mind. 'Captain Jack, that's it . . .'

Mariah took the crumpled paper from his pocket and looked at the writing again.

'Then we have time to meet Charlemagne and he will show us Shanjing.' Biba giggled nervously. Mariah noticed this was something she did often, rubbing her hands together at the same time.

'I don't think we should – I think I need to –' he protested, but she took his hand and dragged him towards the stage.

'Nonsense. You need to meet Shanjing. He can tell you all sorts of things about yourself. I go to see him all the time – it's like seeing someone who can look inside your head. Shanjing is very helpful and quite courteous.'

'Perhaps I am quite happy not knowing,' Mariah replied as she pulled him on.

The theatre was nearly empty. Three elderly ladies huddled around the stage door dressed in black crinoline and fur mufflers. They chatted endlessly and didn't notice Biba and Mariah slip by. The door attendant nodded at Biba. He twitched his long white moustache and eyed them nervously at the same time.

'Is that Mr Blake from the door of the circus?' Mariah asked, sure that he had seen the man before.

'It's Mr Blake but not the one from the circus. In fact, there are four of them – all identical in every way. Quadruplets. My father likes them – he says they confuse the passengers. He puts them to work on different decks – you never know which is which.'

Biba led Mariah to a flight of stairs that connected the back of the Oceanic Theatre with the saloon lounge. The steps were narrow and steep and at one point crossed over the top of the stage before turning upwards towards the dressing rooms.

They were lit by small electric lights that shone down from oyster-shell holders fixed to the ceiling. Every few yards were doors that led off to the left and right. The corridors were all interlinked like a gigantic maze.

'How do you know where you are going?' Mariah asked Biba as she walked on ahead of him.

'Below deck, the *Triton* and the *Ketos* are identical in every way. Father just had more room given for the Zane Generator. I lived on the *Ketos* for a year. I know every inch of the ship.'

'Didn't you get bored?' he asked as they turned the corner of the final staircase, out of breath with the climb.

'Bored?' she asked as if she didn't know what the word meant. 'I sailed around the world and saw things I never thought possible – how could you ever be bored?' she scoffed.

Mariah was about to reply when Biba stopped outside a small doorway and read the nameplate above it.

'This is the place,' she said quickly. She rapped against the door and waited for a reply.

'Who is it?' asked the man inside.

Biba replied in her crisp voice. The door opened and Charlemagne stood in front of them with his arms wide open as if welcoming a long-lost friend.

'So great to see you,' he said as he fussed about the dressing room, tidying things from the chairs so that they could sit down. 'Was your father in the audience? I would love for him to see the show.'

'This is Mariah,' Biba said without being asked. 'He's a friend of mine and I am showing him the ship. I want him to converse with Shanjing.'

Charlemagne sighed deeply and Mariah looked down. There, by Charlemagne's feet and pushed under the dressing table, was a coffin-shaped wooden box.

'Shanjing is resting, my dear Biba – but I am sure we can

arrange another time for him to meet with you both and share his insights,' he said apologetically.

'I told Mariah that you would at least perform for us,' she pleaded, smiling at Charlemagne.

'He'll do it . . .' said a voice that appeared to come from below their feet.

'Shanjing?' Biba asked.

'Of course it is me,' the box replied.

Mariah looked at Charlemagne. The man's lips didn't move, nor was there any tremble in his neck.

'I have brought a friend to see you – will you come out, Shanjing?' Biba asked.

'Only if the fleshy one will let me. Leather hands are no good for getting out of boxes,' the voice quipped eerily.

Mariah studied Charlemagne. He seemed to look as surprised as they were that the voice spoke from the box.

'I have never seen a ventriloquist like you before,' Mariah said as Charlemagne slipped the catch on the wooden box and began to open the lid.

'Neither have I,' said the voice from the box.

Charlemagne laughed. 'Sometimes I cannot think who is really talking to who.'

He opened the lid of the box. There, wrapped in a silk blanket, was a small man. He was perfect in every way. On his head was a black brimless cap, on each hand a leather glove and around his neck a silk scarf. Mariah stared at his face. It was like toughened leather with painted lips and black-rimmed eyes. It looked human, without possessing life. The doll was the best that Mariah had ever seen.

'Where did you have this made?' Mariah asked.

'I found him. I don't know if he was made by man or was the last thing to be created. Shanjing is one thousand years old,' Charlemagne said as he carefully lifted the heavy mannequin from the box. Mariah watched the doll flop from side to side and then, as if life were breathed into it, sit bolt upright and open its eyes.

'Welcome, Shanjing. We have guests,' Charlemagne said as he appeared to work the mechanics inside the doll.

'Biba and . . . Mariah Mundi?' the doll asked hesitantly.

'It knows my name,' Mariah said.

'It? *It? It?*' asked Shanjing in a voice that could cut cold cheese. 'I am not an *it*, Mariah Mundi.'

'Sorry,' he replied, never having been told off by a ventriloquist's dummy before. 'I am just so surprised by you, that's all. You know my name and yet we have never met.'

'Everyone is an open book to me, the Great Shanjing. Did you see my performance?' the doll asked.

'We did, it was amazing,' Biba said excitedly.

'The night of the exploding Frenchman – that is what I shall call it,' the mannequin said as its lifelike eyes flashed from side to side. 'I amazed myself . . .'

'How do you do it?' Mariah asked Charlemagne, who appeared just to sit silently and nod at the right time in the conversation.

'He doesn't do anything. I am a living creature, Mariah Mundi. I am sentient and alive just like you – I only pretend to be a mannequin. The world can accept a doll prophesying to them about their lives, but if a man were to do it he would be burnt for witchcraft.' Shanjing stuttered with his last words, as if he should never have spoken them. 'Do you believe in such things?'

'I believe whatever you are makes you amazing. Be you wood, leather or flesh, I have never seen anything the like of you in the whole world,' Mariah replied.

'Wise words for such a boy,' Shanjing said quietly as he looked Mariah in the eyes. 'You have a difficult future on board this ship. There is a power that seeks . . . to take your life. And it will stop at nothing . . . until you are gone.' The mannequin stuttered slowly as if it were truly breathing.

'We know these things, Shanjing,' Biba said in her matter-of-fact way. 'What of the future for us both?'

'How can you ask such a thing?' he said gruffly, as if he didn't want to answer. 'I see tigers and blood and my head is full of screaming. Is that the future you want to hear about?'

'Tigers? Blood?' Mariah repeated.

'Shanjing tired. I sleep now.' The leather eyelids closed. The creature sighed as if it slumbered.

'Why did you do that?' Mariah asked Charlemagne.

'What?' he asked as if woken from a dream.

'Why did you stop?' Biba broke in.

'He only jokes with you, tells you what he thinks might frighten you. Shanjing does that all the time. Can't be waiting round here all day. He's only a doll – I make up the words,' Charlemagne said as he looked up at the clock on the dressing-room wall. 'I have another show in two hours and I need my sleep. Come back another day and we'll talk more.'

He put the puppet back in the box and stood up. He reached across and opened the dressing-room door.

'I think he wants us to go,' Biba said as Charlemagne turned from them and began to tidy the room once more.

'It was kind of you to speak to us,' Mariah said as he stepped outside. 'Goodbye, Shanjing. Thank you, Charlemagne.'

'Thank you, Mariah Mundi. Survive tonight and you might live to see New York,' came the voice from the box as Charlemagne slammed the door behind them.

[10]

Betelgeuse

THE corridor seemed empty and very quiet. Biba DeFeaux looked at her fingernails and scowled intensely.

'I hate it when he does that – always the same, just when it gets interesting he falls asleep,' she said as she walked off ahead.

'Do you really think that Shanjing isn't just a doll?' Mariah asked.

'Have you ever heard a doll speak like that?' she asked in reply, her face turning red with anger. 'I will tell my father to command him to speak to me for longer.'

'Perhaps it's best that way?'

Mariah was about to go on when Biba stopped, turned and looked scornfully at him.

'Are you really so dim – do you think he is made of leather and wood?' she asked.

'Well . . .' Mariah tried to reply.

'I know different. Shanjing is real – I have seen him, and he can walk.'

'How can a puppet walk?' he asked, his voice about to crack with laughter at the way Biba shrugged her shoulders and stamped her feet when she was angry.

Biba saw the look on Mariah's face, the laughter making her even angrier. 'You're impossible! I didn't want to spend the day with you, but father said I had to. I would have rather been with Lorenzo. At least he is civilised . . . and he believes me about Shanjing.'

She stopped shouting as a dressing-room door opened further along the corridor. The fat Frenchman looked out to see who was arguing.

'My wife is trying to rest,' he said in perfect English. 'We have a performance. Argue elsewhere Miss DeFeaux.'

Biba nodded and walked off, followed by Mariah close at heel.

'They were part of the show?' he asked. He looked at the names on the dressing room door as Biba stormed by. 'They're actors . . .'

'Of course – you don't think my father would allow Frenchmen to be blown from the stage, to strip naked and run around the theatre, do you?' Biba asked, not wanting a reply. 'It may be their national pastime – but not on the *Triton*.'

Mariah looked back along the corridor; the lights flickered as he heard laughter coming from far away.

'How can you believe that Shanjing is real when they use stooges in the show?' Mariah asked as Biba walked even faster in front of him.

'Because I've seen him. At night when I was alone. I saw him walking the passageway between the theatre and the saloon. It was when they were performing on the *Ketos*. Is that good enough for you, Mariah Mundi?' Biba stopped, folded her arms and stared him eye to eye. 'I think you should go and see your Captain Charity. The stairs are right behind you – don't get lost.'

With that she pushed Mariah in the chest and walked off. He waited a moment, not sure if he should follow. He thought it would be best not to pursue her. Mariah could tell that she needed to calm down.

'She's mad, totally mad,' he muttered to himself as he pressed the handle of the door to the stairs.

It opened slowly. Beyond was a steel stairwell that spiralled up and up. Each step was suspended from the wall and a brass rail went round and round, like a serpent reaching to heaven. Mariah's feet clanged against the metal as he walked upwards. On each level was a doorway. Next to each doorway, in a glass-fronted red case, was a fire axe.

Mariah took the treads two at a time. The sound of his footsteps echoed up the stairwell as he counted the decks. He went higher and higher, thinking of Biba as he walked on. He wondered why she was so different from anyone he had ever met. She went from silence to laughter and then immersed herself in anger. Her face changed like the seasons and her eyes showed deep bitterness. How can someone who has everything be so strange? He was wondering about this as he finally reached Boat deck 11.

Mariah took the note from his pocket and read the words again. 2 *p.m. – Lifeboat Station* 1 3, *Boat deck* 1 1.

'This is the place,' he said to himself as he took hold of the steel door and turned the handle. He read the sign: *Crew Only*.

The door gave way slowly. He pushed it open and felt a rush of wind against his face. Far in the distance he could see the white tops of the waves. It was like looking out on to a vast blue and lifeless desert. The sky was grey. The afternoon sun edging its way behind the clouds gave no shadows.

Mariah stepped outside. The sign on the wall in red letters said Lifeboat Station 13. He looked the length of the short deck and saw four lifeboats covered in canvas. They swung gently back and forth as the ship rocked slightly. By each one was the winching handle that would lower them to the deck below, where the passengers would climb aboard should the lifeboats ever be needed.

The wind blew against his face. It was scented with brine and cut at his skin. Taking a fob watch from his pocket he checked the time. Captain Jack was five minutes late. He looked again at the note and then to the sign on the wall – this was the right place, he thought as he waited.

The door to the ship opened slowly. Max Arras looked out.

'Mariah – so glad I've found you. There's been a problem,' Arras said as he stepped outside whilst holding the door open.

'What?' asked Mariah.

'Jack Charity – he's been injured,' Arras said, sounding concerned by his fate, his voice emphatic and intense.

'Where?'

'Come with me – they have him in the infirmary.' Arras spoke with his usual smile that matched his cheap suit. 'We must go this way – it will be quicker.'

Mariah stepped forward to follow and then stopped. He looked down to the sea far, far below. He remembered the night before. He could see it clearly. There was Topher; and standing on the deck, near to him, lurking in the shadows, was a woman. Mariah had seen her before – he knew her face. Just as his mind searched for who she was, the vision went away once more.

'We can't wait,' Max Arras shouted against the wind. 'We'll have to be going.'

Mariah shook his head as if to judder away the hallucination and held tightly to the railing. 'Are you sure Captain Jack will be OK?' he asked as he began to walk towards Arras.

'Fine. He needs you. You must come now – quickly,' Arras replied, waving Mariah towards him.

There was something about the way in which the man spoke that unsettled Mariah. Max Arras was brusque and coarse, with hands stained with dirt. Somehow he didn't seem like an agent of the Bureau of Antiquities – even if he was undercover.

'Have you been to Room 31 at Claridges Hotel?' Mariah asked.

'Of course,' Arras replied.

'Room 31 or 13?' he asked.

'Does it matter which?' Arras said angrily. 'Jack Charity needs to see you, now.'

Mariah walked towards the door and then looked up. On the next deck, looking down, was Madame Zane. She nodded at Max Arras and then at Mariah. It was as if she knew the man. She gave a slight smile and then stepped back out of sight.

Mariah stepped through the door. He could sense someone close. There was a smell of burnt almonds. A sudden and uncontrollable surge of fear swept through him. It was as if every sense in his body told him to run. Mariah dived to the right, hoping to avoid the dark shadow that fell upon him. He was knocked to the floor. A hand smothered his face with rough fingers that gouged his eyes.

'Don't speak, lad,' came the voice of a man much older than Max Arras.

'You got him?' asked Arras. He stepped inside the stairwell and shut the door with a turn of the wheel.

'Better get him below before someone sees us,' said the rough-handed man.

'Deck 1, Locker 17,' whispered Max Arras as he slipped a black hood over Mariah's head.

'Not the fight you told me he would give,' said the man to Arras as he held Mariah in his firm grip.

Mariah slumped to the floor and gasped for air. His hand slipped to the leg of his trouser and clutched the handle of the gun. The man struggled to drag Mariah to his feet. Mariah slipped the gun from the leg holster and pulled back the safety catch as he pressed the barrel against the man's leg.

'Let me go,' Mariah screamed. 'In the name of the Bureau of Antiquities I demand you let me go.'

'Did you hear that? The lad demands I let him go,' the man said as they both laughed.

'I won't warn you again,' Mariah said as he hunched forward with his finger on the trigger.

'Take him down below, Mr Cody – let him see what we have in store for him,' Arras said as he kicked Mariah in the back.

There was a loud crack as Mariah pulled the trigger of the gun. He was thrown back through the air and against the door as a jet of flame exploded from the barrel. He gripped the handle tightly and pulled the trigger again and again. With every shot, more flame exploded in a bright white plume of light.

For an instant he saw the face of the man who had held him mercilessly. It was blistered and unshaven. His coat was smouldering with black smoke as he stared at Mariah with eyes that no longer could express his pain.

Max Arras grabbed his hand as the other man fell to the floor. He twisted Mariah's fingers and tried to wrench the gun from him. Mariah pulled the trigger again. It blasted a sword of fire to the roof of the stairwell. Arras fell back, stumbled over the other man and rolled down the stairs.

'I told you to let me go – but you didn't listen,' Mariah screamed at them as he jumped over Max Arras and ran down the stairwell. 'You should have listened – I gave you a chance,' he went on, his words edged with guilt.

'Mundi – get Mundi!' he heard Arras scream to the other man, whose reply was a dull groan as he tried to dampen his smouldering trousers with his hands.

'Burning,' the man whimpered. 'Burning on the inside . . .'

Mariah ran on as fast as he could. Far above he could hear footsteps chasing him.

'Deck 1, Locker 17,' he said to himself time and again as he tried to catch his breath and fight the fear that churned his stomach.

Three decks lower, he could still hear the feet chasing him down the stairwell. As he ran he looked for places to hide or someone to stop and tell that he was being chased. But he knew that he could trust no one. A horror-filled thought stuck in his mind – what if everyone was the enemy? What if this was just an ambitious trap to get him and Charity in the middle of the Atlantic Ocean? He dare not believe what he thought – he dare not believe that he was on his own.

The stairwell was empty. The steam generator churned with every revolution of the piston. Mariah could hear the great portals on the side of the ship suck in the ocean like the mouth of a whale. The water boiled instantly as it was pushed through the Zane generator and back out into the sea to propel the ship.

Mariah ran faster. He clutched the pistol in his fingers and slid the catch forward so it would fire the eleven bullets in the magazine. The footsteps behind him were getting closer. He stopped for a moment at a door of Deck 6. Mariah twisted the handle, but the door refused to open. He listened to the feet coming ever closer. There were now three men chasing him. Two ran quickly whilst the third followed on some way behind. It sounded as though he dragged his leg and coughed on every landing to regain his breath.

'Stop now, Mariah – you won't get far. We have people throughout the ship. You will never know who to trust,' Max Arras shouted, his words echoing Mariah's own thoughts. 'If you don't stop – Jack Charity will die.'

Mariah ran on. He heard Charity whispering the words he'd said to Mariah one night long ago on the balcony of the Prince Regent: 'They'll use every trick they can think of to deceive you – never believe a word they say. If they say give in or I shall die – wish me farewell, for I know where I am going.'

He stopped at the stairwell of Deck 5 and spun the handle to the hatch. Pulling the portal open and hiding behind the steel frame, he pressed himself against the wall. Mariah aimed the pistol at the top of the stairs and waited. He could smell the stench of the circus coming in through the door. The circus was in full flight and there were screams from the passengers as the trapeze artists swung to and fro, leaping from ladder to ladder.

Max Arras ran into his sights. Mariah pulled the trigger of the pistol three times. Bullets ricocheted against the steel walls. He swung round and dived through the hatch, pulling it behind him and spinning the handle until the two bolts clunked into place.

'What you doing back here?' asked a tall clown with floppy feet and a tomato nose.

'Miss DeFeaux has asked me to come for Rollo,' he said, not knowing what else to say.

'He's busy – the tigers are on next. Can't she wait?' The clown grimaced with disdain for Biba as he spoke. 'Gets everything she wants, that girl. Can't be good for her.'

The audience jeered as the trapeze artist fell to the net for the third time. The clown turned and clumsily walked away as the wheel of the hatch began to turn slowly.

'Max Arras,' said Mariah as he looked around him for a place to hide.

The portal opened. Max Arras stepped inside the circus and looked about him. He was followed by another man in a black suit and then sometime later by Mr Cody. The man limped as he walked, clutching his leg. His trousers were burnt and torn and his jacket still smouldered. Half the hair of his long beard had been burnt away.

'Got to be here somewhere,' he said to Arras, who looked into the tented changing room of the clowns.

'Hiding – somewhere we'd not bother to look,' replied Arras. He stared at the audience from behind the row of tiger cages. 'He's not going to get away – we need them both for what we have to do.'

Mariah listened from above. He had climbed the bars and now hid on the roof of Eduardo's cage. The tiger prowled beneath him as Rollo and the others were pushed along a tube of steel wire and into the circus ring.

'He can't stay here all the time,' Cody said as he sat on the steps of the cage to regain his breath. 'All we have to do is wait for the circus to end and the people to leave and we're bound to find him.'

Max Arras thought for a moment.

'You could be right. You wait inside the stairwell so he can't escape,' he said as he nodded to the other man. 'Mr Saumur, go to the ticket office and tell Blake what we are doing. Don't let Mariah Mundi get away from you.'

Mariah heard the hatch to the stairwell open and close. He could sense that Max Arras was still close by. He peered over the top of the cage. Eduardo growled, angered by the presence above him.

'What's a big cat getting so upset about?' Max Arras joked as he prodded the beast with the cane that hung from the door. 'Won't they let you go and play with the passengers?'

He stopped and looked up to the roof of the circus. As the lights dimmed for the procession of the snow tigers the heights above him shone like a galaxy with miniscule lights that looked like stars.

'What would you give to see this, eh, tiger?' Arras teased as he prodded the beast once more with the stick. 'Betelgeuse and Orion's belt – how fitting that it should be those stars that shine tonight.' Eduardo growled and bared his teeth as he smashed his gigantic paw against the bars of the cage and sniffed the air above him. Max Arras looked up. 'Something bothering you, tiger? Something up there?'

Just as Max Arras smashed the cane against the roof of the cage, the circus fell into complete darkness. The stars faded and a spotlight followed the ghostly pageant of white tigers. Everyone stood up and the circus erupted with applause. Arras walked the length of the cage in the twilight, staring upwards as if he knew someone was there.

'A good place to hide, Mariah Mundi – but not good enough,' he said as he took a pistol from his pocket and aimed it at the roof. 'If you don't come down I will be happy to shoot you – just where you are.'

Mariah realised he was trapped. He slipped from the roof and onto the sawdust floor. He gave no protestation and didn't try to run away.

'Will you shoot me here?' he asked as Max Arras pointed the gun at him.

'Not here – perhaps not at all,' he replied. 'Let's get moving. Back into the stairwell, now! And before we go, I would like your gun.'

Mariah looked towards the hatch. He knew that if he stepped through the doorway, he would never see the light of day again. He felt in his pocket and took out the pistol and stepped towards Arras.

'When can I have it back?' Mariah asked.

'Never. I have always wanted a Bureau pistol. What an invention, a flamethrower and a gun in one weapon. Mr Cody is still smouldering from his encounter with you,' Arras said as he took the weapon from Mariah's hand.

'Then I'll have yours,' Mariah said as he snatched the other gun from Arras.

Arras grabbed him by the throat and both pistols fell to the floor. Although older than Mariah, Arras was lighter and not as strong. Mariah twisted him to the floor and they rolled towards the cage. Arras kicked and punched, not sparing the boy because of his age, but fighting him like a man. Mariah fended the blows from his head and kicked back with his feet as he tried to get away. Arras was the quicker, a seasoned fighter with no care for what pain he inflicted. He punched Mariah again and again. Then, when Mariah could take no more, he dragged the boy to his feet and held him upright.

'Stupid boy,' he said breathlessly. 'To think you could fight me . . .'

'I had to try – I couldn't just give in,' Mariah replied.

'Brave, but foolish. And if I let go will you try to run?' he asked as he pushed Mariah towards the cage.

'I have no strength left – what's done is done,' Mariah replied, his legs shaking.

'Very well. This shall be the place,' Arras said, and he pushed Mariah back and bent to pick up his pistol from the floor.

Mariah seized the moment and grabbed Arras by his long white hair. He kicked the man and then pushed him back against the bars of the tiger cage in one last attempt to break free.

Without warning, Eduardo leapt from the dark corner of the cage. The tiger seized Max Arras by the shoulder. The man kicked and screamed. Mariah let go of him, falling backwards to the floor in panic. He watched in horror as Max Arras was slowly dragged through the bars, screaming and screaming. His cries could not be heard over the shouts of the crowd in the circus as they watched Rollo the tiger dance around the arena to a Viennese waltz.

The last thing that Mariah saw was the booted foot of Max

Arras disappearing into the cage. He turned his head and looked no more as he grabbed his pistol from the sawdust and crawled under the trailer cage and hid. Above his head he heard the growling of the tiger, and then all was silent.

Vulgari Eloquentia

MARIAH didn't know how long he had waited, but from where he was hiding he had heard the tigers return to their cages. No one had seemed to realise what Eduardo had done or could see any remains of Max Arras. They had opened the cages and put the white tigers inside. Mariah could now hear the crowd laughing at the clowns as they tried to chase a kangaroo around the circus ring. He could see nothing. The tarpaulin hung like a thick, heavy curtain around the base of the cage, covering the wheels from view. Occasionally he could hear Eduardo growl and crunch bone in the small sleeping compartment at one end of the tiger cage. Mariah wondered how much of a man a tiger could eat. He knew he would have to explain to Captain Charity what had happened. He lay in shocked silence, knowing he had to move, knowing he must find Captain Jack.

It was soon clear that once the tigers had been put in their cages the wranglers looking after them had other jobs to do. Mariah listened to their bickering conversations. He heard one man say that it would all be over in ten minutes and then the man was to return to his cabin to sleep.

'Don't want to waste more time here than needed,' the man said. 'Better be getting off as soon as this lot has finished.'

Mariah stayed silent. He knew he could only move when the men had gone. In his mind's eye he could see Max Arras struggling with the tiger and then giving up as if he knew he could not fight his fate – it was as if he had allowed Eduardo to drag him through the bars of the cage, as if this was meant to be.

Soon, all was quiet. He could still hear the clowns falling from an exploding carriage. The passengers laughed and cheered as Mariah waited for the moment to escape. Pulling a flap of the tarpaulin, he looked out. There was no one. He slipped from underneath the cage and looked back to see if Eduardo was waiting for him. In seven paces he had crossed the shadows and was by the hatch door.

Mariah knew Cody would be waiting for him. He spun the wheel of the hatch and then stood back. A long shadow crossed the open doorway. It was the size of a man – it was Cody. He was expecting to see Max Arras. Mariah hid behind the hatch, waiting for the right moment. Cody stepped from the door. As Mariah saw his shadow cross the floor he pushed the steel hatch as hard as he could. It slammed shut, knocking Cody from his feet. The man screamed in pain and rolled on the floor, clutching his face. Mariah pulled the pistol from his pocket and aimed it at Cody.

'Promise me you won't follow,' Mariah said, opening the hatch with one hand.

'Where's Max?' asked Cody.

'He's gone,' Mariah replied.

'What you done with him?' the man asked.

'I did nothing,' Mariah answered as he aimed the gun at Cody.

'You burnt me once – you won't be doing that again,' Cody said. He began to get to his feet.

'Don't come after me. I warn you now.' Mariah stepped back and then turned to run.

A hand caught his leg just as he was stepping through the hatch. Cody pulled him back.

'You're not getting away that easy – not until I finish what I was going to do,' the man said as he struggled with Mariah.

'Don't make me –' Mariah gasped as he threw back the hand holding the gun.

Cody collapsed silently. Mariah looked down at him. He was an old man with a half-burned white beard and lined face. He had deep wrinkles and sea-brown skin. Every crease looked as though it had been seeped with ship oil from a life at sea. Cody looked peaceful as he breathed sleepily. He was unconscious. Mariah had knocked him cold.

Mariah looked at the pistol. The tip was covered in blood from the wound on Cody's head. He felt detached, distant, as if it were a dream from which he could not escape. Again he had a vision of himself on the gangplank. He was looking back towards the ship. He could see the outline of the woman who had brought him there. She was tall, thin and elegantly dressed. A shadow covered her face from view. He could hear her words – she was telling him to jump.

It was the shouts of the crowd that broke his dream. The circus had come to an end. The clowns took their bows as the acrobats cartwheeled around the ring. Cody was still unconscious, breathing heavily, snoring and snorting with every other breath. Mariah turned him onto his side so he wouldn't choke. He searched the pockets of his jacket. In the last one he found a strange steel key with a twisted hook on the end. On the black leather fob was the word *Ketos*.

Mariah put it in his pocket and stepped through the hatch, pulling the door shut. He saw the red box to one side, broke the glass with his pistol and took out the axe. He jammed the handle of the axe into the wheel so it couldn't be turned and Cody couldn't follow.

At first he went slowly as he took the stairs down and down. He listened constantly to discover if he was being followed. He saw no one. When he got to the door of Deck 2 he felt the air grow hotter. It smelt of the sea. Mariah could hear the Zane Generator and the pumps pushing the water out of the back of the ship in a steady flow. The generator whirred and hissed as the water boiled. Four flights later he was at Deck 1.

Mariah opened the inner door. He knew he was under the water line. Everything sounded muffled and different; the walls were hot to the touch. There was a creaking of the metal plates, as if the outer skin might be torn off with the speed of the ship. The long passageway led in both directions. It was searing, dank and musty.

Mariah could hear the bilge pumps whirring as they sucked the brine from below his feet. He looked down through the mesh grille of the deck. In the shadows below, he could see the water running back and forth with the motion of the ship.

'Deck 1, Locker 17,' Mariah said out loud as he turned and ran along the passageway, passing a door with number 35 upon it. 'Must be near here somewhere.'

Within a minute he was at the door of Locker 17. It looked just like all the others – a black hatch with a brass wheel and two dead bolts that pinned it to the wall on either side.

'Captain Jack – you in there?' he shouted as he banged on the door. It thudded dimly as if it were a solid wall. Mariah banged again and again. There was no reply.

Mariah began to turn the wheel. At first it wouldn't move. It felt heavy as if gripped by unseen hands that wanted to keep it locked to the world. He pulled harder. The wheel began to move slowly as the bolts slid cautiously from each steel wall.

It was then that he saw the water seeping from the bottom of the door. It bled faster and faster with every turn of the wheel.

'You in there, Captain Jack?' he shouted as he realised the locker was full of water.

There was no reply.

He spun the wheel harder and waited for the bolts to burst from the locks. Suddenly, the door blew open. A surge of water pushed him back along the passageway as it forced its way from Locker 17 in a vast torrent. The bilges whirred even louder as they pumped the deluge. Steam filled the passageway. Mariah got to his feet.

'Captain Jack!' he shouted as he stumbled to the hatch. 'You in there?'

There was no reply. Mariah looked inside the dark locker. It smelt just like the crab-boiling house in the street next to the Prince Regent Hotel. Mariah used to pass it every morning. Large crabs were hung from the doorway, and in winter they steamed and sizzled in the cold air.

Locker 17 was empty. A tap bubbled in the corner of the room. Mariah stepped inside. By the far wall were a raggle of woman's clothes and the arms of a mannequin doll.

'Took your time,' said a voice above him. 'I nearly drowned.'

'Captain Jack,' Mariah said as he looked up at the open hatch above his head. 'How did you get up there?'

'Whoever locked me in here didn't realise that all the lockers are linked. Quite simple, really. I just waited for the water to lift me higher and then undid the hatch.'

'They tried to kill me.' Mariah babbled quickly as Charity slipped through the hatch and dropped to the wet floor. 'A man called Max Arras said he was from the Bureau. He showed me a letter he said was from you, but I didn't trust him. He lied.'

'Max Arras works for Lord Bonham – where is he now?' Charity asked.

Mariah didn't speak. He turned away and stepped outside the hatch. Charity followed.

'Where is he?' he asked again.

'Dead.' Mariah replied reluctantly. 'He was eaten by a tiger. Arras tried to kill me – we had a fight. The tiger dragged him into its cage and I couldn't look.'

'Sometimes these things have to take place. It is never easy.' Charity put his hand on Mariah's shoulder.

'He just let it happen as if it were fate,' Mariah replied as in his mind the event went on, relived over again.

'I knew of Max Arras in the army. Strange he should be involved in such a thing as this. Are you sure it was him?'

'That's what he said – Max Arras. Told me he was in the Bureau. It was Arras who mentioned Deck 1 and Locker 17. They were going to bring me here,' Mariah said as the heat of the Zane Generator caused his clothes to steam.

'I think that there is another side to our dilemma,' Charity said thoughtfully. 'I was brought here by a man called Sachnasun – he works for Lorenzo Zane. It was convenient that this should take place.'

'A trap?' asked Mariah.

'A conspiracy, Mariah, a total conspiracy,' he replied.

Far away, a sea hatch suddenly creaked. Charity looked into the darkness. The heavy footsteps of two men clattered on the steel.

'Cody!' whispered Mariah. 'He was one of the men who was with Arras.'

'Then the hunted shall start to hunt. Quickly, Mariah, inside,' Charity said as he stepped back inside Locker 17, followed by Mariah. Silently he pushed the door and turned the locking wheel. 'Let them get inside and then we attack.'

'Cody is injured – I used the pistol,' Mariah said, half hoping that Charity wouldn't hear him.

'Then he shall be even quicker to catch. Stand by the wall – let them see you first,' Charity said as he jumped, caught hold of the rim of the hatch above and pulled himself through.

Mariah waited as the footsteps clanged against the metal floor of the passageway. Locker 17 steamed with the heat of the generator. A small shaft of light came down from the open hatch in the corner of the room. Mariah stood by the far wall. He held his pistol behind his back, his hand trembling.

He was trepidatious about what would happen next. It was as if all that was his life had passed away, and everything familiar was now no more. Mariah was at war and in war; he knew that men would seize the world with violence. He found the battle hard, foreign, harrowing. Its companion was always fear and anguish. It was far away from the books he had read of valiant heroes, but he knew it was what he had to do. It had been this way since the start of his life at the Prince Regent – one by one his adversaries had come to him and had fallen. Death had made him a man with the heart of a boy. His eyes looked on this new life and still could not comprehend it.

'Locker 17, Mr Brogan,' he heard the muffled voice of Cody say as the hatch lock began to turn. 'No sign of Mariah Mundi – who do you think he's gone to tell?'

'None would believe him. We'll have this ship as soon as we have Charity and Mundi dead,' the man replied. 'We'll be changing course before we get to America and then we'll see.'

The man stopped speaking as if he knew something was wrong. There was a tap, tap, tap on the door of the hatch as if it were being tested.

'Empty already?' Cody asked. 'Thought he was going to fill it with brine when he trapped Charity inside and have him soaked like a turbot?'

'Must have done its job. Take no chances,' Brogan replied through spittle.

The hatch unlocked slowly and steam oozed from the opening.

'Smells like he's dead,' Cody chirped cheerfully. 'All we need now is the boy and –'

Cody stared into the gloom. There before them was the mannequin doll in her ragged and soaked dress. By the far wall was a shadow, still and lifeless.

'Mundi! Get him!' shouted Brogan as he leapt inside.

'Stand or I'll shoot you dead!' Mariah said as he aimed the pistol.

'One of you and two of us,' Brogan said as he drew closer, pulling a knife from inside his jacket. Cody followed close behind. He seemed reluctant and somewhat fearful.

'You don't have to do this, Cody. I warned you before,' Mariah said as he aimed the gun at him.

'Shoot him,' Brogan said without reservation. 'I have no concern for him.'

Cody looked hesitant. He looked at Brogan and then to Mariah.

'They care not for you, Cody,' Mariah went on. 'They would see you dead and think nothing of it.'

'Put down the gun, Mariah Mundi. You won't shoot us,' Brogan said as he cut through the air with his knife.

'He will, Brogan, mark my words,' Cody went on. 'The lad's not frightened of pulling that trigger.'

'And neither am I,' said Charity as he slipped from the upper hatch and landed on the floor behind them. 'Two pistols, one knife and time for you to talk.'

Brogan spun on his heels to face Charity.

'Jack Charity? I am so glad to meet you – but not to talk to you,' he said as he stood his ground. 'I'm sworn on my life not to say a word to the Bureau of Antiquities.'

'Very well,' Charity said as he nodded to Mariah. Then

Brogan's eyes opened widely and he slumped to the floor. 'Well done, Mariah. Take his knife and we shall see what Mr Cody has to say for himself.' Charity threw a pair of silver handcuffs to Mariah. 'Place him in these. We shall see what Captain Tharakan has to say about the mutiny of his crew.'

'You won't get far with Tharakan,' Cody said as Mariah handcuffed Brogan. 'He can't do a thing.'

'He's the captain of the *Triton*,' Mariah said as Brogan moaned.

'That may be so, but –' Cody was about to go on.

'Tell him no more, Cody,' muttered Brogan as he tried to get to his feet. 'You've been well paid for this.'

'Blackmailed and beaten, Mr Brogan. I remember what you said to me. I hold you no favours,' Cody replied.

'Then you'll be cursed and dead before midnight,' Brogan spluttered.

'He is now in the care of the Bureau of Antiquities – what harm can he come to?' Charity asked.

'He swore an oath, just like me. If that old codger says one word –' He stopped and looked at Cody. 'Bob Cody solemnly swears to speak not of our endeavours on pain of death. Remember that, Bob?'

Cody nodded as if he knew a curse would strike him there and then.

'Don't fear him,' said Mariah. 'You'll be safe with us.'

'Of that I can assure you, Cody. You will not see this man again – he can't harm you,' Charity said.

'Wherever, however, whenever . . .' lilted Brogan as if he sang a rhyme in a baby's ear. 'Your death waits . . .'

'I'm old enough for that,' Cody said as he straightened his back. 'I'll tell you what you want – but not here, not in front of that man . . .'

'Then we shall take you both to see Captain Tharakan,'

Charity replied. 'Mariah, you take Mr Cody and I will escort our delightful friend.'

Brogan didn't wait. He smashed Mariah with his manacled hands and as he did so he grabbed the pistol. Then he turned and fired at Cody, striking him in the chest. The man fell to the floor as Brogan jumped at Charity, knocking him out of the way.

'I'll get him – stay with Cody,' Charity shouted as he gave chase.

'Leave me boy,' Cody said. 'Tell Charity that they want the ship – don't be fooled by the gold . . . Quickly, go . . . Stop Brogan for me.' He used his last breath to speak these words.

Mariah gave chase. He could hear Charity far ahead of him. The sound of pistol shots echoed in the steaming gloom. He saw Charity look back just as Mariah got to a steam elevator.

'Steam elevator!' Charity shouted to him. 'Boat Deck 11.'

Mariah knew what he had to do. He pushed the button for the lift. It rattled down and down with a gushing of steam. Mariah could feel the ship adjust its bearing. The Zane Generator whirred even louder and the vapour blasts flustered through the thick conduits that ran in the bilges beneath his feet. The elevator rattled to a halt and the door slid open. He pressed the button for Deck 11 and counted as the elevator shot upwards.

It took just thirteen seconds for the elevator to reach Deck 11. Mariah was still inside the crew area. The passages here were smaller, unpainted, and stank of cabbage and cold tea. There was the odour too of wood oil – it would be painted on every railing and door in the dark of the night by unseen labourers. They would paint and wax, polish the brass and scrub the deck, and no one but the moon would see them. At first light they would vanish like the night mist.

Mariah took the outer door where the staircase from below

opened out to a lifeboat deck. He wondered how Charity knew he should come to that place. Then he saw it – the hanging strap of a lifeboat cover that flapped in the wind. The bolts that held the lifeboat in place had fallen from their mountings and gently rolled back and forth on the deck. Someone had prepared the lifeboat ready to launch.

Mariah looked out to sea. Near to the horizon he could see a pillar of smoke from the *Ketos* far ahead of them. On the deck above, several passengers looked through binoculars to the distant ship. They didn't seem to notice Mariah on the crew deck.

Mariah waited. The door flew open. Brogan leapt outside and ran towards the lifeboat. Charity quickly followed.

'It's no use, Mr Brogan – you will never get from the ship,' he shouted.

Brogan didn't listen. He climbed the gantry and onto the boat. Mariah went to pursue.

'One more step, Captain Charity, and I will shoot the boy,' Brogan spat.

'Stay back, Mariah,' Charity said.

Brogan laughed as he unhooked the craft and began to spin the windlass.

'We are too far from land, Mr Brogan – it's madness.'

'Death on board or death at sea – this way I'll have a chance,' he replied.

'It's not about the gold, but the ship,' Mariah shouted. 'Cody told me everything before he died.'

'Too late for you both – you won't see midnight,' Brogan said as he spun the handle faster and the lifeboat dropped another deck. 'I've been paid well, Captain Charity.'

The windlass stopped suddenly fifty feet above the water. The boat tipped at the stern and Brogan was cast from the lifeboat like a Jonah. He fell to the water far below. The sound of the Zane Generator covered his screams.

As Mariah turned to look at Charity there, on the deck above him, was Madame Zane. She was without her usual smile. Her face scowled at him as she threw a fur wrap around her shoulders. When he looked again, she was gone.

[12]

Isbrae

'I DON'T see why we should give in to them,' Captain Tharakan protested earnestly to the Marquis DeFeaux as the steam elevator opened on Deck 13.

'We give in to them because they will blow up the ship,' DeFeaux replied. Close by him stood Casper Vikash.

'And you let the Bureau of Antiquities take control of the security of my ship,' Tharakan shouted, his eyes bulging with anger.

'Your ship? Your ship?' DeFeaux asked. 'You are the man who just steers the *Triton*. It was my money, my time, my energy – not yours.'

'But the gold is not yours – you cannot just give it away,' Tharakan answered back.

'Under the circumstances the Marquis can give it to whom he wants,' Charity said as he stepped from the elevator, followed by Mariah Mundi.

'It is the prize money for the race, money I was promised a share in if I won. You cannot give away my fortune,' Tharakan said, ignoring Charity.

'If it is the money that worries you, I will pay you from my own purse,' DeFeaux said as he banged the long mahogany table that stretched out before him. 'The *Ketos* is still ahead of us. Lorenzo Zane is having trouble keeping the engine at full power. There is a bomb on the ship and all you worry about is the money?'

'Is the gold in the lifeboat?' Charity asked as he sat at the table and looked about the panelled room.

'They are loading the last ingots as we speak,' said Casper Vikash as his fingers traced the scars on his face.

'Then we should do what they want. I have searched the ship and found nothing,' Charity replied.

'And Sachnasun – what have you done with him? He is missing,' Tharakan snarled angrily, leaning towards Charity.

'We met with some opposition. I have not seen your Third Officer since I was locked in an airtight room and nearly drowned,' Charity replied. 'I have some questions I would like to ask him myself.'

'Then that explains what they found in Eduardo's cage?' DeFeaux asked with a raised eyebrow.

'Sadly, that was a twist of fate. The man tried to kill Mariah and the tiger killed him . . . And before you ask, there is a slight problem with a lifeboat on Deck 11 and a body in Locker 17, Deck 1.'

'You killed my crew?' Tharakan demanded.

'For some reason they appeared to have a strong desire to kill both Mariah and myself,' Charity replied as DeFeaux walked from the table and looked out of the window towards the horizon.

Casper Vikash took a step to follow.

'If you chose your crew wisely,' he said to Tharakan, 'then Charity might not have to resort to such methods. He is only protecting Mariah Mundi as they do the bidding of the Bureau of Antiquities.'

'I didn't. Lorenzo Zane chose them for me. Every man on this ship was hand-picked by him. I had no say in the matter,' Tharakan snapped in reply.

'Only because they had worked on the ship in Greenland and had taken part in the sea trials,' DeFeaux said, turning to face him.

'Then we should ask Lorenzo Zane how he came to have so many trained assassins in one place at one time. I have never known so many military men with the desire to become sailors.' Charity laughed as he spoke.

'What more do you know of these men?' asked Casper Vikash.

'I see from the scars on your face that you are a man prepared to lay down your life for your master?' asked Charity.

'I am,' Vikash replied.

'Then so were the men we encountered today. Before they died they talked about an oath, sworn under the threat of a curse should it ever be broken. One of them was even prepared to die before giving away the secrets to us,' Charity went on. 'These are not common thieves – they are loyal servants of an unknown master. Their intent is to destroy this ship and steal the gold.'

'Then who can we trust?' Vikash asked.

'Perhaps, my dear Vikash, the only people we can trust are in this room,' Charity replied as he looked at each man in turn.

The ship gave a sudden jolt and trembled in the water. It shook the dark wood panelling and rattled the gold chandeliers.

'It is the generator – there is a problem with the force of the water,' said Tharakan.

'And Lorenzo Zane?' Charity asked.

'He has spent the entire voyage in the engine room. He eats there, sleeps there and refuses to come out,' Tharakan replied.

'Then Mariah and I shall pay him a visit,' Charity said as Mariah stood by the elevator door and kept silent.

'Impossible,' muttered Tharakan. 'His guards will not let you in through the door. I went myself and was told to leave immediately – how dare they speak like that to the captain of the ship?'

'These guards, who are they?' Charity asked.

'From Greenland – they have been working on the project for almost five years. They are committed to the task,' DeFeaux interrupted.

'Sachnasun?' asked Mariah.

'Sachnasun,' replied Tharakan.

'The one thing every assassin has had in common is that they were put on this ship by Lorenzo Zane,' Charity said.

'Very well,' said DeFeaux as he returned to the table and smudged the thick wax with his finger. 'I think it is time to speak with Lorenzo Zane.'

'Tell me, Lyon. The Great Race – will the *Triton* win?' Charity asked.

'If the generator cannot be fixed, then the ship will not win and Zane's reputation will be ruined,' DeFeaux replied.

Tharakan looked out of the window of the room at the distant *Ketos*. The *Bicameralist* hovered in the sky to the south of the ship. He appeared to be thinking deeply.

'Strange weather for this time of year,' he said, changing the conversation like a sailboat tack. 'I don't think I have ever known such calm water. It is like the Arctic just before the water is about to freeze.'

'I too noticed that. Perhaps it is the conditions that affect the Zane Generator,' The Marquis said as he looked uncomfortably around the room.

'Tell me, Lyon, do you have access to the *Bicameralist*?' Charity asked.

'For what purpose?' he replied, wondering why he should be asked such a question.

'I noticed that it communicated with the ship via means of light. Is it possible for the skyship to land on the *Triton*?' said Charity. He got up from the table and crossed the room.

'It is very possible and in certain circumstances could be arranged immediately,' Vikash said uncomfortably before DeFeaux could speak. 'You cannot have one of the richest men in the world at the mercy of the Atlantic without an exit route.'

'On a day such as this I would be more in danger on the pond in St James's Park.' Charity laughed. 'Apart from the bomb hidden in the ship, our only peril would be to be struck by a demented seabird.'

'How can you laugh at such a thing? We could be blown into oblivion and it is not a thought I like to hold in my mind,' Tharakan growled.

'Oblivion is not a place I intend to go. I cannot believe in such an empty situation and I do not think we shall be blown up. The Marquis will ensure that the gold leaves the ship and we will continue to search for the bomb. Mariah and I will supervise the launch of the vessel with the gold at midnight. I suggest we keep the ransom a secret. I am sure that we will be watched if we are not already.' Charity smiled at the Marquis and then turned to leave. He walked towards the elevator and before he reached Mariah, he turned momentarily. 'I suggest we all carry on as normal. With so many deaths on the ship we do not want the guests to become worried.'

'I am glad I have your confidence, Captain Charity. After all, we shall sleep safe in our beds knowing the Bureau of Antiquities is protecting us,' Tharakan said sarcastically as he yawned.

'And sleep we shall – what a good idea,' Charity replied as he and Mariah walked through the door and along the elegant passageway.

'Do you really think the ship is safe?' Mariah asked as they neared the apartment given to them by the Marquis.

'We are sailing to hell, Mariah. Whoever is after the gold could blow up the ship as soon as it is delivered. That way there would be no witnesses. We have to find the bomb,' said Charity.

'But Cody said it was not about the gold,' replied Mariah.

'I fear that Lorenzo Zane has something to do with this. The *Triton* is not how it should be. If I were Zane and about to fail, I would have a plan to redeem myself.' Charity wiped the tiredness from his eyes. 'The consequences of such a thought are beyond belief and I can presume that only a madman would do such a thing.'

'Sink the ship if he thought it was going to lose the Great Race?' asked Mariah.

'Then his reputation would not be lost. If it were an act of sabotage, Lorenzo Zane could say it was a jealous rival who set out to destroy his invention.'

'And with the skyship they would be ensured of a means of escape. Biba told me she had travelled on it from Greenland to Nova Scotia,' Mariah replied as they reached the doorway to their apartment.

'My thoughts too, Mariah, and best we keep them to ourselves,' Charity said as he opened the mahogany doors to the room and stepped inside.

They both stopped, equally surprised to see Biba DeFeaux lounging on the sofa by the balcony. Spirals of incense swirled upwards from the table by the door, giving the room a fragrance of myrrh. The lace drapes had been pulled so that the net mellowed the harsh light of the afternoon sun.

Biba was dressed as a Mandarin and had painted her face with lines of kohl to slant the eyes. She fiddled nervously with a large diamond set in a gold necklace.

'I wondered how long you would be,' she said apologetically. 'I came to say . . .'

'Mad as cheese. Crazy as a buffarilla,' muttered Charity as

he smiled benignly and walked into his room, slamming the door behind him.

'Is he always like that?' Biba asked as she stood on the sofa and bounced up and down.

'Only when irate,' Mariah replied as he looked at the long table laid out with cakes and steaming silver pots and China cups. 'Is that chocolate?' he asked.

'Not only is it chocolate – it's Belgian chocolate made by the inscrutable Mr Bonnet,' she whispered, not wanting Charity to hear her. 'I thought I could say sorry by bringing you something nice.'

'Why do you act like that?' he asked as he sat next to her and poured the rich dark liquid into a translucent cup.

'I can't help it. Not a single person ever says no to me . . . and you look like someone who will, just for the sake of it. My father believes me to be spoilt and says I must be indulged and my mother keeps out of the way. The only time we ever touched was when that dreaded polar bear tried to kill me. Even then she seemed more concerned for Vikash.' Biba frowned as she slumped to the leather sofa. 'Madame Zane cares more for me than she does.'

'Do you know her well?' Mariah asked.

'It is planned that at some time in the future our families will come together. I have spent the summer with them and Lorenzo will be with us at Christmas,' she said as she took a piece of cake and crumbled it in her fingers.

'Then your life is planned for you,' said Mariah.

'Isn't that how it is for everyone?' Biba asked, astonished at the suggestion that it could be any other way. She stopped, realising that she was about to do what she had done before. Biba giggled and sipped from Mariah's cup. 'I have never met anyone like you before. There is something strange about you, Mariah Mundi.'

Mariah looked at her in the Mandarin suit and embroidered slippers. Biba smiled at him and screwed up her nose as if she were a rabbit sniffing the air.

'What is Lorenzo's father like?' he asked in as matter-of-fact a way as he could.

'Luscious,' she replied. 'Just like chocolate. I think everyone should be seen as something to eat. You remind me of a parsnip – bitter at first and then quite sweet.'

'Do you know him well?' said Mariah, thinking Charity was right in saying she was mad.

'I saw much of him when we went to Greenland. He spent a lot of time talking to my mother. They share an interest in *Alcatorda* . . .'

Mariah didn't know what she meant but smiled as if he did.

'Why should anyone want to harm Lorenzo Zane?' he asked.

Biba suddenly recoiled like a snake. It was as if she knew a secret that she couldn't share with him. She put her hands over her eyes and sighed. Mariah waited for her to reply. The incense swirled about him like long dark fingers that dripped with strands of torn hair. Then the light in the room dimmed and darkness fell unexpectedly as a gigantic shadow fell across the window.

From outside, Mariah heard the grumbling of the *Bicameralist*'s engines. The skyship hovered above the *Triton*. Mariah went to the window, pulled back the lace and looked out. There, like a gigantic cloud, blotting out the southern sky was the airship. It was the closest it had ever been to the ship. Its vast, whale-like carcass hung in the air, and beneath it the long gondola stretched the length of the *Triton*. Underneath the rear of the ribbed gondola were the steam engines, suspended like church bells. They buzzed as the blades turned and the steam pistons churned. Like the spouting of a whale, a column of smoke blew from a funnel on top of the skyship.

'Look Biba, have you ever seen such a thing?' Mariah asked.

Biba didn't move. She sat with her face in her hands as if in her mind's eye she watched something far more fascinating.

'It was her fault,' she said softly. 'If she hadn't left me behind to go looking for razorbills then the bear would never have come for me . . . She tried to make out that she had nothing to do with it. They left me behind in the village – I went looking for them – they had set off across the bay. I tried to follow – no one told me about the polar bears.'

'So you blame her?' Mariah asked.

'Why am I telling you this?' she replied, as if her speaking were beyond her control.

'We all have to tell someone. I know what it is like to be angry with your parents. You can't expect them to be perfect. Mine put me in the Colonial School and went to Africa. They went missing – some say they are dead. I wish they had taken me with them – at least I would know what happened to them.'

'Do you think they are dead?' she asked.

'Probably,' he said quietly as he watched a set of stairs being lowered from the front of the gondola as it moved closer to the ship.

'I wish my mother was . . . I thought of poisoning her, but Casper Vikash found out. He said it wasn't a kind thing to do,' she replied.

'I think it is better to have a mother alive and hate her, than hate her when she is dead,' said Mariah thinking of his own mother.

'It's better not to hate at all,' Charity said. He stood in the doorway of his room. 'Bitterness can eat you from the inside, Biba. The only way you'll be free from this is if you forgive her and forgive yourself for hating her. Is that why you couldn't speak?' he asked.

Biba nodded as tears filled her eyes.

'I felt so alone. Not natural to leave a child like that. Left me on the edge of Jacobshavn. Lorenzo would walk my mother to a red hut by the Isbrae Glacier. She told me to stay on the beach until they came back. Mother would often disappear for hours with Lorenzo Zane and then just return. Father was working – he didn't know. I waited and waited and then the bear came. At first it just followed me. It knew I was frightened. I tried to run. It chased me along the shingle beach. I thought I had escaped. I climbed a small hill. My heart was pounding. Then it jumped from behind an ice boulder. Casper heard my screams and he shot the bear. When Casper found me, he told me to say nothing to my father and that he wasn't to know where mother had gone. He said it was a secret that I couldn't speak because it would ruin my family.'

'So you didn't speak at all?' Mariah asked.

'It was easier that way. If I didn't speak then I couldn't give away the secret – it was as simple as that,' Biba said. 'Now you know, now you both know. Casper will not be pleased.'

'Have you not told anyone else about it?' Charity asked Biba as she sobbed.

'When you are the daughter of the Marquis DeFeaux, not many people ask. My father pays for children to be my friends. He doesn't let me go to school in case I am kidnapped. There is no one to talk to – but then you wouldn't understand that.'

There was a dull rumble and a grating noise above their heads. It was as if something scraped the roof of the ship.

'I take it that the *Bicameralist* has docked safely with the *Triton*?' asked Charity.

'My father arranged it this morning. He wanted to be sure everything was working and in order. They have come for some papers – to keep them safe. I heard him telling Casper Vikash to make them ready.'

[13]

Midnight

THE *Triton* cut its way through the black, glassy sea. A silver full moon touched the top of the sky. From the forward lifeboat deck, Mariah could see the lights of the *Ketos* near to the horizon. They looked like the glinting of a small town. In the light of the moon, Mariah thought it could be mistaken for New York and the end of the journey.

Biba stood with him, huddled close by. He thought she would see the view as he did, but then again, crossing the Atlantic was not a new experience for her. Biba had sailed many oceans and knew the sea well. For Mariah it was vast, dark, foreboding. He knew not what was beneath the calm waters and his mind conjured creatures greater and more dangerous than the Kraken.

The Marquis DeFeaux, Vikash and Tharakan clustered in deep conversation near to the lifeboat as Captain Jack looked at his watch and counted the minutes to the hour. 'Five minutes to midnight,' he said as three sailors packed the last of the gold ingots into the lifeboat and pulled the tarpaulin back across the boat. The red straps dangled to one side as the small boat rocked back and forth, ready to be lowered to the sea.

There was a commotion on the stairway. The hatch door was flung open.

'They have found Sachnasun,' Mr Ellerby said as he stormed onto the lifeboat deck. 'He is injured – a blow to the head.'

Tharakan turned and looked at him. 'Has he said anything? Does he know how it happened?' he asked.

Mariah and Biba looked at each other and then slipped out of sight.

'He is still not conscious – I don't know if he ever will be,' Ellerby replied as he looked at Charity. 'They found him by the entrance to the steam generator. He seems to have been just left there in the last hour.'

'Then go and be with him,' Tharakan said as two sailors took their places at the lowering wheels. 'It is nearly time to put the lifeboat to sea.'

A small crowd had gathered on the passenger deck above. They watched as the lifeboat was lowered to the water from the speeding ship. Some murmured in discontent, wondering why the Captain of the ship should be so concerned with launching an unmanned lifeboat.

'Should we not stop, Captain Tharakan?' Charity asked. 'If the lifeboat sinks then we are done for.'

'Fret not, Charity,' he replied. 'You shall be amazed how we launch the lifeboats on the *Triton*.'

There was a whir of the capstan as the lifeboat was lowered down towards the turbid water. The sea was disturbed by the wake of the ship that rippled out like the carving of a plough. The water appeared viscous and stiff, the wavelets laborious and cumbersome.

'Then I await to be amazed,' Charity replied as he watched the boat go lower and lower.

'The most expensive lifeboat that ever put to sea,' said Casper Vikash as he caught Charity's eye.

'A ransom worth the life of the people on this ship – wouldn't you think? You have been prepared to give your life for the Marquis – you should know of what I speak,' Charity replied.

'My life would mean nothing to save his,' Casper replied. He touched the piranha scars on his face. 'I would do it again to save him.'

'Such loyalty is worth rewarding – saving the Marquis, Biba and their family life,' Charity replied.

'You know too much, Captain Charity. Someone has been speaking out of turn. I told the Marquis it would be dangerous to have you so close. Madame DeFeaux should know when to be silent.'

'Mergyn has said nothing – the last time I saw her was at dinner with the Marquis,' Charity replied as the Marquis DeFeaux came and stood with them.

'Do you think this is an act of stupidity, Charity, or will it save the ship?' asked the Marquis as he wrapped his checked scarf tightly around his neck.

'I think we shall see in the next twenty-four hours. I only hope the gold is not lost to the sea,' he said.

'You still do not trust me?' Tharakan asked, overhearing the conversation. 'What you are about to see is a miracle of science, an invention of –'

'Lorenzo Zane, by chance?' asked Charity.

'Precisely,' Tharakan replied as the Marquis stiffened his frame.

The lifeboat dangled on the end of two ropes as the *Triton* sped through the water. Captain Tharakan nodded to the man at the lowering wheel. Without speaking he pulled a small brass lever at the front of the cradle that had held the boat in place. There were two loud bangs as the boat touched the water. Incredibly, the lifeboat hit the sea safely and was left behind in the wake of the ship. It remained upright as it rocked violently from side to side.

'Amazing, Charity?' Tharakan asked. 'It is designed so that if anyone falls overboard we can put a lifeboat in the sea immediately. It takes eleven nautical miles for the ship to stop at full speed – this way we have a chance of saving them.'

'Then we shall pray that the gold is safe and whoever is out in this blue desert will find it easily,' Charity replied cordially as he looked for Mariah. 'Biba and Mariah were here – but now they are not.'

'They wanted to see the circus,' said Casper Vikash as he patted Charity on the back. 'Biba likes to see Shanjing – she is fascinated by him.'

DeFeaux watched this gesture silently.

'If she were not promised to young Lorenzo, we could have . . .' mused DeFeaux as he pulled up the fur collar of his coat and nodded to Vikash to open the hatch. 'I expect they will turn up sooner or later. Vikash will go and look for them – Biba can take care of herself.'

'But I never saw them leave. They were by the lifeboat and the hatch never opened,' Charity replied.

'Come, Charity. Let us go to my apartment. Tharakan will come with us. We need to search the ship and find the bomb,' said DeFeaux as he disappeared through the hatch.

Charity took one long look back at the sea. He felt uneasy, as if a small voice spoke to his heart that all was not well. He turned and checked the lifeboat deck once more.

'Mariah! Mariah!' he shouted, sure the boy could hear him.

Left behind by the *Triton*, the lifeboat was rocked gently on the cold, black ocean. Not one ripple broke the surface of the viscous sea. The moon shone down its bitter blue rays and outlined the *Triton* as it sailed away.

Softly, quietly, the forward hatch of the lifeboat was lifted upwards. A white hand, etched in the blue of the moon, reached out and pushed back the red tarpaulin.

'We did it!' Biba said as she looked out and watched the ship sailing into the distance.

'Should never have left the ship – it's madness,' Mariah replied.

'So you don't want to know who is stealing all my father's money?' Biba asked as the *Triton* sailed into the darkness.

'But we'll get caught and they don't know we're here. Don't you ever think?' he said.

'Father will come for us – he always does. I left him a note,' she replied.

'But he doesn't know you are here. They could search the ship and think we have gone overboard,' Mariah said as the gravity of what he had done weighed heavily upon him.

'But . . .' was all Biba could say as her voice faded. 'You came with me . . .'

'I came with you because I knew you were mad enough to go on your own,' he replied.

'You could have told them,' she said, now hoping that he had.

'You jumped into the lifeboat – I had to follow you. Then before I could do anything we were in the sea,' Mariah said, chiding himself for pursuing her.

'But – we will get rescued?' she asked as if suddenly she saw the flaw in her own plan. 'My father will come – won't he?'

Mariah held his face in his hands and sighed. It felt as if he was in a dream – a dream from which he would wake soon and find himself back on the ship. It had seemed right to follow Biba into the lifeboat. He sensed her excitement. The words she had said seemed so convincing – 'Let's find out who the thieves are . . .' It was possible, he could do it without Charity. After all, he too was an agent of the Bureau of Antiquities. Only now, as he sat curled in the forward hatch of the lifeboat, did he have doubts. He should have known that anything Biba suggested could and would go wrong. Charity had warned him that whenever you ventured into enemy territory, you should always make sure you had a way of escape.

Now, Mariah felt like he was the bait on the end of a hook. That he would just have to wait to be captured. Once the thieves realised they had got hold of Biba DeFeaux then he knew she would be ransomed. He also knew that his own fate was uncertain.

'Why did you do it?' he asked indignantly.

'It was a quest and quests are to be followed,' Biba said as she looked again from the hatch. 'It seemed like a good idea – a spur-of-the-moment good idea . . . My necklace! I have lost my diamond necklace!' she gasped as if the weight of her venture now pressed on her heart.

Mariah wasn't listening. His fingers fumbled with the lock on the inside of the hatch that led into the lifeboat.

'There could be a way. It has to be that they will come for the boat. We could hide,' he said, his voice strained. 'They might unload the boat or lift it from the water – just pray they don't decide to sink us.'

He scrabbled through the hatch and into the lifeboat. There, under the thick red tarpaulin, was the gold. The ingots were stacked five high, covering the deck in between the wooden seats. They were wedged in place with life-jackets pushed against the gold. Mariah pulled back the tarpaulin so he could see more. In the corner was a black box. The lid was tied with a rubber seal.

'Flares,' he said to Biba as he pulled the tag on the box and its lid fell open.

There, held in place with a rubber strap, was a brass pistol and five thick cartridges. Mariah pulled the gun from its holder and pushed the cartridges into his pocket.

'We can use this,' he said, closing up the box and replacing the seal the best he could. 'If we're going to get out of this you'll have to do what I say, understand?'

Biba nodded. Then she spoke: 'I think you'd better come and look,' she said, her eyes saying more than her words.

Mariah pulled back the tarpaulin and crawled into the forward hatch. He shut the small door and then reached up to peer out of the top hatch. Coming towards them was an old ship. It had river paddles, one steam funnel and two sail masts, half-rigged. As it cut through the water it looked as if it were a stack of small thatched houses piled on each other. The starboard light glowed dimly as it got nearer.

'Do you think it's them?' Biba asked.

'It's a paddle steamer. Shouldn't be this far out at sea. It'll be lucky if it makes it across the Atlantic,' he said.

'But do you think it's them?' she asked impatiently.

'We'll soon find out,' he said as a small cannon fired high into the night sky.

There was a blinding explosion that lit the horizon. The blast roared towards them, rippling the water with small waves.

'Get down!' Mariah shouted. 'They'll see us.'

Biba pulled the hatch lid and slammed out the light. They sat together in the darkness. The sound of the steam trader got closer and closer. The engine churned relentlessly, paddles beating the water as it drew alongside the lifeboat. Mariah held his breath as the two craft rubbed against each other and footsteps crunched against the side of the boat.

'Hook it on – we have to get the lifeboat into the hold,' a man shouted. 'Then we can signal to the *Triton*.'

Mariah put his hand over Biba's mouth. He knew she was going to speak.

The lifeboat juddered slightly. It felt as if it was being plucked from the water by giant fingers and that the sea wouldn't give it up. There was a moment when the boat didn't move. Then it burst from the water and hung in the air, spinning back and forth as it clattered against the wooden side of the steam trader.

'Be still,' Mariah whispered. 'We are being lowered into the hold.'

The lifeboat went down and down as a winch whirred and crunched. Even inside the forward hatch they could feel the icy cold as they went deeper. Muffled voices shouted overhead and steel cables scraped against the side of the hold. It was as if they were being swallowed into the belly of a gigantic fish. Then suddenly the lifeboat halted. It tipped to one side as the cables slipped from the mooring rings.

Mariah heard the chains rattle as they were pulled from the hold. Men laughed drunkenly.

'Rich, Mr Chamberlain, very rich,' shouted a voice above them.

What light there was that came from the moon through a crack in the hatch soon vanished, as the deck above them slid into place.

'What shall we do?' Biba asked as she gulped back tears. 'I want Casper Vikash . . .'

'We'll wait and see who comes. When they find out who you are, they will realise they have more than gold,' Mariah replied. Just then the cannon on deck fired again, rocking the steam trader from side to side.

'Will they kill me?' she asked.

'Ransom you,' Mariah replied.

A door opened and stopped their conversation. It creaked on its hinges, giving them warning. Mariah tried to work out from which direction it came. Before he could think, a rope was thrown over the boat and then another and another until it was tied down. He could tell there was just one man outside. The man never spoke but occasionally he would whistle the end of a song and then another, changing tunes with every breath.

The red tarpaulin was pulled back. Mariah saw the shining of a lamp through the crack in the hatch. A shadow crossed back and forth. The man stood on the side of the lifeboat and then jumped inside. He lifted a heavy ingot and then threw it to the floor of the hold. It thudded heavily.

'All the gold I'll ever need,' the man said. He jumped from the boat to the deck, opened the creaking door and then slammed it behind him.

They waited until they could wait no more. Mariah spoke first, his mouth dry, yet so close to Biba that he could feel the warmth of her face.

'I'll go and see what I can find. Stay here,' he said.

'I hate the dark . . . I've never never been alone in the dark – I'll have to come with you,' she stuttered anxiously as the blackness of the ship pressed in on her like a tomb.

'You'll have to stay – I promise I won't be long,' Mariah said as he slowly opened the hatch and looked outside.

'Mariah, don't go!' Biba insisted as he climbed from the small opening and onto the deck of the lifeboat.

'Just stay in the hatch. Close your eyes and imagine a light inside your head – that's what I do, it always works for me.'

Leaving Biba inside, Mariah closed the lid of the hatch and pulled back the tarpaulin and then dropped to the floor. It was as if a voice inside him was telling him what to do. Carefully he crossed the floor of the hold to where he had heard the creaking door.

Shadows appeared to grow on shadows and shapes leapt before his eyes. He walked like a blind man, hands outstretched, until he reached the wall. Mariah traced his fingers over the wooden beams, following them sideways until they came to the joist that made the shape of the doorway. He fumbled for the handle, twisted it until it sprung open and then waited.

There was nothing but the thud, thud, thud of the steam piston that turned the ship's paddles. He pulled the door open an inch and peered out into a long passageway. It was lit by two oil lamps where a flight of wooden steps turned towards the door. There was a rancid smell of fish and whale oil. It floated in the air as a fine mist and glistened in the muted light.

He pushed slowly against the door and then waited again. There was nothing, no one. Mariah could feel the flare gun against his ribs. He had rammed it into his black Spiderweb waistcoat. As he closed the hold door behind him, he wished he were not alone.

'Did the *Triton* see the flare?' a voice asked from the corner of the stairs.

'It did. Markesan signalled,' replied another. 'They have not found the bomb and the ship will explode in twenty hours.'

'And his escape?' the man asked.

'He will lower himself to the water and then we shall rescue him,' came the reply as the voices came nearer to Mariah, who had nowhere to hide.

'Good – then we shall watch the fastest ship in the world sink to the bottom of the Atlantic Ocean.' The man laughed.

[14]

Markesan

THE stateroom of Deck 13 was thick with smoke from a chain of Havana cigars smoked by the Marquis DeFeaux as he paced up and down. With every step he puffed the smouldering noxious blue tobacco into the room and coughed as he spoke.

'So where can she be?' he asked Casper Vikash anxiously. 'You said she had gone to the circus with Mariah Mundi.'

'I thought they had,' he replied, seeing the true worry on Biba's father's face.

'Then you should find her – have you spoken to Charlemagne?' he asked.

'Ellerby said that Charlemagne hasn't seen her – she never went backstage after the performance,' said Vikash.

'But she has to be somewhere – she cannot vanish, not Biba DeFeaux,' he shouted angrily as his wife entered the room dressed in a sparkling gown of shimmering ruby. 'Mergyn – Biba is missing.' Mergyn dropped her gaze. She thought for a moment without speaking until the Marquis prodded her shoulder with the tips of his fingers. 'She is missing – don't you understand?'

'I know already,' she said as she held out her hand.

There, draped through her fingers, was an old gold necklace with a cluster of diamonds. It glistened in the light from the chandelier.

'Where?' asked the Marquis quite simply.

'A crewman found it on the lifeboat deck. It was dangling from the cables below. He said it was glinting in the moonlight and that's how he saw it,' Madame DeFeaux replied as she held back her tears.

'It can't be. I will not have it,' he protested. He threw the cigar to the floor, then stamped it into the carpet. 'She will not be lost to the sea . . .'

The steam elevator opened on Deck 13 and Charity stepped out. He was still out of breath. His eyes flicked from the Marquis to Mergyn and then to Vikash. They were all silent and stood like the witnesses to death.

'What do you know?' he asked calmly as their sombre look spoke of a great bereavement.

'Biba has fallen overboard – with Mariah. This has been found. Her necklace. She would never take it off, never,' Mergyn said fretfully.

'We were there and we never saw a thing,' the Marquis said as he stepped away from his wife. Charity looked at them both and realised, in that instant, that all love had been lost between them.

'That is why I know they did not fall into the sea.' Charity spoke firmly and without emotion. 'They would have screamed and we would have known. They are either still on this ship or they hid in the lifeboat.' He kept his eyes fixed on Mergyn as if he looked for something within her heart. 'We can only be sure when we have searched the ship. I suggest Casper and I go together – then we can be sure. If they cannot be found then I think that both of us have lost more than the gold.'

'They will have my daughter as well. Money can be replaced but Biba never – she is all I have,' the Marquis said bitterly as he looked at his wife.

'Marquis, Charity is right – I will go with him,' said Casper Vikash as he fastened the buttons on his jacket, took out his pistol and checked the chamber. 'We *will* find her.'

'Order the ship to slow down – make sure it is done gradually. I fear we are being stalked from afar. Have one of your men be a lookout from the stern of the *Triton*. If we cannot find Biba and Mariah on board – I think I know what to do.' Charity looked at Mergyn. He could see that she was about to cry. He put out a hand to comfort her. The Marquis stared at him sullenly. 'I will find Biba and Mariah. I promise you, Mergyn.'

Vikash and Mariah took the steam elevator to the promenade deck. The doors opened and they were engulfed in crowds of passengers taking the night air as they walked around the ship. A human tide of sharp tuxedos and crinoline gowns pushed them onwards as they made their way towards the stern of the ship. There, they knew, would be the best place to start the search. Soon they stood beneath the upper decks looking out across the still, cold Atlantic. Charity held on to the rail and looked out to the dark horizon.

'I know you have a plan,' Vikash said as he stood next to him.

'I don't think that Mariah and Biba are still on the ship. Something inside me makes me think they got on the lifeboat to go with the gold,' he said.

'Why should they do that?' Vikash asked.

'They are young and foolish and want to change the world,' he replied.

'Biba would never do such a thing,' Vikash replied as he watched the crowds of passengers chattering and walking by.

'From what I can see it would be exactly what she would do. I see a family on the verge of breaking and a woman who spends more time with an eccentric inventor than her own husband.'

'Never say that again,' Vikash replied angrily. 'That is my family – my father . . .'

'But it is true. Mergyn thinks nothing of Lyon DeFeaux and he gives his life to money and more money. Surely it hasn't always been that way?' Charity asked.

'You see things that are not there – they are happy together,' Vikash said as he turned to walk with the crowds.

'You said "father" – I heard you say "father" . . .' Charity asked as he pursued him.

'A mistake, a slip of the tongue,' Vikash replied.

'From you, one who always chooses his words so well?'

'We need to find Biba,' Casper said as he walked on.

'I always thought you were more than just a servant, Vikash,' Charity pursued further.

Vikash stopped and turned. His face was red with rage. He pushed Charity into a darkened doorway, slipped the pistol from his pocket and held it to his throat.

'What do you think you know, Mr Bureau of Antiquities? Can you see what goes on in my mind? Do you see that I am thinking I should just shoot you now?' Vikash growled.

'I see a son who protected his father and then saved his half-sister – is that not so, Casper Vikash? You are the son of the Marquis DeFeaux?'

Vikash released his grip and put the gun back in his pocket.

'How did you know?' he asked.

'I have watched the way you look at him and he at you. It is well known the Marquis worked in India thirty years ago and, I presume, that is about your age. Mergyn is much younger than him and Biba is only fifteen. I last saw Mergyn three days before she married the Marquis. A child was mentioned then and now I know it is you . . .'

149

'Then my heart is laid bare,' said Vikash. 'It was impossible for the Marquis to marry my mother – even though they were in love. As you can see, my skin is different to yours.'

'That may be so – but the heart of every man is the same,' Charity replied.

'Then your thoughts are not of this world. People are more frightened by my dark skin than the scars on my face,' he said. He closed his simmering brown eyes and hoped the situation of his life would be magically transformed.

'Then they are fools and will rot in their ignorance,' Charity said. 'I will keep your secret.'

'And say nothing of Madame DeFeaux and Lorenzo Zane?' Vikash asked suspiciously as they stepped from the doorway together.

'That is none of my business. The Marquis invited the Bureau to protect the gold and not his marriage,' Charity replied.

'It would be simple for me just to kill Lorenzo Zane and then Mergyn would have to love the Marquis once more,' Vikash said as they walked.

'That cannot be done. Sometimes hearts are changed and desires cannot be overcome. It is the way of a fallen world,' Charity replied.

'Not in my world,' said Casper Vikash. 'There is no honour in such a way as this.'

'I think Lorenzo may have his interest fuelled by more things other than the wife of the Marquis DeFeaux,' Charity said as they reached the entrance to the Oceanic Theatre. 'We should ask the Great Shanjing to see if he knows the future.'

The two men opened the theatre door. The third identical Mr Blake nodded as they stepped inside and took a seat. A herd of dancers stomped on the stage and wafted pelican wings back and forth as they tangoed. Soon, the curtain of blood-red velvet was tipped across the stage. The lights above them began to glow brightly as the show ended. Vikash and Charity waited until everyone had departed from the theatre. Three portly Americans struggled to free themselves from their seats and had to be eased from their places with the help of a one-armed juggler.

'Will you be going?' asked yet another of the Blake quadruplets.

'We are here to see Charlemagne,' Vikash said.

'He doesn't want any visitors and is not to be disturbed,' Blake said. He made it clear that he now wanted both men to leave.

'I don't think you understand,' Vikash replied.

'I have orders from Mr Ellerby – no one is to see Charlemagne,' he said as he pointed to the door.

'I have orders from the Marquis DeFeaux,' Vikash said as he got up from his seat and twisted the man's hand. 'Now do you understand?'

Mr Blake nodded, unable to speak. His eyes bulged from his head with the pain and he squeaked and twitched his long moustache.

'Very well,' he said eventually as Vikash eased his grip. 'Through that door.'

Vikash let the man go and nodded for Charity to follow.

'He didn't want any visitors,' Blake shouted defiantly as Vikash and Charity disappeared through the door that led backstage.

Vikash led Charity along the labyrinth of corridors that led to Charlemagne's dressing room. They stank of sweat, grease paint and sticky-sweet tobacco. Dancers and acrobats shouted and squalled at each other in a hundred different languages. They pushed their way through the entertainers in the dim glow of the oyster-shell lamps. Even though Charity had been there before he still could not remember the way. All looked the same, all smelt the same. They turned the final corner and there was the door. It was just how Charity remembered.

Vikash knocked loudly but there was no reply. He turned the handle and opened the door. The room was in darkness. A man sat in front of a long mirror. He didn't move. His head was in his hands and tears trickled through his fingers. Vikash turned the switch and the lamps around the mirror began to glow. There, sobbing was Charlemagne. He looked up pitifully at Vikash and Charity.

'We're looking for Biba DeFeaux and Mariah Mundi – have you seen them?' Vikash asked in a voice that said he was a moment away from using force.

'Gone, everything's gone,' Charlemagne mumbled drunkenly.

'What did you say to Ellerby?' Vikash asked.

'Ellerby? Ellerby? I haven't seen the man in days – he's far too good to come down here,' he replied as he wiped the tears from his face.

'Did you say that you hadn't seen Biba and Mariah?' Charity asked.

'I saw them . . . yes, I saw them. Biba came to talk with Shanjing. He gave the boy a prophecy, a word of knowledge about his life – or his death . . . Has it come true?' he asked as he managed to lift his head from his stick-like fingers and look at Charity through red eyes. 'I saw them after an earlier performance – all Shanjing would say was tiger's blood and a head full of screaming. Is that what you came for – is the boy dead?'

'For your sake I hope not,' Charity said. 'Did they mention to you anything of what they were doing?'

'Not a thing. I was tired. But I did hear them arguing in the passageway when they had gone. That lad didn't believe in Shanjing – I can tell.'

'And where is the mannequin now?' asked Vikash.

'Asleep in his box, as always. Too much wine and brandy for the old leather-skin,' Charlemagne said as he slipped from his chair. He grovelled on the floor as he tried to stand.

Vikash pushed him mercilessly to one side. He pulled open the lid of the box. It was empty.

'Leather-skin is not here,' he said as he looked about the room for the puppet.

Charlemagne looked up at him.

'You know – don't you? – you're eyes aren't clouded like all the others. You believe in such things – don't you?' he asked as he staggered to his feet and attempted to pour himself yet another drink.

'I believe you are drunk. Where is the doll?' Vikash asked as he took Charlemagne by the shirt and lifted him in the air until he dangled a foot from the ground.

'He's gone . . . Ran away, wouldn't perform any more – why do you think I'm drunk?' Charlemagne said.

'Mannequins don't run away – why do you lie to us?' Charity asked.

'He's not a doll, you fool. Shanjing is a man. Perfect in every way – but miniature, smaller than a child. He is a prophet – a seer, a visionary. Shanjing can see the future,' Charlemagne said as if he were the Prince of Denmark.

'Then prophesy for us – tell us where you have hidden Biba and Mariah and we will let you go,' Charity said as Charlemagne slumped to the floor.

'Only Shanjing can do that and he's gone. I am useless. All I do is hold him on my lap and see to his needs. I can't utter a divine word to save my life.' He fumbled for the glass as Vikash reached out to grab him.

'Leave him, Vikash,' Charity said. 'I believe he tells the truth. I have heard of such a man before – but he was not called Shanjing.'

'Do you know everything?' Charlemagne asked as he wondered why they wanted to know so much about Shanjing. 'What name was he given, this small man you had heard of?'

'That I can't recall,' Charity said. 'But I do know that he was similar to your Shanjing.'

'I wish I had never met him,' Charlemagne went on. 'It has been a curse – who'd have thought a Chinese dwarf would ever find their way to Wigan?'

'Does he believe Shanjing is really human?' Casper Vikash asked.

'But he is,' Charlemagne protested. 'Fully human in every way. Go, find him – see for yourself.'

'We search for Biba DeFeaux,' Vikash said angrily as he grabbed Charlemagne by the long strands of hair that were combed over his bald head and twisted them tightly.

'Shanjing talked about the girl when we were alone. He said she was part of the plan – but wouldn't tell me why,' Charlemagne uttered in feverish pain.

'Part of your plan?' Vikash asked as he tightened his grip.

'I tell you, it is not my doing. Shanjing is my master, I do what he says,' Charlemagne muttered in pain. 'He wants to get the girl. He was going to do it tonight but she never came. He has gone looking for her. That is the truth.'

Vikash looked at Charity and then pushed Charlemagne onto the red couch that stretched along the wall.

'Tell your friend that we will find him,' Charity said as he turned to leave. 'If any harm comes to the girl then he will wish he never stepped foot on this ship – and that, my friend, will be your fate also . . .'

Charlemagne slumped back onto the sofa. He curled himself like a small child and sobbed. Vikash looked at him briefly and shook his head. He leant towards him and out of Charity's sight whispered in Charlemagne's ear.

'Pray to whatever god you worship that nothing happens to my sister,' Vikash said softly as if he spoke a lullaby. 'If she is harmed in any way then I will come for you – understand?'

Charlemagne nodded and held out a shaking hand as if to beg friendship. Vikash turned and walked away.

'Don't judge me by what he does,' Charlemagne shouted after him in a rapid, anxious voice.

The two men walked purposefully and ignored the shouting from the room. A small crowd had gathered in the passageway and muttered to each other as Vikash and Charity forced their way through.

'What you done to him?' asked the one-armed juggler as he stood in their way. 'You can't come down here accusing him of things.'

'We accuse him of nothing. It is Shanjing we seek – he is a human and not a mannequin,' Vikash said as he pushed the man to one side. The troubadours gasped that he should say such a thing. 'It is true – ask Charlemagne, he will tell you.'

Vikash had no need to say another word. The troupe that blocked his way soon parted and scurried like mice to see Charlemagne.

Charity turned back and saw them forcing their way into his room. 'It will be about the ship within the hour,' he said, 'but it will help our cause – he will have nowhere to go.'

'You believe him?' asked Vikash.

'I don't doubt what he said. I had my suspicions that all was not well. There was something about Shanjing that was too real. Just before I was trapped I saw the figure of what I thought was a small boy. Now I know that to be Shanjing – *he* is the true ventriloquist,' Charity said as they descended further into the depths of the ship. 'Where would Biba hide in such a place as this?'

'There is a place Biba would always go when she lived on the

Ketos. It was the store where the passengers' luggage not wanted on the voyage was kept. She would look through the cases and dress in the clothes. If she were still on the ship, I'm sure that is the place she would take Mariah,' he said.

'Then we shall go to that place and start our search. With every hour that passes the chance of finding them dwindles,' said Charity.

Casper Vikash led on. Charity watched him as he walked. He was tall and upright with a nimble yet muscular frame. His clothes were functional but had an air of finery that not many men could accomplish. Charity wondered as they walked how Vikash could live with the agony of such a disfigured countenance. It was obvious that he had at one time had distinguished looks. Now his face was torn with a thousand scars.

There was much about the man that intrigued Charity. Now he knew that Vikash was the son of the Marquis DeFeaux he began to understand. It also made him realise that he was the true heir to all of the fortune. The houses, ships, yachts, the castles and factories, all the great wealth that DeFeaux had built into the grandest financial empire since Napoleon, would belong to Vikash on DeFeaux's death. All that stood in the way of the fortune was the true-born daughter – Biba.

[15]

Cartaphilus

O N board the paddle steamer Mariah looked down from his hiding place. He had pressed himself into the narrow gap between the door and the roof of the passageway. The ship was smaller than the *Triton* and had rolled back and forth even though the sea was calm. It made him feel sick – that and the smell of the whale oil that appeared to float in the air like a fine mist. The two men he'd heard talking had walked by without even looking up. Mariah had listened to them arguing as they disappeared from view. They were drunk, he could smell it. Their voices were tinged with anger and echoed through the passageway even when they were long gone. Mariah waited until he could hear them no more.

Dropping to the floor, he stretched out his stiff arms and shook them. The blood began to circulate again and he could feel his fingers. He could see to the end of the corridor where the men had gone. It was dark and empty. The lamps were dim and their light was absorbed by the grey walls. Mariah didn't know which way to go. Now, he regretted even more jumping into the lifeboat with Biba DeFeaux. It had seemed to be the right thing at the time – to come in search of the thieves and have them captured. He had disregarded all that Charity had told him. But now he had no plan and no way out. Mariah didn't know how long Biba would be able to stay alone in the dark. All he wanted to do was find the deck of the ship and think of a way of escape. Biba herself would be safe. When they found out that she was a DeFeaux no one in their right mind would ever harm her – well, not without trying to gain a ransom first.

It even crossed his mind to go straight to the captain of this ship and give themselves up and hope they would not be harmed. But that was not his way and was not the way of the Bureau of Antiquities. As he shook the numbness from his fingertips he thought that he should at least try to make an escape.

The ship must have its own lifeboat, and if they put to sea they might be found. Charity had told him that two ships a day left Southampton for New York and that they kept to the same latitude to avoid the sea ice to the north. Since the explosions in Greenland, the ice had moved further south – pushing the ships with it. There was a good chance, Mariah thought, that if they could escape from the ship they would be seen.

He felt a peculiar disadvantage, searching a ship that he didn't know. He checked the pistol in his pocket and slipped the catch forward. Then he took a deep breath and crept along the corridor towards the light by a flight of steps that led upwards. Mariah went quickly up the run of iron steps, turned at the top and then along another corridor. The smell of cabbage and cooking beetroot spilled from under the galley door in a cloud of thick steam. Next to the galley was an iron door with peeling paint that revealed the metal beneath. Swinging to and fro as the ship moved, never quite closing, there was a small hatch to look in through. The door was bolted from the outside and in faded black paint had the word *Brig* painted above the hatch.

'A jail,' Mariah whispered to himself as he dared to peer in through the hatch.

On a bench on the far wall of a room without light a man was lying. He sprawled across the makeshift bed as if he were dead. His arms were outstretched, his mouth open. Rolling back and forth across the wet floor was an empty bottle. It turned this way and then that, never finding rest. The man opened one eye and stared at him. Mariah ducked out of sight, hoping that he had not been seen. He clung to the door and looked back towards the steps, thinking he should run.

'Gonna let me out, boy?' the man asked. 'Been in here long enough . . . Sober now. I've done no wrong. Said it was for my own good and now my own good is good enough,' the man rambled.

Mariah was silent as he thought of what to do. He had been seen. He was trapped. The prisoner could shout and in the hue and cry Mariah would be found.

'I said, you gonna let me out?' the man asked again. 'Don't care what you doing on the ship. Got a face I never seen before. You a stowaway?' he asked. 'That's what I was – that's why I'm in here.' He laughed in a deep and gruff voice tinged with spit.

Mariah thought for a moment and then stood up. He looked through the hatch. The man could not be seen. It was as if he had been a ghost – the voice of an ancient mariner long dead. He could smell the foul stench of half-digested onions mixed with rum. It hung in the air like vapours of mist. Mariah stared harder into the gloom, hoping to see some sign of the man, but there was nothing – he was gone.

Without warning, a hand grabbed Mariah by the collar of his shirt and pulled him close, choking him as the thick fingers gripped hard.

'Don't you speak, stowaway?' the man asked as he appeared from his hiding place.

'Let me go!' Mariah said.

'Not until you let me out. Don't like it in here and I'm not sailing all the way to America in the brig. Undo the bolt and I'll say nothing and you can go and hide with the rats,' said the man sternly as he tightened his grip.

'Why are you in here?' Mariah asked.

'What's it to you – why you on the ship?' the man asked.

'Stowaway, just like you said,' Mariah replied, thinking fast as he held the man's hand to stop him tightening his grip.

'Well, you gonna let me out or am I to choke you where you stand?' the man asked as he shook Mariah with an arm so thick that it filled the hatch opening.

'I can't reach the lock – you'll have to let me go,' Mariah replied as his face was scraped against the side of the door.

'Then we got a problem. If I let you go you could run away and leave me in here,' the man said.

'You could turn me in and then I'd be locked up with you,' Mariah replied, as the man's grip got even tighter.

'Then we have to find some trust,' the man said through the vapours of rum that billowed from his guts.

Mariah thought for a moment. He was being held by his throat and couldn't escape. The man grasped him with such strength that he could snuff him out there and then.

'If I open the door are you going to turn me in?' he asked.

'Depends on what you have to say for yourself,' the man replied, not releasing his grip.

'Then I promise not to run and I will undo the bolts,' Mariah replied as the breath was being squeezed from him.

'Give me your left hand,' said the man. He loosened his grip on Mariah's throat.

Mariah didn't question him. He knew this would be the only way he could escape being choked by the man's arboreal fingers. He slipped his hand through the hatch. The man grabbed him by the wrist as he let go of his throat. His grip on Mariah's hand was just as tight, just as harsh.

'I can't run,' Mariah said painfully. 'I'll open the door.'

He slid the bolts with his free hand. They were easy to move and slipped quickly from their keepers. The door swung open and the man stepped outside. He kept his grip on Mariah as he looked down at him and smiled.

'Bigger than I thought for a stowaway,' the man said as he pushed the fingers of his free hand through the mass of thick, black curls that covered his head. 'How did you get on the ship?'

Mariah didn't know what to say. It would be easy to lie, but it would be easy to be found out. He was caught, either by a friend or foe, and he didn't know which the man was.

'Does it matter?' Mariah asked.

The man laughed. 'It would be interesting to know – I have never met a fellow stowaway. That's how I started my life at sea – a lad just like you jumping on a ship to see the world.'

'And what are you now?' Mariah asked, as he looked the giant of a man up and down.

'They call me Cartaphilus – I wander the seas of the world in whatever way I can,' he replied as he let go of Mariah's wrist. 'You have honest eyes, too honest to be at sea and I bet you haven't eaten.' Mariah nodded as Cartaphilus smiled again. 'I can smell cabbage. The crew are on watch, either that or drunk in their beds – we can eat and won't get disturbed.'

'What if we get caught?' Mariah asked as the man took him by the shoulder and marched him to the galley, opening the door and pushing him inside.

'Then we'll sleep in the brig until we get to Virginia,' he replied as he took some bread and cheese from a cabinet and gave it to Mariah. 'You alone?'

The question had come suddenly and Mariah answered with his eyes. He looked from Cartaphilus to the door.

'A girl?' asked the giant. Mariah nodded. 'Hiding in the hold?'

As he ate the bread and cheese Mariah told the man how they had got on board the ship. Something made him keep Biba's identity a secret.

'So they'll think you're lost to the sea?' Cartaphilus asked. 'In a lifeboat you say – from the *Triton*?'

Mariah nodded. 'Why did they have you locked up?' he asked.

'Didn't like what I was up to – took five of them to get me in there. Got me drunk first – that's my weakness. We all have a weakness and I love Jamaica juice.' He coughed as he savoured the memory.

'So they'll put you back inside?' asked Mariah as he looked at the faded tattoos on the man's arm.

'Not again – and you're gonna help me,' the man said as he leant forward to Mariah and picked cheese from his plate. 'We're gonna take over this ship, you and me . . . I'll make you first mate.'

'So you're not a stowaway?' Mariah asked.

'I'm the captain,' Cartaphilus replied slowly as he stared Mariah in the eyes. 'Or should I say – I was the captain until I agreed to pick up that lifeboat from the *Triton*. Once it got out that it was packed with gold then other people had ideas beyond their calling.'

'Mutiny?' Mariah asked.

'I would call it cowardice – cheating and stealing what is mine,' Cartaphilus said as he stood up from the table. 'Come on, lad, we are going to take back my ship.'

Cartaphilus pushed Mariah into the passageway and then bade him to follow. It seemed he didn't need to know Mariah's name or much about him at all. Mariah felt a deep unease. Could he believe the man? Cartaphilus didn't look like a captain of a ship. He had the bearing and guise of a soldier, with hands that looked as if they had worked the land for a thousand years.

They crept though the begrimed warren of tunnels until

they came to the stairway that led up to the deck. Mariah could smell the sea.

'This is what I want you to do,' Cartaphilus said as he held Mariah by the shoulder. 'Go up them stairs and along the deck. Behind the bridge you will see a cabin – that's my place. Inside the desk you'll find a gun. Bring it to me . . .'

Mariah did as he said. He had soon climbed the stairs and ran along the empty deck. The moon shone down and far to the west he could see the lights of the *Triton*. Behind the bridge he saw a ladder that led up to a narrow deck with a solitary door. A man with a beard at the wheel of the ship was staring straight ahead, as if he tried to follow in the wake of the *Triton*.

Mariah climbed the ladder, walked the deck and slowly and carefully opened the door of the cabin. Just as Cartaphilus had said, Mariah saw the desk. He opened the drawer and found the gun. It was old, more a small rifle than a pistol, with a short magazine that jutted out from the side. Quickly, Mariah retraced his steps, keeping an eye on the bridge and the man staring out to sea.

'Was there anyone about?' Cartaphilus asked when Mariah returned.

'Just a man on the bridge steering the ship – he didn't see me.' Mariah replied.

'Did he have a beard?' he asked. Mariah nodded. 'That's old Tornado Jones. Blind as a bat – he be sticking to a heading and seeing nothing at all. That means the rest will be drunk and asleep. Better choose the place to do battle,' he said as he took the gun from Mariah and cocked the hammer. 'You'll have to fend for yourself, lad – it could get bad . . .'

Cartaphilus climbed the steps and onto the deck. The night was clear and crisp. For a thousand miles around them the sea was still, as if it were about to freeze. The wake from the ship fell back into the sea like shards of ice.

The captain walked towards the bridge, staggering as if he were still drunk. With every step he looked back and forth, expecting an ambush lay ahead. They edged their way around a stack of barrels filled with lamp oil and then slowly on.

'We'll wait until they change the night watch,' he whispered as he climbed to the deck and got to the door of his cabin. 'You coming or are you going to stand there all night?'

Mariah followed him into the cabin. It was all he could think of to do. He felt as if he were trapped in a game – like a mouse chased by a cat, captured but not killed. The cabin was small. There was a desk by one wall and an old stove by the other. Three leather chairs were nailed to the floor by their claw feet. Maps and charts were pinned to the walls. Cartaphilus lit the whale–oil lamp and put a pot of coffee on to the stove.

'When will the watch be changed?' Mariah asked as he searched nervously for something to say.

Cartaphilus looked up at the clock on the wall of the cabin. Its white face glowed in the golden light. The black hands were unmoving, as if time had stood still.

'Two of the clock now . . . and the watch will be changed in an hour. Time for some coffee,' he replied. He sat in a rickety old chair by the stove and warmed his feet. 'So,' he said with a long, deep sigh. 'What's your name? Where's your friend? And what are you doing on my ship...'

Mariah touched the pistol in his pocket and was tempted to pull the gun and shoot the man there and then. He could feel his breathing deepen as the blood pulsed through his body. His mouthed dried as he stared blankly at the clock. The room was cold and airless and stank of whale oil.

'Mariah,' he found himself saying. 'Mariah Mundi. My friend is Biba DeFeaux – she is in the hold with the lifeboat – we hid and never knew it would be set adrift.'

'Did you see the gold?' Cartaphilus asked.

'A man came and took an ingot. I saw him from our hiding place.'

'That would be Mr Pusey – you may know him, an English-man from Oxford,' Cartaphilus said as he watched the coffee pot steam.

'No.' Mariah stumbled on his words. 'I live in the north – but once lived in London.'

'Do you like thieves?' the man asked as he put the gun by the stove and lifted the coffee pot to fill a mug on his desk. Then he spoke again before Mariah could answer. 'I have just stolen a million pounds from the *Triton*. Mr Pusey then stole it from me. He didn't have the guts to kill me, so he got me drunk and locked me away. Without you, Mariah, I would still be in that brig. How can I repay you?'

'You could put us off at the next port?' Mariah asked.

'Is that all you want? Don't you want a share of the gold?' Cartaphilus asked.

Mariah shook his head as he watched the seconds pass uncomfortably. 'Virginia would be a fine place to be left.'

'No parents to care for you?' the man asked.

Mariah shook his head again. 'Dead,' he said softly, as if the fact had finally been accepted.

'Chance would be a fine thing,' Cartaphilus said. His eyes followed the flickering shadows cast by the oil lamp. 'To rest in such a way would be a sufficient thing.'

'It comes to us all,' Mariah replied.

'For some . . . but not for everyone.' He coughed as he spoke.

Mariah was about to speak when there was a sound outside the cabin. It was as if ropes were being hauled from over the side of the ship. A door slammed shut. A man shouted.

'Now's the time,' Cartaphilus whispered. He cast an eye to the clock. 'Pusey is on night watch.'

Cartaphilus got to his feet, gun in hand, then pushed Mariah to one side. He opened the door a fraction of an inch and peered out. The cold sea air was sucked into the room, flapping the charts that were pinned to the smoke-tainted walls.

Mariah watched as Cartaphilus opened the door even further. It was as if he knew what would happen next. He could see the shadow of a man on the deck below, outlined by the moon. Two others stood nearby. It looked as if they were about to hoist a boat over the side of the ship.

'Thinking of leaving, Mr Pusey?' Cartaphilus asked.

'Captain Cartaphilus! I thought we had locked you away?' the man asked mockingly.

'Alive and well – no thanks to you,' he replied as Mariah kept out of sight.

'Then we shall have to set you adrift and hope you will be saved by Eskimos,' he said.

Cartaphilus said nothing. He slipped the gun from behind the door. Mariah heard the click of the trigger and the explosion of the bullet.

'Not us!' shouted another man. 'Pusey made us follow him.'

The gun fired again.

'And you,' Cartaphilus said, 'will you follow the same way?'

'Not me, Captain – you know that,' the last man said.

'Then throw them both into the sea. I have Mariah Mundi and Biba DeFeaux as guests on this ship. Snuck away in that lifeboat you picked up. She'll be worth more than the gold.'

Cartaphilus turned to Mariah and smiled.

'I thought you would be a man of your word,' Mariah said to the Captain.

'That I am, lad. I have lived so long that my word is worth nothing.'

Rhinoceros Trousers

'RHINOCEROS trousers?' Charity asked as he and Vikash, continuing their search for Mariah and Biba on the *Triton*, entered the long dark room where the passengers' luggage was stored in the depths of the ship. It was like a gigantic library. From wall to wall were avenues of cases stacked upon each other and strapped to the floor by long red cords to stop them moving as the ship rolled.

'I know it is hard to believe, but I heard it myself,' Vikash replied as he remembered the day when he had first met Henry Mitchell, the big game hunter.

'But they can't be bulletproof,' Charity said in disbelief as he looked around at the piles of neatly stacked trunks and cases that filled the room from floor to ceiling.

'His case should be here somewhere. I know that he is one of the greatest hunters in the world and that he always wears a pair of rhinoceros trousers. It is even said that he has a pair of pyjamas made from the same creature,' Vikash went on, laughing to himself. 'Of course, he is English,' he said, as if this was an excuse for insanity.

'Can't understand why anyone should take part in such a

slaughter,' Charity replied as he searched the narrow corridors between the piles of leather cases.

'I heard that he used a machine gun mounted on the back of a carriage,' Vikash said.

'Mariah! Biba!' Charity shouted, his words echoing from the high vaulted ceiling. 'I don't think they are here, Vikash. I am convinced they were on the lifeboat.'

'But why would Biba do such a thing?' Vikash asked.

'They are both young, and foolish in a way,' Charity replied as a fleeting shadow caught his attention. It flickered momentarily between two avenues of travel trunks and then disappeared. 'Did you see that?'

Charity turned. It was obvious that Vikash had also seen the shadow. He signalled to Charity to keep down as he skirted around a tall stack of luggage, piled like coffins to the high roof.

'It's Shanjing,' Charity whispered. 'I know it is . . .'

Suddenly and without warning, the holding cords snapped. Suitcases began to fall. They rained down, crashing to the floor. Vikash was hit, just as Charity shouted out a warning. From above them, the walls of the avenue began to tumble as more and more travelling luggage fell on top of them like a landslide. There was no escape. The passageway was quickly blocked and the cases formed an impenetrable barrier. Vikash was silent, stunned and dazed, his brow cut open and bleeding.

'Vikash,' shouted Charity, 'I can't get to you.'

Charity heard laughter. It seemed to come from everywhere. It was cackling, harsh, old, the ranting of a madman.

'Think you could find me?' the voice asked as if it were right behind him. 'You are such a fool.'

'Shanjing! Shanjing!' shouted Charity as the voice faded.

Laughter came once more. This time it was shrill and monkey-like. More cases fell, kicked down from above.

'Such a fool, Captain Charity,' the voice said before all was silent.

Jack Charity struggled beneath the avalanche of leather and wood. The cases were as heavy as rocks and pressed down upon him. He couldn't see Vikash. Struggling under the weight of the baggage, Charity gasped for breath. He tugged at each case as he tried to pull it aside.

'Charity,' Vikash called from somewhere close by. 'I am injured.'

'I'm here, not but six feet away,' Charity said as he pushed himself under the mountain of luggage and crawled towards the direction of the voice.

Charity found Vikash slumped against the wall. One of the cases had struck him on the head as it fell and Vikash had managed to crawl into a small cave of tumbled luggage. Miraculously he had not been crushed.

'What do people put in these things?' Vikash asked.

'Their lives,' Charity replied.

'But why should Shanjing be here?' he asked.

'I think we found him by coincidence. Looking here for Biba was a chance of fate. Now Shanjing will have to find another hiding place,' Charity said as he struggled to push a case out of his way.

'No!' screamed Vikash. 'They will all fall. They are not safe. There must be at least three tonnes above us – we are blessed to be alive.'

'But we will not be so if we stay in this place,' Charity replied. 'If we stay close to the walls and crawl through we can find a way out.'

'And Shanjing will be long gone,' said Vikash as he turned uncomfortably, his face bleeding.

'We should go on – we could crawl out of here if we take care,' Charity said. He looked about him for a way of escape.

There was no way of seeing where they were going. The fallen trunks and cases had crashed to the ground to form a labyrinth of dark, narrow passages. Some of the cases had burst open, their secrets spilled out like entrails. Charity crawled slowly and carefully, as above him the weight of the luggage creaked and groaned as if it were to soon collapse. Vikash followed, his face streaming with blood. Together they struggled a few yards until they could go no further. A large stuffed antelope that looked at Charity through its glass eye blocked their way.

'Amazing what people bring with them on a voyage,' Charity said as both men managed to sit upright.

'I can see light above us,' Vikash said as he pushed his hand through a gap between a case and a coffin-like trunk. 'There is a way out from this place . . .'

Vikash pushed harder. The gap grew larger until it was the size through which he could squeeze himself. Charity followed and they both scrambled to the surface. It was as if they had escaped from the depths of a glacier. Finally Vikash pushed away the last case and sat on the top of the avalanche.

'Do you think Shanjing got away?' he asked.

'The dwarf is fleet of foot and does not want to be caught – I suspect he is gone,' Charity replied as he pushed his way through to the surface.

From where he was, Charity could see the vastness of the ship's hold. No longer were there avenues of neatly stacked cases. Everything that had once been so neat was now scattered and broken like the crumbling rocks of a mountain. High above, the electric lights clung to the roof. Charity could see the doorway. It was clear of cases; the green exit sign flickered meagrely.

One piece of luggage caught his attention in particular. Unlike the others, it was still attached to the wall of the ship's hold. Charity could see that it had been strapped separately to a thick metal beam. Had the other cases not fallen, it would never have been found. In itself it was quite unremarkable. The case was made of green leather with a gold-coloured handle and even from a distance Charity could make out the owner's name – MARKESAN.

The word brought back a terrible memory to him. He froze. A bead of cold sweat trickled across his forehead. It was as if he stared at death.

Vikash saw the look on his companion's face.

'What is it?' he asked as Charity pointed as if he had seen a ghost.

'Do we have a list of passengers?' Charity asked anxiously as he put his hand to his mouth.

'It can be obtained – what is it?' he asked.

'Oscar Markesan,' he replied. 'He is on this ship . . .'

'There are thousands of people on this ship, Charity. Why should one more make a difference?' Vikash asked, the name of no significance to him.

'Because I now know who intends to blow up the ship,' he replied.

'But the ransom has been paid,' said Vikash as Charity clambered across the ridge of suitcases towards the door.

'Markesan doesn't care. He will have the money and destroy the ship. That is his way.'

Charity got to the door and then began to edge his way towards Markesan's suitcase. Once near, he heard a sound that called dread to his heart. Coming from the green crocodile-skin case was the ticking of a clock.

'This is the bomb,' Charity said as Vikash approached. 'It will blow a hole in the side of the ship.'

'The *Triton* is unsinkable. If water floods the hold the ship will still float,' Vikash replied.

'Markesan didn't place it here by accident, Mr Vikash. There is an expansion joint just at this point to allow the ship to move without the steel plates of the hull bursting. If the bomb explodes, it will split the ship in two and it will sink within minutes.'

'Then?' asked Vikash, not knowing what to say.

'We take the bomb and throw it overboard,' Charity replied as he unhooked the red strap that held the case in place. 'He didn't work alone. It is no coincidence that the suitcase was placed here.'

'Are you sure it is a bomb?' Vikash said.

Charity took the case from the wall, placed it on the floor and opened the brass latches with a flick of his fingers.

'I know Markesan's work. He was meticulous in all things. Look at this,' Charity said, rubbing his hand over the fine, hand-crafted leather. 'This is the most expensive travelling case money can buy.'

With that he lifted the lid open. Inside, as if it were a work of art, was the ornate face of a striking clock. The long black hands were encased inside a glass front that sat on a brass frame filling the case. It was as intricate as it was beautiful, and it looked as though the device had been specially designed to fit in the case.

'Magnificent,' Vikash said as he looked over Charity's shoulder. 'I have never seen such a beautiful thing as this.'

'And to think it is made for death,' Charity replied. 'Jacquier de Paris – 1835, if I am not mistaken. One of the finest clockmakers in the world.'

Charity looked inside. Beneath the beautiful and intricate workings was a lining of explosive. The wires from the clock were placed inside a small glass tube filled with mercury, wax and gunpowder. To one side was a crisp white envelope. It bore the words: *Captain Jack Charity – Bureau of Antiquities*.

'It has your name,' Vikash said as Charity lifted the envelope from the case and looked at the letter inside.

Dear Captain Charity – I leave this note should you find the case – if not you dwell in the deep and this does not matter – once you took something precious from me – now I will take something precious from you . . . like for like. MARKESAN

'He knows you . . . knows you would find the case. What does it mean?' Vikash asked. 'What did you take from him?'

'Something precious – irreplaceable,' Charity replied.

'But what should a man own that he would want revenge for taking it?' asked Vikash.

'His only son,' Charity said. He paused before he went on. 'No one has ever seen Markesan face to face. I followed him through Paris – or so I thought. He had some papers of the seer Nostradamus. The lost Quatrain. The Bureau wanted them. It was dark. I saw the glint of a silvered pistol. I fired, and the man fell. It was not Markesan – but his son.'

'Something precious – like for like – but you do not have a son?' Vikash asked.

'He wants to kill Mariah,' Charity said.

'But he is not your son,' replied Vikash.

Charity said nothing. He looked at the letter once more and then neatly folded the paper and put it in his pocket. Then, as if it had never happened, he examined the case, the clock and the explosives.

'It will be safe to move. The mercury is quite safe,' he said.

'Is it set to explode?' asked Vikash warily as he wiped the blood from his face.

'I cannot be sure. All I can see is that if I remove the wires from the explosive then the bomb will explode. From the clock face, I presume we may have several hours. We should take it to the top deck and throw it into the sea.'

'Could it explode if we move it?' Vikash asked.

'That is a chance we will have to take,' Charity said as he closed the lid and smiled.

'I am not convinced,' said Vikash as he reluctantly took hold of the case and helped Charity lift it up. 'I never thought that I would enter the next life holding a green crocodile-skin bag . . .'

They carried the case carefully across the room until they came to the exit door. For several minutes they followed the labyrinth of tunnels until they came to the steam elevator. They never spoke, putting all their effort into holding the case as steadily as they could. As they walked, the case ticked malignantly. Vikash felt as though he was being watched all the time. To him it was as if he was being tested and if he failed, he would vanish in an explosion of light.

'Does Mergyn know you are the son of the Marquis?' Charity asked as they got to the steam elevator.

'It was never a secret from her, but she chooses to say nothing,' he replied as he pressed the pearled call button for the elevator. 'And the Marquis, he is at best avuncular and at worst . . . Well, I am perhaps a useful reminder of happier times.'

'And your mother?' Charity enquired as they waited for the elevator to arrive.

'She is dead – grief broke her heart,' Vikash replied simply and then laughed. 'You English choose the strangest times to talk of such things. Here we are standing in the bowels of a ship, clutching a bomb powerful enough to blow us to heaven, a madman wants you dead – and you ask me of my life?'

'It was something I desired to know and now seemed a good time,' Charity replied as the elevator chimed its arrival.

Stepping inside they held the case as if it were a fragile small child. Both men tried to avoid the gaze of the other as the elevator rattled higher and higher. The clock ticked on and on.

Charity could feel each second pass as the hands skirted across the clock face.

The elevator stopped suddenly. The doors opened and a woman in a black ball gown stepped inside. She smiled at them both in a way that showed her wonder why two men should stand precariously holding a travelling case.

'They had fireworks from the top deck,' she said unsteadily in her best Tennessee drawl. 'To think I have danced all night.'

Vikash and Charity smiled politely. It was obvious from the look on the woman's pinched face that she would not desist until she knew what they were doing.

'An unusual case – is it yours?' she asked as she stared worriedly at Vikash's blood-soaked and scarred face. 'I enquire because I saw a man with a whole set of luggage just like that coming onto the ship and he certainly didn't look like you.'

'What was this man like?' Charity asked.

'I don't know if I should tell – after all, you could be thieves and stealing what's not yours, wanting to know your victim,' the woman said. Her corset heaved like the creaking timbers of a sailing ship about to strike a reef. 'And I a woman alone . . .' she went on, her voice faded.

'It is of no consequence, Madame. I am the assistant of the Marquis Lyon DeFeaux, the owner of the *Triton*, and in this case is a bomb,' Vikash spoke as if he talked about the price of bread.

'Bomb? Did you say bomb?' the woman stuttered.

'The man – what was he like?' pressed Charity as the woman fell back against the doors.

'Old . . . a beard, spectacles, a top hat . . . beady eyes . . . he was French,' the woman said as she stared at Charity. 'Is it really a bomb?'

Vikash casually opened the lid of the case to expose the clock and the explosive.

'With enough explosive to blow you from your corset,' he said as the woman swooned to the floor.

'An unusual way of informing the passengers there is a bomb on the ship,' quipped Charity as the lift stopped suddenly and the doors opened automatically in the crowded restaurant.

'What shall we do with her?' Vikash asked as they stepped over the woman and left her in the elevator.

The woman got to her knees and looked as if she had just been beaten. 'Bomb!' she screamed. 'They have a bomb.'

The room was silent. A waiter turned and, seeing Vikash and Charity carrying the case, dropped a tray of champagne.

The woman shrieked the warning again.

'Did you hear that? They have a bomb . . .' said a man by the door.

Vikash was about to explain when Charity spoke.

'It's stopped ticking,' he said in disbelief as he opened the lid of the case. He could see the phial of mercury was clouding. It had lost its shimmer and had turned dark brown. Vapour poured from a small cylinder as acid dripped inside the tube. 'We have been tricked, Vikash. Quickly . . .'

'GET DOWN!' screamed Vikash as they ran to the door that led on to the top deck.

Vikash kicked at the door – it burst open. The night was cold and still. Charity stumbled . . . the case fell. Vikash grabbed the handle. With all his might he threw the bomb . . .

The night sky burned brightly as the *Triton* shuddered in the blast of the bomb – then all was still again.

[17]

Carasbandra

THE paddle steamer sailed silently into the night. It had no silhouette as the moon had set in the sea. The ocean slopped icily against the side of the steamer and the engines churned with the monotonous drone of the paddles.

Inside the cabin behind the bridge, Biba DeFeaux stood next to Mariah. She had been found and dragged from the hold to the bridge. Cartaphilus sat in his chair, feet on the black stove and arms folded. Behind him, two of the crew looked on. Biba picked at the strands of fur on her coat.

'How much do you think you are worth to your father?' Cartaphilus asked as she sobbed. 'Stupid thing, getting in the lifeboat – you deserve all you get.'

Biba couldn't speak. She gulped back her tears angrily.

'You've got the gold, isn't that enough?' Mariah asked as he put his arm around her.

'Gold is never enough, Mariah. I have promised the crew a larger share for their loyalty. I can't go back on my word, and I have a partner who will take half of the money if not more. This will be for me.'

'But you can't just kidnap us,' he replied.

'I could have you killed instead – would that suit you?' Cartaphilus asked with a laugh. He turned to Biba. 'I intend to contact your father and tell him that I have you and ask him for a million dollars for your return or else I will send you to him piece by piece.'

Biba sobbed even more. Vikash was not here to protect her. She felt alone.

'He said he would never pay a ransom,' she sobbed. 'Told me that if I was ever kidnapped that would be it. His empire is worth more than family – that's what he said.'

She held tight to Mariah's coat as if it were all she had.

'Then you better pray that he changes his mind. There is a bomb on the *Triton* that will be exploded – I am sure he will pay for that information as well as his daughter,' Cartaphilus said without any sentiment. 'Take them to the brig and make sure they don't get out.'

'But how will you tell him? The *Triton* is far ahead and unmatchable in speed,' Mariah asked.

'We don't work alone in this – it will be as I have said. The *Carasbandra* may look like a rotting hulk, but she can keep pace with the *Triton* – especially if the wonderful Zane Generator should be in difficulty.'

'Sabotage?' asked Mariah.

'I would prefer not to use such a word,' replied Cartaphilus. 'I have lived so long that I have made many friends.'

Biba and Mariah were dragged from the cabin and taken to the brig. The cold night air cut at their skin. It was as if the breeze was tinged with sharp steel and blew like unseen daggers about them.

'Not good, this,' said one of the men as he pointed to the north. 'Sky shouldn't be like that – never seen a green sky in the dead of night.'

The other man just grunted in reply as they dragged their

captives below deck and along the passageway past the galley.

The men locked the door of the brig and Biba and Mariah were left in the gloom of the dim, smoking whale-lamp. Mariah pressed his ear to the door and listened for the men. Their footsteps echoed as they climbed the metal stairs back to the deck.

'We will have to escape,' he said urgently when he was sure they had gone.

'How? Don't you realise we are on a ship in the middle of the ocean?' she snapped.

'As soon as Charity realises I have gone and your father finds the note they will come looking for us. I am sure of it. The *Triton* could ram this ship out of the water. Cartaphilus would have to give you up – he could trade you for the gold,' Mariah said quickly. 'It has to be that way. We have to get out of here and hide in the ship.'

'He said there was a spy on the *Triton* – and a bomb,' Biba said.

'More reason to escape,' replied Mariah. He checked the flare gun deep in the pocket of his thick coat. Without speaking, he then took the other pistol from his pocket and pointed it at the door. 'Stand to the wall and cover your face . . .'

'You have a gun?' asked Biba, surprised.

'I have two. They never thought to search me,' he said.

Mariah pulled the trigger of the pistol. There was a bright flash as the flame shot from the gun. The lock burst open and fell from the door as it opened. Mariah cautiously looked outside the brig. The corridor was empty.

'Where shall we hide?' Biba asked as she tried to rub the burst of the flash from her eyes.

'It will soon be dawn. We have to make them believe we have jumped overboard. I think I know what to do,' Mariah said. He took hold of Biba's hand and led her from the cell. 'We can put a lifeboat over the side of the ship and throw our coats in the water. I'll set off a flare and then we hide.'

Biba raised an unconvinced eyebrow. 'Not my coat,' she said. 'I couldn't.'

'It has to look real if you want to live, Biba,' Mariah replied as they walked towards the metal stairs that led to the deck.

Mariah opened the hatch and stepped outside. It was even colder than before. The drone of the engines seemed louder and the beat of the giant paddles heavier. The night was black like velvet. The moon had gone and the dawn was still far off. To the north was a green glow slit across the horizon like a knife. It appeared that the world was changing, that some force was secretly at work. Mariah looked out to sea. In the faint glow, Biba saw his face change.

'It's Greenland,' she said as if she could read his mind. 'Lorenzo Zane was experimenting with the Isbrae glacier. He was trying to make power from the ice and all I know is that something went wrong.'

'What was he trying to do?' he asked.

'An experiment,' she whispered. 'He would fire a cannon packed with silver dust into the clouds. He told my mother he was trying to make lightning to power the shipyard. The sky turned green and glowed at night. Mother said that it got worse night by night. Zane would tell her in the letters he wrote,' Biba said as if she hated to say his name.

'Can't understand why he would mess with things like that. It could kill us all,' Mariah replied.

'There are worse things than that. My father told him to stop his experiments but he wouldn't listen. I didn't know what he was doing, but I would hear my parents arguing about him,' Biba said quietly.

Mariah walked the narrow boards between the gunwales and the cargo of whale oil stored on deck. Biba followed at a distance, tripping on her coat. When they were at the lifeboat Mariah didn't hesitate. Working alone he undid the rope and pushed the boat over the side.

'When I tell you, throw your coat into the sea,' he said.

'No – never!' Biba said as she pulled the fur coat defiantly about her.

Mariah slipped the rope through his hands as the boat fell to the water.

'All I have to do is release this catch,' he said as his cold fingers fumbled with a brass catch at the end of the rope.

'YOU!' shouted a voice from the darkness.

A pistol shot flew above their heads.

Mariah shouted, 'Get down!'

The shots came again and again from the darkness. Mariah took the flare gun from his pocket and calmly slipped a thick shell into the breach. A shot came again, splintering the wood by his head. Mariah saw a faint shadow standing far away on the cargo deck. He aimed the flare gun and fired. There was a blinding explosion as the gun jolted back and fell from his hand. The flare bounced across the deck, igniting everything it touched. It smashed into a barrel of whale oil, cracking it open. Then it rose up in the air, deflected by the barrel, and set fire to the half sail that hung windless in the night. The cloth burst into flame, tearing open and falling to the deck. Like hot tallow, the whale oil exploded in a cloud of fire and black smoke.

Shots rang out from the other side of the flames. A bullet knocked Mariah to the deck.

'Mariah!' screamed Biba as she ran to him.

Mariah lay motionless. He was without breath. His face was white, his eyes wide open. Biba looked at him and thought he was dead. A shot rang out again from somewhere near. It smashed into the deck rail, blasting shards of wood into the air. Biba rummaged in Mariah's coat as a man jumped from the blazing cargo deck and walked towards her. She found a shell for the flare gun. Picking up the pistol, she broke open the barrel, loaded the cartridge, aimed and then fired.

Just as before, the flare burst from the pistol and shot through the air. It bounced once on the deck, setting fire to the whale oil. The flare bounced just as the man took aim and smashed into his chest, knocking him from his feet. He stumbled backwards, tipped over the rail and fell screaming to the cold, dark sea.

'Who taught you to shoot?' Mariah gasped as he looked at Biba.

'You were shot – I saw you hit by the bullet,' she replied as if she spoke to a ghost.

'Spiderweb,' Mariah said as he pulled the slug from the fibres of his coat. 'Bulletproof.'

There was a large explosion that lit the night sky, sending a ball of fire towards the heavens. Barrels of kerosene blew from the ship, set on fire by the pool of whale oil that seeped across the deck. From the far side of the flames, they could hear the screams of the crew as they jumped from the ship.

Cartaphilus stood on the bridge screaming for them to stop.

'Mariah Mundi, I will kill you for this! I have walked the earth and always had my way. I shall not be stopped by a lad like you.'

Mariah could see him looking down at them. Cartaphilus shook his fist as he ranted and screamed. He looked like a demon burning in hell. His hair blew wildly as the firestorm burned his ship. He clung to the iron railings as he shouted damnation upon them.

'The lifeboat,' Mariah said as he got to his feet. 'Inside, now!'

Biba jumped into the boat as Mariah struggled with the brass latch.

'It's no use,' he said as he took the pistol from his pocket and fired at the lock.

Biba didn't have time to speak. The lifeboat broke free and fell safely to the water. It was soon clear of the *Carasbandra*. The ship paddled on, its large water-wheels churning the sea as the deck burned and kerosene barrels exploded into the air like fireworks.

Mariah climbed onto the deck rail and looked to the water below. Seeing the lifeboat in the distance he knew he could make if he jumped now. But just as he closed his eyes and leant forward towards the sea, a hand grabbed the collar of his coat and pulled him back.

'Don't think you'll get away that easily,' Cartaphilus said as he threw Mariah to the floor. 'Captains and killers go down with the ship and the only difference between you and I is that Cartaphilus will survive no matter what.'

'You'll drown like the rest of them if you don't go now,' Mariah said, scrambling backwards away from him.

'You still don't know who I am, do you?' Cartaphilus said smugly. 'What is death to me but a temporary inconvenience?'

He grabbed Mariah by the coat and threw him towards the flames. It was as if Mariah were but a rag doll to be played with however Cartaphilus wished. He crashed to the deck, winded by the blow. Then Mariah slipped his hand inside his coat, pulled out the pistol given to him by Charity, slipped back the catch and fired. Cartaphilus was jolted by the shot and for a moment staggered back. He wiped his hand across the front of his blood-stained shirt and pulled it open to expose the wound.

Mariah could not believe what he saw. The bullet had passed through the ribs and into the heart – of that he was sure. In the burning light, Mariah could see the wound. Cartaphilus rubbed the wound again and it was gone.

'It can't be,' Mariah said in disbelief.

'I will not take the time to explain. I am weary of this existence and hope beyond hope that you could kill me, to free me from the drudgery of this life,' Cartaphilus said as he sat down next to Mariah. 'Go, leave me here. You have earned your freedom. You are a brave lad, Mariah Mundi, and I no longer have the strength to kill you for the sake of it. Too many deaths add to the weight of my judgement. I fear one more will be too much for me.'

Cartaphilus panted like an old dog. His hair was stuck to his face. His beard was singed by the flames of the inferno.

'Who are you?' Mariah asked.

'A wandering Aramean,' he replied with a sigh and a cough. 'That is all you need to know. I will meet with you again, that is for sure . . . Now go. Take the lifeboat and look out for a man called Markesan . . .'

For a moment Mariah stared him eye to eye. He was not sure if it was the reflection of the raging flames or something within Cartaphilus that shone so brightly in the man's eyes. It was as if he had seen the world and knew the desires of all hearts.

'Come with me,' Mariah said as he got to his feet and ran to the front of the ship.

'I stay to be with my gold. I would just bring a curse on you, Mariah,' Cartaphilus said as he crawled towards a hatch that led below.

Cartaphilus slipped from sight. The ship burned and lit the night sky as it steamed on.

Mariah unhooked the lifeboat. Once inside, he let it fall to the water. The ropes were pulled from the boat as the churning paddles of the burning *Carasbandra* crashed towards him, the water boiling and bubbling in the steaming wake. The paddles turned faster as he looked up at the gigantic steel palms that smashed against the sea and drove the ship on.

Just as they were about to strike, the ship veered to port. A blade of the paddle crashed into the sea, narrowly missing the lifeboat. Mariah looked up. There on the bridge, surrounded by smoke and flames, was Cartaphilus. He had turned the ship away from Mariah, saving his life. As the lifeboat slipped from sight, Cartaphilus looked down and raised his hand.

The ship steamed on into the night. It burnt even brighter as the drone of the engine was suddenly stilled. Mariah watched the fate of the *Carasbandra* from the lifeboat. A vast explosion ripped out the belly of the ship and threw wood and metal high into the air. The sky burnt with a crimson glow as blast followed blast. It shimmered the still, cold water and trembled the air. The flames burnt brightly as the steam engine burst open and hissed and wailed like a dying vixen.

There came a sound like the breaking of bones. The hull cracked open and the sea flooded in. The stern of the ship rose up, the paddles turning slowly. Mariah held his breath as he witnessed the fiery death of the *Carasbandra*, dragged down to the depths by the weight of the ingots in its hold. It was as if he watched a giant creature give up its life.

The water began to boil around the ship as the flames were slowly submerged. The night grew dark. The *Carasbandra* slipped silently beneath the waves about a mile from him.

'Mariah!' shouted a voice from the darkness. 'How did you escape?'

Mariah turned. There was Biba. He said nothing as they stood in their two separate boats watching the ship sink into the sea as if they attended the funeral of an old friend.

'You look wet,' he said as the ship finally vanished.

'How did you escape?' she asked.

'Cartaphilus,' he replied. 'He let me go. I thought he would kill me and then . . .' Mariah saw again the look in the eyes of Cartaphilus. It was as if he had seen much in his life that no man had ever seen before. 'I know I'll see him again.'

'The *Triton* is bound to have seen the explosions – they'll come looking for us,' Biba said as she pulled the two boats together.

'Then we shall wait,' he said. He sat at the tiller as Biba climbed on board slowly. 'It will be dawn within the hour.'

They slept curled in Biba's fur coat, their bodies bringing warmth to each other. Biba woke suddenly as in the half-light of dawn she heard a familiar sound.

'Mariah,' she said excitedly. 'The *Bicameralist* – it's here!'

Mariah opened his eyes. He had dreamed of England and the Prince Regent hotel. He had been warm and dry, eating fish tails and sliced potato. Now he opened his eyes on the cold grey Atlantic Ocean.

'What?' he asked as he rubbed his face with the collar of her coat.

The sound came from the east. It skirted the calm sea like a dragonfly. It moved back and forth, the blades of the gigantic propellers touching the water.

'They can't see us. I know they can't see us,' Biba said, her voice edged with panic.

'We're here!' he shouted as he got to his feet waving his arms.

The *Bicameralist* turned and headed back towards the *Triton* as if its mission had failed.

'They've gone – they can't go!' Biba screamed thinking her one chance had now departed.

Mariah rummaged in the sealed compartment by the hatch. He loaded the flare gun he found and fired it into the air. It cracked with a bright red light as the shell exploded. The *Bicameralist* appeared to hesitate and then turned again. Mariah fired another flare. The skyship beamed its searchlight across the sea, circling them in pure white light. It drew close and then hovered above them.

The dawn broke. From underneath the skyship a flight of steel stairs slid out. A man stood at the very tip, holding fast with one hand and waving with the other. The steps came closer and closer.

'Casper Vikash!' Biba screamed with joy to see him. 'You found us!'

Vikash held out his hand and pulled Biba from the boat and then hooked her to the steps. He took hold of Mariah and lifted him from the lifeboat.

'We have much to tell you Casper,' Biba said as she held back her tears.

'And I you,' he replied as the skyship pulled them ever higher and away from the sea.

[18]

Skyship

THE *Bicameralist* soared like a ghost across the sky. Inside the long gondola Mariah could hear only the faint sound of the wind. It was as if the skyship had no engines and was carried by the jet stream. He looked down upon the Atlantic. It was calm and still. Where the *Carasbandra* had sunk the water appeared to smoke and he could see the debris of the ship floating in the sea. Barrels of whale oil, a broken mast, lifeless swimmers bobbed back and forth. There was no sign of Cartaphilus. Even though he was gone, Mariah could not get the man from his mind. He could still see his piercing eyes and, what was more, could still see all that flickered within. It was as if he looked at a moving picture – the images flashed, bright and clear and very real. It was as if the thoughts of Cartaphilus had spilled out and now danced before him.

'Chocolate?' Vikash asked. He tapped Mariah on the shoulder and presented him with a cup of thick, steaming liquid. 'Biba tells me she hasn't eaten.'

Mariah looked back to the row of leather chairs that were next to the window behind him. Biba slept, sprawled across them, wrapped in her coat. The gondola looked as though it had been hand-carved from a single piece of dark wood and then fitted with grey leather. The seats were softer than anything Mariah had known before. The walls had been covered in gold leaf. They shimmered with every change of light as the skyship moved on. The carpet was the same as that in DeFeaux's stateroom. It was lush and bright.

He couldn't see the pilot, nor knew how the Skyship was sailed through the clouds. Vikash had brought them both to the cabin and locked the door behind them. Mariah knew there were many more rooms to the gondola. The passageway stretched out the length of the ship from where they had entered, but he had seen no other crew than Vikash. It was as if the ship sailed itself silently through the sky.

'They were going to hold her for ransom. I had to get her from the ship,' Mariah said when he had taken in all the detail around him. 'I didn't want her to leave the *Triton*.'

'That would have been impossible. I know Biba too well. When she sets her heart on something she has to do it. I am just thankful you went with her,' Vikash said as he sat in the seat next to him.

'Cartaphilus said that I had to beware a man called Markesan,' Mariah said as he sipped the bitter chocolate. It brightened his mind and took away the tiredness.

'Markesan is on the *Triton* – that we know,' said Vikash.

'There is a bomb on the *Triton* – they are going to explode it even though they took the gold,' Mariah said.

'We found it, there is no need to worry,' replied Vikash.

'And Captain Jack, is he –'

'Fine, in good spirits,' said Vikash. 'And he is not too concerned about your adventure.'

Mariah sighed in relief. 'That is what I feared the most.'

'Then all is well,' said Vikash.

But Mariah knew all was not well. There was a growing

189

dread in his heart as if his world was about to come to an end. As he drank the chocolate he looked out to the sea below like a gigantic sheet of black ice. The morning sun glistened on the water as a dark hand of cloud moved south towards them. He could see the *Triton* in the distance and further still, on the edge of the horizon, the *Ketos*. Both ships billowed steam as they sailed on, rolling out their wakes. It looked as if the *Triton* would never make up time and that the Great Race was already lost.

There was something about the way in which the *Triton* sat in the water that made him look more closely. It was something he hadn't noticed when on the ship, but from the air it looked as if only one engine of the vast ship was working. To hold the vessel in a straight line the rudder had to be forced to one side. As they drew closer, Mariah could see this more clearly. He thought to say something to Vikash, but as Biba slept he stayed silent.

'What are they doing?' he asked as they got nearer to the ship. He could see a vast flapping silk rag hanging over the side of the *Triton* and an army of ant-like men struggling to hold open an envelope of silk.

'The Marquis has decided that the passengers need to be entertained. Business as usual,' Vikash said.

'As usual?' Mariah asked.

'Charity and I found the bomb – it exploded over the side of the ship. There was some damage and the passengers think they are in danger. To keep them quiet the Marquis is going to launch the Montgolfier balloon. He will take the first ride to show them it is safe.'

'From the ship? But how will they land?' Mariah asked.

'The Montgolfier is tethered to the ship and they will be winched back – as simple as that,' he said.

As they got nearer Mariah could see the preparations taking

place on deck. All along the side of the ship stretched a line of eager passengers waiting for the balloon to be inflated with hot air. As the *Bicameralist* approached they stood back. Some began to applaud whilst others looked fearfully at the gigantic craft.

Biba woke from her sleep and, seeing the crowds, began to wave.

'What is father doing?' she asked Vikash as she noticed him on the upper deck by the large wicker basket of the Montgolfier.

'He is riding on the balloon with your mother and Captain Tharakan – it is to show the passengers it is safe,' said Vikash.

'And is it?' Biba asked.

Vikash laughed. 'It is only a balloon trip on the end of a rope – what can go wrong?'

He smiled at Biba and flicked the end of her nose with his finger. It calmed her. She shrugged her shoulders and giggled as the *Bicameralist* began to lower the extending ladder towards the ship.

'Look, it's Lorenzo with his father and mother,' she said excitedly, as if looking forward to greeting an old friend.

Standing near to the Marquis was the Zane family. They wore their best winter coats. Madame Zane pulled her hat close to her as the blast from the propellers of the skyship ruffled the feather collar of her coat. Sir Lorenzo Zane shrugged the chill from his shoulders and didn't even look at the airship. He stared at the Marquis, holding tightly to his son as if to protect him from those around them.

'I must tell you both that there is one problem that I cannot solve,' Vikash said gravely. They both turned to him. 'The mannequin – the puppet, Shanjing – he is not what he seems.'

'I know, Vikash,' Biba said. 'He is a man, a very small man.'

'How did you know?' he asked.

'I saw him when we travelled on the *Ketos* from New York

and once when he was on stage, a fly landed on his face. I've never seen a puppet wince the way he did,' she replied.

'You should have told me,' replied Vikash.

'Would you have believed me?' she asked.

The *Bicameralist* sailed closer to the docking bay at the rear of the ship. It kept pace, yard by yard until it hooked itself to a steel pylon that had been hoisted towards it. The extending ladder was lowered slowly until it reached the deck.

The crowd applauded as if this itself was an entertainment. Casper Vikash led Biba and Mariah to the entrance of the sky-ship. Mariah looked down the steep flight of steps towards the ship. A thousand faces stared eagerly at him. They clapped and cheered as if they knew what he had done.

'It was announced that we were to rescue you,' Vikash said. 'Word had spread that you had been kidnapped. When the ship exploded we knew where you were. It set fire to the sky. We thought you were lost. The Marquis insisted I search for you both. Lorenzo Zane said we could take the *Bicameralist*.' He spoke as if they both needed to know before they left the air-ship. 'You must be careful – both of you. We have two madmen on this ship and you will not be safe until they are found.'

'Do you know what Markesan looks like?' asked Mariah.

'His name is not on the list of passengers on the ship. According to Charity, he has never been seen,' Vikash answered as the engines of the airship dimmed their tone.

'Is Captain Jack waiting for me?' Mariah asked hopefully.

'We will see him later. The bomb went off and there was an explosion. If it had not been thrown over the side many would have been killed,' Vikash said uneasily without looking at Mariah. 'He's alive and well. He wants to see you. I have told him to rest, and he is well guarded.'

'Guarded?' asked Biba as if the world had changed since she had been away.

'A precaution, that's all,' Vikash replied as he gestured for them to walk the long, silver stairway to the ship.

The crowds of passengers waved and cheered as Biba followed Mariah down the steps to the safety of the ship. Mariah hesitated as they thronged towards him, hoping to shake his hand.

'Well done, Mariah Mundi,' said Lorenzo Zane as he took him by the hand. 'You haven't met my son properly have you? He is now fit enough to be out and the wound is healing,' he said as his son smiled at Mariah.

'Lozzy!' said Biba excitedly as she jumped the last steps from the skyship. 'I could see you from right up there. You look so well.'

His mother scowled at Biba. 'He's called Lorenzo – just like his father. Lozzy is such a stupid name.'

'Sorry, Madame Zane, I forgot,' Biba replied as the crowd gathered and jostled around them and the steps of the skyship were retracted.

'You are safe at last,' said Sir Lorenzo. 'Your mother will be pleased.'

Before she could reply, Vikash ushered them away through the crowd towards the bridge. Biba caught a brief glimpse of her father and mother as they stood with Captain Tharakan on a small dais next to where the wicker basket for the Montgolfier was precariously balanced. The *Bicameralist* turned. The propellers span faster and the skyship set off in pursuit of the *Ketos*.

'Your father wants me to take you to Deck 13,' Vikash said as the balloon filled with hot air and rose up like a red, silk cloud behind the ship. 'The journey will not be long.'

Biba tried to see her father again. She was too small to see over the men and women who gathered on the deck, pressed tightly together in their winter coats. Vikash pushed Biba through the crowd as Mariah followed. She turned again and again to try and see her father.

'Can we wait here and watch?' she asked as they got to the flight of steps that led to Deck 13.

'Only for a moment,' Vikash replied. 'Your father doesn't want you on the deck. It will be safer for you in your room.'

But Biba refused to be led inside and they stayed to watch the balloon inflate with hot air. It towered over the back of the ship, blotting out the horizon. The basket was made ready and an acrobat from the circus helped Tharakan and Biba's parents to step inside.

Her father looked up. Biba waved. He smiled softly and silently said the words, 'I love you.'

Her mother looked not to her but to Sir Lorenzo Zane. She bowed to him and giggled, then cast a glance with a raised eyebrow to Biba. With that she and the Marquis stepped into the basket as the ropes that held it to the balloon tightened.

From the deck below, a brass band struck up a German march. The music seemed brash and out of place. People began to clap in time and stamp their feet as the Marquis and his wife made ready for the balloon to set sail. Turned by three sailors in white jackets, a large winch handle cranked and clattered as the ratchet turned slowly. The Montgolfier staggered momentarily. The acrobat pulled a cord attached to a large brass handle and a gush of flames roared upwards, heating the air within the balloon. In the fresh morning light the Montgolfier was illuminated like a gigantic lamp holder.

The crowds gasped as, with every blast of heat, the balloon slowly lifted from the deck of the ship. Madame DeFeaux waved regally, her eyes fixed on Sir Lorenzo Zane. Biba could see her smiling. She waved to her father, but he didn't see her. He talked to the acrobat and rubbed his hands and laughed as the balloon went slowly higher and higher.

The brass band played on as the queue to be next on the Montgolfier got longer. People bustled on the deck below, impatiently waiting their turn. The crewmen turned the handle of the ratchet-winch and let out the rope as thick as a man's arm.

The balloon went up and up, dragged along by the *Triton*. It was a bright and still morning. A faint sun climbed higher above the horizon, reaching up into a cloudless sky.

The winch rolled out the line yard by yard. Every hundred feet the rope was painted with a red mark. Biba counted these as they went by.

'Can you see the icebergs?' a man shouted mockingly from the deck below as the balloon reached three hundred feet above them.

'How high will the balloon go?' Mariah asked Vikash.

'Four hundred feet,' he replied as the rope tightened and the crowds cheered. The last red marker appeared as the line pulled even tighter.

'Is it safe?' Biba asked as her heart beat faster.

'They will pull them back now,' Vikash said as he watched the crewmen stop the winch and reverse the winding.

There was something about a glance that one of the men gave to another that made Mariah feel all was not right. The winch crackled as it turned, as if the teeth were broken inside. The rope juddered. The balloon trembled on the end of the rope, four hundred feet away. Due to the drag of the ship, the Montgolfier was only about a hundred feet above the sea. The Marquis and his wife were still waving and taking in the view. The crewmen pulled at the handles and slipped the catch on the top of the winch back and forth as if it was stuck.

Mariah didn't want to say anything in front of Biba. He looked at Vikash and then to the rope. Vikash had already seen it. He secretly put his finger to his lips, a clear warning for Mariah to say nothing.

'Stay here, I just need to speak with Lorenzo Zane,' he said as he went down the steps to the deck below.

'Is everything all right?' Biba asked. 'Why aren't they pulling them back?'

Mariah was about to reply when the crewman gave a shout of relief. The winch began to turn and the rope was wound tightly onto the capstan. Vikash turned and smiled as if to say all was well. The balloon drew nearer and then stopped. Mariah looked at the capstan – the winch was still turning and he could see the rope going into the winch but the balloon didn't move.

'Stop!' he shouted as he set off after Vikash, his words swallowed by the din of the brass band. No one heard him. Biba gave chase.

'What is it Mariah? What have you seen?' she said as she ran after him, her long fur coat trailing on the deck.

'The rope, stop turning the rope!' he screamed again as he pushed against the crowds.

There was a sudden and sharp crack. It was as if a beam of oak had smashed in two. The people near to the winch began to scream as it spun faster. It was out of control. The weight of the balloon pulled against the rope, drawing out more and more.

'Grab the rope,' Vikash shouted as a crewman was knocked over the side of the deck by the flailing capstan.

Two passengers rushed forward just as the final yard of rope was pulled from the winch. They took hold and were lifted in the air.

Biba began to scream. 'No! No, Father, no!'

He could not hear her words so far away.

As the balloon broke free of the ship it went higher into the sky until the rope dragged along the deck like the pendulum of a large clock. The two men hanging on were now joined by other passengers who frantically tried to hold the balloon. Biba could see her father waving his hands as if to signal the distress.

Casper Vikash took hold of her and tried to turn her away.

'They will be safe,' he said over and over as she fought with him to see what was happening to the balloon.

Mariah ran the length of the deck towards the men holding tightly to the rope. As it reached the front of the ship, one man twisted the rope around the railings. It held fast. The balloon steadied and then, as if it were a hot knife, the rope cut through the railing and slipped from the ship.

Mariah could hear Biba screaming for her father. The mooring rope dangled over the sea, just out of reach of the passengers who frantically tried to seize it. A man in a camel coat leapt from the deck. He took hold of the rope, held fast and then began to climb.

The balloon went higher and higher, carried by the wind. The man began to scream, his words faint as he went further away. Then suddenly he let go of his grip. He fell to the sea and disappeared beneath the water. The crowds screamed. Women covered their faces.

Mariah looked on. He turned to see Biba. Vikash was holding her back. She held out her hand towards the Montgolfier. It was as if she reached out to touch her father one last time. She sobbed as the balloon drifted towards the west. It spun around and around as it was pushed westwards, trapped in an invisible vortex.

Everyone on the deck of the *Triton* stood and watched silently until the balloon was out of sight. The *Bicameralist* had gone at great speed beyond the horizon. A pillar of cloud could be seen far to the west as the *Ketos* billowed steam from its engines.

Biba gripped the wooden deck rail and screamed for her father. When she could see the Montgolfier no more she went silent, gulped her breath and then fell to the deck.

The Dumb Waiter

IN the panic that followed, no one noticed Mariah Mundi as he edged his way through the crowds towards the winching capstan. Vikash carried Biba DeFeaux to Deck 13. She was limp and silent, her eyes were open but she was unable to move. He had told Mariah that the shock of losing her parents had caused her to faint. Mariah had waited purposefully and allowed the frightened passengers to get in his way. The crowds had thronged the walkways, hoping for a glimpse of the lost balloon that had taken the Marquis, his wife and Captain Tharakan over the horizon. Mariah stood by the brass capstan, and when he looked inside he could see the severed strands of rope. The cogs that held the device were broken and three brass bolts lay on the deck. He bent down and, without letting anyone see, picked them up and slipped them into his pocket. He glanced at the last bolt in his hand and noticed that it had been cut through.

'What do you have there?' asked Lorenzo Zane as he stepped from the crowd unexpectedly.

Mariah panicked. 'Nothing . . .'

'I saw you pick something from the deck – what is it?' Zane

insisted angrily as he took hold of Mariah's clenched hand and squeezed until Mariah winced with pain.

'A bolt – I found it on the floor – nothing else,' Mariah said as he tried to pull away from the man.

'Then let me see. If the capstan has failed I need to know.' Zane opened Mariah's hand and snatched the bolt. He studied it carefully as he sniffed and then took a magnifying glass from his pocket. He examined the bolt closely. 'Nothing of consequence. It has fractured under the stress. I advised DeFeaux he would be foolish to use the Mongolfier, but he wouldn't listen.'

'What will happen to them?' Mariah asked.

'With the wind in the right direction I would presume they will get to America. There is enough fuel in the Montgolfier to keep them afloat for two days. I made it myself,' Zane said as he tried to change his face to a smile. 'I will signal to the *Bicameralist* to search for them and if they go down into the sea, then hopefully they shall be rescued.'

'And what about the ship now that Captain Tharakan has gone?' asked Mariah.

'I shall make Ellerby captain. It is only right,' Zane said, then paused as he looked into Mariah's eyes. 'And you, Mariah. What a journey you have had. It appears to have been steeped in trouble.'

'I have to see Captain Charity – I believe he was injured by the bomb,' Mariah replied as he stepped away from the man.

'Ah, the bomb . . . Someone tried to blow up my ship. How inconvenient,' Zane replied just as Ellerby came to him. 'Mr Ellerby, I was just getting to know all about Mariah Mundi. And I was just saying that with Captain Tharakan indisposed, you would have to take his place.'

'It is already done,' Ellerby gloated his reply. 'Do you have any orders for the crew?'

'I think we need to double the guard around the engine

room. With a saboteur on board we cannot be too careful,' Zane said.

'Is there something wrong with the ship?' Mariah asked.

'Why should you ask such a question?' said Ellerby as he pushed Mariah back.

'From the skyship I noticed that the rudder was hard to starboard to keep the ship straight and that only one engine was pushing out steam,' Mariah replied.

'And all this from such a young lad,' said Zane. 'We were testing the engine and had to turn off the power. It is restored again. You must be the same age as my own son. He is no more than sixteen and would never have noticed such a thing.'

'I sailed at school. On the Thames. We had a small steam cruiser,' Mariah replied.

'Then you must be from the Chiswick Colonial School if I am not mistaken?' asked Zane.

'I am,' replied Mariah. 'Do you know of it?'

Zane didn't answer, but turned to Ellerby. 'I think we should give Mariah a tour of the engine room. He is obviously quite bright and we may be interested in what he knows.'

There was something about the way in which Lorenzo Zane spoke that made Mariah feel uncomfortable. He stared at Mariah for too long, as if he was examining him for some fault. His eyes were sharp, like a hawk's. Mariah had never seen a man with such vivid green eyes. They were the colour of spring grass after thunder.

'That can be arranged, Sir Lorenzo,' replied Ellerby. 'If that is what you wish.'

Zane nodded that it was what he wanted. He turned to Mariah.

'You would like that, wouldn't you?' he asked.

Mariah felt he had to agree. The two men stood before him. They would not let him go until he complied with their wishes.

'I need to see Captain Charity – he has been injured,' Mariah said. 'I will be free in the afternoon.'

'Of course you will be free,' Zane laughed. 'This is a ship, you have nowhere to go – not unless you want to jump in another lifeboat . . . Mr Ellerby will collect you from Deck 13.'

With that both men walked away in deep conversation. Mariah watched as they pushed their way through the crowds towards the bridge of the ship. He decided not to go straight to Deck 13 but instead found a windless place overlooking the rear deck and looked out to sea. He watched the waves created by the whirring of the steam engines. They were just as he had seen from the skyship, just the same. Zane had lied to him. The engine was still not working.

Mariah walked once around the entire deck. He heard the passengers talking as they promenaded, linked together in gossiping of the loss of Captain Tharakan. It was his greatest love to watch people as they went about their lives, but now he could sense an edge of fear. They spoke of bombs and rescues and the loss of the Montgolfier. He heard a man in a striped suit telling another that in his opinion the ship was cursed and they would never reach America. He said it was the vengeance of Poseidon, the god of the sea, for the *Triton* being able to sail so quickly across the ocean. Mariah stole upon another conversation in which a woman with a pug face insisted that she would sleep in her life jacket or else she would be drowned in her slumber.

Whatever it was, Mariah could now sense a growing anxiety amongst his fellow travellers. Together, they were trapped on board with not enough lifeboats to save everyone.

By the door of the Saloon Theatre was a poster. Mariah read the words: THE SS TRITON – THE UNSINKABLE – NEVER FEARS THE STORM. It showed the ship crashing through a great storm and those inside drinking and eating as if they were on a millpond. He smiled to himself as he opened the door and went inside. The Saloon Theatre was empty. He walked to the steam elevator, went inside, took his card and slotted it into the aperture.

The lift rattled upwards. It was slower than usual, as if the power was not as great. And then Mariah noticed that the lights inside the ship had dimmed. They were not glaring as bright as they had been the day before. He realised something was wrong with the power of the ship. It was as if it were a leviathan of the sea that was slowly dying.

The elevator stopped at Deck 13 and the doors opened automatically. There was a fresh smell to the air. The flowers that were brought each day from the cold storage room far below had just arrived. He stepped outside and there, on the round table in the vast entrance room, was a vase of pure white lilies. Their red stamens stuck out like tongues of fire. Everything here seemed to be crisp and clean.

Mariah called out for Vikash, but no one came. He walked through the rooms and along the passageway that ran the length of the top of the ship until he reached the door of his own room. Before going inside he had the desire to see Biba once more. Mariah turned and took several paces back to her door. He knocked gently and turned the handle. Biba was on the bed, wrapped in her fur coat. She looked like a Viking girl ready for burial. She was sleeping.

Closing the door, he made his way back down the corridor until he got to his room. The door opened for him. Charity stood there, his hair pushed back, his eye badly bruised from the blast.

'I wondered where you had got to,' said Charity. 'I hear we have had another accident.'

Mariah reached into his pocket and pulled out the two bolts and handed them to Charity. 'It looks as if they have been cut through. The capstan had been sabotaged.'

Charity looked at the bolts. Mariah wondered why he hadn't mentioned him leaving the ship. He wanted to ask him but felt it best that he should keep silent.

'Tell me Mariah,' Charity said, and Mariah knew what words would come next. 'What happened on the other ship?'

Mariah sat in the armchair with a sigh. It was as if he was back at school and had to explain away some misdemeanour. He looked up at Charity and began to tell him everything. The words came easily as he spoke of Cartaphilus and how they had escaped from the ship. Mariah talked for half an hour and Charity listened intently, never interrupting, and making a note in his mind of everything Mariah had said.

'What's more,' Mariah said, 'when I travelled back on the skyship I could see that only one engine of the *Triton* was working and I noticed just now that the lights in the elevator were on half power.'

'I fear we will not reach America,' Charity said. 'This ship is doomed.'

'I heard a man say that on the deck. He insisted that it is cursed,' Mariah replied as his mind raced.

'Is is not a curse that will take it to destruction but someone who does not wish the *Triton* to win the Great Race,' Charity replied. 'Though the gold is no longer with us there is still a prize to the person who wins and many gamblers have already placed bets. This event will make some people very rich. It is in their interest for the *Triton* to lose. The only way they can be sure of this is if the ship is at the bottom of the Atlantic.'

'I think Zane is lying,' Mariah said.

'That is obvious,' Charity replied. 'I don't think that the *Triton* would have been capable of winning the race even if both engines had been working. The Marquis expressed this to me last night.'

'And now he is lost in the sky,' Mariah replied.

'Conveniently,' Charity added. 'With the Marquis and Captain Tharakan out of the way it leaves Lorenzo Zane in charge of the ship.'

'He appointed Ellerby as captain. He told me on deck,' Mariah replied.

As they talked on, neither heard the rumbling of the dumb waiter in the corridor outside. It rattled from the butler's larder on the deck below and then stopped quietly. The small doors opened and Shanjing stepped out.

He was confident and silent with his step. He listened to Charity talking to Mariah. He smiled to himself and twisted his long rat-tail moustache in his fingers. Within a few paces he was at Biba's door. He slowly turned the handle and stepped inside just as Vikash came from his study.

Vikash knocked on the door of the room and then went in. Biba was asleep on the bed. He shook her gently.

'Biba, you must wake soon – it will not be good for you to sleep so long,' he said softly. She opened her eyes and looked at him. Vikash could see that she didn't want to speak. 'I think you should eat something. I will have the butler bring some soup.'

Biba nodded and pleaded with her eyes for any news of her parents.

'Still no word,' he said as he turned to leave. 'I will be back in the hour with some food – rest until then.'

He closed the door behind him and Biba was once again in darkness. She felt alone, more so than she had ever felt before. Now her father was not there, she had no one. All attachment to her mother had left her that day on the ice at Jacobshavn. She had closed her heart and mind to her. Biba knew that her mother felt more for Lorenzo Zane than she did for her father. That was obvious. Her mother changed when in Zane's company. She would laugh and smile, a demeanour which was absent when alone with the Marquis.

Biba pulled the fur coat around her and tried to wake up. She was caught in a world between sleeping and waking. It allowed her to dream with her eyes wide open. She looked about the cabin. It was drained of colour by the lack of light. It reminded Biba of her heart.

It was as if her bed and the warmth of the fur coat wouldn't let her sit up. She lay for a while listening to the sounds of the ship and the sea beyond. Biba wondered about her parents – if they were still alive. She knew she could not give up hope for her father.

The door of her small dressing room opened slightly. Biba heard the handle click. At first she thought it was the movement of the ship and she rested gently, half asleep, half awake. The door opened further. A light footstep touched the wooden floor. Then another. It was more of a dance than someone walking to her. Biba lay still, hoping the sounds were in a dream and that she was alone, but some ancient instinct within her told Biba that someone was near. All was silent. The room was dark.

In the half-light, Biba opened her eyes. She searched the room for some trace of who was there. She could see nothing. The door to the dressing room swung gently with a tremor of motion. Biba relaxed back into the covers of the bed and pulled her fur coat tighter about herself.

'You did well to escape from the ship,' a voice said, as if from inside her own head. 'Don't scream – we are old friends.' Biba couldn't move. Fingers of fear gripped her to the bed. She looked about her to see who it was who spoke. 'I would like you to come with me – I have much to tell you.'

She felt a word come to mind.

'Shanjing?' she asked in a whisper.

'That is one of my many names,' he replied as he stepped from the shadows so he could be seen in the gloom.

'Why are you here?' she said as she gripped tightly to the coat.

'I need your help,' Shanjing said. He pulled a knife from the belt around his narrow waist. 'Just a token from you as proof. A lock of hair, a fingernail – something more perhaps? I need you to come with me. I have a secret place on the ship.'

The door opened suddenly. Mariah stood in the corridor. He looked at Biba.

'I heard you talking to someone. Vikash came and told us you were sleeping. I was just passing,' he said as he looked about the room.

'I was talking in my sleep,' she said.

'But –' Mariah began and then stopped as he saw her gesture for him to be silent. He felt as though he was being watched.

'Vikash should not tell tales. I am quite all right – no one could hurt me here,' she said angrily as she opened her eyes widely and looked to the door. 'I think you should go and let me sleep. You always do this to me. Lozzy would let me sleep. Go away, Mariah.'

'Well, I will – I'll leave you to it then,' Mariah said as he stepped back and closed the door behind him.

The room fell dark again. Shanjing stepped from the shadows behind the door.

'Well done,' he whispered as he took another pace. 'Just what I –'

The door flew open. Shanjing was knocked from his feet towards the bed. The light from the corridor fell on his face.

'Shanjing!' screamed Mariah. 'It was you . . .'

Shanjing jumped to his feet and brandished the knife.

'Mariah Mundi – meddlesome Mariah Mundi,' he said as he danced towards him, kicking out as he spun on his toes.

The knife glanced across Mariah's chest. The Spiderweb held fast. Shanjing leapt at him once more and struck out again. Mariah felt the stab in his side. The dwarf pushed him out of the way as he ran for the door. Footsteps came down the corridor in answer to Mariah's scream.

'Shanjing!' yelled Charity. 'Vikash, quickly . . .'

Shanjing leapt from the room with Mariah close behind. He turned and slashed at Mariah again. Mariah kicked at his hand, knocking the knife to the floor. Charity ran towards them and Shanjing took flight, running as fast as he could.

'Steam elevator,' Charity screamed as Vikash appeared from his room as the dwarf ran towards him.

'Don't stop me, Vikash,' Shanjing screamed. 'It'll be more than your face which is scarred . . .'

Vikash stood his ground. Shanjing charged him, followed by Mariah and Charity gaining ground. Shanjing reached into his pocket as he ran and threw a handful of dust towards Vikash. As it touched the floor it exploded in bright blue sparks that hissed and smoked. It stank of sulphur and hogweed. Smoke billowed from the carpet as if it were ablaze and Vikash grasped his throat, choking on the fumes. In the pall of acrid smoke as thick as a London fog, Shanjing vanished.

'Get Biba from her room,' Vikash coughed as the burning tears poured from his eyes. 'She cannot be left alone.'

Mariah returned to the room. Biba was gone.

[20]

Shanjing

FROM the sound of the engine, Biba knew she was far below Deck 13. Wherever she was being held prisoner, it was dark, warm and smelt of roast nutmeg. How she had got there was a complete blur. She could vaguely remember stumbling out of her door through a cloud of smoke. It was as if she was part of a flamboyant magician's trick – Biba felt that she had been magicked from her bed. There was a memory of her eyes burning, then she could remember falling through a small doorway and down a tunnel. From then, she had stumbled along a narrow black corridor until she had felt a door close behind her. She knew she had slept for some time, but was not sure as to how long.

Biba opened her eyes, fearful of what she might see. Her hands and feet were tied and her mouth was bandaged with a rough gag that cut into her face. Her makeshift bed was made of hessian sacks stuffed with silk. In the dim light the shadows of the room pressed in on her. Hanging from the walls were countless masks. She had seen them before – they had been used by the dancers on the *Ketos* and transferred when her father had bought the *Triton*. There too were the costumes and

208

props from the magician's performance. There was a stuffed donkey that would explode to reveal the magician's assistant. Next to that were the empty cages for the pigeons. From this she realised she must be in a theatrical store. In its own way the room was quite alluring, everything having been laid out and arranged for beauty rather than convenience.

In her memory Biba had a vague recollection that she had been brought here by Shanjing. It was as if she had woken from an interrupted dream. All that had taken place was disjointed, mixed up, and somehow out of time. Biba could not stop asking herself why she was there. She wondered what curse was upon her family that her parents should be sent off in a balloon and she herself captured by an obviously mad mannequin.

It was not long after waking that Biba heard the sound of footsteps in the corridor outside. They were gentle and light, almost a dance. She knew it to be Shanjing.

The door opened slowly. Shanjing looked into the room.

'Sleeping?' he asked with a smile. 'Shanjing has brought you some food.'

Biba stared at him and grunted a reply.

'I will take off the mask – please don't scream, no one will hear you and it will just hurt my ears,' Shanjing joked as he put down a small bag and raised stiff little fingers to his face.

'Why?' she asked as she gasped heavily.

'Always why,' he replied. 'If you had come to see me instead of jumping on the lifeboat then you would have known why. Instead you run off with Mariah Mundi and get into trouble.' Shanjing sounded like a concerned aunt. 'Sometimes it is better for you not to know what is the reason for things.'

Shanjing sat on a sack in front of her and stared at her for a moment. Biba stared back at him. 'You've kidnapped me and I didn't want to be kidnapped. I've just lost my parents so who'll pay a ransom anyway?' she asked.

'Ransom?' Shanjing asked as he rubbed his leathery face. 'I have brought you biscuits and scones and – a sandwich,' he said as he made them appear from the bag like magic. 'If I were to untie your hands, you wouldn't try to hurt me, would you?'

Biba nodded as she tried to scowl at him. She was hungry. Whatever he had used to make her fall asleep had left her feeling ravenous. 'I promise,' she heard herself saying reluctantly.

Shanjing untied her hands and offered her a buttered scone. She took it and ate it quickly. It was the first time she had seen the mannequin so clearly. She hadn't realised before that what covered his face was not skin but an intricate mask. Made of the finest leather without a stitch visible, it formed to the contours of his face and circled his lips. It was obvious that these had been painted with red lead to cover the join twixt skin and leather. It was the same with his eyes. They were outlined in jet-black kohl.

Shanjing realised that Biba was looking at his face as she greedily ate the scone.

'I thought you would wonder what I am,' he said slowly. 'People don't usually see me this closely.'

'I knew you weren't a mannequin. I saw you walking late one night when you performed on the *Ketos*,' she said as she finished a mouthful of food and picked a sandwich from the bag.

'I wasn't sure I had been discovered. It is hard to spend your life in a wooden box. Charlemagne is not the best of company. After all, how much can you talk about with someone from Wigan?' Shanjing asked.

'So it was all pretence, everything. Even the mind reading?' Biba asked.

'Not everything. It is true I am not a mannequin. But I can see the future – well, sometimes,' he replied.

'Have you always worn a leather mask?' Biba asked.

'Not always,' he said as if the thought were a sad memory. 'You would not wish to see what is beneath. The mask protects me – but it also protects you.'

Biba thought for a moment, wondering if she should take the question further. Shanjing sat cross-legged on the hessian sack. He seemed to be no threat to her, nor to wish her harm – or so it seemed as they broke bread.

'How did you get that way?' Biba asked eventually when she had been silent long enough for it to become uncomfortable.

'It was an accident – an explosion. My face is badly burned. The scars have not yet healed.' Shanjing touched the mask and then held out his hands. 'That is why I wear gloves. This is a necessity and not a disguise. My ailment caused me to leave my old life. I had a very wealthy employer, an American, until this happened to me . . .'

Biba felt she could ask him no more. She could sense from his voice that he was still pained by the memory.

'And this is where you have been living? It's a beautiful place,' she said as she looked around the ornate storeroom.

'It was the same on the *Ketos*. I had a hiding place there also. I was on my way to it when you saw me. I love beautiful things and the theatre is a place of great beauty.'

'So will you let me go?' she asked abruptly, her words not fitting with the conversation.

Shanjing stood up and brushed the front of his silk robes. He stood out of arm's reach and leant against the door as if ready to escape.

'Would you like the truth?' he asked.

'Of course,' Biba replied.

'Your parents are gone. It had nothing to do with me,' he insisted, 'but because of that things have changed. If they are dead then you are one of the richest girls in the world. If you are dead then Casper Vikash will be one of the richest men.'

'Casper?' asked Biba quite surprised. 'Why should my death make him rich?'

'He will inherit everything. Casper Vikash is your brother – didn't you know?' Shanjing giggled as if he enjoyed breaking the news to her.

'*Brother?*' asked Biba furiously. 'How?'

'How else do we have brothers, sisters, birds, bees?' replied Shanjing mockingly as he rubbed his leather chin. 'It is well known – and has even been heard from your father's lips. Casper Vikash is your half brother. There is a document in the Bank of Paris. It explains everything. It is signed by your father. A deed of trust, or should I say *mistrust?*'

Biba sighed and lay back against the sack. Suddenly everything made sense. No mere servant would be so loyal to their master. No servant would risk their lives so often. No servant would have been so kind to her.

'He would read me stories as a child. When mother was busy.' Biba paused. 'I feared a monster under my bed. Casper would always look underneath for me and tell me there was nothing hiding. Now I realise why he was so kind.'

Shanjing squealed as if in pain. Biba saw his eyes change. They burned blood red and were full of anger.

'Kind?' he asked venomously. 'Kind? I intend to ask him if he wants me to kill you. Don't you realise with you out of the way he gets every penny of your father's great wealth? Strange, isn't it, that your parents should be cast adrift in a balloon leaving you alone on a ship like this. Casper Vikash will either pay for you dead or pay to have you kept alive. Either way I will be rich.' Shanjing stopped and looked thoughtfully at her. 'I think I will make it cheaper for him to have you killed rather than kept alive. That way you will see if he really is a loving brother.'

Shanjing was about to tie her hands again when there was a tapping at the door. He looked surprised and anxious.

'You've been found. Surely the Great Shanjing could have seen the future?' Biba said, her words cutting.

'Keep quiet if you know what is good for you,' Shanjing replied. 'Only one man knows I am here – pray it is him.'

Shanjing opened the door slightly and looked out.

'Is she here?' asked a man. His voice was deep and caustic. 'Charity is looking for her with the boy – we could set a trap. I have to have Mariah Mundi.'

'Would be too easy – they would think it strange. I have had an idea,' Shanjing replied courteously as if he was in fear of the man.

'It can't go wrong. The *Carasbandra* is lost. Without that vessel we have no way off the *Triton*. We need another way of escape,' the man said.

Shanjing whispered something that Biba DeFeaux couldn't hear.

'Midnight tonight,' answered the man. 'Everything has to be ready for then.'

'Mr Markesan, please, will there be time?' Shanjing pleaded.

'For your sake and mine I hope so,' the man said.

Shanjing closed the door and turned to Biba. He stared at his hands and rubbed them together as if he looked for the answer to a question. The answer did not come.

'Why do you need a way from the ship?' Biba asked. 'We will be in New York and you can escape then.'

Shanjing shrugged his tiny shoulders and folded his arms. He looked like a small child that time had forgotten.

'I have to be quick in what I need to do,' he said as his mind raced. 'How much money does your father have in his safe?'

'I don't know,' replied Biba.

'Does Vikash have a key?'

'Of course,' she said, knowing the reason for asking. 'You'll get as much out of him as you can and then leave the ship.'

'You should be a mind reader,' Shanjing replied. 'With my last breath before I leave I will tell him where you are, alive or dead . . . Now I must go, I must go . . .'

Shanjing rushed through the door and left Biba alone. She could hear the lock being turned and a bolt slid quickly into place. For a while there was silence. In his haste, Shanjing had left her hands untied. Biba quickly removed the binding from her feet and wondered what to do next. She knew she would have to find Mariah and warn him of what was planned. There was something about the voice of Markesan that was familiar. It was as if she had heard it before.

She thought of Vikash and wondered what he would do. It would be easy for him to have her killed so he could have everything. The cost would doubtless be just a proportion of all the wealth he would inherit. Until that moment she had never really thought of money. It was only when it was valued against her life that she realised what power and importance it had. Biba had never wanted for anything that money could buy. Now she wanted that which was free but so hard to find. She had seen how Shanjing's eyes had flamed whenever he spoke of money – his voice quickened, he came alive by the mere mention of its name. Perhaps, she thought, if she was poor then she would think differently about it. But now, the love of money could bring about her death.

Yet, Biba hoped that there was something within Vikash, some pity or even love for her, that would prevail against any greed. He had been kind to her, she thought as she looked for a way out. If he had wanted her dead he could have just watched the bear kill her at Jacobshavn. No one would have known – he could have said he found her on the beach – well, what was left of a carcass picked over by a bear. Vikash had always protected her, even from her own mother and all that she did in the dark and secret nights when Biba's father was away.

'He won't see me dead,' Biba said in a whisper as she ran her hands around the doorframe, looking for a hidden key. She found a box on the floor covered in vanishing handkerchiefs. She pulled back the silks and there, neatly arranged as if they had just been used, was a compendium of magical tricks. There was a knife with a trick blade, a pack of large playing cards and a juggler's baton.

Suddenly, there were footsteps outside. Small, neat, dancing steps – it was Shanjing. Biba began to tremble.

The bolt slid back. The lock was turned. Biba held her breath. Shanjing opened the door. Light flooded in.

'I almost forgot,' he gleefully said and then stopped. Shanjing could not see Biba.

Biba didn't hesitate. She took the juggler's baton and lashed out blindly as she screwed up her eyes. There was a thud. Shanjing moaned. He stumbled to the floor, falling across a hessian sack. His small legs with even tinier feet blocked the door. She pushed them out of the way with her feet. She didn't want to touch him. To her, Shanjing was haram, impure. It was as if by touching him she too would be sullied.

He moaned loudly but couldn't move. Biba pushed him further out of the way and then opened the door. Above her she could hear the dancers hoofing on the stage. It was time for their rehearsal. Biba knew that if she could get from the room she could soon find her way out. She took several slow steps from the room. The corridor was narrow and low. It was as if it was made just for Shanjing. She hunched forward, stooping. Walking was difficult and slow. Ahead she could see another door. She feared it to be locked. But when Biba twisted the handle the door opened. There was a scraping of steel. A knife was drawn in the darkness.

'How far did you think you would get?' Shanjing asked, somewhere near.

Biba looked back over her shoulder. Shanjing was three feet away, holding a long-bladed knife like a Saracen's sword.

'Just let me go and I won't tell anyone,' she said as she edged her fingers around the door.

'Too late for that, my dear.' Shanjing said as he came towards, her ready to strike. 'I may have let you go eventually – but now I think not . . .'

Biba looked again. Shanjing wasn't there. Suddenly the knife flashed by her face. Biba pushed against the door, which opened into the passageway below the stage. Shanjing stabbed at her again. The knife glanced her shoulder and then was embedded in the wall. The dwarf hung from the stiletto. He kicked against the wall to pull it free. Biba got to her feet and slammed the door. She slid the bolt on the outside as she rested against the wall.

'Must find Mariah,' she said as she gained her breath.

There was a splitting of wood – the knife burst through the wall. It sliced through her coat, against the side of her skin. Biba could feel the blade touching her, cold and hard. She didn't move. The blade came again and this time, the knife cut through the boards above her shoulder. She fell to the floor and looked up as the knife was smashed again and again through the wood. Shanjing was cutting his way out. He stabbed and stabbed like a madman. Biba could hear his shrill voice screaming damnation.

'I'll find you, Biba DeFeaux,' he screamed. 'You will never be safe – not even on Deck 13.'

Biba was petrified with fear. She attempted to get to her feet but was frozen to the spot. She could feel her stomach turn as she began to sob. Tears filled her eyes. She wanted her father, wanted Vikash, wanted Mariah. She screamed as she finally forced herself to move. Biba stumbled as the wooden wall splintered and tore and the dagger ripped and ripped. It was as if it slashed through bone.

'Mariah!' she shouted. Her words echoed down the empty corridor.

Shanjing burst through the wall, knife in hand. Blood trickled from his leather fingers.

'I'll find you – no matter where, Biba DeFeaux,' he said as he threw his voice so that it came at her chillingly from all sides.

Biba ran. Her body trembled. She looked back. Shanjing pursued her like a demented child. He would only give up when he had caught her. Biba ran faster. She could see the door at the end of the corridor and prayed it would not be locked – prayed she would not be trapped.

The door opened easily. There was a spiral of dark stairs without any light. She fumbled upwards a tread at a time. It was familiar. The smell of lime and greasepaint filled the air like an autumnal bouquet of wet leaves, and she could hear the sound of dancing. Feet clattered against boards as the whir of a hurdy-gurdy droned on and on.

Biba could see the outline of a door edged in light and pulled frantically to open it. The door was locked. She ran even higher. Far behind her, the sound of miniature footsteps padded on relentlessly. They drew closer. Slowing in speed, as if tiring, they still came. Shanjing would not give up. It was as if he could scent her presence and her only escape would be in death.

21

The Eloquent Captain Ellerby

'I HAVE searched everywhere,' Vikash said as he met with Charity and Mariah by the doors of the Saloon Theatre. 'Biba is nowhere to be found.'

'How did she get from the room?' Mariah asked, having kept watch at the steam elevator whilst Charity and Vikash had searched the ship.

'We can only presume she was taken,' Charity replied as crowds of passengers milled by whilst taking their afternoon walk. 'The lifeboats are all in place, so I don't think she has left the ship.'

'It could only have been Shanjing. There must be a place where he has taken her,' Vikash said.

'I questioned Charlemagne. He says he has not seen the dwarf since he vanished. He knows of no place where he could be hiding,' Charity replied.

'Then I will go and ask him,' Vikash said, cracking the knuckles of his fingers. 'I am sure he will talk for me.'

'A conspiracy?' asked Ellerby, suddenly appearing in his crisp and neat captain's uniform. 'Is there something I should know of?'

The three looked at each other and no one spoke. Ellerby smiled at Mariah.

'You have an appointment. In fact you are already late. I came to Deck 13 and you were gone. Did you forget?' he asked.

'I came to tell Captain Charity that Lorenzo Zane had invited me to see the engine room. I'm sorry,' Mariah said as he stared at Charity.

'Then we shall depart. We cannot keep Zane waiting,' Ellerby said as he gripped Mariah by the arm.

'I too shall enjoy the visit,' said Charity.

'It is just for the boy – not for you. He comes alone,' Ellerby replied.

'But –' protested Charity to no avail as Ellerby walked off holding Mariah.

'I will keep him safe and bring him back to you, don't fear,' Ellerby said.

Neither of them spoke as Ellerby took Mariah out onto the deck of the *Triton*. The sea was thick and icy-black. A bank of Newfoundland murk had overcast the morning sun. It spread like a dark hand from the far horizon. In the distance Mariah could see the tip of an iceberg the size of a mountain. It seemed alone and out of place, slowly dying as it drifted south. He pointed to it with his free hand.

'How far is the iceberg?' he asked.

'Many miles. We shall be out of its way and safe in New York by the time it has drifted this far to the south,' Ellerby replied.

'Did you see the lights to the north? I heard it was the result of an experiment,' said Mariah.

Ellerby shrugged his shoulders as if he didn't care and kept on walking towards the stern of the ship. A small doorway set in a bulkhead was surrounded by empty deck chairs and neatly folded blankets. There were no passengers here. A red cord rope barred entry, but Ellerby stepped over the rope and opened the door. Mariah followed.

'Not many people have been allowed to see this,' he said as he walked down a narrow flight of steps lit by a chain of electric lights. 'Lorenzo Zane must think you are very special.'

Mariah could feel the air getting warmer as they walked. There was a smell of oil and boiled tea. The stairway was claustrophobic and grew smaller the deeper they went. He could see nothing ahead of him as Ellerby blocked his view.

'Much further?' he asked as the narrow stairway turned into a corridor.

'Through the next hatch and we shall be there,' Ellerby replied as he opened the hatch and stepped through. The bright light blinded Mariah. It burnt like a sun as it scorched through the hatch. 'Wear these,' said Ellerby, handing Mariah a pair of spectacles with black lenses. 'You will need them until we pass through the next hatch.'

Mariah put on the glasses and walked on. The light was intense. He held out his hand and was sure he could see the bones under his skin.

'What is it for?' he asked Ellerby.

'A means of security – anyone trapped in here would never escape,' he replied.

Ellerby opened the other hatch and took the glasses from Mariah. They were now in a small sterile room with steel walls. Mariah could hear the sound of the engine louder than he had ever heard it before. Ellerby slid a handle on the wall and to Mariah's surprise the wall opened.

There before him was the gigantic engine room. Three galleries surrounded two vast steam pistons. A large steel tank with gold riveted bands was connected to a boiler that stretched up high above them. Lorenzo Zane stood on a raised dais in front of a control panel of wheels and dials.

'Good to see you, Mariah,' he said as he beckoned him over. 'This is the Zane Generator. Impressive, isn't it?'

Mariah nodded, lost for words.

'I have to go,' Ellerby said. 'The *Bicameralist* is returning to signalling distance.'

Zane nodded and turned to Mariah. 'I wanted you to see this. My son has no interest in engines. In fact he is quite boring. He likes to play cricket and pull the legs from cockroaches. For once in my life I want to share all I have done with someone other than those who have aged and lost their vision of wonder.' Zane held up his arms as if he beheld a god. 'This is my greatest invention and yet . . .' His words faded into a sigh.

'It is beautiful,' Mariah said as he stared up at the monster of steel and chrome that towered above him.

'A good word, Mariah, a good word. An engine can be beautiful. And yet you saw the one flaw in my whole design,' Zane said.

'I did?' asked Mariah.

'When you were in the skyship you noticed that one engine had failed,' Zane said as he bit his lip anxiously and pushed back his thick black hair. 'There was a mishap. One of the crew fell inside the Steam Generator. That engine no longer works and I was wondering . . .' Zane stopped and looked Mariah up and down. 'You see, Mariah, I need someone adventurous to go inside and retrieve something for me. You are just about the right size – would you be willing?' he asked nervously.

'What do you need me to get?' asked Mariah uncomfortably, knowing one man had already died.

'An instrument of great worth. Small, delicate, irreplaceable, incredibly valuable and in the pocket of the idiot who got himself killed,' Zane said as he picked a fleck of dust from Mariah's shoulder.

'How did he die?' Mariah asked.

'Heart failure,' Zane said, avoiding the truth. 'That is really of no importance. He is stuck – jammed – and blocking the outlet pipe valve. Once I have the Thannometer I can flush him from the system. You would like to help me, wouldn't you, Mariah? I even think I know where I could find Biba. I heard she had vanished – in a cloud of smoke?'

Mariah thought for a moment. 'Why me?' he asked. 'You must have many men who could go inside.'

'I do,' Zane replied. 'But I am sure they would end up the same way. I need someone youthful, dexterous and anxious to please.' Zane handed Mariah a white silk overall that had been hanging over the back of the chair. 'I think this is your size.'

Mariah looked at the overall. He realised he would have to do what Zane wanted. Mariah hated to be patronised, especially by someone like Zane. Taking the overall he slipped it on quickly and buttoned up the front.

'The Thannometer – what does it do?' Mariah asked.

'It measures units of force and balances them against their resistance. It is quite a wonderful thing. You can't mistake it. Bring it back and you will be well rewarded,' Zane said eagerly. 'Just take the stepladder.'

Zane pointed to a brass ladder set in the side of a large steel cylinder. At the top was an open brass hatch that appeared to lead into a long funnel. Mariah looked up. It seemed so far away. All around the machinery whirred and churned. He saw no other men apart from Zane. It was as if he was the only one running the ship.

'How does the ship get its power?' Mariah asked.

Zane looked surprised to be asked such a question. He grinned malevolently. 'That is a great secret, but one that I will share with you . . . Ice fusion – but I do not expect you to understand. I have created a device that burns ice so quickly that it creates a dense steam under intense pressure . . . the

Thannolater. It then creates ice and so the circle continues – perpetual motion . . . Perhaps you have seen the emerald tinge to the steam coming from the stack?' Mariah shook his head. He hadn't noticed at all. 'Don't worry, Mariah, once inside the flask there are treads that will take you to the right place. Bring back the Thannometer and you can go, I promise. But first I will stop the engine. The momentum will keep the ship moving for several miles. No one should notice.'

Zane spun a dial on the board. The engine grew still, the room silent. He gestured for Mariah to go, pointing to the ladder and smiling.

Mariah turned, took hold of the ladder and began to climb. He was soon at the top, but didn't care to look down. It seemed pointless. All he could think of was what was ahead – taking the Thannometer from a dead man's pocket and then getting out of the engine room with his life. He had no reason to believe that Zane would have him killed, but this was a secret place, a place that Mariah should never have seen.

He climbed on and just as he reached the brass hatch the door opened below. Ellerby came in, removed the dark glasses and went to Zane. They appeared to wait until Mariah was inside the flask. He lingered out of sight and tried to listen to what was being said.

'The *Bicameralist* will come for you at eleven-thirty. Be ready,' Ellerby said, his whispered words echoing through the engine room.

'And the device?' Zane asked.

'Markesan assures me that it is ready as you asked,' Ellerby replied quietly.

'Good,' said Zane. 'All I need is the Thannometer and we can be gone.'

Mariah had heard enough. He realised that they planned to escape the ship. Far below in the meagre light of the funnel,

Mariah could see the legs of a man. They were covered in white silk just like his own. Each boot was frozen and covered in a thick layer of frost. He stepped from the plate onto the first tread of the descent. It grew colder by the inch until he could feel the ice forming on his lips and eyebrows.

When he came to the bottom tread he could see the man clearly. He was wedged in the neck of the funnel and was completely frozen. Mariah searched the icy pockets of his oversuit. Just below the belt he found the Thannometer. He struggled, took it out and stared at the device. It was made of solid gold. At one end was a glass orb that looked as though it was filled with green smoke. It was then that the Thannometer trembled in his hand, as if the heat of his body gave it life. The orb glowed dimly whilst inside three silver dials turned and then stopped – 636. Mariah read the number several times but did not know what it meant.

Putting the Thannometer in the pocket of his oversuit, Mariah retraced his steps and climbed back down the ladder. Zane was alone. Ellerby had gone.

'Did you find it?' Zane asked as he held out his hands.

Mariah handed over the device and looked at Zane. 'What does it do?' he asked.

'It measures perpetual motion – but that shouldn't concern you,' he said. He paused and looked up to the hatch high above them. 'There is one thing. The hatch is open – I will need your help to close it. First I have to set the generator and as soon as the hatch is closed the problem will be gone.'

'Gone?' asked Mariah. 'The *man* will be gone?'

'Yes,' he said calmly. 'Crunched up, minced – and spat out into the sea,' Zane replied.

'I think I need to go – you said you would tell me where Biba had gone,' Mariah said as he unbuttoned the overall.

'That is what I wanted to talk to you about. Biba is a hysterical girl – like all girls – and not to be trusted. She runs away and hides for effect. When she came to my house in Calgary she vanished for a whole day. When we searched for her, there she was in the larder eating cup cakes.'

'But she vanished from Deck 13,' Mariah protested. 'Someone took her – it was Shanjing.'

By the look on Zane's face, Mariah knew he had said too much.

'Shanjing?' he said as he stepped towards him, his eyes searching every inch of Mariah's face. 'Did you say Shanjing?'

Mariah stiffened himself. He shrugged his shoulders and lifted his head and stared at Zane eye to eye.

'Shanjing. Just like I said before. Everyone thinks he's a puppet, a mannequin, but he's not . . .'

'How surprising,' Zane said as he recovered himself and tried to turn his frown into a smile. 'Mr Ellerby did mention something about a rumour.' Zane looked at Mariah and put his hand on his shoulder. 'So you will help?'

'The hatch?' Mariah replied reluctantly.

'If you would be so kind . . .' Zane replied.

Mariah felt that he had no option other than to help Lorenzo Zane. He took off the overall and turned towards the ladder. Zane went ahead of him and climbed the ladder. He was quick and nimble, and Mariah thought him to be faster than most men of his age. At the top, Zane pulled the suspenders on his trousers and looked down at him.

'Thought you would be faster than that, Mariah Mundi. I need you to reach in and drop the catch whilst I turn on the vacuum.' Zane spoke eagerly as he walked the small gantry just below the roof of the engine room. There were several dials and a steel lever. Zane turned three of the dials and then pushed the lever down. 'Let me know when you've pulled the catch and I'll help with the door.'

Mariah looked in. He could see the catch – it was a small brass handle that held up the hatch door. It was just out of reach. He stretched further inside the hatch, and further . . . There was a sharp kick in his back, then a punch. Mariah was pushed inside. The hatch door was slammed shut behind him.

'Let me out!' he screamed as he scrambled on the treads and tried to open the door.

Zane stared in through a thick plate porthole and smiled.

'Mariah, what an accident . . .' he said with a smile. 'I can't open the door and the vacuum is about to fire. I'm so sorry. The door is – stuck.'

Zane sang the last word. There was a sudden drop in the pressure of the air and from far away Mariah could hear the rushing of water. The sound bubbled, growing in intensity as it vibrated the inside of the chamber. His eyes began to burst as the air was sucked from around him. The rushing air tore at his clothes. The frozen dead crewman began to vibrate as if he were dancing. His stiffened legs jumped back and forth as the whole contraption moved with the force of the air being sucked away. Zane stared in and laughed.

'Don't do this!' Mariah shouted, his words unheard under the deafening sound of the hurricane that now hurtled through the pipes towards him.

The crewman slowly began to disappear down the outlet pipe. His feet began to melt as what was left of the air got hotter and hotter. Beads of sweat trickled down Mariah's face as a burning wind filled the chamber. The man melted faster as he was sucked away. Then, like a bullet blasted from a gun, there was a sudden explosion and the man disappeared in a cloud of fragmenting ice.

Mariah was thrown towards the outlet pipe. The wind surged around him, lifting him from his feet as if he were straw and pushing him towards the outlet where the crewman had disappeared. From deep within he could hear the churning of the blades far below. They cut like sabres through the hurricane.

He glanced back as he spun around and around, lifted in a vortex of air. Zane peered into the chamber and laughed as Mariah was sucked into the funnel. The steel sides closed around him. The air rushed by – it pulled at his skin and jowled his face. He thought his eyes would burst. Mariah put his hands out to steady himself as he went deeper and deeper.

There was the sound of crunching and smashing as the steel blades span faster, and Mariah knew what was to come. He stretched out in an attempt to slow himself down. The steel funnel tore against the Spiderweb of his coat. It held fast. Strands of hair were torn from his head by the force of the vacuum. Mariah reached into his pocket and took hold of the pistol. He fought against the wind as he pressed the gun against the metal wall and aimed it at the approaching blades.

Mariah closed his eyes as he pulled the trigger again and again until he had emptied the magazine of all but one last shot. The blades that had cut up the frozen mariner shattered and broke off, spinning down the tube. They splintered, one after another, as the machine disintegrated.

Mariah held fast to the wall as the air slowed to a breeze. He pressed the gun to the metal and fired the last bullet. It burst through the steel. There was a violent hissing like a thousand snakes as the pipe tore open. The Zane Generator groaned like a dying creature without breath. The lights of the *Triton* flickered and then dimmed. Mariah was spat out of the funnel and onto the floor of the engine room. As he lay in a pool of blood and ice, he could hear Zane screaming, screaming to find and kill Mariah Mundi.

22

Zercidious

STILL fleeing Shanjing, Biba stumbled through the hatch door and on to the stage of the Saloon Theatre. It was in complete darkness. The heavy curtain was stretched across the high arch and she could see nothing at all. It was thick, musty black as if she were blind. But unexpectedly she could sense people near. At first she thought it to be Shanjing. Then she realised that whoever was there was all around her.

Biba heard the tap, tap, tapping of impatient feet. Someone pushed her out of the way but said nothing. She heard the tinkle of beads close to her, and suddenly the curtain opened. Music began to play. Lights burst through the blackness. The audience laughed. She gasped. All around her were dancers. Each was garbed in silver with a tall feather hat and a plumed skirt. They glared at her to leave. Biba looked to the side of the stage. There was Shanjing, hiding in the shadows, waiting for her. He smiled, knowing there was nowhere for her to go.

Biba stood quite still as all about her tall Amazons danced and swirled with grace. They seemed to ignore the girl in the tattered and torn fur coat. Her forlorn smile ebbed as she peered at the laughing faces of the men in the first three rows who shouted and sneered as the band played on. A man to her right, standing in the wings, shouted at her. His words died in the sound of thumping feet and shrill violins.

'Get off! Now!' he said again as she stood petrified by the limelit faces.

'This way, Biba . . .' Shanjing said, taunting her.

No one seemed to be able to see him. He had wrapped himself in the stage curtain, with only the leather skin of his face visible. His red eyes appeared to glow in the crisp white light as he cackled like a miniature madman. Then with no warning and not caring as to his revelation, he sprang from the curtain to the stage.

It was as if the devil had appeared. The dancers, who had seen Shanjing as a puppet in the arms of Charlemagne every night, screamed.

'He's alive,' shouted one as she threw her feather boa to the floor, turned and dived into the audience.

The effect of his appearance as a sentient creature was dramatic. The orchestra stopped playing, threw down their instruments and ran. Shanjing became more excited. It was as if he no longer cared.

'You are going to die!' he screamed as they fled. 'All of you . . . You shall play as the ship sinks.'

The audience surged from their seats, screaming. They tipped tables and chairs as they ran to the doors. They too believed that Shanjing had been transformed from a mannequin to a man. Just as Biba dived from the stage a passenger pulled a small dandy pistol from his pocket and fired at Shanjing. The bullet bounced off his coat and fell to the floor like a squashed fly. The sight of Shanjing repelling the bullet added to the terror. As a cacophony of horrified screams filled the theatre, Shanjing stood on the stage like an old master and held his arms in the air as if he were about to part the sea.

'Get the Captain,' shouted a man. 'The doll is possessed!'

'Possessed?' asked Shanjing as he looked at the terrified man. 'It shall be you who is possessed – possessed by fear as you see the *Triton* sinking beneath your feet and the ocean biting with icy teeth at your body.'

The man fainted with fear. He fell back against a small table, knocking the candle to the floor. Biba tried to hide as the mannequin paced the stage looking for her. The audience ran in terror from the theatre, trampling one another to get through the doors. They howled and screamed as Shanjing barked prophecies from the stage like a dog at the Wailing Wall.

'It is meant to be . . . I am Shanjing – a man, not a puppet!' Shanjing screamed at them as they fled. 'Listen! Listen to me!'

Biba slid quietly to the side of the room. She hid by the stairway door behind the abandoned instruments of the orchestra. The room emptied quickly and Shanjing stood silently with no one to listen to him. His curses became a whisper until he was finally silent.

Biba slowly turned the handle and opened the door. If the ship was designed like the *Ketos*, she knew she would be able to slip through the door, go down several flights of stairs and come to the circus. From there, she knew she could get the steam elevator back to Deck 13. Her hands felt stiff, her fingers were cold and numb with fear. She could see the shadow of Shanjing stretching across the floor, lit by the limelight candles. Faces stared in through the round glass windows in the saloon doors. No one dared enter. She could hear the crowds outside. Shanjing lowered his arms and nodded his head very slowly. It was as if he were listening to a silent voice telling him what to do.

'Yes, yes, that's it,' he said over and over. 'I know what will be . . .' Shanjing turned his head towards where she was hiding as if he had been told where she was. 'Biba – come out.'

Biba turned the handle further and opened the stairway door as quietly as she could. Crowds pressed against the entrance to the saloon, trying to peer in to see what Shanjing would do next. Biba slipped slowly into the blackness of the stairwell and closed the door behind her.

There was a loud crash as the wooden door split and a juggler's spear flew past her face. It had burst through the door, sending shards and splinters into the air. The spear cut through her fur coat, pushing her back. Biba screamed with surprise.

Without thinking she turned and with one hand slipped the latch of the door. It was just in time. Small hands pulled against the handle on the outside. She could hear Shanjing yelling dementedly.

'I'll have to kill you – it is a matter of principle!' Shanjing screamed.

Again there was a splintering of wood as another spear smashed through the door. Biba ducked down as it shot above her head and wedged itself in the opposite wall of the narrow landing.

'Leave me be!' she shouted instinctively, as if ridding herself of a demon inside.

'I am Shanjing,' said the voice as if it were to take her soul. 'I cannot do that . . .'

Biba slipped quickly under the shaft of the spear and ran down the dark stairway. She could hear the churning of the ship's engines. The sound seemed different, slower, laboured, as if they struggled to turn and turn.

Behind her, small hands beat against the door. She knew it was Shanjing. He beat his fists against the door and Biba feared it would give way. She ran further into the gloom. The wall lights were dim, faint and dying. They cast shadows along the corridors and dimmed the sound of her running. Her fur coat caught on a doorway. She pulled, and the coat tore as she ran on. From far away she heard the door open and then close quickly.

She knew Shanjing was now behind her in the relentless chase. Biba ran faster, desperate to get to the circus and then to the steam elevator. She hoped there would be people. They would protect her. But something made her worry, a nagging feeling in her heart that told her Shanjing now cared nothing about what he would do. The secret of him being alive would be about the ship. In her mind she could see him being hunted and chased just as she was.

The hatch to the circus soon came. Biba had run and run until her lungs were bursting and she could run no more. She sobbed, knowing he was behind her. In her heart she wanted to give up, to sit down where she was in the darkness and allow herself to be caught. It was pointless, she thought as she opened the door. He would find her.

The door to the circus opened easily. She could smell the animals and sawdust but when she looked all was dark, empty and silent. No one was there. Biba closed the door and spun the wheel on the hatch as tightly as she could. Her mind raced, wondering where everyone had gone.

'Mr Blake . . . Mr Blake,' she said in a loud whisper, hoping he would be at the door where he always was.

'Biba,' came a voice from the darkness. 'I thought you would come here . . .'

It was as if the words were icy hands that gripped her tightly. Shanjing was close by. Biba could sense him near to her. She stood silently waiting. It was as if she knew he would pounce from the darkness like a cat.

'Come on then, Shanjing. I can run no more,' she said loudly, out of breath, her voice trembling angrily. 'Here and now. I will fight you here and now.'

A sudden breeze lifted the sawdust about her feet. Biba stumbled forward.

'I know you are near,' said Shanjing as if he were close by.

Biba edged her hand along the side of the tiger cage. She could hear the creature sleeping in the compartment at the far end.

'Rollo,' she whispered quietly. 'Rollo . . .'

The tiger purred as it stirred in its dark-eyed sleep. She knew it to be Rollo. Eduardo the man-eater was deaf and couldn't hear her calling.

'The tiger won't protect you,' Shanjing said from inside the cage. 'I am already here and he is nothing but a pussy cat.'

The voice was in her face – then a hand darted from the blackness like a shadow and took hold of her hair. It pulled her to the cage. Biba dropped instinctively to the floor. Shanjing lost his grip as she screamed. Biba ran and found the steps of the next cage. She slid the catch from the door and slipped inside. Trying to hold her laboured and fearful breath, she waited in the darkness.

There was the sound of the striking of a tinderbox. A light burnt in the darkness. Shanjing stood outside the cage. In each hand was a juggler's knife with a burning handle. He held them by the tips of the blades as he waved them back and forth. By his feet were several more burning knives, neatly stacked upon the juggler's rack.

'Do you think I am mad enough to follow you into Eduardo's cage?' he asked. 'That beast is still chomping on the bones of Max Arras. I am only a breakfast morsel for one so great as Eduardo.'

Shanjing spun the blades as if he had done it countless times before. They burnt circles of fire in the darkness and illuminat-ed the man-mannequin like a ghost. He laughed as he stopped, flicked one knife in the air, caught it and then threw it at the cage. It slammed into the trailer board like a fiery razor. The knife dripped fire to the floor below.

'Come out, Biba . . . The cat will wake and eat you,' Shanjing taunted her as he prepared to throw another knife.

'I would rather be eaten alive than allow you to kill me.' Biba shrieked in fear as Shanjing threw another blade. It spun like a fire-wheel and slammed into the wood. The knife juddered the cage. Eduardo the tiger growled in his sleep.

'Then I shall wake the beast and watch in my delight,' he scoffed as he picked up another blade from the ivory stand.

Then another voice – 'Biba! Biba!' – as the far doors opened and Mariah rushed in.

Biba turned. Mariah stood by the door of the circus. The burning knives cast long shadows that flickered and danced across the roof.

'Shanjing is here – beware!' She shouted the warning as Mariah ran across the circus ring towards her. Biba turned. Shanjing was gone.

'Where is he?' shouted Mariah. 'We must go. Lorenzo Zane and Ellerby are searching for me. Zane tried to kill me.'

'Zane?' cried Biba as the tiger growled loudly.

'Stop there!' Shanjing shouted as he appeared from under a tiger cage carrying a flaming knife. 'I will happily kill you, Mariah Mundi.'

'You should stick to sitting in the laps of old men, Shanjing. You'll never get off this ship,' Mariah said as he walked slowly towards him.

'You are either brave or foolish, Mariah Mundi.' Shanjing threw the knife, just missing Mariah. Then he was gone, disappearing yet again into the darkness.

'Get out of the cage,' Mariah shouted to Biba. 'We have to get to Deck 13 before Zane finds me.'

Biba edged her way to the door of the tiger cage. She pushed on it and it opened slowly. Eduardo growled in his sleep. He was old and tired and although he looked much younger, his twenty years had taken their toll upon him.

'I can't see Shanjing,' she said as Mariah walked towards her, still wary of the dwarf's presence somewhere nearby.

As she stepped from the cage, a hand grabbed her leg. It gripped her tightly, taking her off balance and pulling her through the gap in the steps. Biba screamed as she fell. Mariah ran to her. Shanjing leapt into his path. He kicked at Mariah and knocked him to the floor. There was a dull thud and Mariah groaned as blood trickled from his ear. Shanjing appeared at the foot of the steps as Biba struggled to her feet.

'I suggest you come with me,' he said calmly as if it were a pleasant invitation.

Biba scrambled backwards. She pulled open the cage door and crawled in.

'I won't go with you,' she said, sobbing and hoping Mariah would wake.

'Then you leave me no choice,' Shanjing said as he climbed the steps towards her and began slowly to untie the leather mask from his face. 'I want you to see – need you to see – who I really am.'

Eduardo groaned sleepily in the hutch at the back of the cage. Shanjing stepped inside and took off his mask.

'It is a shame Mariah Mundi cannot see this as I am sure he will recognise me.'

Biba stared at the grotesque face of the man-mannequin. The only part untouched by flame were his eyes. The burnt skin was crinkled like a crocodile's, tightly stretched and translucent over the bones. Small pulsing veins ran across the cheeks of a face that had no lips.

'Who did that to you?' Biba asked in horror as she crawled further from him.

235

'I was left for dead,' Shanjing said as he dropped the mask to the floor and took the gloves from his hands. 'Come with me Biba – this is not the right place.'

Biba looked to Mariah. In the faint glow of the tallowed knives she could see him slumped on the ground. He didn't move. She looked to the floor, knowing her eyes would give away the secret thought that came to her.

'Very well,' she said as she got to her feet and held out her hand to Shanjing. 'Just help me . . .'

Shanjing reached out to her. Biba took his hand. She felt the dryness of the burnt fingers against her skin.

'You know it has to be this way?' Shanjing asked in a melancholic way.

'Yes,' she said slowly as she tightened her grip on his fingers and stared at the floor of the cage. 'This way and no other.'

Shanjing grinned. His teeth were lipless and bared, with just a veneer of burnt skin around the edge of what was his mouth. He flicked his tongue like an expectant snake.

'It is time,' he said slowly as he stood before her.

Biba pulled his hand suddenly. She dragged Shanjing towards her, summoning every last morsel of strength. He stumbled as she grabbed his coat with her other hand. Then, without giving him a chance to shout out, Biba pushed him as hard as she could. He fell towards the darkness of the sleeping hutch. The tiger growled as it realised someone was near. Shanjing screamed as he stared face to face at the creature. He fell before it like a sacrifice as Biba leapt from the cage and slammed the door shut.

The tiger lashed out with its gigantic paw, slashing Shanjing across the chest. The man-mannequin screamed as his body twisted. He stared at Biba, holding out his hand to be saved.

'Not like this!' he screamed as Eduardo the tiger bit into his side. 'Biba, no!'

The tiger dragged him into the darkness of its lair. Biba covered her face with her hands, unable to breathe as Shanjing screamed and screamed. The tiger roared as it tore at Shanjing with claws and teeth. It was as if it would not be satisfied until it had found his heart. Then all was silent.

Biba looked into the cage. On the floor was the mannequin's mask. It looked like the discarded chrysalis of a beautiful butterfly that had pupated and flown away. Biba reached inside and took hold of the mask, pulling it to her. She held it in her hands and stared at the empty eye sockets. It was still warm and moulded into the shape of Shanjing's thin face.

In the cage, Eduardo purred and slurped hungrily.

'Biba,' said Mariah as he recovered his mind from Shanjing's blow. 'You're safe?'

'He's dead,' she muttered as she stared at the mask. 'I killed him . . .'

Mariah looked towards the cage in disbelief. He thought of Max Arras and the way he had died. It was as if the tiger acted out the desires of his heart.

'Zane tried to kill me. The *Triton* is damned – I fear it will be scuttled tonight, at midnight...'

'He wouldn't do that – I know him too well,' she said and then thought of what she was saying. 'I suppose he could. He would never want to lose face. My father called him arrogant, but mother wouldn't listen to him.'

'I think it was Madame Zane who tried to kill me,' Mariah said. 'I have a memory of seeing her, hearing her voice. Someone drugged me that night I was on the gantry. I can remember seeing her in the shadows, waiting for me to jump.'

23

Et mon cul, c'est du poulet?

'SO you don't deny it?' Ellerby said as he stepped across the lounge of Deck 13 towards Captain Jack Charity. 'Sachnasun insists you tried to kill him.'

'What?' Charity asked bemused by the cross-examination. '*Et mon cul, c'est du poulet?*'

'If I could understand your question, then I would answer,' Ellerby replied as he walked to the window and looked out over the sea.

'What's more, Captain Charity,' Zane interrupted, 'since you have been on this ship things have happened that cannot be explained. I can only presume that you have something to do with it.'

'Sachnasun is lying. He ran off and I never saw him again. Then I was locked in a chamber and someone tried to drown me. I never assaulted him. I couldn't,' Charity replied as he moved to stand next to Ellerby.

In the far distance he could see the *Bicameralist*. Like a graceful snail, it floated in between the clouds as it came nearer. He saw Ellerby look at his fob watch as if the skyship's reappearance had been timed. Ellerby turned from him and gave a nod to Lorenzo Zane like a signal to start some pre-ordained strategy.

'The thing is, Charity,' Zane said, stumbling with his words, 'it would not be safe to leave you at liberty to walk the ship. We are in a race with the *Ketos* and I cannot take the chance that you are in fact an agent of Lord Bonham, sent here to stop us from winning.'

'Isn't it obvious you will lose? The *Triton* has been unable to keep pace with the *Ketos* since leaving Liverpool. With every league we fall further behind. This ship is unfit for the sea, Lorenzo, and you know it.'

Charity looked at Vikash, who had been silently watching from the doorway of the room. 'Someone wants this ship to sink. We found a bomb, as you well know, and we saved the ship. If anyone should want the *Triton* to be sunk it is you, Lorenzo Zane.'

'For what purpose would I want such a thing?' he asked calmly.

'The Zane Generator doesn't work and you know it. You will be disgraced and no one will employ you again. It was conven- ient for you that DeFeaux should come to such a fateful end – did he know too much and you needed him out of the way?'

Zane bristled angrily. He looked at Ellerby and then to the door. Down the corridor, the steam elevator shuddered slowly. It was as if it were dying.

'Who is there?' Ellerby asked Vikash.

Vikash looked. Biba and Mariah stood by the door.

'No one,' he replied. 'I think the ship is doing strange things. I noticed the power is fading. Mr Zane, do you think Charity is really guilty of these things?'

Mariah opened the cupboard door next to the steam elevator and he and Biba slipped silently inside.

'It is quite possible,' Zane replied.

'Then how is it that I can vouch for him on two occasions?' Vikash asked.

'An accomplice, Mariah Mundi. He was found in the engine room tampering with the Zane Generator,' Ellerby replied. 'It is obvious he works for Charity and does what he is asked. Did Bonham pay you well for this?'

Charity leant against the glass and laughed. It was as if he realised what was to come. He held out his hands, touching them at the wrists as if to be manacled.

'I think you should do what you have to do and spare me the betrayal. It is obvious, Vikash, that no matter what you say, our friends have the will to arrest me and Mariah Mundi.' Charity spoke loudly as if he knew Mariah were near. 'I may be an easy catch, but Mariah will prove more difficult.'

'Then you admit it?' Ellerby asked.

'Dear Ellerby, you and I both know that this is preposterous. Take me away and have done with it. Does the *Triton* have a brig?' Charity asked.

'You will be confined to Tharakan's cabin. You will find it is secure enough to keep you,' he said. 'Mr Vikash, you will be confined to Deck 13 for the remainder of the voyage. The steam elevator will be disabled and food will be sent up to you. There will be a guard to make sure you don't come looking for Captain Charity. As for Biba DeFeaux and Mariah Mundi – when they are caught they too will be kept from you both.'

'So even children are a threat to the ship?' Charity asked.

'Only when they are employed as saboteurs,' Zane replied as he walked from the room.

Ellerby followed. He tugged Charity by the sleeve as if to take him along. It was a tentative touch, as if he didn't dare take hold of him. Charity brushed off the hand as if it were a fly. He straightened his tie and took a step in front of Ellerby.

'I shall enjoy the view from Tharakan's cabin,' he said loudly. 'I believe the only way to it is through the bridge?'

'I will see you in New York, Jack,' Vikash said as he winked at him. 'Don't worry about Mariah – I will look after him.'

'If you see Mariah Mundi, I would suggest that you hand him to me. That boy has a lot to answer for,' Zane muttered in a spitting voice.

'I will, I will,' said Vikash in reply. 'It will be the first thought that enters my head.'

Vikash watched them take Charity to the steam elevator. Zane slid open the doors and stepped inside, anxiously looking around him as if he somehow feared the device would crash to the bilges of the ship. Ellerby pushed Charity inside and slid shut the gate. Charity lifted his hand slightly as a gesture of goodbye. He smiled at Vikash and then looked to Zane, who fumbled to press the button for three decks below.

'I think you will find it helps to keep a steady finger,' Charity said as he pushed the button for Deck 10. 'Goodbye, Vikash – see you in New York.'

The steam elevator rattled to feeble life. It juddered more than usual and sounded as if it were gasping for breath. All its power had dissipated. It dropped slowly from view, leaving Vikash to stare on a dark void. He waited until it had vanished completely and then opened the cupboard door.

'You are lucky that you are both not skinned alive,' he said as he took Biba by the ear and pulled her from the hiding place. 'As for you, Mariah Mundi – what have you done to the ship?'

'Zane tried to kill me,' he said as he held Biba's hand, hoping they would stay together.

Biba squeezed his fingers tightly for him to stop speaking. She looked at Vikash with eyes that spoke of a revealed secret.

'I know who you are,' she said, and she stared at his face as if for the first time.

'Of course you know who I am,' Vikash replied as if to shrug off the words and stop her from going further. 'I am Casper Vikash – the servant and bodyguard of your father.'

Mariah stood back, as if it wasn't his place to be there any longer.

'You are more than that. Shanjing told me everything,' Biba said as she took a guarded pace towards him.

'How can I be more than that?' Vikash asked. He turned away.

'Shanjing said you are my brother,' she said, whispering the word.

Vikash stopped. Mariah could see a tear in his eye that glinted as it rolled across his scarred cheek.

'Does that change anything?' he asked Biba.

'I understand why you have done the things you have. Saving my father – saving me – covering up for mother.' Biba reached out and caught the tear with the tip of her finger. 'It all makes sense. You would have rather died than see my father killed by the piranha and you fought a bear to save me.'

'I would have done it anyway,' he said as he took her hand from his face. 'I always wanted you to know, but our father swore me to secrecy until the time was right. Why did Shanjing tell you this?'

'He was trying to kill me and blackmail you,' she said. 'He was going to offer to do it for you for all the money in the safe. I heard him talk to a man – he called him Markesan.'

'I wish Jack Charity had heard that name. There is more than one person who wants to see the *Triton* at the bottom of the ocean.'

'And it will happen tonight. I heard Ellerby talking to Zane. The *Bicameralist* is coming back for them tonight. They are going to leave the ship,' said Mariah.

'No captain and no inventor – we shall be left to our own fate,' said Vikash as he went to the window and looked out. 'It is very dangerous for you, Mariah. I cannot be there to protect you – please understand I have to look after Biba. If there is to be a problem with the *Triton* I have to make sure she is safe.'

'I understand,' Mariah replied as he looked at Biba. 'I would do the same for her. I will take my chance and find Captain Jack.'

'The cabin on the bridge will be well guarded. If you get caught then I do not think you will leave the ship alive,' replied Vikash.

'The *Triton* is going nowhere. I smashed the Zane Generator. There was a man stuck inside. Zane sent me in to bring out a device, then he tried to kill me and the turbine was smashed.' Mariah started to laugh. 'I have never seen anyone so angry – I escaped through the air vents – they run throughout the ship. I know a way of finding Captain Jack.'

'Then you must wait here until it's dark,' Biba said. 'The lights on the ship are fading – they won't be able to see you.'

'By that time the ship will be dead in the water. It is slowing all the time,' said Mariah as Vikash went to the window and looked out to sea.

'And panic will set in and the passengers will wonder what is happening,' said Vikash 'How will you get from Deck 13?'

'Easy,' said Mariah. 'The same way Shanjing did without any of us seeing him.'

He walked into the corridor. There, near to the steam elevator, was the dumb waiter, its wooden panel door fitting neatly into the partition. By the side was a mahogany button that looked like a stud in the wall.

Biba pressed the button. It rang far below and echoed through the dark shaft.

'They could be waiting for you,' she said slowly.

'I will have to find that out for myself, Biba,' Mariah replied as the dumb waiter stopped and the door opened automatically.

'Tell me one thing, Mariah. This hotel of yours – can I come and stay there?' Biba asked as he squeezed himself inside the compartment.

'I insist,' he replied. 'You will find the Prince Regent far safer than the *Triton* . . . and not as crowded.'

Mariah looked to Vikash. He signalled for him to press the button.

'If the *Bicameralist* is to return I will try to get Biba on board. The docking gantry was made so that it can be accessed from Deck 13. Good luck, Mariah, and we will see you in New York.'

'Luck? No such thing – Captain Jack told me that. Masters of our own fortune or victims of fate – that's what he said,' Mariah replied as the door shut suddenly and he was plunged into darkness as the dumb waiter slowly descended. Luck was a thing he didn't believe in. Topher had carried an elephant amulet, sent by his mother from darkest Africa. She had said it would protect him from all evil. He would go nowhere without it and slept with it under his pillow. On the day he had drowned in the Thames he had worn it around his neck. It became a millstone on his life and never brought him luck.

Mariah heard Biba whisper a faint goodbye as the lift rattled down. There was a nagging doubt in his mind. He had hoped in his heart that the apparition of his friend was long gone and that it would haunt him no more. Mariah knew he would have to find Charity and set him free from Tharakan's cabin. He knew too that the *Triton* would be sunk that night, scuppered by Lorenzo Zane in the dark Atlantic Ocean.

The dumb waiter eventually stopped several floors below. Mariah could smell the sweet scent of the ship's kitchens and hear the sound of the chefs screaming orders to their battalions. There was the clanging of pots and pans as the evening dinner was being prepared. As the doors to the dumb waiter opened steam flooded in from the churning of the metal pot-washer that hissed and spurted near by.

Mariah slipped out into a scullery with steel walls and a tiled floor. The pot-washer filled one wall. It was a monstrous silver machine, the size of a large grizzly bear. It rattled and shook as steam shot from around its doorway. In the centre of its door was a red dial to indicate the temperature of the water. Mariah read the dial: 127 degrees Fahrenheit.

Hanging on a neat row of brass hooks were several waiter's jackets. Each was of bright white cloth with gold braid collars and cuffs. Mariah slipped on the nearest jacket, which covered his coat and was a size too big. He knew he would have to walk through the kitchen. He picked up a tray from the side of the pot-washer and held it just how he had seen it done by the waiters at the Prince Regent. He flicked back his hair and stood as tall as he could, then he stepped from the room and into the vast kitchen. It shone and gleamed. A hundred white-clad chefs dashed this way and that. Fat sizzled, water boiled, and to his right several large swans hissed on the oven-spit.

Mariah took a deep breath and walked on. He nimbly made his way, head down, towards the far end of the kitchen. He strode past several sous-chefs without catching their eye. Mariah was ever nearer to the double doors that led to the restaurant, but it was hard to avoid the phalanx of croutoniers who chopped and fried the bread. At the end of the row was the chef de battalion, a tall, thin man with a lined face who barked orders and snarled as he flashed a long-bladed knife back and forth.

'You!' he screamed at Mariah. 'How dare you come into the kitchen?'

'I was asked for,' Mariah said quickly, trying to think of something that a waiter would risk his life for by entering a kitchen uninvited.

'Then you will leave now and not come back. Your domain begins on the other side of the door. This is a place of creation, not fit for the likes of you,' scoffed the chef de battalion as the soupers and croutoniers laughed at Mariah.

Mariah coughed apologetically, bowed his head and rushed to the door. He took hold of the handle just as the door was pushed briskly towards him. He fell back, dropping the empty tray, and the chef applauded and laughed.

A man with a thin beard and greased hair leered down at him.

'What are you doing?' he asked as he held out a white, gloved hand. 'I do not recall seeing you before.'

Mariah got to his feet. 'I –'

'Are you from the saloon café?' the man asked with a raised brow.

Mariah nodded and tried to smile. He could feel a shiver run through his spine, as if he were to be found out and captured.

'He is a penguin without ice,' said the chef de battalion. 'Another dumb waiter . . .'

Both men laughed as Mariah got to his feet.

'He is just what I need,' said the head waiter. 'Captain Eller-by has asked for food. It is plated and ready. Take it at once.'

The man pointed to a small hatch in the wall. Mariah looked across and saw a tray with a large silver tureen. He took it with both hands, turned and left the kitchen.

The chef de battalion shouted, 'The captain is the man at the top of the ship.'

Mariah walked quickly through the restaurant and out on to the deck. Above, the *Bicameralist* hovered menacingly. Far to the west the sun was touching the ocean. Again the northern sky was tinged with a green glow. The *Triton* was hardly moving in the calm sea, the engines were still and silent. The only sound was that of a gentle breeze sighing through the rigging above him and the droning of the engines of the skyship. He wasn't sure, but far on the horizon it looked as if there was a ship coming towards them.

As he climbed the steps he clutched the tray tightly. It was a good excuse to be there, he thought, but Mariah knew he would be recognised immediately by Captain Ellerby. He walked by the guard who had been placed on the stairway to the bridge. He wasn't challenged. It was as if he had been expected – the guard stopped him briefly and looked under the cover of the tureen and then let him go on. Mariah slipped quickly up the steps and then, when he was out of sight, hid in the dark shadows of the gantry.

The bridge door opened. Ellerby and Zane stepped out on to the landing.

'We shall get the *Bicameralist* now. My wife and son are already aboard,' said Zane as he took hold of the ladder that would lead him to Deck 13.

'Vikash has asked if he and Biba can go with us,' Ellerby said as Zane climbed higher.

'How did he know? Are we to invite the whole ship?' Zane replied sarcastically.

'I knew that is what you would say,' Ellerby said as he followed on. 'I took the liberty of locking the doors to Deck 13 so that they cannot get out. They will go down with the ship.'

'And Markesan?' asked Zane.

'He will not be coming – just as you instructed,' replied Ellerby.

'Soldiers of fortune have their uses, but make abominable flying companions,' Zane said, not realising Mariah was hiding just feet away. 'Just think, Ellerby. Tomorrow we will be in New York. The only survivors of this awesome tragedy.'

'Are you sure no one will survive?' he asked.

'I have reason to believe that will be the case,' Zane replied. 'At least, not after dinner.'

[24]

Ruinis Inminentibus Musculi Praemigrant

IT was not long before the *Bicameralist* whirred its engines and began to move away from the ship. It passed over Mariah's head like a sky-whale and then turned to the west before making towards the horizon. He watched as it glided on. Then when it was some miles from the ship and travelling at great speed, it turned to the south as if to avoid the lights of the vessel that was now closer than before.

Mariah tapped on the door to the bridge. The door opened. An officer of the watch looked him up and down.

'Ellerby has left the bridge,' he snarled. 'He won't want feeding until later.'

'I know,' Mariah said calmly as his stomach churned and his knees trembled. 'He told me to bring this to the man in Captain Tharakan's cabin. Lorenzo Zane said I had to take it myself.'

'Are you sure he told you to come here?' asked the man.

'Just now when I brought the food – they came out. Said it was too good to waste the food so give it to the man in Tharakan's cabin.'

'Didn't mention that to me,' the man snapped as he looked

over his shoulder. 'What did he say to you?' he asked the man at the wheel of the ship.

'Who cares,' said the man. 'How else would the lad know we had someone locked in there if Ellerby hadn't told him? We have no power and Zane said he was going to fix it. Let the lad in and get him out of the way.'

The man on the door nodded to Mariah and let him in. He pointed to a door at the rear of the bridge.

'You'll find him in there. Down the corridor at the end. Don't let him out.'

Mariah smiled at the man and kept his head down as he walked through the bridge, opened the door and once inside breathed a sigh. Ahead of him was a short corridor with a doorway at the end. He quickly pulled the handle of the door and went inside. The lights of the *Triton* were fading and the room was dimly lit. He could see the back of a man's head. The man was tied roughly to a chair with thick rope.

'Captain Jack,' Mariah whispered.

'Mariah?' he answered. 'How did you get in here?'

'I'm an agent of the Bureau of Antiquities,' he said as he began to undo the thick cords that held Charity fast. 'Zane and Ellerby have left the ship. They have escaped in the *Bicameralist*. The ship is to be sunk – scuppered. I heard Zane tell Ellerby.'

'I thought that would be the case,' Charity replied. 'Did they say anything else?'

'They talked of Markesan. Ellerby said he wouldn't be joining them. Zane said he was a soldier of fortune.'

'Just what we needed. *Ruinis inminentibus musculi praemigrant* – the small rodent deserts the falling building . . . It looks as though Markesan will have the same fate as ourselves.'

'How can we stop the ship from sinking?' asked Mariah.

'We can't – there isn't time. To make sure the *Triton* goes to the bottom of the ocean it will be blown from the water.'

249

'But there aren't enough lifeboats for the passengers and Biba is locked on Deck 13. Zane said there would be no survivors,' Mariah replied.

'Then Zane was wrong. I will not see a single soul lost. Not one shall perish. We must act quickly,' Charity said in a whisper. 'I want you to scream and scream loudly, now!'

Mariah screamed as if he was being murdered. Charity threw the chair to the floor and tipped over Tharakan's desk. He hid behind the door as the officer of the watch rushed in. Mariah stood against the far wall with his arms folded.

'What's happening here?' asked the man.

Mariah pointed behind him. The man turned, just as Charity punched him. He slumped backwards, falling onto the overturned chair.

'To the bridge,' Charity said as they left the officer of the watch groaning in the room.

Just as they set foot on the bridge there was a sudden and powerful explosion. It ripped through the front of the ship and sent waves shuddering around it. The *Triton* moaned as metal beams twisted. The officer at the helm was thrown to the floor.

'You're being scuppered by your own captain,' Charity said as the man got to his feet about to attack. 'Sound the alarm.'

The officer reached out to a red lever on the control panel and pushed it back as far as it would go. The sound of a whirring siren came from below their feet. From above them, flares shot from the roof one after the other like lightning in the night sky.

There was another sudden explosion from the port side amidships. It was like a Trafalgar cannon. The roar billowed far across the calm sea to the distant icebergs that haunted them like ghostly cliffs of steel.

'I must find the captain,' the officer said as he made for the door.

'He's gone – took the Skyship and left you to your fate,' Mariah said.

'You must seal all watertight doors,' Charity demanded as the man tried to leave the bridge.

'They don't work,' the man said as he dashed by. 'Nothing works any more – the ship is dead and has been all day. It will sink within three hours and there's nothing I or anyone can do.'

'But what of the passengers?' asked Mariah.

'What of them?' replied the man as he pushed open the door and ran outside. 'They will die. The sea is so cold it will kill them.'

'Is there nothing you can do?' Mariah shouted after him.

There was no reply. He heard the officer running down the metal steps to the deck below. Mariah looked about the bridge. Lights flashed. An alarm sounded. From the rear of the ship came another explosion. It ripped through the steel plates, cutting a hole in the side of the ship and spilling the cargo of travelling trunks and cases into the sea. Even on the bridge they could hear the passengers screaming below. Charity looked down. The decks were empty but for the crew who were lowering the lifeboats into the water and leaving the passengers behind.

'The passengers are trapped,' Charity said as he suddenly realised what Zane had meant by no one surviving. 'They are locked below in the dining rooms, unable to escape.'

Together they rushed from the bridge and down the steps to the lower deck. The outer doorways were all locked. Charity shouted at the crew to help but they ignored his pleas and continued to lower the lifeboats.

Mariah stared into the large dining room through the window of toughened glass. He could see a stampede of people pushing towards the doors not caring who would be trampled. Mariah screamed for them to be calm, but he could see their eyes watching the lifeboats being lowered to the sea and with it their hopes fading. Gone were their cares for each other as the instinct for self-preservation took its place and thrilled each man with the need to survive. In the corner of the dining room Mariah could see a small boy. He was alone, abandoned by his guardian who now beat at the door with her fists to be set free.

'How do we get in?' Mariah asked.

'Shoot out the locks and then stand back,' Charity said.

Mariah drew his pistol and aimed it at the lock. He pulled the trigger. The lock exploded and a sea of people pushed outwards from their confinement.

'Don't panic!' screamed Charity above the melee, his words falling on deaf ears and screaming mouths.

The crowd surged forward, spilling onto the deck. Like lemmings they leapt over the side of the ship and into the cold sea. Men dived for the lifeboats before they had even taken to the water. Crewmen were thrown to the deep below. The *Triton* slowly tilted to one side as the flood engulfed the engine room. Mariah was pushed back, further and further from Charity, separated by a sea of people. They clung to the railings for dear life. The water bubbled all around them as the ship settled in the calm sea. Gushes of black soot shot from the funnels into the star-filled sky as the Zane Generator was submerged. A complete silence descended. Not a word was spoken. It was as if everyone was listening for the hope of rescue.

Then they came – first in ones and twos, then a handful and then a mob. They scurried along the walkways, some dripping with water, others fresh-faced and preened. People began to scream as the rats clung to long coats to escape the sea. In a swarm they ran across the decks and climbed the gantries. A black army of long-tails was invading the ship, biting and snatching at everyone who came near as they climbed higher to escape the rising tide.

From far below the sound of roaring tigers echoed through the cavernous and now empty rooms of the stricken vessel. The passengers now began to scream, as if a madness had taken hold of them all. Mariah watched as one man stood before him crying like a small child before throwing himself to the water below.

'Don't do this!' he shouted. 'Just be calm and we will be safe.'

No one listened. On the wall near to him Mariah saw an emergency cupboard. He smashed the glass with his elbow, took out the key and opened the small door. Inside was a bull-horn and flare gun. Mariah loaded the gun and fired the bright red flare high into the sky. Taking the bullhorn he shouted to the passengers.

The shock of the exploding flare had silenced them again. The rats ran about their feet as they listened to Mariah speak.

'Keep calm!' he shouted. 'We will get you from the ship. A rescue vessel is on its way.'

Mariah pointed to the far horizon. There in the distance were the lights of a ship. Since he'd first seen them from the bridge, Mariah realised they were coming closer, coming towards the *Triton*. 'If you can stay calm we will all be rescued. The ship is only two hours away. Everyone get to a higher deck and from there we will load the lifeboats.'

'But the crew have gone,' shouted a man angrily.

'Then we shall rescue ourselves,' shouted Charity from the other side of the crowd. 'The lad is right. We can all be saved – we just need faith.'

'There are enough lifeboats and jackets if we just take our time,' Mariah hollered through the bullhorn. 'We must all go to the upper decks.'

Mariah led on. The ship was now tilted in the water. A line of frightened passengers climbed the slanting stairs to the front of the ship. They gathered below the bridge, high enough to see the lights of the far off ship.

'Will it get here before we sink?' asked a woman carrying a small child.

'It will. I am sure of it,' replied Mariah as he prayed it would be so.

'Then we will play for you all,' said an Austrian musician clutching a violin. 'An hour will pass quickly with the music of Vienna.'

Charity pushed his way through the crowds to Mariah. People looking out to sea and the faraway lights surrounded them.

'Is it what I think it is?' Mariah asked quietly so as not to be overheard.

'The *Ketos*?' he asked. 'I think so – but whether it will get here in time I don't know. The ship has been badly damaged. Whoever planted the explosives knew how to destroy a ship. The only thing keeping us afloat is a calm sea and the air trapped below. I want you to go and find Biba and then get off the ship.'

'I can't,' replied Mariah. 'What about the passengers?'

'I will stay until the last. You must go, Mariah,' Charity said.

Mariah looked about him. Gatherings of passengers clustered about the deck wrapped in blankets. The crew had gone. They had abandoned ship and saved themselves, and now drifted far away in the lifeboats. A small orchestra gathered under the eaves of the bridge played sonatas in the moonlight. A woman danced as a man by the railings drank whisky from a jar. All seemed well. It was as if a calm had descended upon the passengers as they awaited their fate.

The *Triton* had sunk no further. It was lurched in the water, listing to one side. Mariah looked up to Deck 13. It was in darkness, and looked like the front of a large impregnable castle.

'Promise me you will leave the ship?' he asked Charity.

'I promise,' Charity replied as Mariah turned to walk away. 'Mariah,' he said. 'There is something I need to tell you about your father.'

Mariah stopped and turned as the ship creaked and groaned. 'What is it?' he asked.

Charity thought for a moment. It was as if he had changed his mind about what he had intended to say. He looked embarrassed, uncomfortable, out of place.

'I am . . .' He stopped what he was saying. 'He . . .will always love you. I know that to be true,' Charity said. 'Now go – find Biba – do what you have to do – all will be well . . .' Mariah looked at him for a moment, and it was as if he stared at his companion for the first time. He had never heard Charity speak like that before. His heart raced. Mariah was fearful that Charity was saying goodbye and they would never see each other again. Charity turned and walked away. 'I will see to the lifeboats. Go, find Biba – quickly.'

The ship groaned as it settled deeper in the water. What peace there had been was now broken as screams of fear came from all around him. Mariah looked up at the high metal walls that rose up from where he stood to Deck 13. He tried the door to the stairs, but like every other it had been automatically locked when the explosion happened.

'I'll have to climb,' he said to himself as he eyed the route to the top of the ship.

Taking hold of the window outside the Saloon Theatre, Mariah started to climb. He edged his way slowly up and up. His fingers gripped the cracks between the metal plates. He gripped the bolts and used each ledge as a foothold. The wind whistled about him as if it hoped to drag him from the ship. Mariah dared not to look down but he turned and looked over his shoulder. In the distance he could see the lights of the ship getting closer. It gave him strength and hope.

Mariah heard the lifeboats being launched on the far side of the ship. They scraped as they slid down the listing metal plates and into the water. The passengers were shouting as the *Triton* slowly deepened its draught.

Soon he had climbed three decks. He looked up. There was the balcony where the Marquis had talked with Charity on the night Mariah had first met Biba DeFeaux. Mariah stretched out his hands to reach for the railing. He gripped the cold brass rod in his fingers and pulled as hard as he could. Quickly he was on the balcony. The door was open. The room drapes still covered the opening.

'Biba! Casper!' Mariah shouted as he went to the door.

It was as if Deck 13 was empty. He searched the first room and found no one. Then he checked Biba's suite. It too was empty. He shouted again but there was no reply. Yet Mariah was sure he was not alone. He could feel someone nearby. He walked through the rooms of the apartment until he had nearly come to the rear of the ship but still he couldn't find Biba nor Casper Vikash. The rooms were dark, eerie and cold – unlike when he had first stood on the marble floor and wondered what kind of a man could afford a suite of rooms such as this on the most expensive ocean liner in the world.

It was then that he saw that one of the oak panels on the wall was slightly open. In the dim light he made out three fingers curled around the wood. For a moment he wondered what to do and then without further hesitation he kicked the panel shut.

A girl screamed. It was Biba.

'Biba?' he asked as the panel swung open and Biba sat in the darkness crying and clutching her hand.

'You could have broken my fingers,' she said angrily, unafraid to speak. 'Why did you do that?'

'I didn't know it was you. I called out your name and no one replied – you could have been anyone.'

'Anyone with a broken finger,' she snapped.

'Where's Casper?' Mariah asked.

'Four men took him. He fought them so I could hide. They had guns and explosives,' she said as she rubbed her hand.

'Who were they?' asked Mariah.

'I heard them call one Markesan.'

'But how could they have got in? All the doors are locked and the steam elevator isn't working,' Mariah asked.

'Through there,' she said as she pointed to a large picture of a Greek sea god in an ornate gold frame on the wall opposite. 'It's an escape ladder my father had fitted to all his ships. It takes you to the lifeboat deck. The only people who knew about it were Captain Tharakan and Lorenzo Zane.'

'Then we have a way of escape. The ship is sinking, we have to get to a lifeboat,' Mariah said as he examined the picture.

The frame opened from the wall to reveal a small room and a ladder descending into the darkness. Mariah looked down; it was like staring into a dark abyss. Far below he could hear the screams of the passengers as they leapt into the remaining lifeboats. He turned to Biba. She knew from his look what he was about to say.

'I can't do it,' she said nervously. 'They have Casper and could be waiting for me.'

'We have to go, now. The *Triton* will be at the bottom of the ocean within the hour.'

25

Excelsis Aliquando Videbimus

IT was Mariah who led the way through the darkness. Biba followed, gripping the ladder with both hands, frightened to let go. The tunnel was narrow and cold and it echoed with the sound of distressed voices far below. Mariah kept talking, reassuring Biba that all would be well, but in his heart he doubted his own words. From far away he could hear the sound of the orchestra. Their music was carried by the wind and matched the rumble of the bubbling seawater that boiled with the heat of the Zane Generator.

'How much further?' Biba asked when they reached a small landing and looked down.

'I can see some light,' Mariah replied, pointing to a faint glimmer of light below them.

The ship groaned and juddered. It was as if it were splitting in two. They heard the crack of the metal plates. Mariah couldn't understand how the *Triton* was still afloat.

'It's designed not to sink,' Biba said as if she could read his mind. 'I heard Lorenzo Zane tell my father that even if the side of the ship fell off then it would still float for several hours.'

'Do you think he was right?' Mariah asked hopefully.

'For our sake, yes,' she said as Mariah again took to the ladder and climbed down to the deck below.

The shouting grew steadily louder. They could hear the sound of the sea and the scraping of lifeboats on the side of the hull. They were soon on deck amongst the chaos of people.

A man recognised Biba. 'You should be ashamed, bringing us on a ship like this. If your father was here . . .' he snarled as he pushed by her towards the front of the ship.

'Ignore them,' Mariah said as Biba pulled up the collar of her coat to cover her face.

'There aren't enough boats, are there?' she asked.

Mariah nodded. Ahead he could see Charity by the lifeboat station. An orderly queue of women processed as if at the entrance to a jumble sale. They filled the lifeboats one by one. Charity turned and waved.

'Biba! Here, there is a seat for you here,' he said. She looked at Mariah, unsure if she wanted to meet her fate alone. 'Women only – you'll have to go.'

Biba took her place at the end of the line and waited. Mariah put his arm around her shoulder.

'Now the men – line here,' Charity shouted as three clowns in full make-up and costume trudged the deck towards them. They looked out of place with their masked, lopsided smiles and gigantic shoes. 'Once this boat is at sea we have ten more lifeboats. Keep calm, there is enough room for you all.'

Charity tried to count the men who lined up before him. He took Biba's hand and then turned to Mariah. He was gone.

'Did you see where Mariah went to?' he asked.

'I felt his arm around me and then nothing more,' she replied as she turned to see where he was.

'I will find him. Now get in the boat, you will have to go,' Charity said as Biba stepped into the lifeboat and took the last seat. The boat was lowered quickly and two men with long oars pushed the boat away from the keel. Biba looked back up to the ship that grew in size as she reached the water. It smelt of brine and engine oil. It steamed and sizzled as the lifeboat touched the water.

No one saw the hand that had snatched Mariah into the shadows of the quarterdeck lounge. He was dragged quickly, his heels dragging along the carpet as two men pulled him across the floor. He tried to speak but a hand squeezed his mouth tightly shut. The man smelt of French cologne that was bitter and stale.

'Say nothing,' whispered the voice. 'You belong to me.'

He was taken down several flights of stairs until he reached the door of the circus. There was the empty space where Mr Blake would always stand and collect the tickets. The doors were forced open and Mariah was pushed inside. He fell to the wet floor, which was covered by an inch of cold seawater. He looked up. Casper Vikash was locked in an empty tiger cage. He had been beaten. His face was bloody and bruised. Vikash looked as though he were dying.

In a large sedan chair sat a clown whom Mariah thought he had seen before. He was dressed as a pierrot, clad in white silk with a painted face and sad red lips.

'Markesan,' Mariah said as the man let go of him and dropped him into the water.

'How very true, Mariah Mundi. But not my real name,' he replied.

'Why have you brought me here?' Mariah asked. 'The ship is sinking.'

'Because, my dear friend, you are the most important thing in the whole world to me,' Markesan jabbered, throwing his voice about the room to sound like a mighty echo. 'You don't know how hard it has been for me to see you on this ship. The very presence of your face pains me greatly.'

260

'But I don't know you,' Mariah replied.

'But you should. I am the curse of your family and the Bureau of Antiquities,' he said in the voice of a child. 'Captain Charity once took something very precious from me and now I will do the same for him. Do you know his secret?'

'This is not the place or the time,' Vikash shouted breathlessly. 'Don't believe him, Mariah, he is a liar.'

'A dying man protecting the boy's feelings, Vikash? How gallant,' Markesan said. 'You see, Mariah, I once had a son. He joined the family business – a business of secrets, sold to the highest bidder. Captain Charity killed my son one starlit night in Paris. Now I will do the same.'

'Don't listen, Mariah it is all lies,' Vikash said.

'You are the son of Captain Jack Charity – the man you called your father took you and your mother as his wife and child for the sake of the good name of the Bureau. You are Mariah Charity . . .'

'My father is dead,' Mariah said.

'Oh, how I wish he were,' Markesan said painfully. 'I have waited for this day for many years and now that it has come I will rejoice and sleep at last.'

Mariah looked at Vikash.

'Is it true?' he asked.

'This is Markesan – he is a liar,' Vikash said as he slumped to the floor of the cage.

'Put him in with scarface – let them be drowned together,' Markesan said. 'Look at me, for not many have seen me or known my real name. You will both take this sight to the grave. And be thankful for it. As you can see, the water is rising quickly. I think you have perhaps only ten minutes of life – make good your time.'

The door to the cage was opened and Mariah was thrown in. Vikash lay on the floor. Mariah could see the marks of his beating. The cage was locked, bolted and then pushed against the wall.

'My ribs are broken,' Vikash whispered as Mariah knelt to help him. 'I have to get you from this place.'

'There shall be no escape,' Markesan said. 'My assistant knows the tigers well. They shall be released from their cage and guard you whilst the water rises. In the meantime I shall take my place on deck and pray to Hades for a rescue. Don't worry, Mariah. I will think of you down here with no air. How very, very sad.'

Markesan got up from the sedan chair. The water was now to his knees. He smiled at them both and waded to the door.

'Charity will find you, Markesan – your wages will be death,' Vikash shouted as his broken ribs cut at his lungs.

'Let out the tigers and follow me – make haste, my men, the ship is sinking.' Markesan laughed madly as he pushed open the doors and vanished into the darkness.

Mariah watched as two men pushed the tiger cage towards the exit. A rope was slung across the roof from the door. The two men stood behind the cage and then pulled on the rope and fastened it. Then the door opened and they ran from the circus.

Eduardo leapt out of the cage with Rollo close behind. They could sense danger and sought a way of escape.

'Did you find Biba?' Vikash asked. 'I knew you would look for her – is she safe?'

'She is on a lifeboat, away from the ship,' Mariah said. 'We have to get out of here.'

'There is a way,' Vikash said, 'but only for you – my time is near.'

Mariah looked down. The water was rising quicker than before. The ship moaned and juddered as the tigers sought higher ground on the bank of seats that surrounded the circus. Vikash staggered to his feet and took hold of the bars of the cage.

'If I can hold open the bars then you can escape,' Vikash said as he gripped a metal rod in each hand. 'When I pull the bars open you must squeeze through.'

'I won't go without you,' Mariah answered.

'You have to save yourself and help Charity. He is a good man,' Vikash replied.

'Is he my father?' Mariah asked as the ship creaked and a metal beam fell from the ceiling.

'Now!' Vikash shouted as he pulled against the bars with all his might, screaming in pain. Mariah pushed himself through the opening. He could feel Vikash weakening as he strained to keep the bars apart. 'I can't hold . . .'

Mariah slipped through just as Vikash lost his grip and fell to the floor. He jumped from the cage. The water was up to Mariah's waist. Vikash waved him on.

'I can't leave you,' Mariah protested as Eduardo roared and slashed the air with his claws.

'I don't cling to this world, Mariah. Eum in excelsis aliquando videbimus coelis. Life is about another place far greater than here . . . Go!'

Vikash breathed a deep sigh and his head fell to one side. All life was gone from him. As Mariah stared at his face it was as if the scars mellowed and fused back into his skin. Vikash gazed upwards. Mariah reached in and touched his eyelids to close them.

'Sleep well . . .' he said as he stepped back. Eduardo the tiger roared louder than Mariah had ever heard. He knew he could not save the beasts and would have to leave them to their fate.

He was soon on the walkway that led from the circus to the grand hallway at the centre of the ship. A double staircase of gold leaf swirled up and round to form a balcony, lit by the fading lights of the ship's emergency batteries. It was eerily empty. The water here was only a foot deep. Mariah took the stairs two at a time. It was bitterly cold. His sodden clothes stuck to him, drawing the heat from his body.

The *Triton* clung to life, even though he could hear the weight of the ship falling in on itself. It was as if it were about to split in two. By the grand staircase, a large crack ran up the walls and across the ceiling. Plaster dust fell like snow and the vast chandelier of glass and gold had already crashed to the floor. Mariah knew he was running out of time. From far away he could hear the sudden blasting of a steam whistle. It couldn't be? He thought – the *Ketos* . . .

Mariah remembered the sound when they had left Liverpool, sharp and shrill like the whistle of a steam train. It was the *Ketos* – he knew it.

He ran faster towards the outer deck. The battery lights were fading fast and the water was rising quickly. There was the sound of gunfire as salvage lines were fired at the *Triton*. Mariah could hear the crowds of passengers cheering and shouting as their fear turned to hope of rescue. Searchlights flashed across the water. The bow waves of the *Ketos* broke against the side of the ship; as it rocked sideways the deck was tilted towards the sea. The doorway on to the deck had been smashed open, and pieces of cloth hung from the broken glass of a nearby window. There was a crack that ran along the deck as far as he could see. The ship was breaking up. It was slow and silent but Mariah knew instinctively that its end would come suddenly.

'Mariah!' shouted Charity as he tied on a rope to the metal foremast. 'We must leave the ship.'

Mariah looked up. The *Ketos* now towered above them as the *Triton* took on more water. He looked about the deck. A handful of men waited to be hoist across the ravine of water to the liner.

'Is this it?' he asked.

264

'All safe as far as I can tell. Fifty lines strapped to the ship and we should have everyone off in no time at all. Where did you go?'

'Markesan – he found me. Casper Vikash . . . He's dead . . .' It was all that Mariah could say.

'Markesan – did you see him?' Charity asked.

'He said you were my father and because of that I had to die. Did you kill his son?' asked Mariah as the rescue buoy came closer.

'We sometimes do things that come back to haunt us,' Charity replied as the searchlight fixed upon them. 'This is for you – you must go now.'

Mariah strapped himself into the buoy as the rope took the strain. He looked back at Charity.

There was a sudden crashing sound as a crack ripped through the deck of the ship. It splintered the wood into a hail of shrapnel that blew upwards. Water exploded through the funnel, which blasted soot and ash high into the air and showered burning coals to the deck. The landing on which they stood began to break away from the ship as it began to sink.

'Hold on!' Mariah shouted to Charity as the rope tightened.

Charity grasped the buoy. He was pulled from his feet high into the air as he and Mariah dangled like flies trapped in a web. The sea bubbled beneath them. The *Triton* slipped slowly deeper and deeper into the cold, dark sea. The searchlight kept them in its glare. Mariah heard people screaming and he looked back to the swirling depths. Just for a moment, in the flickering lamplight, he thought he saw a tiger reaching up to him, claws outstretched.

In an instant it was gone. The rope was heaved and pulled as the winch spun faster. They shot higher until they landed on the deck of the *Ketos* in a pile of cargo nets.

Mariah didn't see the death of the *Triton*, but he heard its dying screams as it clung to life. It was as if the ship was crunched and chewed by a leviathan of the deep. The metal twisted as water spouted high into the air. The foghorn blasted several times until the water vanquished it. Within a minute, the *Triton* was no more. Like Atlantis, the glittering city now rested in the deep ocean.

Rushing to the side of the *Ketos*, Mariah looked down to where the *Triton* had once been. The water bubbled and boiled as the darkness of the sea finally consumed all that was the ship. There was a faint glow deep within the ocean that slowly dimmed. Then, as if from the sky, came a rumble of thunder. All around the *Ketos* was the debris of the ship. The flotsam bobbed on the wavelets – discarded travelling cases, crates of gin and a multitude of lost chattels floating on the sea.

'Charity – you are safe,' shouted the Marquis DeFeaux. Mariah looked up. On the balcony above them was the Marquis, and safe in his arms was Biba. 'Any news of Casper?' he asked.

Charity looked back to the sea and said nothing.

'How did you get here?' Mariah asked the Marquis.

'It was the goodness of the wind and the fortune of Tharakan,' he said. 'We were blown over the horizon and straight towards the *Ketos*. Tharakan brought the balloon down on the back of the ship. The only injury was to my wife. She broke her jaw. Quite fitting really, considering.' The Marquis looked down at Mariah. 'I owe you a debt of gratitude, Mariah Mundi. You saved my child.'

The Marquis let go of Biba and bade her to stay where she was. He walked down the steps and took Charity and Mariah to one side. The throngs of passengers from the *Triton* littered the deck in dishevelled but thankful huddles.

'Is he dead?' the Marquis asked boldly.

'He saved my life,' Mariah replied knowing he spoke of

Casper Vikash. 'He had been beaten by Markesan and his men – he would not have lived.'

The Marquis looked to the deck.

'He was a good son. I am only ashamed that I could not share him with the world. These are sad times, Mariah. People are people regardless of the colour of their skin. I am thankful I have one child left. Despite my riches, my life has been such a bitter experience,' he said solemnly as he took Mariah by the hand.

Mariah could feel the warmth of his fingers. It was as if the Marquis wished to impart something to him but words would not suffice. He looked him in the eyes.

'He was brave to the last,' Mariah said.

'I am sure of it,' the Marquis replied. 'As in life so in death.'

'Lorenzo Zane and Ellerby abandoned the ship before the explosions,' Charity said.

'We saw the *Bicameralist* pass over the ship en route to New York. I take it you think he was responsible?'

'The Zane Generator didn't work,' said Mariah.

'I know,' replied the Marquis. 'That is most probably why I was set adrift. I had argued with Zane about the very thing. He told me I was mad – to be patient and that his ship would win the race. I knew he was lying. I had the Captain turn the *Ketos*. Sad, what people will do for money – especially for gold.'

'The gold is quite safe,' Charity said to their surprise.

'But it was stolen from the *Triton* – a blackmail,' said the Marquis, quite astonished.

'It was never on the *Triton* to be stolen. It rests in Coutts Bank, Pall Mall, London,' Charity replied with a smile.

'But I saw it loaded onto the lifeboat, ingot by ingot,' he replied.

'That is what you thought you saw. The Bureau knew of a plan to steal the gold so I took the liberty of replacing it with lead and gold leaf,' Charity said. 'The money is quite safe.'

'And I took the liberty of winning the *Ketos* back from Lord Bonham when we played poker last night,' said the Marquis. 'One thing troubles me – Markesan . . . Does he work for Zane?'

'It is certain,' Charity said quietly. 'Until he is captured then none of us are safe, and I am sure he is now on the *Ketos*.'

26

Grimm & Grendel

MARIAH had never seen anything like the crystal ball-room of the *Ketos*. If he had thought that the *Triton* was grand and magnificent, the *Ketos* was astounding. The ball-room was three storeys high with a vast crystal chandelier that moved like a procession of stars across the night sky. The walls were decorated with gigantic crystal mirrors. In the centre of the room was a mahogany dance floor that remained level, regardless of the pounding of the sea, having a balancing mechanism that counteracted the movement of the ship. On a night like this, that didn't matter. The sea was still calm. Mariah's last glimpse of the ocean had been when the Marquis DeFeaux had invited Charity and Mariah to dinner. He had told them to be there within the hour and had arranged fresh clothes for them both and a cabin in which to change.

Mariah had wanted to ask Charity more about him being his father. He was sure that Casper Vikash had wanted to save him from harm. He had waited for the right moment but, like so many things, that moment never came. Now they stood at the entrance to the crystal ballroom and waited to be seated.

Life on board the *Ketos* appeared different. It was brighter, bolder and more alive. The ship echoed with laughter and the air smelt of lilies and lavender. The crew nodded politely when they passed by and would often stop and engage the passengers in conversation. The passengers from the *Triton* had been accommodated immediately, the passengers on the *Ketos* offering to share their cabins and what clothes they had. All in all, Mariah now wished he had travelled on this ship. The only thing that took the thought from his mind was that he knew he would not have met Biba DeFeaux. She was now all he could think of. When he had seen her standing next to her father, his heart had raced. But Mariah had not had the chance to speak to her since their escape from the *Triton*. He searched the ballroom with his eyes, hoping to get a glimpse of her. She was nowhere to be seen.

'Who are we eating with?' Mariah asked impatiently.

'I presume the Marquis,' Charity said as the waiter approached with a swagger. 'He invited us here.'

The waiter sneered at Charity. He looked at the ill-fitting suit.

'From the *Triton*?' he asked. They both nodded. 'Messrs Charity and Mundi, by chance? This way . . .'

The waiter didn't need a reply. He led them across the ballroom to a large alcove with its own brass-framed picture window overlooking the sea. In the centre of the large leather-clad booth was a long table gowned in crisp white linen. As Mariah approached he saw the Marquis, his wife and a younger man with bright blue eyes.

'Lord Bonham,' Charity whispered without being seen. 'He was once an actor – star of the London stage.'

Bonham got to his feet and began to applaud their arrival. He nodded to the band. Instinctively, they ended the waltz they were playing. Those gathered before them stopped dancing and turned to Bonham. He took a deep breath.

'Ladies, gentlemen, friends . . . We are honoured to have with us Captain Jack Charity and Mariah Mundi – saviours of the *Triton*.' Lord Bonham applauded yet again as everyone in the room stood and clapped.

Charity tried to look grateful. He hated the limelight. Mariah stood in his shadow and stared at the hundreds of faces that looked straight at him.

'Thank you,' Charity said as he bade them to stop. 'There were others far braver than we . . .'

'Nonsense,' Bonham said as he offered them both their seats at the table. 'I have heard that you stopped a disaster and saved Biba – what could be more heroic than that?'

There was something about him that Mariah didn't like. He sensed Charity felt the same. Bonham was flash and had a smile tinged with arrogance and eyes that never rested upon you. He was taller than Charity and fatter, with twisted locks of auburn hair and a ruddy face. He looked constantly about the room with eyes that danced to see the next and more exciting thing.

'She is a friend,' Mariah said naively.

'We have had the crew locked away – I hear they abandoned ship and didn't help the passengers,' Bonham said, ignoring Mariah. 'What a dastardly thing – were they French?'

'Is Biba well?' Mariah asked the Marquis.

He smiled benignly. 'She has not taken the news of Casper's death at all well. And she is still disturbed by her encounter with Shanjing.'

Mariah attempted a reply.

'Fancy that – the whole world thought he was a puppet and all along it was a man in disguise – a man-mannequin. I would have paid more to see him than watch a ventriloquist,' Bonham interrupted.

Mergyn DeFeaux could say nothing. She sat at the end of the table, her jaw wired into a steel cradle. A device looking like a globe of the world had been placed on her head; it held her chin rigidly in its grip and stopped the head from moving.

'I hope you will soon be well,' Charity said politely.

'When they crashed, Mergyn hit the deck so hard it broke her jaw,' Bonham blustered like a schoolboy fresh from vacation. 'Tharakan landed on top of her and they all spilled out on to the rear of the ship. Best entertainment I have had in years.' Mergyn DeFeaux winced painfully. Mariah wished Lorenzo Zane could see her now.

'I hear you have lost the ship at cards, Lord Bonham,' Charity replied hoping the reminder would still his hyperactivity.

'But we play again tonight. This time I hope to win it back,' Bonham said. 'DeFeaux tells me the gold is safe in London. Inspired work, Charity, inspired work.'

The food was served. Mariah didn't want to eat. He slipped back into the oval bench seat and watched the dancing. He felt as if he were on the edge of a dream. Lord Bonham talked and told tales, seldom stopping for food or breath as one course after another came and went. Mergyn DeFeaux couldn't eat. She sat quite still. Her head was firmly held in the wired cage that pushed out her cheeks so that she resembled a Thanksgiving turkey.

As the others talked, Mariah watched the dancers. They swirled back and forth with seldom a foot out of place. In their own way they were mesmerising. They allowed him to dream comfortably as if he were barely part of the dinner gathering. Bonham talked, cigars were lit and the dancing slowed. The lamps on the chandelier were dimmed and a starball glittered, sending shards of light hypnotically around the room.

It was then that Mariah noticed a rather odd couple dancing in the far corner of the room. Unlike the others who swept about the ballroom floor as if they were wildebeest on a savannah, these two kept to one place.

The man who danced appeared to be very uncomfortable, as if he wore the shoes of someone else. His partner, a tall woman with a billow of curls, dragged him around and around in smaller circles.

Mariah gulped and took a sharp breath. He stared at the man in disbelief and shuddered. Charity was engrossed in conversation with the Marquis as Bonham talked on, not realising that neither was listening. Mariah stared and stared.

'Mr Grimm,' he muttered to himself as he remembered the man who on several occasions had tried to kill him. 'It can't be.'

But there was no doubt – it was Grimm. Mariah could never forget a face, especially one as sharp and keen as Mr Grimm's. This had been the man who with his partner Grendel had assisted Gormenberg and then the wicked Bardolph in all their treachery. Yet even though they had been the enemy of Jack Charity and the Bureau for so long, Mariah pitied them. They had left England to start a new life in San Francisco. He now knew that they had chosen the *Ketos* on which to make the journey.

It was when Mariah gave particular attention to Mr Grimm's dancing companion that he realised who it was. Under the fine long dress and bouffant curls lurked another familiar face. This was Mr Grendel. His nails had been trimmed and face shaved, but the eyes – the eyes that stared through you as if they looked on another world – were the same.

Mariah looked to Charity and wondered if he should interrupt him to tell him the news. Grimm and Grendel danced to an even darker place in the shadows. Mariah watched them intently. They seemed to be actually enjoying what they were doing. Grendel made a particularly fine lady. So much so that he even caught the admiring eye of a drunken Hussar standing nearby.

Mariah slipped unnoticed from the table, followed by a small waiter with a towel over his arm and a glass of soda on a silver tray. Charity, the Marquis and now Bonham had drawn close together, deep in conversation, wrapped in a cocoon of thick blue cigar smoke. He crossed the ballroom, weaving in and out of the dancers until he came to near where Grimm and Grendel danced passionately. Grendel swirled Mr Grimm until his feet spun from the floor. Grimm giggled as he danced. Mariah thought he had never seen anyone so happy.

The music was silenced. Grimm turned to applaud and then stopped. His hands were motionless. He stared as if he had seen a ghost.

'Is it really *you*?' he asked Mariah as Grendel pulled a fan from his purse to cover his face.

'I've missed you, Mr Grimm,' Mariah said as the music started again for the next dance.

Grimm looked at Grendel.

'We are undone,' he hissed feverishly as his face turned crimson.

Grendel fanned frantically. He stared at Mariah and then to the door as if he were about to take to his high heels and run.

'You are on a ship, Mr Grendel,' Mariah said as he took a step closer to avoid being trampled by the hoards of dancers milling around him. 'There is nowhere to hide. Anyway, I wouldn't stop you. Not when you're trying to make a new start in America.'

'Is Captain Charity with you?' Grendel asked, resting the fan on his nose.

'Of course,' replied Mariah as Grendel took a step further into the shadows.

'And the Bureau of Antiquities?'

'Everywhere – as we speak,' Mariah said as he grinned elfishly.

'Then, Mr Grimm, we are certainly undone and shall be

returned to England for our crimes.' Grendel sat heavily on a chair and sighed.

'But we were to start a new life away from all that we had done. I would never have killed you – you do know that. I did have my chance but would never have done it,' Grimm pleaded.

'Then why did you work for them?' Mariah asked. 'You knew Gormenberg was a madman and Bardolph a murderer.'

'They knew things . . . things about Grimm and I that would have made life very difficult,' Grendel said as he looked up at Mariah, knowing that it was pointless lying. 'Leaving England is all we can do. Now you have found us life will be over.'

'Why should that be?' Mariah asked.

'Wanted men, that's what we are,' Grimm replied sadly, as if a full understanding of his life flashed before him.

'Only if someone saw you. All I can see is a gentleman and his lady dancing on an ocean voyage. I see no villains – or detectives,' Mariah said as he laughed.

Grimm looked tearfully at Grendel.

'Do you mean –' Grimm asked.

'Forgiven,' replied Mariah. 'As far as I am concerned. But you better keep out of Captain Jack's way until New York.'

'Confined to cabin,' Grimm chirped thankfully.

'Never to be seen until Pier 91 on the Hudson River,' added Grendel. 'Why are you here?'

Mariah was taken by surprise. He hadn't thought he would be asked this question by Grendel.

'Bureau business,' he said politely, knowing he should say no more.

'You wouldn't be looking for a Mr Markesan, would you?' Grimm asked. He could see from the look on Mariah's face that this was the case. 'Thing is,' he went on, 'I once saw Gormenberg talking to a man called Markesan at the Prince Regent. It was not long before you arrived. Next time I saw him, he was getting off a lifeboat and onto the *Ketos* . . . I couldn't believe my eyes. Now it all makes sense.'

'So you know what he looks like?' Mariah asked in disbelief.

'Would never forget a face. You know me, Mariah. I am a detective,' Grimm said proudly as if it were a badge of honour. 'Funny thing was that he didn't stay close with the passengers. It was as if he'd done something on the *Triton*.'

'And,' Grendel added, 'I saw him clearly. Accompanied by a man dressed as a clown.'

A waiter stepped forward, as if from nowhere. He looked at Mariah and offered him the glass of soda.

'With the regards of Captain Charity,' he said as he disappeared quickly.

Mariah thought nothing of taking the glass and drinking from it. The soda was ice cold and bitter and fizzed in his mouth. Grimm and Grendel saw the look on Mariah's face. It was as if he was reliving all that had gone on in the circus – the colour bleached from him and his head swam as he stared at the floor.

'Did he do something terrible?' Grimm asked, his voice swift and concerned.

Mariah nodded. The heat of the room seemed suddenly to clutch at him with burning fingers. His collar tightened and hands throbbed with pain.

'Then you better be finding him, Mariah. You look not well – I'll tell Charity,' Grendel said as he stood up and took a step forward.

'No . . . I just need some air. I don't know what it is,' Mariah said as he handed Grendel his glass and stepped towards the doors. The waiter followed. He pushed a trolley covered with half-eaten desserts.

Grendel watched as Mariah pushed open the doors to the deck and stepped outside.

'Do you think he is well?' he asked Grimm.

'We will have to stay in our cabin until we are in New York. I can't see Charity being so charitable.' Grimm laughed.

Grendel turned again. Mariah was gone. He sniffed the glass from which Mariah had drunk – there was the faint aroma of beetroot and burnt wax.

'Poisoned! The waiter,' he said as he gave chase. 'Quickly, Grimm – he has Mariah.'

The detective realised what had taken place. Mariah had been given laudanum. They rushed from the ballroom.

From the far side of the ballroom Charity saw the commotion. 'Grimm!' he shouted as he leapt to his feet and ran after them.

Grimm and Grendel were ahead of him. Despite being six feet tall, wearing a long dress and stiletto heels, Grendel was quite sprightly. He was a yard faster than Grimm, who found it difficult to run. Ahead of them they saw the waiter running with the trolley of food. An arm flopped out from underneath the white cloth.

'Look, he has him,' shouted Grimm as they gave chase through the promenading passengers taking the night air.

'Stop! Stop that man!' Grendel shouted in a deep voice as a woman looked at him and then fainted.

They ran on. Grimm and Grendel chased the waiter and Charity chased them.

The waiter ran faster. The trolley was out of control but he soon reached the end of the deck. Grimm saw him pull Mariah's limp body from under the cart.

'No!' screamed Grendel as he careered towards the waiter at great speed on the polished deck.

The waiter lifted Mariah towards the railings. He heaved him over the top and then grabbed hold of his legs as if to tip him in the sea. Turning, he was taken aback by the sight of a

277

giant, screaming woman with the voice of a man coming towards him.

Grendel skated towards him on the polished wooden deck with Grimm close behind. The waiter pushed Mariah as hard as he could. Grendel slid towards him, unable to stop, and hit the waiter with such force that the sound of the man's groan echoed across the deck. Grimm grabbed Mariah just as he was about to fall, clutching at his legs and holding tight. The boy slumped forward as his weight pulled him to the sea below. The waiter fell into a crumpled heap on the deck with Grendel on top of him.

'Got you!' Grimm screamed as he pulled Mariah back on to the ship.

Charity took aim with his pistol. 'Let go and you will be a dead man, Mr Grimm,' he said with a hate-filled voice. 'Nothing would give me greater pleasure.'

Grimm clutched Mariah even tighter as Grendel struggled to his feet. Red lipstick was now smeared across his face and his curled, bouffant wig was torn to one side. It made him look like a macabre monster, a half-man, half-woman vampire that never slept.

'It's not as it seems, Mr Charity,' Grimm pleaded.

'Then say nothing more and do not let go of Mariah Mundi,' Charity said.

27

Pier 91

THE sun was barely breaking through the mist of the eastern horizon as the *Ketos* sailed quietly towards Bedloe's Island in the bay of New York. Liberty reached upwards with her flaming hand and her words of righteousness as if to welcome them. The deck of the ship was crowded with those passengers wanting to look at New York for the first time. The city was shrouded in smog. The large finger of a skyscraper reached upwards. At its very top, tied to the scaffolding of the newly built tower, was the *Bicameralist*. It floated above the world unashamed and arrogant.

In the captain's wardroom in the aft of the ship, Mariah Mundi banged his fist on to the long, oak table.

'You can't send them back, Captain Jack. They saved my life,' he shouted angrily.

'They are wanted men – wanted by the Bureau of Antiquities,' he replied. He clicked the lock of a pair of handcuffs as he spoke.

'But they helped me . . . They are leaving the old life behind and starting again – what good would it be to take them back?' Mariah pleaded.

'He's right, Captain. We have no intention of going back to what we did,' Grimm said as Grendel nursed his bloody nose from where he had struck the waiter.

'That is not the case. You have been arrested and I am duty bound –' Charity was about to go on before Mariah broke in.

'They have seen Markesan,' he said, remembering what Grendel had told him.

Charity looked at him, surprised.

'I was captured by Markeson myself on the *Triton*,' Mariah went on. 'But he was dressed as a pierrot and his face was painted. These men have seen him as he is, and would recognise him again.'

Charity turned to Grimm and Grendel. 'Markesan – do you know him?' he asked hurriedly, as if the mention of his name would bring a curse on them all.

'Saw him at the Prince Regent. Honest, Captain Charity, we could help you,' said Grendel with a smile.

Charity looked at him. Grendel was still wearing the wig and the long dress. His face was smeared in gaudy make-up. In the morning light he looked like an aberration of humanity.

'It would not be right, Mariah. Just think of what these men have done – think of what they are,' Charity replied.

'They want to be different – to live a different life and put the past behind them. I know they would have killed me given the chance, but don't their actions prove the state of their heart? It would have been easier for them to allow that man to take me and cast me to the deep. Instead they chose to run after me and risk being captured – to save me.'

'He argues well,' said the Marquis from the back of the room. 'And they are our only hope of finding Markesan – the man who killed Casper.'

Charity thought for a moment as he looked at Grimm and Grendel. They sat meekly, looking at the floor. Grimm picked the skin of his fingertips as Grendel flickered his tongue like a snake.

'If you were to escape once you had helped us – where would you go?' he asked quietly.

Grimm did not hear him. Grendel nudged his companion in the side with a sharp elbow.

'Where would we go if we escaped?' he asked.

'If we tell them they will find us,' Grimm replied in a whisper.

'Charity wants to know – what city are we bound for?' Grendel asked.

Grimm looked confused. He stared blankly at Grendel, hoping he would speak for him.

'It's not that I would follow you, but I have to be convinced that I would never see you again,' Charity said as he walked towards them and stared Grimm in the face, nose to nose. 'Where are you bound?'

'San Francisco,' Grimm said nervously.

'And you promise you will never return?' he asked.

'Promise,' Grendel said as he nudged Grimm again.

'Very well, Mariah – set them free,' Charity said as he turned from them. 'If they find Markesan they will have earned their freedom.'

Mariah felt unsure. There was something about the way that Charity spoke that made him feel uneasy. He had given in too quickly; Mariah knew that was not like him. He knew he had a plan.

'But how will we find Markesan?' Mariah asked.

'We will put our new friends by the gangplank when we dock at Pier 91. They will be able to see everyone who leaves the ship and tell us if they find Markesan. We will have men ready and waiting,' Charity replied.

Mariah could see there was more to the plan than this. Charity schemed. Mariah could see it in his face. Whenever

Charity plotted, he would never look at Mariah and always scratched the back of his hand.

'Shall I see to it?' Mariah asked. Charity nodded. 'And leave them just as they are?'

'Of course. This is how they intend to lead a new life – so let it be from now.' Charity smiled.

'We dock in one hour. The *Ketos* will deliver its passengers on the port side on Deck 6. Just by the grand staircase,' said the Marquis.

'So, Mariah, I will leave it all to you,' Charity said as if he were exasperated with him for some misdeed.

'You will leave the boy alone?' asked the Marquis.

'If he can plead the case so eloquently for those who would see him dead, he is capable of looking after them for the next hour,' Charity moaned puckishly as he and the Marquis left the room.

'He doesn't trust us,' said Grendel nervously. 'I could tell it from his face. I'm not a detective for nothing.'

'Then you better make sure you can identify Markesan when he leaves the ship,' replied Mariah.

'Well,' protested Grimm. 'It might not be that easy. People do change – he could have put on another disguise.'

For the next hour Mariah listened to their excuses. The ship got nearer and nearer to Pier 91. The crowds on the quayside cheered and rockets were launched in celebration. Grimm, Grendel and Mariah went to the grand staircase and waited for the sea doors to be opened. They could hear the shouting, the brass bands and the cannons being fired in Central Park.

Inside the ship the passengers waited. The Marquis had arranged for all those who had travelled on the *Ketos* to disembark first. He knew that they would tell those waiting of the disaster they had seen on the ocean and the loss of the *Triton*. He knew it would give time for the Press to lie in wait for all who were survivors of the disaster. It would also give time for news of the strange guard on the door of the ship to spread through the crew. He had made it no secret that they were on the lookout for a stowaway – a dangerous man whom only they could recognise.

The final cannon fired and its blast echoed through the streets of New York. Grimm and Grendel stood by the sea doors. To those leaving the ship they were a marvellous spectacle – 'the painted lady and her beau', as one American woman with a small pug dog with a prettier face than her own remarked cordially.

Grimm and Grendel watched everyone who left the ship. They did not see Markesan. He was not in the long line of fine ladies who had travelled alone, neither was he with the bedraggled survivors who had come from the *Triton*. He was not, as was soon discovered, hiding in the petticoats of a rather large lady who insisted that Grimm searched her for a stowaway.

Outside the ship on the quay, the brass band had stopped playing. The lines were almost at an end when three men came towards the exit near the grand staircase carrying a long narrow trunk made of leather and wood. Mariah watched them approach. They neither spoke to each other nor glanced at their companions, but kept their gaze fixed on the door and the world outside.

Grendel looked at each one of them and shook his head.

'Not them,' he said as he saw the handful of people that were left. 'He is not here.'

'But he has to be – he can't have got away from the ship,' Mariah replied. 'There are guards on the quayside.'

The three men pushed the case towards the door. One of them brushed close to Mariah. He smelt of cologne – it was bitter and stale. He had smelt it before on the night Markesan had tried to kill him.

'You!' he shouted 'It was you!'

The man looked surprised and turned away to hide his face.

'He doesn't speak English,' said his companion. 'He is a stranger to this land.'

'Let me see his hands,' Mariah demanded.

'No,' said the man as he pushed Mariah away from him and made for the doors.

'It's him!' he cried as he gave chase.

The man grabbed hold of Grendel and threw him to the floor. His companions ran to the gangway. One jumped from the ship to the river below. The swell moved the *Ketos* back towards the quayside as the man fell, and he was caught by the hull of the ship against the wooden balustrade of Pier 91. There was a sound like the crushing of a snail shell. A cry and a scream came from those still leaving the customs house. No one dared to look.

Mariah gave chase after the others, quickly followed by Grimm and Grendel who now felt they were his protectors.

They never saw the case of leather and wood open by itself. The lid slammed to the carpeted floor and a man stood up at the back of the crowd that had gathered by the door to watch the distraction. He straightened the tie and collar of his crisp white shirt and pulled the lapels of his checked jacket into place. With one hand he squeezed the ribs of an umbrella tightly. Without being seen he joined the crowd of onlookers who watched young Mariah chase the fleeing men into the arms of several waiting customs officers.

Charity approached and tapped the man on his shoulders. 'I thought you would find a more exciting way of escaping?' he said.

'You must be Jack Charity,' the man said without turning.

'Charlemagne – or is it Markesan?' Charity asked.

'What would you like to call me?' the man replied.

'Eric Bloodstone . . . from Wigan,' Charity said as he clicked a handcuff onto the man's wrist. 'Why didn't you kill me when you had the chance?'

'It would have taken all the fun out of the game,' Markesan replied. 'I enjoyed being close to you. It gave me satisfaction in a way you would never understand.'

'But you were caught,' he said.

'The only people who could recognise me just happened to be on this ship. I noticed them when I came aboard from the *Triton*. I thought I had escaped. Gormenberg assured me that Grimm and Grendel would be disposed of,' he said solemnly as he turned to look at Charity. 'A twist of fate?'

'I prayed that I would find you,' Charity said as he took him by the arm.

'So all this was just an elaborate way of having me caught?' Markesan asked as he fumbled discreetly in his pocket.

'Of course,' Charity replied.

Mariah pushed his way through the host of people who had gathered by the sea doors. Grimm and Grendel appeared to be more reluctant to show their faces.

'So now you can see me face to face, Mariah Mundi,' Markesan said as Charity twisted his arm into his back. 'Tell me one thing before this brute beast does what he has been waiting to do for years. How did you escape from the circus?'

'Casper Vikash – he died so that I could live,' said Mariah. 'So it was you all along. You wanted me dead. I sat with you and talked to Shanjing and you never said.'

'One day you will understand – revenge is best done when the blood runs hot,' Markesan said as Charity pushed him towards the doors. 'And Shanjing, what was his fate?'

'Eaten by tigers when he tried to kill Biba DeFeaux,' said Mariah as he looked hard at Markesan so he would never forget his face.

'I am surprised he didn't try to escape – perhaps like this . . .'

Markesan threw a handful of purple dust high into the air. It fell like snow until it touched the floor and then there was a sudden, loud, blinding explosion and a ball of silver fire engulfed the crowd. Charity was blown back, his hands locked together by an unseen force. The fireball overwhelmed them all. The magician's flames were cold as ice, the smoke like thick treacle. Charity reached out to grab the shadow of Markesan. He found his hands were manacled together.

'Mariah, quickly!' he shouted. 'The key is in my pocket.'

Mariah wiped the smoke from his face. He found the key and fumbled to unlock the handcuffs. Charity struggled to break free as he set off to give chase after Markesan.

'Leave him to me,' Charity shouted as he ran down the grand staircase to the lower deck. 'He is mine . . .'

No one moved. Everyone stood in awe of the explosion. Grimm and Grendel lay dazed on the floor as others tried to get to their feet.

Mariah looked at them momentarily and then gave chase. He could hear Charity shouting for Markesan to stop. Explosion after explosion rang out as Markesan threw more of the coloured dust as he ran. Mariah followed on. He ran faster, gaining ground on them quickly, and soon he could see Markesan ahead. He burst through the heavy wooden doors and onto the lower deck.

'Don't be stupid, Mariah,' Charity shouted, out of breath. 'Leave him to me.'

'Not this time,' Mariah bellowed as he ran. 'He was going to kill me and for that he will not get away.'

As he emerged onto the deck Mariah looked up and glimpsed the New York skyline. The *Bicameralist* was high above him, still tethered to the Manhattan tower. Markesan gave it little thought. He twisted in and out of the scattered canvas chairs that littered the sun deck as he ran on. Every now and then he reached into his pocket and threw a handful of dust. It exploded in silver flames and momentarily blocked him from view.

Charity was three paces behind and out of breath. Mariah pressed on, running faster than ever. He gained on Markesan and was now just a few yards behind him. Markesan turned. He looked at Mariah and laughed as he took hold of a ladder that led up to the next deck. It was as if he waited for Mariah to get near.

'You'll have to be quicker than that to catch me,' Markesan shouted just as Mariah took hold of his leg.

'Let him go!' shouted Charity from behind as Mariah looked up.

He saw Markesan reach into the pocket of his coat, pull out a handful of dust and throw it like a salt curse over his shoulder. Mariah couldn't escape. The dust fell about him. It exploded on his chest, knocking him to the floor. The Spiderweb took the force of the blast. He heard a gunshot. Markesan shrieked.

'You cheated, Jack Charity . . . you shot me,' Markesan shouted indignantly as he clutched the bleeding wound on his leg. 'That is not how it was to be.'

'I've given up on your games, Markesan,' replied Charity as he took aim again.

Mariah could just see Markesan as he leapt from the ladder to the bridge of the ship. It was as if he were a large plaid cat in a checked suit and dazzling shoes. He vanished above them, only to be seen again on the long red ladder that led to the top of the funnel.

'My turn,' Charity said as he went after Markesan with Mariah close behind.

'We have to catch him before he escapes,' said Mariah, climbing to the bridge as fast as he could.

'That's not what I intend to do,' Charity replied as he ran across the roof of the bridge towards the funnel.

'He'll never escape from up there, there's nowhere to go,' said Mariah as he looked at Markesan high above them, almost at the top of the funnel.

'He has a plan of escape – Markesan is not a cornered cat,' Charity replied as he took aim and then quickly fired. The bullet smashed into the metal just below Markesan's feet.

'Too late,' he shouted as he began to pull at the sleeves of his coat. 'I will be away from this place.'

Charity took to the ladder as Mariah watched from the roof of the bridge. He climbed quickly as up above him Markesan pulled more at his sleeves until a furl of cloth hung down from under both arms.

'He's going to fly!' Mariah shouted as he realised what Markesan had planned.

'So right, Mariah – you work for the wrong side,' Markesan said as he held out his arms to the sky and stood on the edge of the funnel high above Pier 91.

Charity stopped on the ladder. He raised his pistol and took aim. Markesan looked back and smiled just as he pulled the trigger.

Mariah watched him fall like a stone as the silk batwings released from his coat swirled about him.

'No!' he screamed as the man crashed towards the earth.

It was as if Markesan heard his cry. Just before he crashed to the deck of the *Ketos*, Markesan opened his arms as wide as he could.

The wind roared across the batwings. Markesan pitched to one side. Instead of smashing to the deck, he suddenly flew towards Mariah. He laughed manically.

'Never too late for a perfect escape,' he shouted as he soared ʰˢ the Hudson River.

There was a crack as a pistol shot rang out. It echoed from the high walls of the Manhattan buildings. Markesan instinctively pulled his arm towards him and span quickly over the side of the ship. Mariah ran to the railings and looked down.

On the dark water of the Hudson River were the remains of Markesan's flying jacket. They floated momentarily before sinking into the murky water.

'Dead,' he said as Charity stood beside him.

'He would have done the same to you if he had the chance,' Charity replied.

'Then it's over?' Mariah asked.

Charity turned and looked up at the *Bicameralist* tied high above them to the tallest building in the world. It reached up from the streets below as the mist swirled around its base.

'Over?' asked Charity in his relentless way. 'It's only just beginning.'

[28]

The Eulogian Tower

THE smell of easy-over eggs and thin slices of bacon filled the stateroom. The Marquis DeFeaux and his daughter Biba sat at the oak table by the window. Madame DeFeaux was not to be seen. As soon as the ship had docked she had left by the private gangway reserved for the owner of the ship. She had taken a set of cases packed with clothes and had left a note to say that she would not return. Biba didn't seem to care very much about the news as she sat close to her father trying to read his copy of the *Tribune* that had been given to him by Lord Bonham.

Mariah sat on the long leather sofa in the window bay looking out at the streets below. He didn't feel hungry, even though the sweet smell of hot eggs made him think of home. He had two preoccupations that erased the desire to eat or sleep. When he closed his eyes, he could still see Topher standing in his cabin on the *Triton*. That night he had been so real, more than a ghost or apparition. He had talked to him, followed him, and if he hadn't been found would have gladly followed him into the sea.

Captain Jack had told him that he had been poisoned and

that the thoughts would leave him as the narcotic subsided. But now, as he sat looking at the vast buildings around him, he knew it was not the case. Topher seemed real, alive and still there. He was on the edge of dreaming, waiting for Mariah to fall asleep.

The other thought that plagued him concerned Captain Charity. Since he had asked him if he was his father, Charity had grown distant. It was as if he no longer wanted to share those things which before had come so naturally. The mention of what Markesan had said had been a shard of ice that had cut into his heart. But Mariah knew he could not rest or be at peace until he had the truth. Even if it destroyed what they had, he would have to know.

The room was comfortably silent. The Marquis ate his eggs and Biba read the newspaper. Mariah was envious of them. They were content with each other and even in their lament for the loss of Casper Vikash it was as if they still had hope.

'The tower where the *Bicameralist* is – what is it called?' Mariah asked, wanting to spoil their silence together.

The Marquis looked up. 'That is the Eulogian Tower. It is the tallest building in the world.'

'Is that where Zane will be?' he asked.

'I should think Zane will be long gone. If he has found out that I am alive then he will flee to Greenland and take Mergyn with him,' the Marquis said as he sipped his coffee.

'Charity told father he was going after him,' Biba said as she got up from the table, crossed the room and stood by the window. 'Will you go as well?'

'Forbidden,' he replied tersely. 'Too young to die for the Bureau of Antiquities, I'm told. Charity is preparing now. He says I have to stay on the ship until he returns. The *Ketos* is returning to England in the morning and we will be on the ship.'

'Is that true, father?' she asked.

'It is so,' the Marquis said reluctantly. 'The life of Mariah Mundi has become a valuable thing. It would be too dangerous to allow him to go after Ellerby and Zane.'

'Then we can stay together. Since mother has left, we will return also. My father wants to build a new ship, bigger than before. It'll be called the *Biba*.'

'A ship named after you?' Mariah said, trying hard to sound enthused by the prospect.

'He has promised to have a swimming pool of heated sea-water to swim in and a circus without animals,' she replied wickedly.

'Who owns the Eulogian Tower?' Mariah asked as he looked out.

The Marquis wiped his mouth and neatly folded the napkin. He wrapped it in the silver ring embossed with a design of an old skull and two crossed bones.

'Theodore Backus,' he said calmly as he stood with Biba and looked up at the tallest building in the world.

It stood to the height of a mountain and was made of slabs of granite. There was still scaffolding on the lower floors. The tower seemed to grow like the neck of a gigantic dragon from a squat building with four turrets on the thirtieth floor that looked like the carved heads of Greek warriors. They stared down at the street below. The windows in each turret shone in the misty sunlight like glazed eyes. The building reminded Mariah of a pyramid that looked as though it were built on another pyramid. Even at that quiet time of the morning, he could see men working on the scaffolding, taking it down piece by piece.

It was impossible for them to see the full height of the tower. It had been shrouded in mist since the *Ketos* had docked at Pier 91. The *Bicameralist* appeared to be tethered to the side of the tower with several long ropes. It hung in the air, sometimes wrapped in grey cloud, sometimes completely invisible.

Mariah was surprised by the throngs of people that bustled in the streets below the ship. To those below, the *Ketos* must have looked like a gigantic skyscraper. It overshadowed every ship in the harbour and was the biggest liner ever to dock in New York. Even now, many hours after its arrival, people still stood on the quay and stared.

'Do they ever go away, the people down there?' Mariah asked. 'They have been on the quay for hours.'

'When we first came here, they lit fires and camped on the streets,' said the Marquis proudly. 'They even sang for us.'

The door of the stateroom opened and Charity stepped inside. He didn't look at Mariah. He stood in the doorway dressed for war in his brown boots, twill suit and waxed overcoat.

'I have made contact with our New York office,' he said to the Marquis. 'I intend to call on Lorenzo Zane. I shall not be alone. If you would be so kind as to care for Mariah until I return . . .'

He said nothing more. Without saying goodbye he turned and left the room.

'Thinks he's going to die,' Biba said strangely. 'That's what he means.'

'Nonsense, Biba. He has a lot on his mind. He can't take Mariah to a place like that. Not with Zane and Ellerby. It's best if he keeps it to the men of the Bureau.'

Mariah couldn't speak. He squeezed his lips together and clenched his teeth. This was not the place for tears. His anger surged as his thoughts raged at being left behind.

The Marquis seemed to know his mind.

'It wouldn't be good for you. Stay with us until he returns,' he said.

'And if he doesn't? If he dies – what then?' Mariah asked.

They both looked at Mariah. A single tear broke across his cheek as he breathed deeply. He turned and looked out of the window. Charity crossed the deck at that moment to the outer gangway. He turned back, stopped for an instant and raised his hand. It was more of a gesture to stay than a goodbye. It hurt like a knife to the heart.

'Go, you stupid man,' Mariah heard himself saying. 'Go and don't come back, just like fathers always do. I lost you once – will it be different this time? Bureau of Antiquities – Honour and Blood – what does it all mean?'

Biba tried to take hold of him. She put a hand on his shoulder. Mariah shrugged off her sympathy and ran from the room. He would not cry in front of them. It was not the way. He didn't care, Mariah told himself as he stood on the deck and watched.

On the quayside Charity met with a man in a dark suit and got into an open horseless carriage. It drove off through the crowded streets towards the Eulogian Tower, which seemed to loom over him like a dark sword about to fall. Mariah hated this town, the stink of the streets, the people who ran this way and that like rats. All he wanted to do was go back to the Prince Regent Hotel and the beautiful town by the sea.

'He will be back,' Biba said as she came from the stateroom and stood on the deck with him.

'That's a lie. He'll be dead. Charity against Lorenzo Zane and whoever else is in that tower – don't kid me, Biba.' Mariah started to walk away.

'He's left orders not to let you go from the ship. The deck guards will stop you – they know what you look like,' she said as Mariah walked down the steps to the promenade below. 'You'll never get from the ship . . . but I know a way.'

Mariah stopped and turned.

'How?' he asked suspiciously.

'There is one door that is never watched. I used it all the time when I lived on the ship. It's easy to find if you know the way,' Biba said as she smiled.

He knew she wanted to come with him. Mariah thought for a moment as he stared at her white face framed by the red curls of her hair that fell about her shoulders.

'But only to the Eulogian Tower. No further. It would be too dangerous for you,' he said.

Biba beckoned for him to follow. Soon they were several decks below the promenade in the darkest part of the ship. It was cold, damp and smelt of the sea. Mariah felt as though the whole ship was pressing in on him and would not let him escape. It was like being in a vast cavern whose chambers were linked by intricate and dangerous passageways. On every corner was a dim electric light that shone meagrely into the darkness.

'Soon be there,' Biba said as she took him down another set of iron steps to an even narrower passageway.

'I think you should stay here – what would your father say?' Mariah asked.

'I'm coming with you. I know you, Mariah Mundi. You will find yourself in trouble and I will raise the alarm,' Biba replied.

'But you won't come into the Tower?' he asked. 'Promise?'

Biba laughed.

The door from the ship was not what he expected. It was a small hatch where the rubbish was dumped at sea. The floor was covered with discarded trifle and cabbage leaves. A rat sat on an empty box chewing the leg of a roast chicken. It didn't seem to care as they got near, and continued to eat.

'No one will be watching this place. When I open the door we have to be quick. There's a ladder that will drop us onto the quayside. We have to keep our heads down and walk as if we are supposed to be there,' Biba said quickly as she turned the wheel of the hatch.

The door opened and the bustle and noise of New York billowed in like a breeze. Mariah climbed down the ladder and jumped the gap onto the quay. No one even bothered to look. A newspaper vendor shouted as he held up a paper with news of the sinking of the *Triton*. He read the headline: *Heiress Saved from Sinking Ship* . . . He looked at Biba and wondered if he would have to save her again.

The streets of New York were full of people and it took time to walk the several blocks towards the Eulogian Tower. The lower west side of Manhattan smelt like a giant restaurant. There seemed to be a coffee shop on every corner. They filled the streets with the bitter aroma of coffee and the sweet smell of hot waffles. Gangs of men stood in the doorways in shirt-sleeves and waistcoats. They ignored Mariah and Biba as they passed by, shouting to each other in Irish and Dutch.

The road from Pier 91 took them up a slight rise. The Eulogian Tower loomed over them, visible from the corner of every street. Mariah and Biba stopped and stepped back into a doorway to let a cart go by. There was no pavement and the street was so full that it was hard for anything to move. Mariah looked across the street to yet another coffee shop. This one seemed different. It had English windows with bubbled glass and there were seats outside under a candy-striped canopy. The waiter wore a white shirt with a black waistcoat that was neatly pressed. He saw them and smiled.

From inside the shop, just in the shadow of the canopy, Mariah could see someone waving to him.

'Grendel,' he said to Biba as he looked at the shady outline.

They slipped through the hordes of people, horses and carts and crossed the muddy road. Once inside the coffee shop, Mariah shivered as the warmth from the fire in the corner took away the chill of the street. Grimm and Grendel were perched like two large black crows next to the fireplace. They squatted on tall chairs, their long coats falling to the floor like black wings.

'A twist of fate,' said Grimm.

'An aberration of the ether,' replied Grendel.

'We have just seen Mr Charity. He came up this very street in a motor carriage. I take it you are on his track?' Grimm asked.

Mariah was reluctant to speak. He shrugged his shoulders.

'We are taking in the sights,' said Biba. 'Mariah will be taking the *Ketos* back to England. I said I would show him some of New York.'

'I love it when people tell lies,' Grimm said as he tugged the waiter by his arm and ordered them two hot chocolates. 'I don't think Hell's Kitchen is a place for sightseeing – do you, Mr Grendel?'

Grendel nodded in agreement as he slurped his coffee.

'You wouldn't be looking for the *Bicameralist*, would you?' he asked as the chocolate arrived in a large pot on a tray with two cups.

'He is . . . I told him not to come but I knew he wouldn't listen,' Biba said as Mariah kept silent.

Grimm and Grendel looked at each other and then drew very close. They spoke so quietly that neither Mariah nor Biba could hear them. They drank the chocolate and waited until the two men had finished their conversation.

'I think it would only be wise to offer our services as detectives. It would of course be for free as we feel you should be repaid for your kindness,' Grimm said as if he were addressing a judge.

'We could offer you protection and an insight into the criminal mind,' Grendel added.

Mariah looked scornfully at Biba. If she had kept silent then it would not be like this, he thought.

'On one condition. That when we get to the Eulogian Tower you leave me there and take Biba back to the *Ketos* safely,' Mariah said as Biba tried to protest.

Grimm and Grendel thought for a moment.

'I think that could be accommodated,' said Grimm as he sipped the last of his coffee from the cup. 'Whilst we are travelling, Grendel and I shall make a plan. You can't walk into such places without knowing what your enemies will do.'

Grimm seemed to be pleased with himself. He smiled cheerfully and warmed his back against the fire until his coat smouldered.

Outside the coffee shop, Grendel flagged down a taxi carriage. As it rattled through the streets towards Broadway, Grimm and Grendel were silent. Biba slipped her hand into Mariah's and held it tightly. He couldn't look at her for fear his eyes would give away his secret.

Grendel looked on wistfully. For the first time he saw Mariah in a new light. It was a pleasure to his eyes.

The carriage was soon on Broadway. The *Bicameralist* cast its shadow over the street. It clung to the Eulogian Tower like a broken branch swaying in the wind, caught only by the last tendon of wood. It was as if it would soon blow away and never be seen again.

As they got out of the carriage, Grimm watched Mariah looking up. 'You don't know where you are going – how to get there or what to do . . . Is that right?' he asked Mariah.

'I need to find Charity. I know he will be in trouble,' Mariah replied.

'But you can't be sure. He could walk out of the building at any moment with Lorenzo Zane under arrest,' Grendel said.

'We could wait,' added Biba thoughtfully. 'If he isn't out within the hour then we could look for him.'

'But you don't have a plan – life never works without a plan,'

Grimm said furiously. 'Gormenberg always had a plan – so did Inspector Walpole – but Mariah Mundi just turns up not knowing what to do . . .'

Biba laughed as Grimm jumped up and down like a frustrated child. His face was red with anger and he clenched his fists in rage.

'Just let me go alone and you can take Biba back to the *Ketos*,' Mariah said. He was watching the door to the Eulogian Tower, where one of the men he had seen Charity with stood by the motor carriage with his back to them.

'Shall I go and ask his driver what time Captain Charity will be coming out?' Grimm asked as he pointed to the man. 'It's obvious what he is doing – I am surprised the whole of New York doesn't know.'

Just as he spoke, two men walked down the steps from the door of the Tower. They wore long leather coats and small black hats. One of the men looked up and then down the busy street, then signalled the other to walk on. The man then talked to the Bureau agent standing by the motor carriage. Mariah could see that at first the agent didn't want to speak. The man from the Tower kept talking.

'Doesn't look good,' Grendel said. 'Seen that thing before – just watch, any moment now and they'll take him inside. If they do then Charity is caught – that's for sure.'

It was as if Grendel could see the future. All happened just as he said. The agent was led up the steps and back into the Tower. Mariah caught a glimpse of the man's face, and suddenly he realised who it was.

'It's Isambard Black,' Mariah said to Grimm, knowing what the name would mean to him.

'Then you are in even more distress than I first thought. How do you expect to get into the Tower?' Grimm asked.

'Perhaps there is a way,' said Grendel as he reached into his pocket and pulled out a small pistol that he cupped in his large hand.

Grimm laughed.

'Mariah Mundi, Biba DeFeaux – you are now our prisoners. Don't protest. I am sure that Grendel would be very prepared to use it should all else fail . . .'

'But –' said Mariah incredulously. 'You cheated us!'

'I never did such a thing. We brought you here and now we take you further. I am sure that Lorenzo Zane will be quite happy with what we have done and very financially rewarding.'

The Burning of
Theodore Backus

ON the thirty-eighth floor of the Eulogian Tower, Jack Charity sat in the office of Lorenzo Zane. It was minimal and neat, with a desk overlooking the window. There were three comfortable leather chairs spaced equally across the room. This didn't include the one in which Jack Charity was tied to by his hands and feet. As he waited for Lorenzo Zane he could hear an elevator whir back and forth.

'I have a friend of yours,' Zane said as he stepped from the elevator and came into the room with three other men. 'You left him in the street and we just picked him up – easy as that.'

'I am sorry, Isambard, I thought that I could convince Zane to come with us,' Charity said reluctantly.

'It is no problem, Jack,' he replied. 'They were very convincing with their arguments to accompany them.'

'We said we would throw you out of the window if he didn't come,' said the man in the long leather coat.

'Including the chair,' added his equally gothic companion.

Charity smiled. 'Then you have the upper hand,' he said nonchalantly. 'I suppose this is where we shall say goodbye to life?'

'On the contrary,' Zane said. 'Now I am a wanted man I will take you with me to Isbrae. It is the only place I will be safe. If I have two of the most important agents of the Bureau of Antiquities then I know I will be left alone.'

'Prisoners for life?' asked Isambard Black as one of the men tied his hands with coarse, rough string.

'Or until I can strike a deal with your employers. It would be far better in Isbrae than at the Prince Regent hotel. I stayed there once when it was owned by a man named Otto Luger,' Zane replied as the telephone on his desk began to ring. He picked up the receiver and listened. Charity could not hear what was being said to him. 'Tell her to go away and find someone else – tell her she is not wanted here.'

'Trouble?' Charity asked.

'Just a woman who left everything to be with me but didn't realise I only favoured her to get what I wanted,' Zane replied arrogantly.

'Mergyn DeFeaux?' asked Charity.

'Yes . . . an old friend of yours, if I am not mistaken. Were you not her beau?' Zane asked.

Charity said nothing as he looked at Black. He knew there was no way of escape. His hands and feet were tightly bound and he and Black were outnumbered.

'It seems strange that you should be in this situation. Surely you were the world's most celebrated inventor,' Black asked to gain time.

Zane shrivelled angrily.

'You wouldn't know what it is like to fall from grace, would you?' he asked sneeringly. 'I had everything I ever wanted until I was let down by a man falling into the generator. From then on the ship was destined to be a failure and that I could not accept. My career would be in ruins.'

'But your plan with Markesan –' Charity said.

'Was a coincidence. I now know he had planned to try and steal the gold and that sinking the *Triton* would be an added bonus,' he replied.

'And did you scheme to kill the Marquis in the hot air balloon?' Charity asked.

'That was Markesan. I just wanted to sink the ship. It is quite amazing how things in life can become so complicated,' Zane said as he looked at the man in the leather coat and smiled smugly. 'Sometimes, Charity, the chase is often better than the kill.'

'So how did you get Theodore Backus involved in your plot?' asked Isambard Black.

'There is no such person – it is me. I created him. He is a fiction, a front for all the money I stole from DeFeaux,' replied Zane.

'You sound quite pleased,' said Charity.

'I am. When I built the *Triton* and the *Bicameralist* I just added a few thousand dollars here and there. It soon adds up. Quite amazing how much you can steal. Enough to build the Eulogian Tower on prime New York real estate,' Zane gloated.

'And all with DeFeaux's money?' asked Charity.

'Every penny,' he replied as he nodded to the man in the leather coat. 'I set up the account with the help of Rhett Piper – perhaps you know him as Dedalus Zogel?'

'Skull and Bones?' said Charity.

'Precisely. This building is dedicated to our fine society. It is our grand tomb – a window on the world. It is our intention to provide the presidents of the United States and prime ministers of England for the next three hundred years. I am surprised no one has given you the tap,' said Zane. 'Zogel is the richest man in the world and gained that place through the Bones. He would be nothing without it.'

'A dangerous club for boys,' said Black sarcastically. 'As my close friend once said, I wouldn't be a part of any club that would have me as a member.'

Zane did not reply. He looked at the guards.

'I think it is time we departed to Isbrae. There is a storm coming and I would hate anything to happen to these fine men,' he said as he walked towards the elevator.

At that precise moment the doors opened and Ellerby threw two men into the room.

'I found these on the ground floor. They said they want to do a deal over something they have found,' said Ellerby as Grimm and Grendel got up from the floor and brushed themselves off. 'They have brought Mariah Mundi and Biba DeFeaux – thought you might be interested.'

'We kidnapped them – took them from the street by the ship and brought them here. Thought they might be of some use to you,' Grimm gabbled quickly as if he were short of breath. 'We met you once before, with Otto . . .'

Zane smiled.

'So it was you . . .' he said. 'I never forget a face. You are detectives.'

Ellerby came back into the room dragging Mariah Mundi and Biba DeFeaux with him.

'You may be detectives but you are also liars,' snarled Charity. 'You promised me and now you break that promise.' Then he looked at Mariah. 'I told you to stay on the ship.'

'And I knew you would get caught,' Mariah replied.

'But I can care for myself,' snapped Charity angrily.

'Gentlemen,' said Zane. 'This is not the time or the place. My good friends have done me a great favour for which they will be rewarded.'

'I will reward them with their eyes cut out on a plate,' shouted Charity as he tried to tear his hands from the bindings on the chair.

'Captain Jack Charity bound in a chair like a senile old man – what a sight for the world,' sneered Grendel.

'If I were not bound you would never dare speak that way. You are but a fat fool and a freak,' he said.

'Freak? Freak? Don't call me a freak, you feckwit,' screamed Grendel. He spat his words with bloodstained spittle and pulled a bear-blade from his coat. 'I will cut your throat . . .'

'Gentlemen!' bellowed Zane just as Grendel leapt onto the chair and pushed Charity back to the floor.

Isambard Black wasted no time. He kicked out at the guard, who crumpled to the floor. He dashed to Grendel, who was slashing at the chair with his knife. Mariah kicked Ellerby and ran to push Grendel from Jack Charity. He grabbed him by the waist but noticed that somehow the strands that had bound Charity had been cut through.

Grendel span around, grabbed Mariah by the coat and lifted him into the air.

'Do what I say,' he whispered. 'We will set Charity free.'

With that he threw Mariah across the room. He collided with Ellerby, pushing him from Black whom he had by the throat.

'Now,' Grendel said as he threw the knife to Mariah, 'cut him free.'

Mariah grabbed the knife from the air. He slashed at Black's binding just as Ellerby got up from the floor. Grendel picked Charity from the chair and pulled the cords from his wrists as Grimm gripped the man in the leather coat so he couldn't move.

'Stop them!' shouted Zane as he stepped back from the fight and searched the drawers of his desk.

In the heat of battle Biba had picked a large bronze statue of the Eulogian Tower from the table by the lift and had somehow managed to give a blinding blow to the other guard. He sat in a crumpled heap by the doors of the elevator.

'It was the only thing we could think to do,' Grendel said to Charity. 'Mariah had to believe he was our prisoner.'

'I would have killed you,' Charity said.

'I know,' said Grendel as the fighting went on and Ellerby tried to escape.

Black lashed out, hitting Ellerby as he began to run. He turned to see Zane by the far door that led to a circular staircase set in the wall of the building.

'You won't follow me from here,' Zane said as he pulled a brass lever by the side of the door. 'Very soon you will all be burnt to a crisp.'

Zane slammed the lever. All the doors and windows began to slowly close as lead shutters came down.

'Get from the room,' shouted Charity to Black. 'Take them with you.'

Black pushed Biba DeFeaux towards the open doors of the elevator. Grimm and Grendel ran to the stairs, managing to dive beneath the lead shutter before it closed. Sparks began to dance from the ceiling of the room. Just as the elevator doors closed, Charity saw Mariah on the floor. He realised there was no way of escape for them.

Zane stood by the door laughing.

'Lightning, my very own St Elmo's fire. But this time it will burn any man who gets in its way,' Zane said.

'Is that what you did in Greenland?' Mariah asked.

'Precisely. And that is what now burns through the ice and causes the sky to blaze at night,' replied Zane. 'But it will not bother you now, as you will become its victims.'

With that, Zane slammed the door. The room glistened with a radiant light that appeared to dance upon the furniture with a green glow. The was a dull buzzing that echoed as the ball-lightning danced about them. It floated around the room as if seeking them, growing more intense.

'Stay close to the floor,' Charity shouted. 'Don't let it touch you.'

Mariah crawled as low as he could towards the door through which Zane had escaped. He reached up and pulled the handle. A shard of blue static shot across the room and seared through his fingers. Mariah screamed in pain.

'Stay down!' Charity shouted. He sheltered behind Zane's desk as the corposant electricity fired at everything around him.

'We're trapped,' shouted Mariah as a blue flash struck the wall above him and ignited the picture of Zane's son.

'It's becoming more powerful – stay down,' shouted Charity anxiously, now hiding under the desk.

The lightning struck everything about him. As its power grew so it sparked the walls until they burst into flames. The room was slowly becoming enveloped in acrid smoke as the wallpaper dribbled like melting ice cream. The heat grew more intense as the corposants divided and divided, hovering above them like a hoard of baneful wasps.

Charity looked from his hiding place and saw the lights begin to gather above where Mariah huddled near to the door. It was as if they assembled by conscious thought, as if they had the power to communicate and knew whom they would kill.

One by one the glowing corposants joined together until they throbbed and boiled above Mariah. They became a blistering mass of fire that scorched the ceiling and shot bolts of lightning from their core. Charity watched as Mariah stared up at the core of fire above his head.

'It can see me,' Mariah shouted, covering his face with his hands.

Charity broke cover from the desk and ran across the room as fast as he could. He dived against the door, smashing it from its hinges. Then, without turning, he grabbed Mariah and pulled him through the opening.

'Run!' screamed Charity as he picked Mariah to his feet and pushed the broken door back into the burning room.

Mariah took to flight. The steps were steep and made of granite slabs tied into one another. Charity waited a moment before he followed. The acrid smoke was suddenly sucked towards the door as it found a way from the room. It was as if a ball of burning smoke rumbled towards him, flashing lightning as it rolled on.

Charity ran up the steps as Mariah raced ahead. He looked behind as the smoke billowed behind him like the head of a giant snake.

'Keep running,' he shouted as the flaming, sparking cloud drew closer.

Mariah pressed on, running for his life, too frightened to look back. He could smell the smoke. His coat and hair were singed from hiding below the fireball. Looking up he could see only a few feet ahead. The staircase spiralled out of sight. In the wall, every few feet were small leaded windows that allowed him to look at the city below. He cast a glance down. It was as if he were on a mountain. From behind he could hear Charity scream as he was engulfed in smoke. Mariah ran on. Then something inside him made him stop, a voice in his head screaming for him to go back. As he went on further, the voice grew louder. Mariah turned. The crackling ball of smoke and flame billowed towards him like a demon. He slipped down, pressing his face against the cold granite and covering his head with his arms.

The fireball crackled over him. It singed his coat. All was silent.

'Charity!' he shouted.

'Here,' came the reply.

Mariah ran down the steps. There was Charity. The smoke blackened his face.

'Thought you were dead,' Mariah said.

'So did I,' Charity replied with a laugh.

'I'm sorry – I'm sorry for the way I have been,' Mariah said as he gripped Charity's hand. 'It was because I thought you were my father.'

Charity said nothing as he looked at him.

'This isn't the time or place. When we get to the Prince Regent I will tell you everything,' Charity said. 'But now we have to stop Zane from leaving New York. If he gets to Isbrae he will never be found.'

They spoke no more. Mariah turned and began to run up the steps as fast as he could. Charity dragged on behind, unable to keep up with his pace.

High above, Mariah could hear the whirring of the engines of the *Bicameralist*. Smoke began to be drawn up the staircase as the room below burned. Mariah looked out of a window and saw that the clouds all around them were tinged with soot. He knew the building was on fire far below.

Mariah got to the open door that led to the roof of the tower. The wind gusted about him as he stepped out, gripping him like an icy hand. Above him the engines of the *Bicameralist* strained as it pulled against the building. Looking up, he could see Zane on a ledge outside the gondola struggling to untie the skyship in the wind. There was no one else on the craft.

Zane pulled the final knot from the metal ring and dropped the rope to the floor. Flames exploded from the other side of the tower as Zane jumped quickly back through the door of the gondola.

Charity burst through the doorway and saw the fire around them.

'There's only one way off this building,' he said as the *Bicameralist* began to pull slowly away. 'Grab the towing rope – quickly, Mariah.'

Mariah could see the thick rope being dragged across the roof of the tower as the skyship floated slowly upwards, its tip trailing across the stone. He ran towards it with Charity keeping pace at his side. He reached out – his fingertips touched the rope. Charity grabbed the line to steady it. The skyship lurched backwards as an explosion below sent a thermal of hot vapour into the sky. It pulled the towing rope away from the roof and Charity, still clinging on, dangled high above the city as the skyship hovered, its engines straining.

'I'm trapped!' screamed Mariah as the flames ruptured through the granite slabs beneath his feet.

'Have faith – you'll have to jump for the rope.'

'I can't – I can't do it,' Mariah said as he felt the building begin to crumble beneath his feet.

'Run for the rope,' Charity shouted as the *Bicameralist* revved its engines.

Mariah paced back. His face was torn with fear. He looked to the rope. Charity held out his hand. The building began to shake and tremble.

'Go on, Jack. Leave me here,' he shouted to Charity.

'Have faith . . .' Charity replied.

Mariah steeled himself. He could feel the building start to fall. He began to run. Just as he reached the lip of the ledge the stone gave way. He leapt out into the air as below him the Eulogian Tower fell to the ground like a deck of cards.

It felt to Mariah as if he was in the sky alone. That he flew like an eagle. He reached out, his eyes fixed on Jack Charity. The skyship lurched towards him with the upward blast from the falling building.

Charity grabbed his arm and gripped his coat as if to squeeze the life from him.

'Thank God for your madness,' Charity screamed as Mariah looked to the ground. What was left of the Eulogian Tower stuck up from the ground like a gigantic broken cross. The streets below were filled with dust and ash.

'Will they have got away?' he asked.

'Isambard Black would have seen to that,' Charity replied. 'We need to get in the skyship.'

Mariah climbed first. The rope cut at his hands. It was crisp with sea salt and burnt his skin. They were soon under the gondola and Mariah swung onto a small ledge with a narrow window. To his right was an inspection door used for mooring the skyship.

Charity wasted no time kicking it in. The door splintered as it burst open and Mariah jumped inside.

The gondola was empty. It smelt of leather and fresh oak, just as it had done on the night he and Biba were rescued from the sea. The ship rocked from side to side as the turbulence plucked it up and down and the engines churned faster.

'I never thought you would get away,' Zane said as he came through a hatch above them. 'This makes things difficult . . .'

Mariah saw he was holding a small harpoon in one hand.

'Guns cannot be used on the *Bicameralist* for fear we would all be blown up. I only have one arrow and I don't know which one of you I should kill,' Zane said eagerly as he eyed them both.

'The one who will do you the most harm if he lays his hands on your throat,' Charity replied as he stepped towards him.

'Choice made,' Zane said quickly as he pulled the trigger of the harpoon.

The arrow flew forward. Mariah dived into its path. Zane gasped as it struck the boy in the chest.

Without warning, Charity grabbed Zane by the arm and pulled him towards him. Zane stumbled forward, unable to resist. Then Charity turned and pushed the man towards the open door at the back of the gondola. Zane fell through. His cries grew fainter and fainter as he spun faster and faster towards Manhattan. It was as if an angel fell from heaven.

Inside the gondola Mariah lay on the deck, not moving. His face was white, his eyes closed. The arrow lay beside him. Charity feared to look.

Taking the arrow in his hand Charity broke it in two. He looked at the shaft. There was no blood.

'Spiderweb! It worked . . .' he said as he pulled Mariah by the front of his waistcoat, shaking life into him. 'Mariah . . . Mariah . . .'

Mariah opened his eyes.

'I want to go home . . .' he said as he held his chest.

'We shall fly there,' said Charity as he lifted Mariah onto a leather bench and leant him against the window.

'A trip to Scarborough?' Mariah asked.